BLOOD WILL
BE BORN

By Gary Donnelly

DI Owen Sheen series
Blood Will Be Born
Killing in Your Name

BLOOD WILL
BE BORN

GARY DONNELLY

Allison & Busby Limited
11 Wardour Mews
London W1F 8AN
allisonandbusby.com

First published in Great Britain in 2017.
This edition first published by Allison & Busby in 2020.

Grateful acknowledgement is made for permission to include the following
copyrighted material:
'The Trigger Men' by Martin Dillon. Copyright © Martin Dillon, 2003.
'Belfast Born, Bred and Buttered' by Joe Graham. © Joe Graham 1990.
A Rushlight Publication.

A CIP catalogue record for this book is available from
the British Library.

First Edition

ISBN 978-0-7490-2521-2

Typeset in 11/16 pt Sabon LT Pro by
Allison & Busby Ltd.

The paper used for this Allison & Busby publication
has been produced from trees that have been legally sourced
from well-managed and credibly certified forests.

Printed and bound by
CPI Group (UK) Ltd, Croydon, CR0 4YY

For Sacha
who always believed

You who are bent, and bald, and blind,
With a heavy heart and a wandering mind,
Have known three centuries, poets sing,
Of dalliance with a demon thing.

William Butler Yeats, *The Wanderings of Oisin: Book I*

It was as if the normal rules and definitions of sanity were pushed aside. Aggressive psychopaths operated without constraint . . . The psychiatric unit of Downpatrick Hospital, with a brief to treat aggressive psychopaths, had to close during the Troubles because of a lack of patients.

Martin Dillon, *The Trigger Men*

[In 1790s Belfast] There were many strange 'disappearances' of people . . . known to have been taken by Moiley, as though Moiley was some kind of phantom who took people away . . . Mothers for years afterwards would scare their children to behave with threats of 'If you don't behave Moiley will get you' . . . but truth is Moiley did take away quite a few informers, some never heard of again . . .

Joe Graham, *Belfast Born, Bred and Buttered*

PROLOGUE

Bog land, Co. Monaghan, Republic of Ireland
1976

Nothing's as heavy as a dead body.

Better to keep them alive, make them walk, easier over ground like this. Fryer kept his eyes down, careful on each step. The path they were on was barely that: a thin snake of semi-swamped moss and turf, broken up by the odd grey rock or half-dead tree. On either side the bog: black and boundary-less in the dead of night. The wind was in voice, it howled across the land, sending salt spray into his face.

Romantic bloody Ireland: people had killed for this, many more had died.

Mooney's light faltered, and then faded, fast. He had been leading the way, the boy between them, Fryer's gun pointed at his back. Fryer stopped, Mooney must have changed direction. Within a minute, a man could be lost. It was the whole point of this place: things came to disappear.

Fryer squinted into the rain. No sign of him. Hovering to his left, for a moment, was the ghost of a light, and then it was gone, obscured by the mist. The spray surged towards him, blanketing even the ground, leaving him without bearings. Fryer staggered drunkenly. He held out both arms like a tightrope walker and slid his finger off the trigger, hissing a prayer of expletives under his breath. He could smell the oily looking water pooled at his feet, mineral, decomposed. No way was he going in that.

Fryer's eyes widened; no longer seeing the bog water. His shoulders hunched and he turned, finger back on the trigger.

'Mooney!' he yelled, dropping down on his right knee, gun pointed.

The hairs on the back of his neck raised in an angry heckle, he felt them shiver and crawl; something had been behind him. Close enough to touch him. And now, something was watching him. He stared, unblinking into the blackness, training the shooter between ten and two.

'Mooney!' he screamed, but the wind sucked his words away.

His mind raced, recounting the journey that had taken them to this point. They had not been tailed. Fryer was certain of it. Mooney said the Brits were sending in the SAS, men who would lie in wait for weeks on end, then *bang bang*. Fryer told Mooney he was scared of fuck all, and that was true. But now, Fryer was scared.

He waited, every sense on edge, but heard only the wind. He watched the path. That's where it was. And he could feel it watching him. Fryer stole a glance in the direction of Mooney's light. He could see it again, but it was very faint, a hazy yellow glow. If he stopped here any longer, he might not find them. He might end up waist deep in the dark water.

With IT.

He slowly raised himself up, gun still trained on the path, and took a few tentative steps forward. He peered intently, but there was only blackness and the spray on his face. He slowly lowered the gun. Nothing. It was time to go. Fryer turned, and walked, one eye on the dissipating halo of Mooney's lamp. He would not run, no need, and if he ran he could twist an ankle, break a leg.

And then it will catch you, because it is still there, you know it. You can feel it on you, watching.

And then Mooney would have to drag him back to the cottage, and Mooney couldn't drive, there'd be no way to get back to Belfast.

Squelch, sink, suck – next foot, and repeat. Wetter here, less of a path. Fryer panted hard. He checked, but Mooney's light was no closer, so he set off again, faster, until he was running, or what passed for it, arms swinging at his side, the gun gripped in the wet claw of his hand, eyes on the light, to catch Mooney, get this dirty job done.

A hand, bony and preternaturally strong, hooked round his left foot, and held it under the cold water. Fryer yelped and fell forward, the bog rushed up, his brain manically ordering his numb body to kick, roll and shoot.

Freezing, earthy ditchwater stung his eyes, filling his ears, his nose and mouth, drowning him in blackness. His left ankle exploded with agony, something holding and turning. It was going to twist off his foot, pull his leg from its socket. Fryer screamed into the mud, his finger pumping the pistol's trigger. Instead, he felt the cold squelch of mossy water in his right fist. He had lost the gun. He pushed himself up and turned, choking out bog water and gasping, crying. Fryer started to tug his leg by the calf, his left ankle exploding with agony as he yanked. Fryer looked down, panting, but no longer sobbing.

His foot was caught on a twisted old root; he could see its shiny blackness where it broke the lip of the water like a mummified forehead. Not the bogeyman after all, he thought. Fryer shuffled on his arse, getting closer to it, then turned himself round and dislodged his foot, shoe coming off in the process. He submerged his hand into the black pool, retrieved it. Grimacing, he squeezed his foot in, leaving the laces undone. He turned, and groped about frantically on his hands and knees in the muddy water for the gun, finding nothing but sediment. Finally, he stood up, panting, spitting away the flat, iodine taste of the water. Time to catch himself on here. He'd lost his cool, and now he'd lost a piece. He was going to balls up this operation if he was not careful.

'Find Mooney, do the job,' he said into the rain.

He cupped his hands to his mouth, ready to bellow Mooney's name, though it would have done little good. Then he looked right. Maybe a hundred feet away, he could see it: Mooney's light, moving ever so slightly, the size of an old penny. Must have tracked too far to his left, overshot them, but he had made up the ground. If anything, he was a bit ahead of them now. Fryer started to move towards the light, trying to keep the weight off his left ankle, but not able to. He gritted his teeth, and welcomed the pain. It was keeping him alert; it was bigger than the wind, a distraction from the foundering cold that wanted him to stop. Fryer plodded on, his gaze fixed on the glow, not looking down. And not looking back.

His feet found a firmer path, the light cleaner, closer. About ten yards further on, there was Mooney, the boy still in tow. Fryer called him. Mooney stopped, turned round and looked him up and down as he approached. He took a fist full of the boy's soaking T-shirt and shoved him down, hard. Ahead was only bog; this was the end of the road.

'State of you, you're soaked,' Mooney said.

'Fell,' said Fryer, looking over his shoulder into the dark. 'Foot caught. On a root.'

'Gun?' asked Mooney.

Fryer shook his head, not meeting Mooney's eyes. The boy was sitting on a flat stone, rocking back and forth, whimpering like a wounded cub.

'Never mind, use mine,' said Mooney.

The boy squinted up at Fryer, taking him in. He raised both his hands, tightly bound by a piece of nylon rope, and pointed a finger at him.

'Ha ha you fell, you fell. You're all wet,' he said. His face had broken into a stupid smile and then he started to laugh, snot swinging off his nose in a white rope, he was in fits.

Fryer limped over, fast as he could, his gun hand balling into a fist. If not for him, he would not be here, his ankle up like a bap and a missing gun to explain back in Belfast. Fryer got to him, launched a punch and decked him in the mouth, feeling his lips squash and split, the bony barrier of his teeth crunch and give way, loosening under Fryer's knuckles. His hand was ringing. The boy was screeching, his bound hands muffling the sound as he pressed them against his mouth. He started shaking, and crying loudly, strings of saliva and blood pouring from his mouth. Mooney had his gun out, pointed at the boy's head.

'Shut you the fuck up!' he said.

The boy stared at the gun, eyes wide, whining, but not crying. Mooney lowered the gun.

'Mammy, I want my mammy,' he said, the tears back on.

Mooney raised the piece and cracked him once on the top of the head with the base of the grip. Hit him hard. The boy slumped off the rock, his tongue lolling out of his mouth, lips swelling. Out cold, but probably still alive. Mooney turned to Fryer, a look of genuine apology.

'I should have gagged him, Fryer. He was quiet, you know, since last night,' he said.

Fryer sighed, nodded. Mooney understood. Worse than carrying their dead weight was listening to them plead and cry for their lives. Got on your nerves. An informer would say anything to save his skin. He will go to England, and never return. He will never say a word; never, ever talk. It was sort of funny when you thought about it. Talking was usually their problem. It explained why Fryer and Mooney usually dumped their bodies in a public place. The message was as important as the punishment: touts will be found and shot. This was different. This boy was never going to be found. He was to be disappeared. He would not be claimed. That was their orders. Mooney was holding the gun out to him by the barrel. Fryer took it.

'I did the last one,' he said. He checked Mooney's Colt, found six in the chamber and then cocked it. Mooney stepped away from where the boy lay.

'Where will we bury the—'

Three shots from Fryer in quick succession, the crack of the gun silencing Mooney's question, the boy's body jerking as though electrified with each shot, and then he was absolutely still. Three holes in the side of his head, darker even than his wet hair, each indented and each still smoking. More smoke and cordite hung in the air momentarily, then was cleaned away by the breeze.

'We'll weigh him down in the water,' said Fryer.

'You take his feet,' he said, setting the gun next to the lamp.

Mooney nodded and grabbed the boy's ankles. Fryer grunted, hoisting the boy up by the nylon rope. As they raised him off the ground, a portion of skull flapped open, grey mash and blood within. Fryer raised his eyes to Mooney and nodded. Mooney's face was pale going on green, but he did what Fryer wanted and turned so they were side on to the where the path ended and the bog water began.

'One, two,' counted Fryer, swinging the body with Mooney, and then they both let go, throwing it into the water on three. It hit with a small splash then started to sink, face down.

'Help me,' said Fryer, returning to where the boy had been sitting. He squatted over the flat rock. He dug his fingers under it, feeling his nails fill and compact with the soft, black earth, until he felt a turn in the stone. Mooney was doing the same on the other side.

'Got it?' said Fryer.

'Yes,' nodded Mooney.

'On three again,' said Fryer and again they counted, this time heaving and lifting the stone from its resting place and carefully bringing it up. Fryer's ankle felt like it was made of rusty shards of metal and nerves, but he kept moving, he wanted this over. They walked the boulder into the black water, up to their knees, and then reached the place where the boy's body had hit.

'Go,' gasped Fryer.

They pushed the weight of the boulder away from them and it splashed into the water, sinking, on top of the body. Now it would never rise. It was over. They sloshed back to the path. Fryer stopped and took the weight off his ankle. Mooney picked up the gun, and kept walking, moving quickly.

'Where are you going?' asked Fryer.

'Piss,' said Mooney, not looking back.

Fryer felt inside his pocket and took out a busted pack of filter tips. They were drenched, like him. He squeezed the paper packet in his hand and watched as water dripped between his fingers. He pocketed the smokes. He had already left a gun out there somewhere, best to leave nothing else. From a fair bit off he heard the sound of retching and vomiting: Mooney. Fryer lifted up the lamp and started to move in that direction. His ankle blasted mercilessly each time he put weight on it. More sounds of retching. Fryer froze, every cell in his body alive and alert. It was back, watching him, but not from the path like before. It was in the bog, it was behind him.

'Nothing there,' said Fryer, to himself, and started to walk.

He heard something over the wind: a slow splash and slop of bog water being disturbed close behind him. Then he smelt it. It was wild, feral as fox piss but also of the bog, wet and cloying as a bag of spoilt potatoes. He ran, swinging the paraffin lamp, crazy shadows lunging at him from the path. The splinters of pain from his ankle were just distant echoes. It was coming for him. It was real but not human and if he turned round he would be able to see it, but that might just take his mind, aye, before it killed him it would do just that.

His left ankle buckled beneath him and Fryer was falling, for the second time that night, this time letting go a small scream as the path surged up to meet him. He hit the ground hard, and heard the paraffin lamp crack. The fuel ignited with a whoosh and Fryer's face was hit with light and heat. The spilt oil started to burn brightly on the path, just inches from Fryer's face. Fryer rolled over and scrabbled away on his back, panting and pushing at the earth with his feet. His eyes were wide, searching for it, but the flash of light hung in his vision, blinding him. It was close, he knew it, its smell was coming at him in waves, fierce as shit, stagnant as a drain.

'No!' he screamed, and waved his right arm in front of him.

There was something spraying out of him, cascading through the air. He lowered his arm and saw a shard of glass from the lamp had embedded in his wrist, the blood still pumping out, hot and black. His vision was clearer. He looked up, waiting for the thing to be looming over him, but it was Mooney looming over him, Mooney who was calling his name, cursing, and stripping off to his white vest. He tore it apart and tied it tight above Fryer's elbow, Fryer groaned, tried to complain, but nothing came out. The blood stopped pumping, and as it did, the first wave of pain hit Fryer, dull and everlasting.

Mooney dragged him up, put Fryer's good arm round his neck and tugged the back of Fryer's strides, keeping him on his feet. Fryer's legs gave up, and then steadied. Mooney was speaking to him. Could he walk, as far as the cottage? Fryer nodded, and they started moving. Fryer could smell the boke on his breath, but that was OK, it was better than

17

the other smell. Fryer stopped. He looked back. The oil was sputtering out now, but still burning. He could not see the 'thing', but it was there. And it was watching, from the darkness. Its name came to him, as the last flames died.

'It's the Moley,' said Fryer, gritting his teeth on the words, but too late, he had spoken. He had given it a name, and a life.

It knew what he had done and had followed him. If not for the blood, it would have taken him.

PART ONE

BLOOD ON THE BLADE

CHAPTER ONE

Belfast, Northern Ireland, present day
Friday 9th July

John Fryer slouched in the pee pee chair. He was in the wet room, wearing the disposable paper bib they gave you when it was time for the Friday afternoon sponge down. The garment covered his bits but not much more. Along the hem, printed in blue capitals, Fryer read:

PROPERTY OF BELFAST HEIGHTS
PSYCHIATRIC HOSPITAL

Not for too much longer, thought Fryer, staring at the pale, hairy outcrops of his knees. Beneath the stamp of ownership it read:

DESTROY AFTER USE

His hands hung heavily at his sides. He could feel a cool draught on his behind, sagging out of the cavity beneath the seat. He stared at his knees, saliva beginning to drool from the left corner of his half-open mouth. But he was alert, sharper than he had been in years. For near three months he had palmed the pink pills he was meant to swallow three times a day, hid them under his mattress.

The door slammed behind him, the sound clean and brittle in the small, tiled chamber followed by the squeak of rubber-soled shoes, getting closer. Ade, the big African fella who had wheeled him in, walked across the room to where a black hose was wound round taps on the wall. He unfurled a length. Fryer was as still as a reptile; only his eyes moved. He heard a sharp screech, and then the hose pulsed and stiffened, water spurted over the tiled floor. When he turned Fryer dropped his eyes, felt icy rain fall on the tops of his bare feet as Ade lumbered towards him. Ade hosed Fryer's legs, cold water. The paper bib quickly saturated and stuck to his skin, chilling him, but Fryer did not move.

'OK, Mr Fryer, now's the time to pee pee or poo poo if you want to.' Ade squatted down and sponged Fryer's shanks and did a quick wipe over what protruded through the hole in the chair.

'No? OK then, easier for me that way.' He was breathing in short gasps as he went about his chore, his rubber shoes squeaking in complaint as he trudged around the chair. He tossed the running hose into the middle of the room where the floor sloped down. The water gurgled into the open mouth of a drainage hole. It sounded like it was falling a long way down. Ade shuffled round and started to carefully scrub Fryer's feet. It tickled like fuck, but Fryer only stared at his knees, drool slipping from his slack jaw. 'Why you never talk to me no more Mr Fryer, huh? You make me sad. Maybe I'd give you a pedicure if you talked to me, no? Lots of nice gentlemen they do it these days,' Ade chuckled, his jest offering Fryer a welcome but momentary warmth, quickly replaced by the hollow echo of the water, falling into that deep, dark drain.

Fryer shivered, gritted his back teeth as Ade's wet sponge did its work up and down his legs. A man was singing, across the courtyard. The sound leaked in with the dusky Belfast light through the single window above Fryer, steel bars visible through opaque glass.

Your man could hold a tune, but hard to make it out.

Bars on a cell and singing at twilight, just like when he was in the H-Blocks, when he had been surrounded by comrades, and friends, men he had fought alongside with rifle and grenade, men like himself who had taken an oath to one another, to Ireland, to the IRA.

But those boys could sing back then. They had filled up the dead zone of that prison, its galleys and cells and featureless courtyards. They had filled it with songs from the heart, rebel songs, made a home in a place designed to break a man, isolate an army, to destroy resistance.

North and south men had stood side by side, comrades and friends. They'd been on the one road, singing 'The Soldier's Song' together.

Fryer blinked. Your man had started to scream, like a trapped animal.

The H-Blocks were closed up now, empty. He'd heard it was going to be a museum. All his comrades were gone. Some dead though many were free men, but all on different roads now, not on the one road. No one wanted to sing 'The Soldier's Song' any more. No one wanted

23

to know him, not even so-called blood brothers like Jim Dempsey, a man he would have died for, the man he had killed for many times. Dempsey had dumped him here ten years ago and left him to rot.

Fryer's chest tightened under the wet paper. He clenched his teeth once more, but this time not because of the cold.

'I leave the pedicure for next time, Mr Fryer,' said Ade, wheezing as he stood up. He trudged to the spewing hose pipe on the floor, still feeding water into that hole. Fryer relaxed his fists, which were balled at his sides, tried to calm his breathing, think of something else, not Dempsey. But no matter what, he would not look at that drain. It was very deep, which meant it was also very dark. And the dark spelt danger for John Fryer. The milky light from the small window was weaker now, and twilight shadows had pooled in the wet room where, minutes before, none had been.

Fryer's heart gave an unpleasant wallop, and he reluctantly lifted his gaze to the darkening room. Ade bent down and picked up the hose, and as he did so, Fryer caught a glimpse of the black drain. It held his attention as only an awful thing can and he stared into it, unblinking. Sweat pimpled Fryer's forehead, in spite of the numbing cold. Every nerve cell screamed in unison for him to jump up, run and get the fuck away. Because IT was coming for him, out of the darkness, always from the darkness. And it was close. He caught a whiff, very faint, but unmistakable: something decayed, and yet lively, like a monkey enclosure on a hot day. His pulse beat in his ears, *bump, bump, bump*, and he breathed in laboured rasps. The cords in his neck stood out as though straining to carry a dead weight. Yes, still time to run, to hide, but to what end? It would find him again sooner or later, as it always did. And aside from letting it devour his body, his soul, there was only one thing which John Fryer could feed it, to keep it at bay. Blood, only freshly spilt blood.

The smell hit him. It was thick and damp: wet pelt and black fungus. It had found him.

It was the Moley.

He looked up to the high bars of the solitary window, not caring now if Ade noticed him move or not. The meagre light was fading fast, but any light at all was good. The waves of stink kept coming.

The Moley was closer.

Ade yanked on the hose and pushed Fryer's wheelchair out of his way. The wheels screeched, and his medical chart clacked against the back of the seat. Fryer glanced there, two words caught his eye, before he turned his attention back to the drain, a man in a living nightmare, not wanting to see but powerless to resist. The Moley's smell filled the air, coated his sinuses, his throat. Any second now he would see it coming up and out of the darkness. Running was not the answer. It needed to be fed.

It needed blood.

Ade stopped dead and dropped the hose, icy water sprayed Fryer's feet. He spun round and started very cautiously back in the direction of the drain, head cocked to one side like a man listening for a rare bird call. He froze. Fryer could see that his left hand was trembling. Fryer listened too: the beat of blood in his ears, the hiss of the hose, Ade's wheezing breaths. Ade's voice faltering:

'You hear dat sound, Mr Fryer? You hear that sound just now, yes?' Fryer was motionless, staring past his knees to a cracked tile on the floor. The smell was hammering him in thick waves. If he looked at the drain he would see it now. On cue, Fryer heard Ade gasp, and then watched as he back-stepped. He said something in a foreign tongue and made a gesture with his right hand. He turned back to Fryer.

'OK, Mr Fryer, let's get you finished. And then let's get out of here. It too cold here,' he said. Fryer was shaking, not from the chill. Ade picked up the sponge and hose. He sprayed Fryer's upper body, and hastily scrubbed Fryer's armpits, top of his shoulders, and the back of Fryer's neck, faster and rougher than before. He ran the sponge down Fryer's left arm, stopped, then stepped away. Fryer heard him gasp again.

'Oh, Mr Fryer, I am so sorry, I should be more careful, Mr Fryer.'

Now Fryer felt the sting from his arm, the warmth of his blood, coursing from him. He'd cut him, maybe just pressure from the big sponge. It did not take a lot. His skin was paper thin in parts, a lattice work of scars, like the damaged surface of one of Jupiter's frozen moons. Countless episodes of cut and heal, blood offering to keep the Moley away. He could see the black ribbon of his blood on the tiled floor, mixing now with the stream of water from the hose. As his blood approached the hole, the stench of the Moley started to recede, and then it disappeared as the blood flowed into the blackness below.

Ade snorted, dropped the sponge to the floor and cast the hose down. Fryer heard Ade slam the wet-room door open, and his huge brown paws encased Fryer's cold hands and gently guided him into the wheelchair. Ade ripped the paper bib from Fryer and carefully wrapped a soft, white towel twice round his lower arm. It throbbed comfortingly under its new duvet. Ade pushed the chair, the wheels squeaked high and low, and Fryer was freed from the shadows of the wet room at last. His chart clacked against his back, reminding Fryer of the two words he had read.

Two words: NO SHARPS.

CHAPTER TWO

Christopher Aaron Moore killed the engine of the London black taxi after pulling to a stop outside his granny's terraced house in Tiger's Bay, North Belfast. His hands and lower arms buzzed with the ghost of the old engine's rattle. He flexed his gloved fingers, the tingling stopped, and the sudden silence was replaced by the faint flutter of the Union Jack bunting, draped between lamp posts the length of the terraced street.

It looked smaller now, and there were more cars, at least one per house, plus satellite dishes pointed skyward, so different from what he recalled. Until now, in his mind's eye, Granny's street was an endless corridor flanked by kerbstones; children swinging on ropes from the lamp posts, ball games and dogs chasing. The first, and until now the only, time he had been here, Christopher had been a child too. It had not ended well. Everyone on the street had stopped and stared, to see what the commotion was. The commotion was Granny Moore's shrill voice, coming from this very doorway, breaking like dinner plates down the street, directed at him, and at his daddy.

Don't either of you come back here! You or that mongrel Fenian taig bastard.

'Fenian' and 'taig' – the insults were directed at him. What 'nigger' was for black America, 'Fenian' and 'taig' were for the Catholics of Northern Ireland. In his case, not strictly true, but Christopher's daddy, though a decorated member of the RUC, had also married a Catholic, Christopher's mother.

Her house looked the same. The window frames had been freshly painted in the same shade of royal blue. The sill was smooth and gleaming white as a surgeon's smock. Her front door was a glossy fresh red, proud as a postbox in the afternoon light. Red white and blue, the colours of a loyal Ulster Protestant and one who had no room at her hearth for a half-blood like Christopher. Christopher was here to have a word with her about that day. But it was not petty revenge, or at least not completely that, which had brought Christopher back to her door after so many years. Daddy had explained exactly what must be done, told him he had a special mission. The fact that Daddy was dead did not bother Christopher unduly. He had spent too long wandering in the wilderness. Daddy had called him in the night, and he had answered, and he had listened. Daddy told him that Belfast was a fallen place, a Gomorrah of hypocrisy and perverted justice, where evil men now ruled and the just, like him, had been cast asunder. Daddy told him he must bring the refiner's fire to Belfast, and where better to set the flame alight but here?

Granny's front door opened first a crack, then wide. A man with a thick brush of grey hair filled the frame, facing in. He said something Christopher could not make out. Christopher stayed still, but he did not hide. The man tugged the door shut, turned and walked past the taxi, his face briefly visible as he pulled out a mobile phone and gave it his full attention.

Uncle Cecil.

Older, a few more saddle bags and much more grey. No paintbrush moustache these days but definitely him. Cecil had been there that day too, arm round his mother as she ranted, burning contempt in his eyes. Christopher watched in his left wing mirror until Uncle Cecil turned the corner and passed out of sight. Let him go, for now. Cecil had his own part to play. When he discovered what Christopher would leave of his mother he could be relied on to wreak more havoc than Christopher could ever start. When his usefulness had expired, Christopher would deal with him too and then a fire would rage in Belfast, the hypocrites and traitors would be consumed.

But first, the spark. He reached into the passenger footwell for his black mahogany truncheon, tucked it into the inside lining of his jacket and touched the front pocket of his jeans, felt the folded hunting knife. He grabbed the holdall with his change of clothes and towel and got out.

He was wearing what he thought of as the unofficial uniform of a Belfast street Provo from the 1980s (something he was not, had not even been born). Black Doc Martens, a pair of stone-washed blue jeans, a padded bomber jacket and a pair of leather gloves. He unrolled the black beanie down his face to reveal a balaclava, two eye holes and one for his mouth. Christopher looked up and down the empty street, closed his eyes and listened to the flapping applause from the bunting, started to smile. The stage was set. Christopher raised one gloved fist to Granny's gleaming door.

BANG, BANG, BANG!

A policeman's knock, as Daddy used to say. He heard a muffled voice from within. Christopher moved his mouth to the letter slot and gently pushed it open.

'It's Cecil. Forgot something.'

Faintly from within: 'I only just sat down. Use yer key.' A litany of muffled curses followed, then the clack and creak of a walking stick or a frame. He released the letter slot and turned his back to the door. The red, white and blue bunting, a sudden riot of colour in his eyes, like so many of his earlier oil-covered canvases. They were now gathering dust in the attic of his childhood home, not hanging in galleries as he had once dreamt. That work was naive, like his wanting to become an artist, of that kind, in the first place.

And yet, Christopher's face flushed beneath the balaclava; art college rejection letters from Belfast and London, softly worded glasses in the face. He breathed it out, felt his rippling pulse flatten, as the front door unlatched behind him. His calling was higher than all that, and he was about to create a different kind of art, his masterpiece. He could hear her creak and shuffle off, a fair pace on her. She must have warmed up a bit. 'You are some sort of spastic, son. The age of me, my knees may be shot but least I have my marbles. Hurry you up, my show's about to start.' Christopher turned to the open

31

door, slipped in. He clicked it closed with the heel of his boot, and slowly walked down the hall.

The smell of an Ulster Fry hung in the hall: fried bacon, sausage, egg and greasy bread. The sound of a television turned way up coming from the parlour further back. A wooden shield with dozens of miniature spoons hung on the wall. On each spoon was a flag of the world. The tricolour of Eire was not amongst them.

To his left, a white door with rectangular glass panels was slightly ajar. The sound of the television blared. The air here was stale with smoked cigarettes. Christopher nudged the door open. Granny was in a high-backed chair diagonally opposite. A grey plastic crutch leant against one of the arms, and a small table was on the other side, with a full ashtray. She was wearing a pair of horn-rimmed glasses and a nylon kitchen coat.

Christopher stepped into the room, reached behind the television and pulled the plug. All was suddenly quiet, only the tick of the clock on the mantelpiece. She stared at him, her mouth open.

'You're . . . you're not Cecil,' she said.

'No, unlucky for you, Esther, I am not.'

CHAPTER THREE

DC Aoife McCusker tapped the big fish tank at the back of the booth where she and Sergeant Charlie Donaldson sat, finishing their Chinese. The lunchtime throng of Belfast Friday office workers and early bank holiday bargain hunters had come and gone, and the place was quiet. Charlie was already drunk. He had polished off five large Bushmills in the time it had taken her to work through one small rosé wine. She could smell the sourness of the whiskey wafting over from across the table and feel his bleary gaze on her.

This was a mistake. She should never have agreed to meet him, the poor guy obviously could not handle it. In the three months since their affair had ended she had shared only a few professional meetings with him, always with others present, despite the fact that he was her boss. Since the last one a month ago, he had lost half a stone of handsome muscle and had black bags under his eyes. In contrast, she was flourishing. First week working Serious Crimes, the promotion she had waited for, had worked for. Charlie was no longer her boss. He was just an old flame, and sputtering out before her eyes.

She heard the ice clink as Charlie finished off the dregs of his drink and then a rattle as he shook it in the direction of the young waitress, waiting in the shadows. She lifted a finger and tapped the thick wall of the fish tank again with the tips of her fingernails three times: one for her little girl Ava, one for her job, and one for luck. Another drink arrived.

'You're not supposed to tap the tank,' said Charlie, gesturing to the peeling sign beneath the fish tank. 'It upsets them,' Charlie said, his bloodshot eyes meeting Aoife's over his wire-rimmed glasses. He drained half his glass, smacked his lips. 'Even fish have feelings you know,' he said. She glanced at Charlie's hand, wedding ring still on. Charlie spotted her looking.

'I know. I should take it off. But I'm not divorced yet.'

'I am so sorry, Charlie, about everything. I shouldn't have come today, this is bad for both of us,' she said. Her apology had escaped unchecked, left a sour residue in her mouth. She picked up her water glass and took a sip.

'We have been over this. The end of my and Lisa's marriage was not your fault,' he said, beginning to slur.

'Look, you said you needed to talk to me about something, something important. So just talk, and then I should go,' she said. He raised a hand, shaking his head at her mention of leaving, then picked up a white cloth napkin and padded his greasy lips.

'Jesus, Charlie, talk to me. You said on the phone that it was serious, you sounded serious.' Charlie studied the table mat and palmed the air between them in a slowdown gesture.

'We can get to that,' he said, gravely. 'Yes, we need to have a serious chat, about something serious,' he said, his stoned eyes fixed on the blue world of the fish tank. This was pointless, if Charlie had important news he was patently too smashed to deliver it.

'Firstly, however,' he said, a big grin spreading over his face, 'firstly we should celebrate. Young lady! Champagne, your best,' he called, and the waitress promptly scurried away.

'Charlie, listen to me, I don't want champagne. I don't want anything. In fact, I think it best I leave,' she said. Charlie wagged a finger at her. He drained the rest of his whiskey and set the glass down with a rap.

'Nonsense, champagne it must be. This is a celebration, Aoife, for a well-deserved promotion. Serious Crimes is lucky to have you,' he said.

'Charlie, you are very sweet, and you are a good man, and thank you for all the coaching and help you gave me, I know I would never have got the job without your help, but—'

'They are lucky to have you. I have never in my days worked with someone who was able to do the job in Community Relations as well as you. You're smart, you're fair and you,' he said, pointing at her, 'are going to be a great detective.'

But in Community Relations her name was dirt, and reputations had a habit of following you, especially as a woman. The waitress arrived with a bottle of cheap-looking fizz in a silver bucket. She set two flutes down and uncorked it with a muted pop, filled their glasses. Aoife picked up one of the fortune cookies from a small bowl in the middle of the table and cradled its delicate shell between her palms.

'To you, Aoife, you knock them dead, kiddo,' said Charlie. He was smiling, holding up the flute, his eyes glazed. What a waste of time. Whatever his supposed news for her was, it could not be that important, probably just a ruse to get her back in the sack. She crushed the shell of the cookie between her hands and then dusted the broken bits on the stained white tablecloth, reached for her purse and pulled out twenty quid, looked at the bottle on ice and then took out another twenty plus a ten. She dropped it on the table on top of the cookie dust. Charlie was watching her, mouth open, eyes not understanding.

'Aoife, darling, what are you doing? We're having a toast here. To you,' he said, weakly lifting his glass. She stood up, grabbed her bag and coat and took the bit of paper from the fortune cookie, then shuffled out of the booth.

'I have to go, Charlie, and I think it's best if you and I are not in touch, for a while,' she said, turning before he could say anything else. She marched away, past the waitress in the shadows who stared at her with big, brown eyes, past the bar with no one serving. She paused to read her fortune, frowned then dropped it on the floor and kept walking. From behind her, Charlie's voice, loud and full of afternoon drink:

'Aoife, stop. We need to talk. I've messed up, badly, I need to explain. Aoife! Aoife! Wait, I'm sorry. Whatever happens, I want you to know that I'm sorry,' he called. She pushed the restaurant door open and stepped out into the bustle of a Belfast Friday afternoon, creating her destiny with confident strides, and leaving Charlie Donaldson's apologies and the warning she'd found in the fortune cookie behind her.

CHAPTER FOUR

Granny stared at him, open-mouthed, then snapped it closed like a turtle. Christopher eased himself into the two-seater settee opposite her chair.

'Who are you? What do you think you're doing in my home?' Then, before Christopher had a chance to respond: 'I was just about to watch my show.'

'Well, let's go back to who I am not. As you said, I am not Cecil,' said Christopher.

'If it's money you're after you may sling your hook, for I have none,' she said, face set. Christopher told her that theft was not his intention, though he noted she was sporting a fair-sized sapphire on her right hand, too big to be the real thing. Something like that could go for a grand in the Cash Exchange in the city centre. She squinted at him through her thick spectacles.

'You know my name. So do I know you? Let me get a better look at them eyes.'

She adjusted her position, craning forward, moving her arm from the chair as she did so. She seized something from the table, faster than Christopher had given her credit for. Like a rat. Christopher could only stare at the plastic alarm on a drawstring now clasped in her hand. It was concealed behind the ashtray. She jabbed the red button, glared at him triumphantly.

Christopher's paralysis broke. He whipped the truncheon from the smooth nylon lining of his jacket, pouncing up from the settee as he did so. He swung it through the air in a tight arc, all of him lasered in on the blinking alarm and the scrawny claw that continued to jab at it. The hard wood truncheon connected and Granny's hand gave a brittle crunch, the alarm dropped to the floor, and she threw her head back, the cords in her neck like metal rods sheathed in thin paper. Her first scream, hoarse and brief, was followed by a big, gasping inhalation, then a long, sharp howl which tailed off first into a whimper.

'Bastard! Cecil will take your life for this.' Her left hand was swelling and turning purple.

'That was worth a rap on the knuckles, Esther,' said Christopher, voice steady, but his heart was yammering. He needed to switch on. The old woman had managed to check him, his next move needed to be smarter still, and fast. He rested the truncheon on the settee, then scooped the alarm off the floor and examined it. He found the number he was looking for.

'Here's the deal, Esther. I'm going to make a phone call and tell them that everything is A-OK. You are going to keep your wee mouth closed and in exchange I will keep this' – pointing at the truncheon – 'away from that.' He pointed to her damaged hand. 'Then, you and I will be able to have a civilised chat. Deal?' She blinked away tears from her eyes and nodded once.

Christopher got up and lifted a cordless phone from its cradle by the door. He punched in the number printed on the back of the alarm and a woman's voice answered. He gave Granny's user ID that was written on a sticker under the emergency number, confirmed the address and identified himself as Cecil Moore, Esther's son.

'Ma accidently pushed the button. Aye, she surely was wearing it. Just glad I was here, she got herself into a right fluster, you know how they get? OK, thanks very much for your help. You have a good weekend. Oh, aye, thanks love, you enjoy the 12th weekend too, we will,' he said and ended the call, his eyes on Granny throughout. Christopher held the alarm, still flashing, by the string and let it pendulum back and forth, like an old-fashioned hypnotist. Granny watched it move and blink. Seconds passed. The alarm stopped blinking.

'Now, that's magic,' said Christopher.

The laughter erupted, surprising him almost as much as his granny, who flinched and then shrunk away, as though it were a contaminant. He wanted to stop, but Christopher simply could not. He laughed until his face ached and his eyes streamed, leaving the balaclava damp against his cheeks. He screeched until he was gasping for air. Christopher tossed the alarm on the carpet and gripped the settee. His outbursts had been a problem since puberty, but recently things had started to get much worse, and in moments like this Christopher was certain he was—

Mad?

He was losing control, in a way that he may not be

40

able to regain it at all. Hearing Daddy's voice was one thing, a welcome gift of great value. But this was bad, and if he didn't catch a grip soon, the old witch would make another move, she had it in her. If she somehow got the better of him (an absurd idea, and a truly horrible one which, until this moment, he had not even conceived of), he would never complete Daddy's mission, he'd be dead if she managed to call Cecil. But there were worse things than death. If he lived he'd end up locked away. People would not understand, they'd say he was nuts, like his mother. At that, the boiling spring inside him went cold and quiet again, the laughter stopped as abruptly as it had begun.

'Who are you?' said Granny.

'Don't you know, Esther? You can't remember me?'

'I know what you look like, sitting there.'

'What's that?' Granny did not reply but eyed his attire up and down, disgust evident, but no more afraid now than she had been when he first surprised her. 'An IRA man you mean? Yes, I suppose I do at that. But this here is not exactly an Armalite rifle, is it?' He lifted the truncheon from the settee and slowly waved it at her. She did not respond. 'This is police issue and proper: RUC. This is a skull cracker.' He thwacked the stick into his gloved palm. 'A Provo, or maybe I should say a mongrel Fenian taig bastard with an RUC truncheon, that's something you don't see every day.' Granny's face shifted from confusion to recognition, and then, most pleasingly, to fear. Her voice small and quaking:

'Christopher? Christopher, is that you?' she asked. Christopher slowly unrolled the balaclava from his face and made it a beanie hat again. He observed her coldly, the residue of his false tears cold on his skin.

41

'I'm sorry,' she said.

'What for?' asked Christopher. She paused before answering, choosing her words like chocolates from a mostly empty box.

'For what was said. What I said. That time, to you and your da.' Straight to the nub; she remembered. But did she recall it as Christopher could? The memories planted in fear by a child have the deepest roots of all and they live on, nourished by the bitter waters of injustice.

Twenty-five years ago, her skin more taut, more meat on her bones, her hair fuller and still a lot of depth and thickness to her grey. She had her Bible under one arm and Uncle Cecil by her side, while his daddy marched him away from her door.

Don't bring him back here! Don't either of you come back here! You or that mongrel Fenian taig bastard.

'Where's your Bible, Esther?' asked Christopher.

Her eyes moved to the shelves on the wall to his left. He saw it: top shelf, big book, bound by brown crenelated leather. He got up and slid the book from the shelf, just about able to hold its weight with one hand. He rested it on his knees.

'That was a long time ago, Christopher,' she said. Christopher noted her tone, reasonable, gentle and the fact that she had started to use his first name. But she was not going to oil her way out of this. She had outfoxed Christopher once, and once was enough. Her puffed-up hand was twitching to a beat of its own. He would never be able to get that ring off easily now, even if he had wanted to.

'A long time ago, Granny dear, but that diatribe of yours caused a lot of damage, a lot of pain. Not that you are interested.'

'I am,' she said.

'No matter, that's not the real reason I am here. The real reason, you could say, is that.' He nodded to the wall above the mantelpiece where a rectangle of orange, bobbled wallpaper was a deeper shade than the rest of the chimney breast. Christopher recalled the big print of Ian Paisley, the firebrand preacher, in full voice outside Belfast City Hall, the epitome of all that was fixed and immutable in the world. The sign behind him in massive red letters:

ULSTER SAYS NO!

'I don't understand,' she said.

'Last time I was here, it was Ulster Says NO! No?'

'It didn't work there no more,' she said, sniffing and raising her eyes to the ceiling, haughty on matters of hearth and home. Then, back to sweetness and reason, 'I told you I'm sorry. About all of it.'

'The big Ian we used to know has gone away – from his pulpit, from your wall and from your mouth, Esther. I heard you interviewed in the news a while back saying what a great thing it was that all parties had voted to work together to support our "wonderful new PSNI",' he said. No response from Granny.

'What they did, when they destroyed the RUC, it killed my daddy,' he said, pointing the finger at her. She looked away, but answered this time, wire in her words.

'Your beloved daddy killed himself,' she said.

'Shut your mouth!' he yelled, and she did, but the words stayed as Christopher opened the Bible and thumbed through the pages, then stabbed his finger on the passage he wanted.

'What I said on the TV was no different from anyone else, Christopher,' she said.

'It was different from you. The old you,' said Christopher.

'God's sake, boy, grow up!' she shouted. 'Times change, sometimes everything changes!'

'But not for the better,' whispered Christopher. He started to read:

'*Whatsoever causes you to sin, cut it out. If your arm causes you to sin, cut it off*—'

'Stop it! Listen to me,' she said. She was crying again.

'*If your eye causes you to sin, pluck it out.*'

'I said sorry. They will know it's you, that you've been here,' she said.

Christopher clapped the Bible closed, stood up. He rolled the balaclava over his face, pulled out the hunting knife, and unlocked the blade with a click. The upper portion was serrated, like a saw. He put the knife on the mantel beside the clock, still crunching off the seconds. Granny whimpered.

'It's that tongue of yours, Esther,' said Christopher, lifting the truncheon from the sofa. 'Always was your problem.'

'Your Fenian cunt of a mother stole my son! Nothin' good could come from it, and look at ye! Look at ye!' She spat loudly, and a string of saliva landed and clung precariously to the head of the truncheon. Christopher flicked it to the floor.

'Ah, Granny,' he said and raised the truncheon over his head like a tennis player ready to serve. She started to scream. 'Flattery will get you nowhere,' he said.

One good hit, a policeman's whack, was all it took.

PART TWO

BLOOD ON THE STREETS

CHAPTER FIVE

Belfast, Northern Ireland, present day
Saturday 10th July

Fryer was awake.

The only sound in his hospital cell was the faint drone from the overhead fluorescent tube. It cast a sickly, yellow light but shadows remained. Outside the clock tower struck two bells. Fryer was sat on the thin mattress, watching a shadow in the space beneath his desk. He did not blink, and his eyes slowly filled with tears that trickled down his face. His vision started to blur and as it did he saw something slither in that pocket of darkness. Fryer scrubbed his eyes with the back of his hand, scrabbling for the Buzz Lightyear torch. It was child friendly; tough, moulded plastic, no glass or removable sharp-edged lens.

Weak, white light filled the cavity. There was nothing there. The painted green floor merged seamlessly into the wall of the same colour. He lifted his nose and inhaled slowly, got the lingering farty smell of overcooked cabbage, the ever-present liquorish undercurrent of disinfectant. But he could not detect its smell: the caged animal smell, mixed with rotten potato mould.

The Moley had been close in the wet room, Ade sensed it, spooked him. Made sense. When you owned a dog, some were going to hear it bark, and hear it howl. Bark and howl, like Shane, his boxer cross. A memory, glinting like a poison shell on the shore of Fryer's mind: Fryer rushing to decant the blood from Shane's still-warm body, crying as he did it and saying sorry over and over again. He had needed to work fast, before the blood thickened and spoilt, painting himself into a safe space.

Fryer shook the thoughts away. Without the pink pills he could remember things that he would gladly bury for ever, some good, most bad. Cradling his baby son in the night so many years before, and the news that the young man he had become had died. Killing Shane and using his blood, Jim Dempsey leaving him here, comrades no more. And the night him and Mooney had killed that young fella, McKenna. That was his name. Killed him and Disappeared him in the bog. Killing was never a problem for Fryer, but he had a code, and that night, he broke it. And he had to pay: the very same night the Moley had found him. Fryer had even recalled where he had locked up his old black taxi. So much else was gone, but these things he knew. And he recalled what the kid, Christopher, had said: *By 1st July be ready, be clean; no pills.*

'If you play catatonic, play a dummy, John. They will soon start to treat you like one, and that's going to help us get you out. But those pills cloud your brain, John,' the kid had said, tapping his forehead, looking at Fryer. To Fryer, anyone whose chin and temples were not yet grey was a kid, even though most of the black Irish still remained in him. But Fryer was no kid. That he knew all too well.

When Christopher first started to visit, Fryer was suspicious. After a few weeks of silence from Fryer and lots of talk from the kid, Fryer looked forward to seeing him as Christopher brought rolling tobacco. He was always on time, Friday morning, 10 a.m. That mattered, another living soul you could depend on. You lived and died by routines in the Heights.

The kid appreciated that the world had fallen down the rabbit hole. IRA men who had been in prison with Fryer, men like Jim Dempsey, were wearing suits and ties and in government with true blue loyalists, and all of them sucking on the tit of Westminster, pumped full of money, making them fat and sleepy and corrupt. You had to hand it to the kid, he had a way with words. He told Fryer the story of his peeler father and how he had strung himself up after the RUC was disbanded, his medals worthless, his commendations defunct.

'How would you feel about shaking things up a little, John? How would you feel about shaking things up a lot, starting with Jim Dempsey?' said Christopher, smiling at him.

'Are you a Dissident?' Fryer had asked.

'Do I look like I am some kind of drug dealing half-wit, being run by Special Branch?' he asked. Fryer had shook his head. 'No, you are correct. I am not. I am the orphan child of the Good Friday Agreement, John. I am the new you, but in a world where there are no more rebels and no real loyalists. Follow me, John. I will set you free.' Fryer said he could be persuaded, anything to pay Dempsey a visit.

After that, Fryer had started to talk; he told him

everything. He explained how to plan and carry out a good operation, how to wire together a simple booby trap, and an incendiary bomb, how to petrol-bomb a vehicle (not as easy as it sounds). Fryer gave him the location of arms dumps, information that no interrogator was ever able to break from him in Castlereagh. Finally, Fryer told him about the Moley, its need for blood, and how he fed it. The kid showed no surprise, and told him not to fear.

'Blood will be born, John. With the chaos to come, blood will be born. You won't need those pills, the Moley will be well fed.'

That had been over three months ago. The kid had asked him to be patient; but July 1st had come and gone and Fryer was still in his cell. The shadow beneath the desk was definitely darker now, and yes, something had just moved. Any second now, the smell would hit him, hormonal and dank. The kid had let him down after all. There was only one visitor Fryer could depend on: the Moley. He ripped the dressing off his injured arm. He needed blood.

Then Fryer heard it.

He froze, dead still, ready to open the cut.

Outside his cell the fire alarm was going off.

CHAPTER SIX

Outside the patients were marshalled into rows, each headed by a member of staff wearing a Day-Glo yellow jacket. Ade pushed Fryer in the wheelchair, the dew from the grass splashed his socked feet as a light drizzle fell. He could smell the acrid tang of smoke as the wind shifted and changed. Definitely not a drill and that meant this was going to take a bit of time. They approached a line of inmates and the big fella parked Fryer at the front, his breath coming in wet gasps.

A voice from behind him, telling Ade he was needed at Line A, someone had fallen down. Fryer felt the weight lift off the back of the chair, and watched as Ade lumbered off up the lines in search of A. Fryer's chair creaked as another pair of hands took control. A voice spoke from behind him. He recognised it immediately.

'Hello, John. It's me, mate. Are you ready to go?' Fryer kept still, but replied to Christopher, his first words for three months.

'You're late, kid.'

'Sorry, John, I've been busy. Had a few things to take care of.'

'So I see. Nice work,' said Fryer, nodding in the direction of the black smoke he could now see billowing over the darkened outline of the Height's secure wing. Christopher's hand on Fryer's right shoulder, his mouth now close to Fryer's left ear.

'Oh, John, believe me, you don't know the half of it,' he said.

'I'm ready, kid,' said Fryer.

Christopher wheeled him briskly past dead-eyed patients, none took an interest. They passed the last man in line, open grass beyond, headed for the copse of trees in the dip of the slope. The squeak of the wheels accompanied them all the way. Fryer turned his head as they trundled down the hill. The kid was dressed in whites, like the rest of the staff; he even had the Day-Glo overcoat on too. Head shaved, his flaxen Jesus hair all gone.

'I see you've been bapped,' said Fryer.

'Disguise,' he said, scrubbing the stubble on his head.

'I know that it's dark here, John, but do you think you can stand it till we reach the cover of the trees? Then you'll be able to use your wee torch.' Fryer turned away from the kid, faced the black copse, too dark to make out any details.

'Didn't bring it, kid. I'll be all right.'

'Ah, good man, not far,' he said.

The dry leaves crunched crisply under the wheels. Fryer's eyes started to adjust. They were on a hard-packed path, no wider than the rear wheels of his wheelchair. The fir trees crowded to its edge on each side, their lower trunks dry and bald and dead looking.

'Stop,' said Fryer.

He stood up and stretched, swiped the drizzle from his face and breathed in the dry, mulchy scent of the woodland night. For the first time in ages he felt good.

'I can walk.'

Fryer led, Christopher pushed the chair. They could have been father and son, the shorter, stocky figure followed by the leaner, younger man. After a few minutes they came to a wooden fence and eased out between its horizontal slats. Christopher lifted the chair over to Fryer.

The sound of a heavy engine gunned to life, the rattling cough of an old London black cab. The taillights turned the drizzly air into a blood-red mist. As the taxi drove away, they faded to two red points, evil eyes watching from the dark.

CHAPTER SEVEN

As his plane approached Belfast International, the words of his chief inspector in London replayed again and again in his mind: 'A three-month break is a big risk, Sheen. Even your friends will circle like vultures for your spot on the Murder Squad. If you're gone long enough, the only things you'll be remembered for is your mistakes.'

The plane banked sharply, pale Saturday morning light danced over the luggage lockers and ceiling. His stomach lurched.

'Cabin crew, prepare for landing,' said a male voice over the intercom. He could feel the whole plane roll and fall, to the right. He shut his eyes.

I know that I shall meet my fate.

Somewhere in the clouds above.

The plane dropped to the left. A jittering vibration went up his arms and Sheen opened his eyes in time to see a swathe of rain-darkened fields, partitioned with bramble hedges and one-track roads before they descended into white mist, the scene gone.

'Well, I hope you're not talking about today,' said the woman on his right. She was old, her silver hair cropped short, no make-up. A thin, gold wedding band was her only adornment.

'Sure, we are nearly landed now,' she added. The man beside her had florid cheeks and wore thick glasses. He had a flat cap on his head. He turned to Sheen.

'Relax, Seamus Heaney, it'll be all right.'

'Can't stand flying,' said Sheen.

'Sure, who can, pet?' the woman said. 'The only reason we bother is it's easier than the boat.'

'You should try a glass or two before you board, son,' said the man, showing a red-stained plastic cup to Sheen. 'Might even help with your poetry.'

'In your case one glass too many,' she said. The man returned to his free copy of the *Daily Mail*. She smiled at Sheen.

'We have been visiting our son, he lives in Cambridge. That's where he studied, he has a fellowship there and a wife too.' A pause. 'She's Chinese.'

Sheen nodded. 'That's nice.'

'Yes, well as long as he is happy and healthy. That's the main thing.'

'Health's your wealth,' suggested Sheen.

'Well said, Seamus,' said the man, not looking up from his paper.

'Have you been to Northern Ireland before?' she asked.

'I was born in Belfast, but we moved.'

'I would not have known it. Not a trace of an accent left.

And what brings you back? Have you still got family here?'

'A few relatives, not many. My brother died when he was a child, and his grave is in Belfast. It's been a long time since I visited him.'

'Oh, I am sorry to hear that.'

'Long time ago. Anyway, I am taking a break from work for a few months.'

'And what work do you do? My son, he is a mechanical engineer. I have no idea where he got the brains from, not from him, that's for sure.'

'Police. The Met.'

'Not the flying squad then?' said the husband. His wife angled her face to him. The man plucked a biro from his breast pocket and started the crossword.

'Sorry about him. You were saying? Your job?'

'Police, Homicide actually.'

'Oh my. Though that must be very interesting?'

'Less than you might imagine. More knocking on doors than car chases.' The woman leant closer, and dropped her voice to a whisper: 'Are you sure it's a break, or is it homicide work that brings you here?'

The chief inspector's voice in his mind again: 'I know this is personal, Sheen, but be careful digging round in Belfast for answers. There's a lot of past there, not all of it is yours.'

'Research,' Sheen lied. This conversation had already gone too far, he should never have said he was a copper. Why not come out and tell her he was here to lead a Serious Historical Offences Team, oh and maybe find the bastard who murdered his brother?

'I'm researching a history of Irish folklore and beliefs,

the Banshee, Changelings, the Leprechaun. The Linen Hall Library in Belfast is a fantastic repository. I want to know how stories have been passed down, oral traditions. Link it with real historical events. Like wakes,' he said.

'Waking the body, you mean? That's a country tradition mostly.'

'Exactly. People think that it started during the Potato Famine, a way of checking if a person was really dead and not in a deep coma. So, the family sat in vigil over the body. In time it became a tradition: an open casket, a way of venting grief.'

A memory, awful but cherished. His mother, thin and drunken at his brother's wake. She leaps on the coffin, scattering wreaths and Mass cards, scratching at the tightly screwed down lid, crying out *who destroyed my son, who would do this to a boy?*

'And leprechauns?'

'Sorry?'

'What about the leprechauns?' she said.

'I can't say I know a lot about them. Not now, but that's what I am hoping to discover.'

The man made a scoffing sound. 'A Londoner come to Norn Ireland in search of a leprechaun? Are you expecting the crock of gold too?' The woman put a hand on the man's arm.

'Well, it sounds like a very interesting idea to me. I wish you well,' she said.

'Thanks.' Sheen felt his cheeks redden and turned his face to the window, away from the simple sincerity of his companion. A break in the fog: a roundabout, a car park, a corrugated roof sped by, shockingly close. He adjusted his posture, heard the robotic winching as the wheels descended. Sheen gripped the arm rests, counted long seconds. A jolt, right under his feet, then weightlessness and drifting, a subdued cry from the passengers. A heavier thump and screeching, and Sheen pushed tight against his seat belt, as the plane slowed, and then stopped. He was safe.

Even before the seat belt sign was switched off, commotion had started. Sheen felt the weight of the woman on his right lift. He gave her a couple of seconds to fully extricate herself, then he would say farewell. He would say something about her son, that he hoped she got to see him again soon. When he looked, she was gone.

Her husband stood at the entrance of the row, checking the fasteners on his hand luggage. He pushed his goggles up his flattened nose and looked down at Sheen, small but solid, the arms of his jacket foreshortened by the tight fit round his chest and shoulders.

'She's a decent woman, my wife. Bit naive if I am to be honest with you.'

'Well, I am sure she is – decent, I mean.' Sheen gave him a tight smile and started to move. The man did not respond to this. He looked at Sheen. Sheen hesitated. The plane had mostly emptied, the sounds now came mainly from people and vehicles outside.

'*An Irish Airman Foresees His Death*.'

'Beg your pardon?'

'Yeats's poem. The one you tried to quote when you were bricking yerself earlier.'

Sheen's smile dropped.

'Excuse me, please,' said Sheen, beginning to move across the seats. The man put out his arm, blocked his way.

'*The years to come seemed waste of breath, a waste of breath the years behind, in balance with this life, this death,*' said the man. 'That's the ending.'

'I know.'

'Just saying,' he said. 'I'll get out of your way. Sure we are the last out. Chatting like a pair of old women.' He hoisted his bag on his shoulder and started up the aisle.

'Thanks,' said Sheen, sliding out. His leather bag was on its side in the luggage compartment. He reached in and slid it out.

'No bother, Seamus,' the man shouted, striding up the plane.

'My name is not Seamus,' he called after the man.

'Oh, I know it's not your name, Seamus,' the man replied, marching on, his back to Sheen. He turned now from the front door of the aircraft. 'I know it's not.'

CHAPTER EIGHT

Aoife awoke in her own bed in Randalstown, a village just outside Belfast. The bedsheets were tangled round her waist. She tasted the stale air, eyes crusted with sleep. The dream retreated from her, she tried to catch it, sensed only the blackness and panic, and a beeping sound. It started to call again and Aoife closed her eyes, followed it, let herself slip away, then her thinking mind screamed in panic, the beeping recognised and confirmed.

It was her alarm.

Eyes open, she blinked the sleep away and grabbed her phone, saw it was past eight o'clock. She was late. Christ almighty, how had this happened? The alarm was loud enough to crack a glass. It read 'snooze', she must have dismissed it several times. Her first weekend working Serious Crimes and she was late – great. Three missed calls, plus texts. Two of the calls were from the duty desk, the texts were from her DCI, Irwin Kirkcaldy:

Are you awake, DC McCusker?

Her fingers worked speedily on the surface of the phone: *On my way, sir.*

Though to where, she had no idea. She typed an apology, decided against it and sent the message. She threw the phone down on the bed and headed for the bathroom. Aoife gently pushed open Ava's bedroom door, careful not to startle her by rattling the assortment of bangles she had decorated her door handle with. She read the warning: *Ava's room! Trespassers will be fed to the goldfish.*

Something was wrong.

Curtains open, morning light filled the room, her toys on the floor and a half-completed jigsaw, but bed empty and no Ava. She rushed inside, let out a cry as she stabbed the sole of her foot on a bit of stray Lego.

'Ah, God!' She grabbed her foot in a hand, massaged the pain away. Her momentary panic levelled off too; she cursed her foolishness. Ava had stopped over with her friend Sinead, the one who attended the Irish language school with her, the Bunscoil. The faces of both girls, smiling and framed in pink letters: *Cáirde Is Fearr* (Best Friends) stared at her from the wall opposite. Sinead red-haired and freckled, Ava brown-skinned and hair in thick, dark bunches. Both were attending the Irish language summer school at the Culturlann centre on the Falls road in west Belfast, over the 12th July weekend. In exchange, Aoife would bring Sinead away with them to a caravan in Donegal she had booked in late August for the next bank holiday.

Instead of the shower, she returned to her bedroom, picked up her phone and called Marie, Sinead's mum. Moments later, Ava's voice was in her ear.

'Hiya, Mummy,' she said. Instant warmth, filling her up.

'Hello, baby girl, did you have a good sleep?' In response Ava took her on a rolling disclosure starting with Marie collecting her and Sinead from school, a litany of sugary treats and orange food, ending with both friends top and tailing in Sinead's single bed (not the comfortable sleeping arrangement Marie had gone to some lengths to arrange), together with a staggering array of soft toys and private diaries which were scribbled in and swapped between them until sleep. Whatever time that had been.

'Mummy there's a blackout. Tonight we're going to make a camp, and use torches. I can't wait,' said Ava. Aoife's brow creased, a dark spool of anxiety unravelling in her gut.

'Ava, honey, put Marie back on for a minute,' she said. But in reply the phone filled with the chattering commotion made only by little girls greeting the arrival of one of their own. The sound scratched and muffled, no doubt the result of a group hug.

'Ava, can you hear me? Put Marie back on,' said Aoife, aware of the edge in her voice, trying to check it. Ava's voice, breathless and excited, clearly she had not heard or was not listening.

'Bye, Mummy, we're leaving now, love you, speak to you later on,' she said, and then she was gone, dead line. Aoife cancelled the call, was about to redial, but stopped. Ava was fine, the child needed to be with her friends. And she was already late. Reluctantly, Aoife tossed the phone back on the bed, hobbled into the bathroom.

The coffee machine purred as she listened to her messages and then called the duty desk. She wrote the victim's name and details of the job on a pad of paper and tore the sheet off. Woman found dead in her home in Tiger's Bay, late eighties, mutilation. No sign of forced entry. Aoife poured then sipped the espresso. The victim's age, and the location in Tiger's Bay had set off an alarm, but too faint to say why. Her thoughts were broken by the sound of another text alert. Irwin again: *PRESS R HERE, HURRY UP.* Christ that man was going to give himself a heart attack.

She holstered her personal protection weapon, and paused as yet another message arrived from Irwin. She read it and immediately gagged on her mouthful of coffee: *Bring the new boy. I have a job for him.* The new boy was DI Owen Sheen, who was on a transfer from the Met. He was arriving this morning and she was supposed to pick him up at the airport, the first real responsibility Irwin had trusted to her since she started Serious Crimes. She scanned her missed calls, saw Sheen's name.

Both late and incompetent, she had really stuck a knife in her career today.

At that moment, a text from Sheen, telling her he had arrived, and was making his way into Belfast, would be at his hotel. She knew where it was, had helped arrange the booking. With a bit of luck, he would be there by the time she reached Belfast. She could pick him up, limit the damage. Aoife threw the last of her coffee into the sink, went out and checked under her car, then drove off.

The early morning mist had burnt off, just the remnants clung to the top of the mountains to her right. Above was the bluest sky with billowing white clouds moving across the city, west to east. As she sped down the M2 motorway into the city she could see the twin yellow cranes, Samson and Goliath, in the shipyard below, and giant bonfires marking loyalist territory, dry and ready to burn on the 11th night. She had felt the tension rise in Belfast over recent weeks, always the same in the build-up to the 12th. The city was like a powder keg.

The light was clean, Nordic sharp. She reached for her shades and the world toned down. Shadowy drabness, the real hue of Belfast city. To the east, hidden from view, was the ladder of terraced streets making up the loyalist district of Tiger's Bay: the location of the murder, also the haunt of Cecil Moore, someone she had dealt with during her time with Community Relations. She shuddered at the thought of him. He masqueraded as a community advisor who worked as a go-between for authorities and loyalist groups who had the guns but did not use them, for now at least. In the double speak of Northern Irish politics, Aoife knew that made him a top brass for the outlawed paramilitary Ulster Defence Association or UDA. The PSNI suspected him of involvement in the drugs trade between Scotland and Northern Ireland, but so far could not prove it.

'Shit,' she whispered, turned off the radio. She glanced at the scrap of paper she'd jotted the case details on from the duty desk. The victim's name was Moore, also from Tiger's Bay. She made the connection. It must be Cecil Moore's mother – he had no other relatives she knew of – now mutilated, killed. There was going to be trouble.

Someone had just lit a fuse under the powder keg.

CHAPTER NINE

A wet gust of wind smacked Sheen in the face as he exited the airport through the automatic sliding doors.

Christ, it's cold here, he thought, *and this is July.*

Another gust followed, coating his face in dank mist. Sheen ran a hand over his eyes, the better to see. The fog broiled around the line of private taxi cabs to his right, their headlights on.

This place was wild.

His chief inspector's voice again, 'And another thing, Sheen, don't come crying if it buckets down on you all summer long. Shitty weather over there, s'why it's so green, mate.'

Sheen had checked his phone, nothing from the elusive Aoife McCusker, the name that had been emailed to him as his meet and greet. He had her number and had given her a call after collecting his luggage, got no reply, left no message. He wrote a quick text telling McCusker that he had arrived, made his own way into Belfast and would be at his hotel. The wind delivered a damp upper cut, actually wetting his chin, water trickling horribly under his collar. He thought about the airport shuttle bus which would take him into the centre of Belfast, then looked at his big suitcase, the heavy leather carry-on satchel which rested on top of it and decided no. Sod this. The PSNI had promised him a ride and they could pay for one. He wheeled his luggage towards the line of waiting taxis, and the driver of the first cab in line rolled out and was round the car without being prompted. The boot of the cab popped open as he did so.

He was lean, with thinning white hair, a grey moustache, dense but trimmed, pale grey eyes set under a high forehead. He lifted the heft of Sheen's luggage, without breaking the rolling sweep of this run, and deposited it into the deep hold of his saloon. He slipped back into the driver's seat, Sheen's signal to get into the car or lose his luggage for ever.

'City centre, sir?' He must have 'outsider' written all over him.

From the back of the cab Sheen gave the name and street address of the hotel he had reserved in Belfast. The driver responded with a small nod, navigated out of the airport and emerged onto a two-lane road, shrouded in hill fog. On either side, boggy hinterland dotted with sheep.

'If it's Harland and Wolff shipyard you were expecting to see, you should have opted for the City Airport,' said the driver. Sheen smiled, nodded at him through the rear-view.

'Been here before?' asked the driver.

'No, first time,' lied Sheen. Sheen's father had forbidden him from returning to Belfast. *Over my dead body, son. Losing one child is enough for any man.* Sheen respected the old man enough not to argue, and he was right. One dead child is one too many. But the old man had passed away, so too was his prohibition. As soon as Dad was buried and mourned he put his transfer in for the PSNI. Over his dead body it was to be.

'Belfast International should really be called Antrim International, that's the nearest town. But politics and all that, you know,' said the driver, not a question.

The two-lane road and fields gave way to a four-lane motorway, the M2 according to the blue sign that flashed by. It plunged steeply down, cut a line from north to south, Belfast's harbour in the basin below. On Sheen's right he could see the sheer rock face of Cave Hill, and beyond, the smooth, green side of the Black Mountain, and the slopes of Divis behind cupping Belfast from the north and west. As they descended, the vista of the city spread open, place names Sheen knew well, though if he'd ever visited them he could not recall.

To his west, the republican heartland of the Falls road, tooth and jowl with the loyalist Shankill, and further west the Glen road, and Poleglass; Catholic and nationalist. East and over the River Lagan were loyalist heartlands; the Newtownards road, Castlereagh. To the north was a patchwork of political and religious territories, including Tiger's Bay, the Crumlin road and Ardoyne – places that saw the worst sectarian murders of the Troubles, and now a seat of new conflict and standoff between nationalist residents and loyalist Orange Order marchers.

Belfast – this was the town of his birth, about which he had read and researched obsessively, but of which he had no real memories. Somewhere deep inside himself, his childhood was locked in a room. Perhaps Belfast was the key. Or perhaps those memories were a bag of ashes, dust in the wind and never to be known.

White letters that spelt out a slogan, now in view on the side of the Black Mountain: VIVA GAZA.

'What's that about?' asked Sheen. The driver glanced at Sheen and followed his gaze to the mountain in the distance.

'That's a political thing. One lot like to support Israel, the others support the Palestinians. It's crackers when you think about, but there you go.'

'Whatever happened to Brits Out?' asked Sheen. The driver coughed out a laugh.

'Aye, well I suppose that there's progress, you know?' They shared a laugh and then shared their silence. In the harbour below Sheen spotted the iconic yellow cranes, and thought of the sea, and docks. That was one place, one memory, more than any other, he wanted to know. Sailortown: try as he might, he could not recall it.

'Say again,' said the driver. Sheen was not aware he had spoken.

'Sailortown?' said Sheen, turned it into a question.

'Aye?' said the driver. The concrete bollards adjacent to the carriageway created weird acoustics in the car and Sheen closed his window.

'Have you ever heard of it?' asked Sheen.

'Over there,' said the driver, nodding to the left. Sheen could see nothing but the concrete high side of the motorway as they sped on, into the centre of the city.

'Not a lot left of it now, redevelopment and all,' continued the driver.

'I was at uni with a Belfast lad, he was from there. He always said I should look him up, if I was ever to visit.' The newborn lie slipped from him like a calf from a cow.

'You in a hurry?' asked the driver and he flicked on his left indicator before Sheen replied, cut across the lanes, down a slip road. Green signs with white letters spelt the various options. Small, on the far left was a sign with a little arrow, appearing to suggest they do a 360-degree turn at the end of the road. The destination: Sailortown.

'I'll take you on a quick run past. It's practically en route,' said the driver.

'Look, you don't have to go to any trouble,' said Sheen.

'No trouble, sir. And no extra charge, in case you were wondering.' He smiled, his face lit like a child's crayon drawing of the sun. They emerged on a deserted street lined with warehouses, the rumble of cobbles beneath the wheels. They navigated a maze of streets and pulled to a stop.

'This is it, or what's left of it.'

Sheen got out of the car and looked up and down the dockside street. It was warmer now he was down in the city, bright morning sunshine pleasantly heating his face. The tide was out and the only water was a lonely trickle ten or more feet below, ensconced by mud flats. The terraced houses were derelict, windows and front doors protected by shiny stainless-steel covers, red stickers that warned against trespassing. He could hear the hum from the motorway, the cry of gulls, and the wind. He tasted the fresh yet stagnant whiff of the dock, breathed it in, but it conjured no images or episodes. On the corner, was Muldoon's Pub (Your friendly local, ceol and craic!). Outside was a dented aluminium table with two chairs containing what had to be the last two locals, both unshaven and smoking cigarettes. The door was closed and windows shuttered.

'Is this it?' asked Sheen. The driver answered through the open passenger window.

'Not all of it. But there's not much more of Sailortown than this left.' Sheen returned to the car and got in.

'This was all built on reclaimed land you know, a lot of the original residents came from across Ireland and settled in this wee district during the Potato Famine. It was very mixed, different than other parts of Belfast. Did you know that?' Sheen said he did not. The driver went on, enjoying being teacher.

'Place has been in decline since the '50s, then, after the bomb here in the early '90s that was really it. Terrible, it sort of killed off what remained of the community, not just the kids who got murdered.' The bomb that had killed his brother, he had been in Belfast for less than an hour and already it was mentioned. The past, it was an invisible presence here, a ghost in the works. Which meant the truth was here, all he had to do was look.

'Can I ask your name?' he said. The driver turned from the front seat, appraised Sheen momentarily.

'Gerard,' he said, and reached into the space between them and handed Sheen a business card with his full name, company logo and mobile phone number. Sheen took the card, nodded. The man's hands were veined, knuckles prominent, nails clean and clipped.

'My name's Sheen, Gerard, and I need a driver on call this weekend, someone reliable, discreet. I can pay you well, might only be a few runs,' he said. Gerard's pale, grey eyes remained on Sheen, and he did not reply. Sheen added, 'All above board, purely for my convenience,' he said. Gerard nodded ever so slightly.

'I work for the company and I'm on duty this weekend. Their calls will have to come first. And if they find out, they won't be happy,' said Gerard. Sheen reached into his pocket, got his wallet and took out the money he had drawn down in Stansted before getting on the plane. He left himself two twenties and a ten and held the rest of the sheets to Gerard.

'Discretion is my middle name. I don't want you to get into a jam. If you are busy, I can wait,' he said. Gerard moved his gaze to the notes in Sheen's hand, returned his eyes to Sheen. He nodded, and blinked, took the money from Sheen and secreted it into his jacket pocket.

'If you call, I will come. Agreed,' he said.

Before Sheen could say anything else, Gerard turned in his seat and started up the engine, quickly pulling the saloon through a tight U-turn. He took the same route back to the motorway. As they climbed the slip road, Sheen looked back, at the sorry line of houses, at the slouching ruin of Muldoon's. A single gull was perched at the apex of the warehouse at the end of the street. Beyond, Sheen could see the well-planned newness of a Belfast reborn. The gull spread its gigantic wings, flapped once, flew away. Sheen watched the remains of Sailortown until it dropped out of sight. He was thinking about his dead brother, about finding the man who left the car bomb, about reclaiming some justice from the past, no matter what the cost.

CHAPTER TEN

Aoife quickly spotted Sheen sitting in the lobby of his chain hotel in the Markets area in the centre of Belfast. He was folded into the armchair in the corner, reading a copy of the *Daily Mail*, probably free from the airport. He had his back to the wall, a good view of the front door (had he been looking) and a line of sight on the window to the street. All points covered and no way to be approached from behind – that was a copper's choice.

Plus he didn't look local, but not in the same way the aged American couple seated on the chairs beside him stood out with their knee-length socks and shorts. Aoife thought he was probably plenty tough, wide at the shoulder. Lean doorman powerful, a look accentuated by his appalling tan leather jacket. No, it was the poise and suppleness that betrayed his otherness. The relaxed way he hung his shoulders, the ease in his limbs, like they were attached to his torso by thick rubber bands. Belfast boys were more hunched and defensive; they sat with a crouch, duck and cover built in. A pose that waited for things to happen because in Belfast they always did, the last resort usually rolled out as the first choice.

Closer now, she could almost see his face. It was still half concealed behind the newspaper. He had his own hair, most of it, face clean-shaven. He glanced up, looked right at her, surprise, then annoyance, in his eyes; very fast, then gone. There was a trace of something else too, that vanished as he started to smile as he stood up, a flash of something cold.

'You must be McCusker?' he said. He was old-style policeman: tall, not a giant, but big enough to have a natural dominance over most. Aoife stood her ground, raised her chin.

'Which means that you are Detective Inspector Owen Sheen from the Metropolitan Police,' she said. He took her hand in his and gave a good squeeze, pumping it twice. Big hand, warm, and dry, and a firm grip, but not too tight. Up close his face was well worn, though not weathered, and while well shy of movie-star stunning he was nonetheless a handsome man, maybe the most dangerous sort, intriguing.

'Good spot, you picked me out easily. It's just Sheen by the way,' he said.

'In which case, it's just Aoife, only my PE teacher called me by my surname,' she said and returned his smile. He nodded.

'Weren't you supposed to meet me at the airport?' he said. She paused, just for a beat before answering.

'I planned to, but—'

Sheen interrupted her, waved the newspaper between them. 'No, I can see you have had your hands full,' he said.

'What do you mean?' she said. Sheen showed her the front page. Big headline: BUTCHERED. Under it a grainy photograph, showing what appeared to be the body of an elderly woman, her head hatched out to disguise the full details, much of that blurred section of the image in red.

'I probably would have left me at the airport too, if I had to deal with that,' said Sheen.

Aoife quickly scanned the short report looking for a clue on who compromised their crime scene. Her lips moved as she sped through the text. No mention of Esther Moore by name, but alluded to, location given. Then she found what she needed, smaller print at the bottom left of the image. Sheen answered her question just as she saw the by line, referencing the source.

'It was uploaded on Freeroller, last night,' he said.

'Freeloader?' she replied, incredulous, not confused.

'Anti-social micro blogging site, all offshore, based out of Eastern Europe—'

'We know about it,' she said. 'Revenge porn, cyber bullying, it's on our radar—' She stopped. Yesterday, meaning it was posted before the body was discovered this morning, before it became a sealed-off crime scene.

'He posted it online? The killer?' she asked.

'It looks like it,' said Sheen. 'Not a subscriber myself, but I have a feeling after this morning, there are going to be a lot of new ones. Said the image was posted by @TedDead81,' said Sheen. He took the paper from her and flicked to the third page. He started to read.

'"The sick post was uploaded by someone using the tag name @TedDead81, thought to be a reference to the ten IRA and republican prisoners who died on hunger strike in 1981 in the Maze Prison. Mainstream republicans have condemned the attack and called for calm, leaving suggestions that the butchery was the work of a Dissident republican splinter group, perhaps new to the stage and eager to make their mark in blood. Cecil Moore, speaking near the scene of the crime, said the sectarian murder of innocent Protestants was nothing new, recalling the massacre of ten Protestant workmen in 1976 in Kingsmill at the hands of the IRA,"' continued Sheen.

'Jesus,' she said. The Internet was the new gable wall, where political slogans had been replaced with instant uploads. Her phone rang: Irwin. Now she was really late, and if she had managed to see the front pages, by now he probably had too. 'We need to go. Irwin is at the crime scene, he wants to meet you,' she said.

'We? No, listen, I'm here for—'

'The Serious Historical Offences Team, I know. But until you start next week, Historical remains with Serious Crimes, meaning you are too,' she said. The look on Sheen's face almost raised a smile on her own.

'PSNI are armed, right? I don't have a gun, I've barely even been trained,' he said.

'I'll keep you safe,' she said, patted her jacket. They exited into sunlight. The church bells from across the street started to toll a wedding melody as she led the way to her car.

'Welcome to Belfast, Sheen,' she said. 'Let's go and meet the dead, what do you say?' Sheen fell into the passenger seat beside her. She started to smile, but when he glanced she saw that the coldness had returned to his eyes, enough for her smile to fall away.

CHAPTER ELEVEN

As Aoife McCusker awoke in her bed, John Fryer stubbed out his roll-up in an ashtray which was overloaded with butts. His throat burnt. He reached for his pouch and started the makings of another. He was in the kid's house in Bangor, twenty miles up the coast and a million light years away from the Heights and the streets of west Belfast Fryer had once stalked. The sort of quiet suburban street Fryer expected a peeler and his family to live, but the house was a mess, sparsely furnished and filthy. Apart from a big framed picture of what Fryer took to be the kid's da in his RUC uniform. Looked like a self-righteous cunt. It was fixed over the mantelpiece, brass frame gleaming.

When they arrived in the night the kid took him upstairs to what he said was the armoury. Not exactly, but evidently the kid had found the arms dump. They had two one-pound blocks of Semtex plastic, which looked like orange plasticine. A finger of very old Nobel 808, sweating in its grease paper, its marzipan smell filled the room. There were a handful of detonators, three ancient timers from New York parking meters, 24-HOUR TIME LIMIT printed on their outer edge, and a reminder USE QUARTERS ONLY.

The kid must have been shopping too, rest looked new. There were three large shopping bags filled up with bolts and six-inch nails, six giant canisters of petrol, each looked like it held at least five litres, several fat 30V batteries and rolls of wire. There were also two sturdy nylon backpacks and a folded Union Jack flag. The kid said that the flag was part of the plan, though if Fryer had been told one, he could not remember. Fryer saw plastic zip ties and beside them, a set of cuffs, keys in the lock. The only weapons were a ′.38 Ruger revolver (that was old issue RUC, the da's, same as the cuffs) and Fryer's Armalite rifle, with half a belt of ammunition.

His old piece, God he had loved that gun. The kid said not to but Fryer took it downstairs with him, sat with the lights on all night, one hand on his old piece. The kid had gone to bed and Fryer heard him shout out in his sleep, and was pretty sure he'd heard him crying too. A dim glow now leaked through the living-room curtains. His Moley vigil was over, soon he could sleep. The kid was up and he appeared from the kitchen carrying two steaming mugs, a bad night's sleep written under his eyes.

'Tea,' he said. Fryer grunted thanks, lifted the chipped mug and helped himself to a good slurp. It was a nice cup of tea, hot and strong. Fryer exhaled a steamy breath, almost scalding his mouth before he released the vapour. He glanced up. The kid was standing there, just looking at him. The line of his jaw, the wisp of hair on his chin and over his lip. In that instance he was the ghost of the boy McKenna, who Fryer had Disappeared in the bog so long ago. Fryer looked away, washed the thought back down with another mouthful of hot tea. He looked up at the kid again, who was still staring at him, but though Christopher looked young he was no longer McKenna. A stupid thought. He must be twice that boy's age. And his baby face looked strained, drawn. Still, his baggy eyes twinkled and danced over Fryer's face, a smile playing on his lips. A distant alarm bell sounded in Fryer's head, warning him to take care, there was something not right here.

'Pull up a pew,' said Fryer, and watched the kid sit down. Tea sloshed over the rim of his mug as he set it down heavily. Fryer took another swallow, fire in his throat, eyes on the kid, one hand still on his gun. He registered, peripherally, that his grip had tightened, no longer only resting on the Armalite's shaft. From the kitchen radio, an oldie: 'Street Fighting Man' by the Stones. The kid was staring at the table. Fryer could feel the vibration of his tapping foot. He hadn't touched his tea. Like a man waiting for something to happen. Fryer slowly and carefully nudged his chair away from the table using his feet. Making space, should space be needed. Fryer did not recall the kid being this wired when he had visited. But then, there was a lot Fryer could not recall. With the taste of tea lingering in his mouth, John Fryer briefly considered just how much he really knew about this kid, Christopher. The answer, spoken in the mind of a man free from a cell and chemical restraints for the first time in a decade was not a lot.

'You OK, kid?' said Fryer. Christopher said he was dead

on, lifted his mug, and took his first sip. His hand was steady but his eyes danced. He asked Fryer if the tea was all right.

'Tea's good,' said Fryer. They drank their brews without speaking, quiet punctuated by noisy, big slurps from Fryer, quieter sips and blows from the kid. Fryer did not take his eyes from him, or his hand from the piece. His mug drained, Fryer's nicotine craving itched, in charge again after so many weeks dormant. He resisted, then lifted his hand off the gun and reached for his makings, his yellowed fingertips doing their accustomed work.

The kid was up, off his chair, quick as a mouse, into the kitchen. Fryer dropped the unrolled tab, tobacco spilt, and closed his fist over the Armalite's grip. The radio went way up. He slipped his index finger round the trigger guard and watched the kitchen door. Mick Jagger protested that there's no place for a street fighting man. The song faded, replaced by the start of an hourly news bulletin. The kid appeared at the kitchen door. He wasn't armed, Fryer let his shoulders drop a little, but his hand stayed on the rifle. The kid was smiling at him, staring, and wringing both hands together. Fryer held his dancing gaze, waiting. He listened to the headlines.

An eighty-five-year-old woman had been found dead in her north Belfast home. The woman has been named locally as Esther Moore, the mother of alleged loyalist Godfather, and former UDA prisoner, Cecil Moore.

The kid exploded into high-pitched, jagged laughter, enormous and unannounced. Fryer jumped up, Armalite raised and pointed on reflex, took a step back, finger on the trigger. The kid kept going, he pointed a finger at Fryer's gun and his laughter increased. It was a godawful sound.

In the Heights he'd heard similar, but this was worse. Fryer thought: *He's fucking mental.*

'What the fuck are you playing at, kid?' But Christopher did not answer, he kept laughing, tears streamed down his face. He gasped for breath. Fryer kept the gun on him. At last, he stopped, panting hard.

'What about that, John, what do you say to that?' he gasped.

'That was you?' said Fryer, nodding at the kitchen. Fryer struggled to remember ever agreeing to this, but drew a blank. 'Name a fuck? She's eighty-five years old.'

'Was,' corrected the kid, still grinning. 'Me and my granny had a bit of unfinished business. But it still plays into the bigger plan, John, and let me tell you, I did it in style. I think it was a great opener, personally.' Fryer let the kid's words sink in. He had called that woman his 'granny'. Fryer replayed the news report struggling to make sense, then he did.

'You never said that Cecil Moore is your uncle, kid,' said Fryer.

'Never came up, John.'

'It should have come up. He's Tiger's Bay UDA, top boy.'

'I know, I know,' said the kid. He shook his head, looked regretful. 'You can't choose your family, John, only your friends.'

If Fryer had known he was Moore's kin, he might have thought twice. Better to cut and run now perhaps, let him manage his own fucking mess? Perhaps, but as he said, you can't choose your family. And most importantly, the kid had chosen him, after those he had once called kin had left him to rot. Christopher had told him he would get him out, and he had been good as his word. So what if he had Moore's blood, plus some faulty wiring?

And once upon a terrible night Fryer could have given another kid a second chance and he had not. He could have walked that boy McKenna out of the bog, drove him to the docks in Dublin and given him a one-way ticket to England and he would never have come back. Now McKenna, and the Moley, would never go away. Fryer relaxed his grip on the gun, took his finger off the trigger, back to the guard. But he kept it raised.

'We're gonna need to be careful, kid. Your uncle's a bad boy, he won't let that lie,' said Fryer. The kid's face creased into a smile, but he was calmer now and assured, the same young man who had visited Fryer in the Heights.

'They need to be careful. Uncle Cecil, and all the peace traitors, they better get ready, they have no clue what's going to hit them.' A moment of quiet settled: Christopher smiling, Fryer still thinking. The newsreader's voice spoke, a reported explosion at an NIE electricity substation on the outskirts of Belfast. One NIE employee killed. Much of west Belfast expected to remain in blackout for days. The kid was no longer smiling.

'You did that too?' he asked.

Christopher slowly nodded. 'Now that I've turned out the lights, it's going to be a lot easier to sneak up on your old mucker Jim Dempsey. Daddy told me to kill the lights, but he hasn't said how we can get at him,' said the kid.

Fryer lowered the gun, looked over at the framed portrait of the man in police uniform, then back to the kid. He was taking orders from his dead da. Jesus help us. First Uncle fucking Cecil, and now this. And they said he was nuts. But these things he would come back to. Dempsey's name had been spoken, and with it, a craving even more powerful than his need for a smoke.

'I'll tell you how we can get to him,' said Fryer. As his mind cleared these past weeks, he had thought of little else. The blackout would make things a lot easier. It was a great move, the kid done well. Fryer set the Armalite on the table, sat down. 'You're gonna have to do a run to the shops for me, kid. I'll tell you what to buy,' he said. The kid said he would be happy to. Fryer gathered his spilt tobacco from the tabletop and rolled one.

'I'll make us another brew. You can tell me how we are going to get to Dempsey. Then I can explain the rest of the plan,' said Christopher. He collected their cups, and walked back into the kitchen. Aye, thought Fryer, he'd have another brew, and then he would put his head down. Because tonight he was going to be busy. He was going to pay a long overdue visit to Jim Judas Dempsey. Rock blared again from the radio, another old one, about the cat in the cradle.

CHAPTER TWELVE

Aoife parked beside a large, wooden arch which straddled a street at the entrance to Tiger's Bay. It depicted William of Orange on horseback, was draped with Union Jack bunting and the command: Remember 1690. She walked the short distance with Sheen until they reached Esther Moore's street, the way ahead blocked by two white armoured Land Rovers and sectioned off with police tape. She saw a man at the head of a small crowd of young people, remonstrating with one of the uniformed officers standing guard. He had his finger pointed in the police constable's face, demanding to be let by. She recognised him even from behind. Small man, wide shoulders, that thick mop of hair: Cecil Moore. Aoife pointed him out to Sheen. She had filled him in on what she knew about the crime and about Moore as they drove over.

They stayed on the other side of the street. She showed her warrant card to the other uniform on duty and they ducked under. A swell of noise rose from the crowd, formed into a sectarian football chant:

'No Surrender!
No Surrender!
No Surrender to the IRA!
Scum!'

Bit late for that, she thought, *those dogs are dead and gone.* On the other side she saw the white tent, secured like an alien carbuncle to the side of one of the red-brick terraced houses on the right-hand side about a quarter of the way down. Two uniformed officers stood guard. At the far end of the street, a similar set-up was in place, two white Land Rovers blocked the street. A Tactical Aid Unit was working on their hands and knees, inching along the length of the road. A line of police tape formed a safe passage from where they stood to the entrance of the forensic tent.

DCI Irwin Kirkcaldy emerged from where he had been hidden from view adjacent to the tent. Irwin was farmyard big with a chubby, round face, usually a redder shade of the pink he currently sported. He stared at Aoife. His eyes, black and glassy, were hooded behind folds of flesh that gave him a piggy appearance, more boar than porker.

'You take your time, Detective, call Mother if you must, this is just a murder investigation,' he said by way of greeting. The two uniforms on guard started to chortle. She stabbed a glance at them, they shut up.

'Quick as I could make it, sir,' she said. Irwin grunted, and then looked to Sheen, one eyebrow raised.

'Sir, this is DI Sheen, from the Metropolitan Police.' Sheen offered his hand and Irwin pumped it.

'Irwin Kirkcaldy. We spoke. DC McCusker got you down from the airport in one piece I hope?' said Irwin. Aoife tensed, ready for what would follow.

'Please, just call me Sheen, sir, everyone does. And yes, she did, sir, and it was most appreciated. Thanks again, Aoife,' said Sheen. Aoife quietly said not to mention it.

'You will have your work cut out with the historical stuff, let me tell you, Sheen. It's a political minefield. But until you begin there, we have you under Serious Crimes. A man like you will understand the necessity of efficient allocation of resources when the clock is ticking on a murder investigation,' continued Irwin. Aoife shuffled, this was not moving in the direction she had anticipated.

'Of course, but I have a lot of things that need to be—' Sheen started, but he was cut short.

'Good to have you on board. We need another experienced man on deck,' replied Irwin, and his eyes briefly turned to rest on her. 'This is DC McCusker's first murder investigation. I want you to stay with her, like a coach. It will do her good, show her how a murder is solved, but from a safe distance,' he said. Sheen looked like he was ready to protest, but Aoife got in there first. Her heart throbbed in her throat and she could feel a light shake in her arms as the angry spike of adrenalin jagged through her system.

'Sir, I really think I have more to offer than that. I know Cecil Moore from my work in Community Relations. I can speak to him, ask the right questions. You do not need to hire some babysitter to look after me,' she continued, but then Irwin spoke.

'I am SIO, and I say who does what. Don't tell me my job, DC McCusker, and never tell me what I need to do,' he said, a thick fingertip pointed at her. He glanced at the rolled newspaper in her hand. 'Oh, I understand what we are up against and how we are going to deal with it,' he said, then sighed. 'I suppose we should probably be grateful that they did not post a beheading video up as well,' said Irwin. She looked at the red hatched area in the image on the front page, all of a sudden felt no ambition whatsoever. She wanted to turn and walk away from the white tent and get far away from here. But it was too late for such musings. Irwin turned and started inside the tent.

'Come on. Get yourselves suited and booted,' he said.

CHAPTER THIRTEEN

Aoife put on the protective suit, shoe covers and mask, signed and timed the scene log. A CSI was dusting the outside of the front door, kneeling on the front step of the house. It was scrubbed and spotless, worn down to a gentle dip in the middle from years of visiting feet.

Irwin waited in the small hallway. White plastic foot markers led a forensically secure path from the front door, and disappeared into a room ahead on the left, probably a parlour and kitchen. Aoife had been in similar homes countless times, Catholic and Protestant, the only thing that differed was the religious icons on the walls and a holy water font by the door. The general layout, ordered cleanliness, and lack of luxuries were usually identical.

'OK. No sign of breaking and entering, so she must have opened the door, and money and jewellery left untouched. No murder weapon, no secretions as yet and I don't hold my breath. Lots of prints, probably the victim's or family, we will do the checks. So far, only those shoe prints which are conspicuous enough to have been left purposely I think. There are more inside,' said Irwin. She looked down at the worn, cream carpet. Boot or shoe prints, the colour of dried blood, emerged from the parlour and stopped at the base of the stairs.

'Like a signature,' said Sheen.

'MacBride's managing the CSIs, right?' she asked.

'He's in there,' said Irwin, cocking his thumb towards the parlour room.

A man appeared from the doorway at which Irwin had gestured. He was like a canvas puppet, overalls stretched over a wiry frame. His bushy ginger eyebrows sprouted from behind a pair of glasses, very thick lenses. He eyed Aoife, lifted his dust mask, to reveal a bird's nest of red goatee beard.

'If I'd have known you were coming down, Detective, I would have splashed on a bit of the old Blue Stratos,' he said and started to smile. Aoife offered a small smile in return, then quickly introduced Sheen.

'Is this big fella my competition? With that sexy cockney accent, sure that's hardly fair? Maybe I should have went the whole hog and taken a bath this morning,' he said.

'Don't you spruce yourself up on my account, MacBride. It's the corpse I am interested in, every time,' she said, though in fairness this would be only the third body she had seen. The other two were during a one-month training placement when Irwin had her making tea and filing for nearly three weeks. Paddy Laverty, Irwin's second in command, had taken pity on her and let her tag along to actual murder scenes. One domestic incident involving a dumbbell and a teenager kicked to death outside a house party.

'Kinky girl,' said MacBride, nodding his head, not holding back on the grin in return. Irwin straightened himself to his full agricultural elevation.

'Have a bit of respect, if you know how,' he said, looking down at the CSI, but resting the full weight of his eyes on Aoife.

'I'll do you better than that for you, sir,' said MacBride. 'I just found her tongue.'

CHAPTER FOURTEEN

'Creative, huh?' said Irwin, his voice muffled behind the thin mask. She turned to him. His eyes were fixed on the horror which lay on the floor before them.

'Bloody hell, Irwin,' she replied, shook her head. This time he did not chastise her for using ungodly expletives. The small room was thick with the heavy, coppery stench of drying blood. Just beneath it was the sharper odour of human excrement, and worst of all, a still-present smell of cooked breakfast. The strong coffee of an hour before was suddenly in the frame. She swallowed hard. *Concentrate, keep calm, be in control.* She forced her eyes back to the remains on the parlour floor.

'You all right, Detective? You look like you have gone a touch pale,' said Irwin.

'Fine, sir,' she said. But that was not true, because this was very bad.

The old woman, dressed in a nylon housecoat, was

positioned in a crouching kneel, with her buttocks raised and pointing towards Aoife and the other observers. Her arms were stretched out at right angles at her sides, like an obscene parody of how little children play at being fighter planes. Her face, which should have been naturally facing to the left or right or buried in the carpet was looking almost vertically straight up. Her neck had been all but severed and her head was attached by a thin hinge of spinal column and tissue. A clean, white gleam of bone shone from the exposed gore under her chin. A pool of thick, congealed black blood had spread in a near perfect circle around her head and upper torso.

'Been posed this way, obviously,' said Irwin.

'There's more,' said MacBride. He carefully lifted the nylon housecoat and dress beneath, revealing first the backs of her legs covered in tan-coloured nylon tights, then her buttocks. Aoife could see the outline of her white pants and a darker circle, sagging from within. She raised a hand and covered her mouth, pressing the flimsy paper mask to her face. Aoife heard Esther Moore's clothes unstick from her back as MacBride tenderly tugged the dress and top coat free from where they had been stuck, a sound like a Velcro fastener on an umbrella being opened.

'Oh my God,' said Aoife. She could see what had caused the dress to adhere to Esther Moore's back. Three letters, carved deep and wide into the smooth skin of the dead woman, each one blurred with dried blood.

UDA

'Ulster Defence Association,' said Sheen, looking down at the wounds. Aoife nodded, but she could not speak.

Cecil Moore was a Brigadier, one of its godfathers.

'Looks like somebody doesn't approve of Cecil's choice of country club,' said Irwin. MacBride lowered Esther Moore's clothes back in place. She gratefully took her eyes off the dead woman's body, looked to the wall above the fireplace facing them, before which Esther Moore had been laid, giving nightmarish homage.

'That's Latin,' said Irwin.

Big letters, brown and thick against the dirty cream of the wood-chipped wallpaper, covered the space above the mantelpiece. Brown now, but they would have been red, clean and stark. The bottom of each letter had run, the blood had dripped down the wall obscenely, pooled on the small wooden shelf beneath.

'Googled it,' he said.

'From Chaos Comes Order,' said Aoife before Irwin could announce it. She returned her gaze to the atrocity before her, not wanting to, but unable to stop looking at Esther Moore. 'I had the convent education, remember sir?' she said weakly.

'That's what it means, Detective, but what does it mean here?' said MacBride, gesturing at the wall and the woman's body. They were silent for a few seconds, birdsong from a sunny July morning audible from the open front door. MacBride walked gingerly over to the small table beside the high-backed easy chair, careful not to step in the pool of blood. He lifted up the heavy leather-backed Bible.

'This is where I found the tongue,' he said. 'Mark, Chapter 9, to be exact.' Irwin's brow flushed behind his mask.

'Sacrilege!' said Irwin. Murdering aged ladies was one thing but using the Bible in the process, criminals beware.

'He's used the tongue to write on the wall, like a paint brush. Probably got her on the ground, then held her head, cut the neck, let her bleed out and then took the tongue. I'm no blood spatter expert, but you can see the spray marks on the fireplace.' MacBride performed a series of charades from hell to help them understand.

'Thank you, MacBride, that's enough for now. If you could get on with tagging and photographing and maybe leave the police work to us?' said Irwin.

'Yes, boss,' he said, sticking his tongue out after Irwin had looked away from him, before putting on his mask and disappearing into the kitchen.

'You can see the footprints here and here,' said Irwin, pointing to the tiles that bordered the fireplace. 'No attempt to conceal or be careful. They are probably the same as those in the hallway.' Aoife asked about the prints, whether there was anything distinctive or different to mark them out. Sheen was close to the ground, shifting position, taking numerous photographs of the clean outline of the print left on the fireplace, as he had done across the whole crime scene. MacBride answered her question before Irwin could.

'Boots by the look, standard size, probably a nine, maybe larger, no obvious blemishes or identifiers,' said MacBride.

'If he was as forensically aware as I think he was, the boots and any other evidence is probably long gone. We will submit them to the National Footwear Database, might get lucky on a match,' said Irwin.

'But no footprints near the front door, just to the bottom of the stairs, then they vanish?' she said. Irwin nodded.

'Might suggest whoever did this changed at the scene.

Someone insane enough to do this on a Friday afternoon might be bold enough to take a shower. If he was as careful as we think there's probably nothing, but definitely check the bathroom for evidence,' said Sheen.

'Good idea, Sheen,' said Irwin. And it was, but something else had snagged Aoife's attention. She positioned herself over Esther Moore's body, each foot on a white plastic island, leant down, examined at the top of the woman's head. There was a nasty bruise big as a duck egg on her forehead, extending under her hairline where it erupted in a bloody gash over her temporal lobe. One question answered: Esther Moore had probably been unconscious when the worst of the mutilation took place, probably. Aoife carefully raised herself up to stand but stopped halfway.

She turned so she could reach Esther Moore's right arm and lifted it up. Dark bruising on her hand, it was swollen and misshapen, broken. She frowned, the woman had been duped into letting the killer in, hit on the head and then he went to work. So why break her hand, unless she attacked him? But that did not ring true. She was eighty-five years old and probably terrified. Aoife stood up, and despite the cloying air of the parlour, she pulled off her mask and frantically looked around the room, unsure of what she was searching for until her eyes stopped. There, on the small sofa, she saw it. A panic alarm, the kind the elderly use to call emergency services when they needed help.

'Whoever did this broke her hand before killing her. Maybe Esther managed to press her alarm? Normally they are linked up to a support centre, there might be a record,' she said, pointing to the sofa. MacBride was on his knees, inspecting Esther Moore's smashed hand, then her bruised head, nodding.

'Good thinking, I'll look into it,' Irwin said, and Aoife's heart sank. Man give, and man take away. She turned to MacBride.

'What might have caused these injuries, have you seen them before?' she asked. MacBride said he'd seen it all, no jesting in his voice.

'Could have been any blunt instrument, something long and hard, DC McCusker,' he said, a smile crept in, then faded fast when she did not respond. 'Maybe a baseball bat, I've seen a few similar bruises on bodies from police-issue truncheons in my day, but as I said before, I'm no pathologist,' he said. Irwin motioned them out. They shed their protective suits and exited the tent.

'This is where we now stand. Cecil Moore has been up to his neck in bad drug deals with Dissident republicans for years, and it looks like one has come home to roost. So far these scumbags have not been in the business of ritualistically murdering old women, but then think about those Mexican drug cartels. I have seen enough in twenty-five years on the job to know some people will always sink lower. I shall speak to Cecil Moore, DC McCusker, size out if there are any other grudges that could bring this upon him, but I doubt if this has come from other loyalists, it's been quiet on that front for ages. Plus, I will follow up with the alarm company,' he said.

'Sheen, I want you two to head down to the community centre at the bottom of the road and get statements from any neighbours the uniforms down there have not spoken to,' said Irwin.

'Detective work is about knocking on doors,' said Sheen.

'Yes indeed. After that, I want you both to take a run up to the Black Mountain. There was an explosion at a substation this morning, does not look like an accident. It killed some poor sinner who was doing a bit of honest overtime. Paddy Laverty is looking into it. See if he needs a hand. If the Dissidents are stepping things up, and it looks very much like they are, there may be a link,' he said.

'Sir, the substation is a million miles from this investigation, it's a dead end. And if Paddy is working it, then it is already in safe hands.' Irwin ignored her, but his colour rose as he listened to her. He shook his head.

'I want it looked into and I want you both back to see me in Ladas Drive for debrief later on. I have asked to speak with Special Branch because of the Dissident angle, so be there in case they have a bone to throw our way. Lord knows they may step in, but for now these are our babies, so let's rock them,' said Irwin. He walked away, phone out already, starting a call.

'Not exactly the welcome you were expecting from Belfast this morning, eh?' she asked. Sheen was looking at the images he had just taken on his phone, looking confused.

'A fresh murder victim was not on my agenda, no. Not before breakfast anyway,' he said.

'You look troubled. Something not right in there?' she asked.

'Lots, but yes, something does not quite fit. Can't say what,' he said.

MacBride emerged from the front doorway. 'Good, you're still here. From Chaos Comes Order. It comes from this guy, Frederic Nietzsche, a German philosopher,' he said, holding up his phone.

'God is dead,' said Aoife.

'Just so, but don't be letting Irwin hear you say that, DC McCusker. I think you will find that it is Nietzsche who is dead, Detective,' he said, doing a pretty good imitation of her DCI.

'Dead he may well be, MacBride,' said Aoife, looking over his shoulder at the bloody footprints. 'But some sick boy out there is showing us that his ideas most definitely are not.'

CHAPTER FIFTEEN

The Tiger's Bay community centre was a breeze-block building with a wooden facade that gave the false impression of an apex roof. It was painted white, but its exterior was marked by years of dirt and the scrawl of numerous graffiti tags. In large letters, sprayed in red paint, he read: TOMMY IS A HERON DEALER.

Sheen smiled, wondered what the market was in north Belfast for fish-eating birds. A PSNI car was parked outside, and a group of young people, some wearing pyjama bottoms, puffer coats on top, watched them as they approached the entrance, then returned to their conversations and their phones. Sheen looked up and read the dedication: Lawrence 'Lucky' Anderson Community Centre, Tiger's Bay. A painted portrait of a man's face in black and white, caught for ever in a mid-chuckle, 1970s hairstyle. Below it was a printed list of the various leisure activities which could be found within.

They stepped inside. A small stage ran across the opposite wall, people seated on chairs along its length, some wearing dressing gowns, women with hair in rollers and nets. To the right of the stage was a small tuck shop where a line of people queued. Sheen could smell fried bacon. Aoife showed her warrant card to the uniformed officer standing by the entrance and asked if they needed any assistance. He told her they were all but done. He asked if the street would be open anytime soon.

'CSIs are still gathering evidence, body is still at the scene,' she said. The officer nodded, yawned.

A man caught Sheen's eye. He was standing by the tuck shop, had been obscured from Sheen's view by the people queuing, but Sheen could see him now. He was watching the crowd of people, his eyes darting from one group to the next, like a kestrel on a branch preparing to pick out fresh meat. Skinhead, mid-forties, he had two fat gold hoops, one in each ear, and his arms were dark with tattoos. On one muscular arm, Sheen could make out an armed and masked figure. He was holding a small tablet, and each time the uniformed officers moved on from interviewing a person, he added a note on his device. He was making a tally of who had spoken to the police. He clocked Sheen, held his gaze momentarily. Sheen felt the hair on his neck bristle, his shoulders tense, more fight than flight. The man looked away.

'Who's that?' he said to Aoife quietly, giving her a chance to follow his eyes, hoped she would pick out the odd man as he had done. She did not disappoint.

'Name's Nelson McKinty, he is Cecil Moore's right-hand man, bodyguard, and more,' she said.

'He lives on the street?' asked Sheen.

'Nope,' she said.

Nelson the skinhead was on the move, swooping with a slicing grace through the queue of people. For a big guy he was fast and precise. Sheen searched the room. He caught a brief glimpse of sunlight, white bright, then gone from the left of the stage on the far wall. Must be another door, it had been obscured from Sheen's view. He tracked his eyes left a little; a uniformed officer was close by, introducing herself to a group of people. She had just finished with someone else, and Nelson was following whoever it was. Sheen turned on his heels and ran out the front and sprinted round the left side of the building, searching for Nelson or the person he was following, but could see nothing. Aoife caught up with him.

'Who was he after?' she asked. Sheen shrugged. An engine gunned to life and a metallic blue Range Rover screeched off. Sheen walked to the middle of the road, squinted to see who was inside, saw nothing. It disappeared round the far corner of the street, its engine revving into the distance. Sheen rejoined Aoife on the pavement.

'Come on,' said Aoife. They went back inside the community centre using the side exit and found the female officer. She flicked back a couple of pages in her black notebook and gave them the name of the last person she had spoken to, the person McKinty had followed, perhaps just drove off with.

'Jamie Anderson, aged fifteen,' she said, and gave the house address. Aoife's brow creased, forming a faint indent between her eyebrows, there and then gone, Sheen noted.

'That's the house opposite Esther Moore,' she said.

Sheen nodded. That made sense, no wonder Nelson was interested. If anyone saw what had happened, Jamie Anderson might have.

'What did he say?' asked Aoife.

The officer shook her head. 'Said he saw and heard nothing. He was home alone, his parents are away for the evening, back later,' she said. Hear no evil, see no evil. Sheen did not buy it. Neither, it seemed, did Aoife.

'I want that youth brought in again. We have his address, and he probably won't have gone far. Ask Nelson McKinty if you hit a wall, OK?' she said. The woman in uniform nodded, said she would and made a note in her book.

'Right, are you ready for a wild goose chase up the Black Mountain, Sheen?' she said, as they exited and walked back to where she had parked. Sheen nodded, looked up at the wooden sign where Lucky Anderson smiled down at him and hoped that his luck ran in the family.

CHAPTER SIXTEEN

The Bad Bet was empty and smelt of the ghost of Friday night: stale beer, and BO. Cecil looked at the inverted bottles of spirits behind the bar. Their optics were primed and ready. He licked his lips, checked his watch. Not yet gone ten; still too early. There was a rap on the pub door, from the street. The sound echoed sharply through the empty void of the bar.

'Come,' said Cecil. Nelson entered, leading with his shaved head, like a street brawler. He closed the door behind him, softly and correctly, using the handle to turn and fasten the clasp in the lock, Cecil's preference. He stood, not quite to attention, but not speaking.

'Well?' said Cecil.

'One witness,' he said.

'Who?'

'Kid from across the road from your mother's. He's in the car,' said Nelson.

'Spoken to the peelers?' asked Cecil.

'Aye, but said kept his mouth shut,' said Nelson.

'Good boy,' said Cecil. Nelson nodded, accepted the boy's accolade as his own, Cecil let it pass. He noticed Nelson was wearing his skinny jeans, the ones that clung to his crotch. Cecil stole a quick glance.

'Bring him in,' he said. Nelson disappeared out the door and returned a moment later with a teenage boy, who looked thin as a stick against Nelson's heft. The boy's hair was half long, half not, the way the Royal Princes had it when they were at that posh boarding school. The boy stood very still and looked at the floor.

'What's your name?' said Cecil.

'Jamie, Jamie Anderson.'

'Are you Lucky Anderson's boy?' said Cecil.

'That was my granda. I'm Scotty's son.' Jesus and where did the time go? Lucky did a bit of time with Cecil in Long Kesh, back in the '70s. He remembered Lucky had a fair-sized litter. The kid must be from one of them, fucked if he could remember their names.

'How's your nana doing, Jamie?'

'OK,' he said. 'She has dementia now. She is up in the Heights, the general part, not the secure part. Keeps asking after my granda.' Lucky Anderson blew himself up carrying a bomb in a milk float in 1982, fucking terrible mess.

'Not doing that OK, eh?' said Cecil. The boy shook his head slowly, eyes down. Cecil caught Nelson's eye, and he left the bar.

'Where's my manners got to?' said Cecil, smiling. 'Come over here, son, sit yourself down,' he gestured to the round upholstered little stool adjacent to the table. The boy sat.

Cecil eased back on the cushioned bench, above the boy.

'Nelson tells me you have something to share,' said Cecil. Jamie nodded, did not speak.

'Speak up, sonny,' said Cecil, grandfatherly, nurturing. The boy did not speak up. This time with a little more grit in his voice, Cecil said: 'That's my mother who was murdered, are you aware of that?' The boy nodded again and reached into the inside pocket of his jacket. Cecil was on him instantly, a strong fist locked round the boy's wrist. He yelped and Cecil felt his breath on his mouth. He pulled the boy's hand from the jacket: a mobile phone. 'You gotta be careful making sudden movements like that, not a good idea round an old dog like me.' Cecil squeezed the boy's knee, felt its bony hardness, the firm muscle of the boy's thigh meat just above. 'Sorry about that, I didn't mean to frighten you,' he said. The kid's eyes were down and Cecil saw him tremble.

'I'm sorry,' he whispered. Cecil leant in closer, ran his hand up the lad's thigh, stroking, soothing him. His thumb curled up, flicked against the weight available between the kid's open legs. Skinny lads usually packed a long length.

'Don't be sorry, son. You just talk to me,' said Cecil.

'I know what happened,' he said. Cecil leant in closer still, his thumb doing the work.

'I was in my room. It looks out over your mother's house. I was online gaming,' he continued.

'Doing what?' said Cecil.

'Playing computer games, but online, with other people, different countries.' Cecil shook his head, dismissed it.

'Never mind, just go on,' he said.

'There was a black taxi parked outside her house.'

'OK,' said Cecil. This was new, this was important.

'It distracted me, so I looked over. I saw you leave, so I thought it was for you.'

Cecil closed his eyes and spun his thoughts back. No way had he walked past the bastard, no way he did not spot a taxi sitting outside his ma's. He remembered leaving, he had been in a hurry, told her something about locking up before he shut the door. Then he was on his phone, that app that sent you mug shots of possible fucks. He had been sliding pictures back and forth as he went down the road, mostly to the left, one or two to the right. He opened his eyes. He was gripping the boy's thigh, hard. He released his clench, returned to strokes, smooth strokes, needed to keep calm.

'But the taxi wasn't for me,' he prompted.

'No, you just walked down the street,' he said.

'And then,' said Cecil, stroking a fat rope growing in his own trousers.

'Then the man got out of the taxi,' said the kid. Cecil stopped and lifted the boy's face so he was staring into his eyes.

'What did he look like?'

'He looked like a bit of a tough nut. Black jacket, woollen hat,' he said.

'And you got a good look at his face? Could you describe him?' The boy nodded, hair swishing over his forehead and eyes.

'I took a video.' Cecil sat back on the bench, one hand still on the boy's knee.

'Did you, by fuck? Good boy, clever boy.' He was a spying little piece of shit. How many other videos had he taken? Who the fuck did he think he was?

'This fella, was he alone?' asked Cecil. The boy nodded. 'Then what happened?'

'He pulled the hat down over his face, when he was at the front door.'

'You watched a man put on a woolly mask at my mother's home? Without running down here to tell me?' said Cecil. Jamie Anderson did not reply. His eyes were full of tears, his lip quivered. Cecil waited, he spoke.

'I didn't know what to do,' he said. The boy had gone very pale, his voice hardly louder than a whisper. Cecil let go of his knee, and slumped back on his seat, deep into the well of cool shadows.

'Where's the video?' said Cecil. The boy held the phone up.

'Give,' said Cecil. The boy did. Cecil looked at the phone. The screen was cracked. It had gel stickers on the back.

'Did you make a copy of the video?' he said.

'No, that's it, and I don't use a cloud backup either,' said the kid, pointing at the phone.

'And you did not mention this to the peelers?' he asked.

'No, said I didn't see anything.'

'That is because you did not see anything, understand me.' The boy nodded his head three times in quick succession.

'I need this,' said Cecil, holding the phone up. 'Just for a while, you'll get it back.' More nods from the boy, more colour in his cheeks now. Cecil got up and walked over to the door, rapped the glass twice with the pinky ring on his right hand. Nelson came in. Cecil turned to look at the boy.

'This young man has been very helpful,' he said. 'See that he gets back OK.'

'Dead on,' said Nelson. He stared at the boy, unblinking.

Cecil pulled his wallet from his back pocket and took out two fifties from the wad inside.

'Here,' he said, jerking his head towards the door. The boy got up quickly and took the notes, moved for the exit.

'You done well, son. Now just keep your mouth sealed,' he said. 'Off you trot,' said Cecil. The boy left, closed the pub door with a crash. Cecil gritted his teeth, turned to Nelson.

'Looks like Prince Harry here saw the bastard,' he said. 'And he seems to think it's all right to shoot videos of my mother's home.' Nelson nodded slowly, but did not speak.

'Get him off the streets Nelson, away from the peelers. Take him to the lock-up, work on him. Not the head, he lives, but he hurts, understand? Dump him outside the area. Blame Fenians if possible,' he said. Nelson nodded.

'Go,' said Cecil, and Nelson did. He closed the door quietly. Cecil walked down the length of the bar, took a glass from the clean stack beneath the beer pumps and pumped it three times in succession under the Bacardi's optic, its gurgling refill the only sound. He sat down again in his preferred spot, his brimming glass on the table in front of him.

When he was at his most angry, his most volatile, his mother had been there, but not today. He closed his eyes, waited for her voice: *You use your hate, let it keep you cold and clear when the fight is on. It's your best weapon. Let your enemies fear it.*

Cecil opened his eyes and raised the drink to his lips and took a slow, lengthy draw, feeling the clear fire burn his throat. His first shot was drained, gauged to the measure, a decision was now in place.

It was time to call in an old debt from Turk Bates, his Ulster Volunteer Force counterpart, and sometimes enemy, on the Shankill road. With Mother's demise, Cecil's stock would be high. No request, however large, would likely be refused. But the tide of sympathy quickly recedes, so if he was to act, it must be now. If the Turk complied, Cecil would win control of the lower Shankill from his UDA 'comrade' Scotty Woods, who had got a bit too big for his boots of late. What he was going to ask was risky, it would mean destruction for him, and the Turk if it was ever proven. But the spoils of Scotty's territory for street deals and the chance to show the Fenians as aggressors over the 12th weekend. It was too good a chance to pass.

Thank you, Mother.

Cecil lifted the glass to his mouth for the second time, already enjoying the background tingle of the first dispensed shot. He sucked his second shot, licked his top lip and held the liquid in his mouth, before flushing the medicine into his throat.

His second move would be to pin Mother's murder on the Fenians, whatever the truth may be. The loyalist people would be ready for the message, the cry that republicans, Dissidents, the Real IRA, Continuity IRA, New Improved IRA, who cares what name was used, it was the same old enemy, the same old bogeyman, they must be responsible for butchering Mother. Loyalists would listen, they would be more than ready; it was what they needed.

If Cecil came out and said it, it would be little use (though of course he would). What this needed was someone neutral, a peeler for instance, to point the finger at Fenians, turn all eyes on the rebels beyond the walls. So it was time to cash in an investment that was just coming to maturity. Like his debt with the Turk, timing was everything.

Thank you again, Mother.

Cecil lifted his glass for the final time, and slowly emptied the last of the lukewarm firewater into his mouth. Part three of his plan was inside Jamie Anderson's phone. He tapped it gently against the tabletop. The screen came to life, an animated cave woman, barely clothed, looked lustfully out at him. Cecil touched the camera icon and scrolled to the most recent video.

In here was the face of the man who came to the door of his blessed mother and carved her like a stuck pig. In here was the person who was soon to have Cecil Moore's attention, all his hatred and black fire. It made him into the most dangerous animal in this city. Cecil pressed play and settled into the nook of shadows, and watched what Jamie Anderson had spied from his window.

Thank you, Mother. For the third time today, thank you.

CHAPTER SEVENTEEN

Aoife had driven beyond the estates and streets of the upper Glen road in west Belfast, en route for the substation on the Black Mountain. Sheen was in the passenger seat, and he was looking out the window, as streets gave way to boggy fields and barren farmland.

They passed a Gaelic Football club on the left, large playing field, frugal clubhouse, with a red hand of Ulster emblazoned over the front door. The team's name in Gaelic, Lamh Dhearg, meaning 'red hand', was written in acrylic-style lettering. Sheen nodded in its direction.

'Lam Derg?' he attempted. Aoife corrected him, the pronunciation correctly spoken sounding more like 'lave jarag'.

'Means red hand as in red hand of Ulster,' she said, laughed. Gaelic pronunciation was not easy. 'Surely you know the legend?' she asked. Sheen shook his head. 'Call yourself an Ulsterman? Did you never have a history lesson when you were a child here?' she said, the laugh still in her voice.

'The story goes that the Kingdom of Ulster had no rightful heir. It was decided that whosoever's hand should touch the shore of Ireland first would be made the king. The race came down between two brothers. Niall realised that he was losing, took a sword and cut off his right hand and threw it from his boat. The bloody hand landed on the shore before his opponent could touch land. Niall was crowned King of Ulster. That's your free history lesson. Fact is they're still arguing over who owns this place. Both sides claim Ulster as theirs, both claim the bloody hand as their symbol too,' she said, but when she glanced at Sheen, he had looked away, as though he was not listening, or was in a huff.

Aoife indicated right and climbed a steep, single track that levelled off at a small car park of pressed stone and quarry dust. There were two PSNI Land Rovers parked and an NIE van with its rear door open, a workshop of tools and rolls of plastic insulated wire on show. Next to the van, but a few spaces further on, was a battered-looking Ford Escort, its original red paint pockmarked with rust, and sun bleached on its corners to a scorched white. Two officers in uniform, one male and one female, were standing guard at the mouth of the path which cut a way up towards the higher ground, and, she assumed, the flat plateau near the summit of the Black Mountain. Aoife showed her warrant card and said Irwin had requested they enter the crime scene. They pulled on protective suits in the tented enclosure at the foot of the path and signed in.

At the head of the path she saw a white CSI tent, pegged down with drawstrings, its side fluttering in the breeze. It was fixed to the side of a green electricity transformer box, size of a large family caravan. Blue and white police tape formed a cordoned-off section of hillside. Small, white flags like mini golf hole markers were scattered across the slope. Two white-suited CSI were bagging and marking the evidence as they found it. One was in the process of taking a photo of something on the grass. He lifted it up and dropped it into a small, transparent plastic bag and wrote a number on the side with a permanent marker.

It looked like a lump of steak.

A man emerged from the tent, same protective suit, dark moustache visible either side of his mask. He was looking down at them, one hand shielding his eyes from the glare of the sun hanging in the east behind her.

'Morning, sir,' she said as he approached. DS Paddy Laverty raised one hand in a momentary greeting.

'Aoife, what about ye,' he said. He strode past her nonetheless, straight to Sheen.

'DS Paddy Laverty,' he said. 'Are you the new boyo from the Met drafted in to help this weekend?'

'Detective Inspector Sheen. I am here to oversee the Serious Historical Offences Team,' replied Sheen. Paddy dropped his eyes, sniffed, then coughed.

'Sorry, no disrespect intended,' he said.

'None taken,' said Sheen. Paddy looked around the hillside, appeared a bit lost.

Aoife said: 'What happened here, Paddy?'

'Smallish explosion,' he replied. 'One fatality. The NIE worker, who was called out to inspect the breach of the gate. We think his name is O'Reilly, local guy from the west. NIE confirm a Sean O'Reilly was on call-out this morning, though we have yet to formally ID him,' he said. 'That might take a bit of time, know what I'm saying?'

Aoife surveyed the scattered white markers across the hillside, and thought, yes, formal ID of Mr O'Reilly could be a very long time coming. Perhaps best to call for dental records.

'The governor thinks the murder in Tiger's Bay is Dissident work, and if so there might be a link to this. Was O'Reilly the likely target, or a Dissident?'

'O'Reilly's background draws a blank. No connections, no history, no red lights on the screen next to his name,' said Paddy. She nodded. In short, O'Reilly neither killed himself planting a bomb for Dissidents, nor was he likely their intended target. Bad for him, but also bad for them. The crime scene felt cold. Paddy nodded back down the hill in the direction of the car park.

'Might mean nothing, but there is a six pack of beer in the passenger footwell of the Ford, one bottle missing.'

'So this was some kind of drunken accident?' asked Sheen.

'Well, not unless he brought a few pounds of plastic explosives along with him and detonated it,' said Paddy. Sheen looked up to where the substation stood, squat and green like a medieval keep.

'So the substation was the target. O'Reilly might just be collateral damage. Question is: why?' said Sheen. Paddy shrugged and nodded. The wind made the small flags flutter, and pushing the coarse grass one way then the other, rolling waves of bright and lighter green as the blades were swished back and forward. They started up the hill.

Inside the shelter of the tent, the wind sucked and pushed the material over their heads, crackling and scrunching. The trapped air inside was heavy with the burnt, metallic odour of fried circuitry, faint but unmistakable. There was also the dank, musty smell from the CSI tent itself. The ground under their feet was sodden with the remains of the flame-retardant foam, thick clumps of the stuff remained in the longer grass that surrounded the structure. Paddy pointed to the scorched side of the transformer. The graffiti-covered face was charred and blackened as a hearth around its midpoint, where the heavy steel doors had been ripped open like a can of sardines, clean sliver edges that looked sharp as glass. Inside was a mess of wires and what looked like relay switches or resistors – she had no idea. It was clear that the innards of the substation were badly damaged. The NIE could take that to the bank.

'If you look just here, you'll see that the damage was caused from the outside,' said Paddy. 'Though, to be fair, the late Mr O Reilly appears to have taken the brunt of the explosion. That said, whoever was responsible also managed to knock the substation out entirely. NIE say they will do their best, but chances are by the time we open the crime scene and they get to work, west Belfast and beyond will be blacked out,' said Paddy. Sheen stepped back a few yards, took a photo of the length of the station, and then proceeded to take more close-up shots of the side of the structure. Aoife stepped back too, frowned. This was simple but not. The details did not add up. Why O'Reilly? What had they missed? She looked at the ruptured door.

'Murdering the guy like this, just to damage the transformer. It's a big hammer to crack a small nut,' said

Paddy. Which was exactly the point. She looked closely at the vertical slot which she assumed served as a keyhole. Inside, something silver and gleaming. Between the seams of the doors, she could see that the thick iron latch was released. The door had been unlocked. O'Reilly was the key holder.

'His hand, Paddy, was there anything in his hand?' she said.

Paddy pointed down to the square of concrete paving she was standing on. There was a white flag marker, with a number written on it, planted just to her left. What looked like dried blood had stained the paving. There was something else too, something that looked like the burnt and blackened scrapings that come off a hot plate. He took out a digital camera and handed her a colour photo of a human hand, palm down, there on the same square of grey paving stone now occupied by the flag. Prongs of bone extended from the wrist, and a small pool of blood neatly pooled like gravy on a plate, covering the palm. The fingers and thumb were intact, clasped what looked like a steel knuckle duster, but with just one, not several protrusions at the business end, pointed up.

'That's the key,' said Aoife. 'When O' Reilly opened the door, he must have set the explosion off, that's why he was needed. Those doors are two, maybe three inches thick?'

'Callous bastards,' said Paddy. He pointed down to the place where the explosion had done its peak damage. 'Looks like the device was hidden in a cardboard box. We found remnants of one near the blast zone,' said Paddy, and showed her another photo, burnt fragments. 'Reminded me of a Doc Martens box. We used to wear them when we were kids. You know, plain cardboard, like that,' he said. 'And there was this,' he walked her round the side of the substation, on the white plastic stepping plates to a patch of sodden ground, grass free and muddy. She stopped dead, eyes wide. It was a print.

'This is the only one we found. No fingerprints,' he said. Aoife stared at the boot print, clean and fresh. It was identical to the one which had been made in blood on Esther Moore's hallway carpet: groves running from left to right, a boat-shaped tongue up the middle. She shouted Sheen's name. He joined them, snapped several shots on his phone. He nodded and she could see the recognition in his eyes. Paddy looked from her to Sheen. He sensed their excitement.

'Mean anything to you?' he asked.

'There was a boot print at the Tiger's Bay murder scene, very similar,' she said.

'Very average, no blemishes or identifiers. Fresh, but could have been left by the kids who sprayed the front of this place,' said Paddy, waving his hand towards the front face of the substation. Aoife thought about the horror of the blood-painted words on Esther Moore's chimney breast. Another flutter of excitement, a bird trapped in her chest. Maybe Irwin's move to deflect her had backfired. There were links – tenuous, but links all the same. She looked at Sheen and he nodded. They were done. She left the tent, breathed in the fresh mountain air. A CSI waved them over.

'This was snagged up in the long grass,' he said. It was a beige bra. 'It looks like it has not been in the elements for long either, no signs of degradation or weathering.'

'Someone must have a sick sense of humour,' said Sheen. Paddy paused, his brow creased, and then a smile slowly spread over his face. He shook his head.

'Or you do more like,' he said, grinning, 'I get it. It was a booby trap.' Paddy glanced at her. His smile evaporated. He turned back to Sheen. 'You two might want to take a walk up to the top of the hill. I bet you can see the whole of Belfast, on a clear morning like this,' he said.

'I'll pass, but thanks. Good to meet you, Paddy,' said Sheen.

'And you. Aoife, good to have you on side,' he said, then turned and went back into his tented domain.

'Thanks, sir,' she said. She looked down at the death markers. Never mind a walk to the top of the hill, the whole of Belfast was right here as far as she could make out: the past, the present and probably future.

'Don't think badly of me, Aoife, but I could do with some food. There was a little Italian cafe near my hotel, have we time for a break?' Sheen asked. Despite her immediate impulse to say she was not hungry, her stomach responded at his mention of breakfast, despite all the grotesque horrors the day had already delivered.

'I think we can do better than that. How does an Ulster Fry sound?'

'Sounds like a plan,' he said, and they started back down the path. She thought about the bra, the sick joke and then Esther Moore's mutilated back, the letters etched deeply into her flesh. She stopped.

'When MacBride pulled up Esther Moore's dress, and we saw what was carved into her, was she wearing a bra?' Sheen told her he did not see one. 'Coincidence, don't you think?' she said.

'Some priest once told me coincidences are put there by God to remind us he's about,' said Sheen.

117

'You believe that?' said Aoife. Sheen did not answer immediately.

'I believe what my DCI in London said. Coincidences happen because there's no such thing as a smart murderer,' said Sheen.

CHAPTER EIGHTEEN

TK One was on the Andersonstown road in west Belfast and, to Sheen, it looked like an illegal drinking den, but the front of house man was friendly, and the place smelt heavenly: fried bacon, salty and rich; eggs, warm and thick in the air.

Aoife ordered an Ulster Fry for them both. Drinks first, steaming hot and smelling just fine. Coffee for her, tea for Sheen, served in a big tin pot. He transferred most of it into a massive builder's mug. One slurp raised him up.

'I think I upset you earlier,' she said.

'No, you didn't,' he replied. Then, 'When did you upset me?'

'On the mountain, a throwaway comment about you not knowing your own history,' she said. Sheen studied his tea. Yes, he knew what she meant, but had no idea he had been so transparent.

'I am a touchy sod when it comes to memory, not my

Irish history,' he said with a smile. Aoife watched him, said nothing. When he looked back on their first real conversation, he marvelled at how easy he had found it to speak to her, effortless when so much else was hard work.

'The thing is, I can't remember. Or should I say I can't access some of my memories. Like when you have a word right on the tip of your tongue. You know that you know it, whatever it is, but you can't get to it. It's like it's there, but not there at the same time.'

'I see,' she said. Sheen thought she clearly did not. He ran his palm over his cheek, the first rasping tug of new stubble, sharp as glass.

'I know that I was born here. I know that I lived here until I was seven, and that I went to Saint Aidan's Primary School.'

'That's in the Markets area. It's close to your hotel, you know?'

'I know it,' he replied, but the words weighed heavy on his tongue, like they did not belong. 'I know a lot of details, but I don't actually remember them. Sometimes, over the years, I get cues from smells, sounds, like keys that unlock those old doors: there it is a fully formed little memory.' The consultant said that his amnesia was probably psychological, not physiological, though the two were linked. After what had happened to his brother, Sheen's mind had cauterised itself, wrapped the red police tape across the synapses and neural pathways leading to Belfast and made it a no-entry point.

'Why are your memories blocked?' she asked. Aoife paused, but her pale blue eyes remained on his face, uninhibited. 'I know you lost someone. It was the

Sailortown bomb, right?' she asked gently. A memory, played out in his mind's eye, one of the very few, familiar and awful. He was flat on his face, lying on the street, his ears ringing, hands stinging from the fall he had taken, and stretching before him was the giant terrain of the concrete road surface. There were a dozen small fires, including the ball he had been chasing, punctured and burning with an orange flame. Debris floated down from above, charred Belfast confetti, coating his seven-year-old's hands and arms like black snowflakes.

'Yeah, Sailortown,' said Sheen, his chest suddenly felt tight, his palms greasy, but he kept his voice cool. 'My brother, Kevin, he took the brunt of the car bomb blast. We had been playing football with other kids on the street. He never had a chance. Afterwards, things changed and the family broke up. Within the year my father and I had moved away to London.'

'Where your memories begin,' she said.

'Where I start to remember them anyway,' he said.

'So is that why you are back here, to rediscover yourself?' she asked. Breakfast arrived, a welcome distraction. Sheen did not reply.

'So, does this breakfast give you any triggers, or what did you call them? Clues?' she asked.

'Cues,' said Sheen, knife and fork in hand, tucking in. 'It's reminded me just how bloody hungry I am,' said Sheen through a mouthful of food. The rashers of bacon looked thick and properly charred to crispy perfection, two fried eggs cooked just right, sausage, fried soda and wheaten bread, golden and giving off a warm, wondrous smell. Sheen speared a sausage and popped it in his mouth.

121

It burst richly between his teeth, delicious. They ate, no talking. Sheen wiped grease and brown sauce from the corner of his mouth with the napkin and sat back with a satisfied sigh.

'So that was the life and times of Owen Sheen, abridged version,' Sheen said.

'You haven't told me if you have a wife, or kids,' she said. She had cleaned her plate too. Same eyes on his, same brave stare, a trace of playfulness. Sheen, whose London apartment was so empty and utilitarian, found himself for once pleased with the reply he could give.

'No wife. And no kids – well, none that I know of,' said Sheen, raising an eyebrow.

'So you have come back to the land of your birth, just like John Wayne in *The Quiet Man*. Only you are a cockney, not a yank. Are you over here looking to settle down with a Colleen? Or I wonder, do you have a dark secret you are running away from like John Thornton, Sheen? Did you kill a man in the ring?'

'Nothing so Hollywood to be honest,' he said, but he felt his neck flush, and not at her tease about wanting a woman.

'So it's all business, but a detective looking for cues, rather than clues. Or maybe you are back looking for other answers. I know if I were you, I'd want some. They never got anyone for the Sailortown bomb.'

'I know that,' said Sheen. His mouth was suddenly parchment dry, the room around them felt too close and too loud.

'The Serious Historical Offences job is a chance to deal with the past. I'd be lying if I said I wasn't interested in uncovering some of my own in the process. Can you blame me?' He could hear the argument trying to crowd his tone, swallowed it down. She was taking a genuine interest, and Sheen wanted it, wanted to talk, keep those calm, pale eyes on him, watch as her long, slim fingers touched the lip of her coffee cup.

'No,' she said softly. 'I'd probably want the same myself,' she said. For an awful second Sheen thought she was going to reach over and hold his hand when she said it, but she did not. He folded his arms, cleared his throat.

'What about you? Married, kids?' he asked.

'It's a bit complicated,' she said.

'Go on,' said Sheen.

'I have a little girl, Ava, she's nine. I am her legal guardian, but Ava's not mine. Her dad was my stepbrother. He died before she was born. Drugs, twenty-five-years old,' she said. Her voice was steady; her eyes blinked rapidly.

'Sounds like a tough deal,' he said.

'Kieran got the deal he chose. Sounds harsh, but he made bad choices and got involved with bad people. He was offered help, but he kept going back to the scag,' she said.

'So Ava is Kieran's daughter?' he asked.

'That's right, so why am I her legal guardian?' she said, pre-empting his question about her biological mother. Sheen nodded. 'Ava's biological mother was given a one-way ticket back to Trinidad when she completed her prison term in Maghaberry for drug smuggling. She will never be back in the country and made it apparent that she wanted nothing to do with Ava after she was born. If Ava had not been carried and born in prison, more than likely she would have been born an addict.

She released her for adoption and my mum took her.' Aoife sighed, dropped her eyes to the table and lifted a sachet of sugar, started to twist it. 'Mum died of breast cancer five years ago, so here we are,' she said.

'Sounds like a lot of shit has come your way these last few years.'

'That's one way of seeing it. But my mum did not suffer and linger, and I still have Ava,' she said. He felt the sincerity in her words about the little girl, but not in the reasoning about her mother. She was still raw, and angry, maybe always would be. He understood. Both at crime scenes and in conversation this morning, Aoife had impressed him.

'While we are revealing all, Sheen, I want you to know that I slept with my former boss and everyone thinks I did it for a promotion. His name was Charlie Donaldson. He's head of Community Relations. Now divorced, my fault, I do regret it, don't plan to repeat the same mistake,' she said, and flashed him a brief smile. Sheen let out a laugh, shook his head. And absurd impulse to take her hand in his. Christ Jesus.

'I appreciate your candour. For the record, I am not interested in gossip, but forewarned is forearmed,' he said.

'Bollocks, Sheen, we are all interested in gossip, that's why it spreads so well. Better to get in first with the truth,' she said, pushed back her chair and excused herself. She appeared a few moments later, pulled on her coat.

'Bill's paid, let's go,' said Aoife.

He was going to protest, decided there was no point. 'Thanks,' he said.

'Welcome,' she said. His eyes rested on hers. She pulled

away, led him through the crowded restaurant, exited. Aoife was reading something on her phone.

'News?' said Sheen.

'Maybe,' she replied, and Sheen could hear the tremor of excitement in her voice. 'Looks like Esther Moore did push her panic button yesterday afternoon. Irwin had it checked out, came back as a positive,' she said.

'Bloody hell, they should have sent a message through to emergency services,' said Sheen.

'And they were about to. But someone called it in as a false alarm,' she said.

'They have a recording?' asked Sheen.

'Yes, but Irwin says the person on duty at the SecuriTel doesn't know how to download the recording from their system as a voice file and email it us. Unbelievable! Ava could do it if she was there,' she said. They got in her car, she crunched into reverse and drove out onto the Andersonstown road. 'We need to go to their office. I'll take a recording there. And show the eejit on duty how to email it. Unbelievable,' she repeated.

'Unbelievable,' agreed Sheen. He did not have the first idea of how to complete the task she had just outlined.

'That's more than likely our murderer speaking. Who did he ID himself as, Mickey Mouse from the gas board?' asked Sheen.

'He identified himself as Cecil Moore,' she said.

'Smart, it was enough to call the dogs off,' said Sheen. It could be a turning point. But he also knew that Irwin had sent her after the recording because it was a glorified tea run, it would take time, and Sheen had other things on his mind, things that he could spend that time on.

'Mind if you drop me back at the hotel? I need to sort out a few things, get some of my photographs printed up, start to get my thoughts organised a bit. It's how I like to work,' he said.

She nodded, eyes on the road, but her thoughts already blatantly far away. They accelerated along the M1, headed back into the city centre. 'Yeah, no worries, whatever you want. This won't take me very long. I'll pick you up in an hour or so,' she said.

'Fine,' said Sheen. He glanced left and saw the boggy undulations of Milltown Cemetery, grave upon grave marked by marble headstones that winked silently at him, reflecting the sunlight, each momentarily dazzling his eye as the car sped on. It was where his brother's bones lay, beneath his mother's. Bobby Sands, the IRA hunger striker and his comrades were also buried here. It was the scene of a loyalist attack on a three-coffin IRA funeral in 1988 that led to two terrible weeks of violence. The place had almost collapsed into civil war and ethnic cleansing. It looked peaceful now, the buffering waves of wind crashed softly against the car. He felt warm wetness on his fingertips. He removed his left hand from his pocket. A bead of fresh blood in the middle of his thumb pad. It was from Gerard's card, sharp as a pin. He pressed it away.

'What was it that was written on Mrs Moore's wall, something in Latin?'

'Rough translation: Out of Chaos Comes Order,' she said, pumping the brakes as they approached a line of standing traffic.

'Got any ideas?' she asked. Sheen could feel something beginning to germinate, spreading small roots in his mind. But it was too soon to know what fruit it might yield, or how bitter it would be.

'Nothing definite, but I'm already convinced it's not true,' he said. Aoife edged the car on, taking them from daylight into the shadow of the underpass.

CHAPTER NINETEEN

Aoife sat in her car outside SecriTel's main office in the Titanic quarter. She had just finished listening to the voice of their murderer, recorded from the call made from Esther Moore's home. She pressed stop on her phone, shivered. Whoever made that call had probably just broken an old woman's hand, and was about to murder her. Did Esther know she was about to die? Maybe not, but she must have known that help was not going to arrive after that call was made. Worst of all, the killer sounded like he was having fun.

One thing she did know, the voice was definitely not Cecil Moore. She had spent many unpleasant hours in his presence during cross-community meetings over parades and flags and paramilitary murals and funding. The man on the phone sounded younger, but there was something about the way he talked, the turn of phrase, or his accent, it rang a bell way far back in her mind. A cue as Sheen would say. The thought of accents brought her back to the creep she had just met, the one who needed her to be there to complete the simple task of emailing the voice recording.

Danny Burgoyne (dirty grey tracksuit, a heart attack waiting to happen) had undressed her with his flat bovine eyes in SecuriTel's control room, where he was the mysterious single Saturday worker, who just happened to be around when the request for the voice recording arrived. Serendipity was what he had called it, which to Aoife sounded dangerously close to a coincidence. His accent was not Belfast, maybe Donegal, or Leitrim, out of place. Like the unconvincing excuse he had given for not emailing the recording in the first place. She looked up to where a CCTV camera pointed into her car from the corner of the building. No doubt he was watching her now. What was it he had said?

'It is a pleasure to meet you, DC McCusker, and so nice to do so in person. So much of my work is digital, I rarely get to see people in the flesh.' Class A creep. Aoife started her car, drove away from the watching eye of the camera.

She stopped short of the exit, checked the time, and decided she had plenty. The voice was not Moore, but it did not mean, however, Moore had nothing more to give. She could get to him, and if she brought home a lead, Irwin would see what she was capable of, a chance to step out of Sheen's shadow. In this business, a woman needed to make her own luck. She pulled away and drove in the direction of Tiger's Bay. There was a match on, Celtic v Rangers, big day for a Belfast publican and good news for her. She knew where she'd find Cecil Moore.

CHAPTER TWENTY

After Aoife dropped Sheen at his hotel, he had made a quick run into the nearby city centre shopping area, where he had purchased the things he wanted from a stationery store: a large cork pinboard, a block of A4 white paper, adhesive putty, a set of permanent marker pens, drawing pins and a small assortment of other stationery. He had also found a quiet self-service photo developer a few shops down where he printed a selection of images from his phone from the two crime scenes they had visited. He took care to shield them from passing eyes as they dried in the collection tray.

Later he would draw together the disparate ideas which were already taking shape in his mind, form them into a visual narrative which he could reshape and rethink as the case evolved. This method had worked for him in the past, and he needed it to work in Belfast. The case had moved fast in several different directions. That, however, was for later. Right now he had another agenda to pursue, a private investigation. When he dumped his purchases in the hotel room he called Gerard, his personal chauffeur, who arrived promptly. Sheen told him to go back to Sailortown. Soon after he was once again parked outside Muldoon's, still slumped like a washed-up drunk at low tide near the water's edge. Sheen said he needed to be back at the hotel in an hour.

'I'll stick around as long as I can for you. As agreed. But if I get another call through the company I'll have to take it, but I'll come back,' said Gerard. Sheen opened the door and got out. Gerard beckoned him back with a twitch of his head. Sheen bent down.

'None of my business, boss, but there are lots of other places in town where you can get a jar. Friendly pubs, welcoming to strangers. Small town, and this is a small part of it. Strangers stand out. Not always in a good way,' said Gerard.

'Thanks, Gerard. I'll keep that in mind, mate,' he said, closing the door. He would too, though perhaps he was not so much of a stranger after all. Sheen had been to enough flat-nosed boozers from Stratford to the Isle of Dogs to know how to cope with a frosty welcome. You just needed to be able to speak the local lingo.

As he approached the entrance, Sheen could hear music from within, country or western, Sheen had no idea what the difference was. The singer crooned that it was five o'clock somewhere. He reached and pulled open one of the double doors by its cold brass handle. The music got instantly louder, under it the sound of ribaldry and clanking glasses and the crack of pool balls breaking. Definitely already five o' clock in Muldoon's. The music did not stop abruptly, nor did punters pause, and stare at him reproachfully, but Sheen was clocked as he entered.

The barman, short-sleeved white shirt, black pencil tie glanced over as he pulled a pint behind the long wooden bar that occupied the right side of the room as Sheen entered. There were two punters, their backs to Sheen. He set half poured pints of stout on the bar, before them. Two men in their early twenties stared at him. They were at a three-quarter-sized snooker table which was directly opposite Sheen. It was on a raised plinth, six inches off the main floor, which extended most of the length of the far wall. A stage, or at least it was at some point.

Sheen strolled across the floor, could smell the ammonia pong of stale urine from the toilet to his right. The wall to Sheen's left was lined with stable box booths of dark, varnished wood. The little snugs were paned in small squares of stained glass which cast faint squares of colour on the floor. A big television over the bar showed the run-up to the Celtic and Rangers match, on mute.

Sheen glanced at the young men at the snooker table who were still staring at him. Both wore dark jeans and polo tops with a brand logo on the breast. One wore white, the other wore black. As Sheen got a bit closer, he could see that they were identical twins, buzz cuts. Both were big men, over six feet and with workout bodies that told of hours in the gym: wide shoulders, trunk biceps, lean waists. Sheen looked away, stayed alert for sudden movements, none came.

A second later he heard the sharp crack of a break. They were back at their game, Sheen discarded.

Sheen took a stool at the bar. The rake-thin men to his right, broken blood vessels on their cheeks, their attention fixed on an open racing supplement from a newspaper, were the men who had been waiting outside the pub earlier this morning.

Sheen's shoulders dropped, then he noticed a single punter who was sitting in the far corner of the bar, to his left. A brown tweed cap was visible above the parapet of his open copy of the *Irish News*, a fresh pint waited. The barman nodded once to Sheen and he ordered a pint of stout. As he counted Sheen's coins into the till, Sheen nodded to his tattooed forearms, slabs of muscle that sported a black panther and a tiger, full of colour.

'Spent a bit of time in the forces, I see,' said Sheen. 'Army, navy?' he added. The barman closed the tap and set Sheen's pint down between them. His eyes were green, flecked with chips of orange, broken brake lights.

'Army,' he said quietly, and Sheen picked up the sharp dip on the first letter. This guy was a Dubliner.

'Irish Army,' he qualified. *Orish*.

'Any place interesting?' said Sheen. The stout had settled from cloudy yellow to black, the white head forming a perfect line between day and night.

'I was in the Balkans, mate, eighteen years old. It was an education I can tell you,' he said.

'You from Dublin, right? Many of your city men in Belfast or are you an exception?' asked Sheen. The barman stopped walking and turned again to Sheen.

'And you are from London. And you ask a lot of questions,' he said.

Sheen smiled, dropped his gaze, trying to keep it friendly. The barman had left a shamrock motif in the head of his beer.

133

'Yes, I am and I suppose I do. But maybe that's the Irish in me. You see my family was from these parts, Sailortown, not just Belfast. Name's Sheen. I want to trace a few of them, get in touch with old relatives if possible. You reckon you might be able to point me in the right direction?'

'Same again, fellas?' said the barman in response. The question was directed over his head. On either side he could see long legs in blue jeans: the twins. He raised his pint, took a sip, and glanced behind him. Sheen had not heard or even sensed their approach. The barman stepped along the bar to the larger taps and started pouring two pints of beer simultaneously, one in each hand.

'You say you're trying to find someone, mate?'

Sheen turned to face the voice.

CHAPTER TWENTY-ONE

When Aoife reached the Bad Bet, Cecil Moore's pub in Tiger's Bay, it was rammed with Rangers' supporters, some already in full song. A massive projection screen took up an entire wall of the bar. The pre-match report was on, volume turned way up, and the punters were shouting in one another's faces, a barrage of sound.

She scanned the place, trying to zone out the distraction of the noise, looking for Moore but not seeing him. Nelson was behind the bar, serving drinks and taking payment, working hard, his bald skull shining in the light of the overhead. He did not look at her. In the far-right corner, adjacent to two doors with male and female signs was another marked PRIVATE. It was slightly ajar. If she could get in she could get upstairs, and Cecil would be there. Nelson started pouring two pints of lager and turned his back to reach the optics. This was her moment.

She skirted round a group of men, each holding two

pints of beer, shouting and laughing animatedly, followed the smell of urine and bleach, but instead of entering the toilets she turned right and pushed the PRIVATE door, felt it give. A vice grip on her right upper arm, tight enough to hold her back, but not hurting, at least not yet.

She stared at the big hand which now enclosed her arm: darkly tanned, a gold chaps bracelet draped across a thick wrist, grey hair abundant, like a fingerless glove. The hand led to an arm, same rash of grey hair, a short-sleeved tangerine-coloured shirt, open at the neck, where more grey hair sprouted, laced with gold.

'Where are you off to, young lady?'

Pale grey eyes, bushy grey brows, an old scar, white and indented, ran from his chin round his right cheek, tapering away into wrinkles near his ear. His accent was thick Glaswegian. He was one of a group of three who were sitting round a small card table, clothed in shadow, concealed in a little snug. They were in their fifties, dressed like the one who still clasped her arm in his fist: short-sleeved shirts, jeans, soft leather shoes, no football tops for these guys. All eyes rested on her, dead and emotionless. She looked back to the big paw that still clasped her right arm, then shrugged hard and pulled away. He dropped his hand, feigning alarm.

'Wooo, wee lass, don't be getting bargy with me, I'm just asking your business. Can you nay read?' he said, jerking his thumb at the door marked PRIVATE.

'I'm here to see Cecil Moore. He's expecting me,' she said. She was about to pull her warrant card, but instead she waited for his reply. If he lifted his hand again, she'd pull her protection pistol.

'Oh, aye, is that so? Yeah, well, Cecil is a pal of ours. He's kindly putting us up over the 12th – I'm Kyle, and that's my business here,' he said, big smile, white-capped teeth.

'So who are you? And what is your business here? Cecil made no mention he was expecting anyone. That makes me a wee bit concerned, and that'll make me unpredictable,' he said, no longer smiling.

Aoife saw a mobile phone on the table. She nodded to it. 'Call Cecil and tell him Aoife McCusker is here and I want a word,' she said.

Kyle's face darkened and his eyes narrowed. 'Aoife, you say? I doubt Cecil has any business with anyone called Aoife. Sounds like you might be in the wrong part of Belfast, Aoife McCusker. You run on home now. Before something should happen,' he said, not moving for his phone.

'Detective Constable Aoife McCusker,' she said, this time withdrawing her warrant card and holding it in his face. Call him, or don't. That door is open and I'm going up.' She pushed hard on the PRIVATE door and it gave easily, revealing a carpeted staircase beyond. Kyle had the phone to his ear, speaking.

She stood on the first step of the staircase and closed the door, from pub to home in one step. The stairs were carpeted in magnolia wool, thin stubble. A varnished mahogany rail extended at a steep angle. The walls were painted light clay, the ceiling white, the overall impression was one of sparse domestic neutrality, at odds with the busy, public space of the bar she had come from. Aoife walked up the staircase, the sounds from the pub below becoming more muted and muffled as she ascended. The small square of carpet that marked the top of the stairs was illuminated from above by an old-fashioned skylight window, iron and glass.

'Hello, Mr Moore? This is DC McCusker, PSNI,' she called.

A small passage extended in both directions, ten feet to the left and about fifteen to her right. The passage had the same decor as the staircase, but was floored in thinly cut hardwood planks. Overhead spots softly illuminating the way in both directions. On the left the passage ended with a closed door, half paned in glass. Light was seeping through, made cloudy by a mask of opaque plastic which covered the pane. The door at the end of the passage to her right was open. The hardwood floor extended seamlessly into this room, a sash window visible, again shielded. Cecil Moore's voice answered from within.

'DC McCusker. Sure our stars must be aligned,' he called and laughed, sounding genuinely amused. Not a good sound. A shiver sneaked down the back of her neck. Perhaps this was not such a brilliant idea after all. She turned and looked back down the stairs. There was still time to make an excuse, to get away from here. Moore appeared in the doorway from the left, roller neck woollen jumper, cream slacks and expensive-looking leather brogues.

'Come into my office. I'm trying to catch up with myself,' he said, then turned and walked out of sight. Aoife hesitated, then followed.

Moore was sitting behind the desk, doing something on his computer. At the opposite end of the room a large, flat-screen TV was mounted on the wall, a leather sofa and bean bags positioned around it. The room was finished in the same neutral colours as the staircase and landing. No paramilitary regalia or flags, no photographs of old comrades standing shoulder to shoulder in a prison cell or exercise yard. Instead, on the wall next to the window, was an oil painting of a woman's torso, breasts stretched and full, a rainbow of colour for her skin. Moore looked up from his desk where he was sitting on a comfortable-looking swivel chair and nodded at the painting.

'Art lover?' he said.

'If it's good,' she replied, looking at the flecks of colour, the thick dabs of wet-looking oil. It was good, tasteful and subtly executed. She was about to offer her sympathies for the loss of his mother, but instinct told her it was the wrong move. Instead, she said: 'This is a nice place you have here,' she said.

'Nicer than you expected?' he said, flashed her smile. Moore stretched back in his chair. 'Well, you have to enjoy your home comforts while you can, and there's sense in keeping the public and private apart. Something learnt a long time ago, DC McCusker,' he said. 'Now what can I do for you? I have already spoken to Irwin Kirkcaldy. Went over all the nasty details,' he said.

'I appreciate this is a hard time, a difficult time, but I need to ask you a few questions,' she said. The phrase sounded as false as a badly delivered line in a school play.

'Please, call me Cecil,' he said.

She nodded, returned his smile with a thin reply. 'Cecil, I'd like to ask you about your whereabouts last night. And also, I wanted to know whether you believe there are any enemies, anyone who would want to get to you though your mother?' The muffled commentary from the big screen downstairs vibrated through the floor. After a second or

139

two he looked away from her and tapped the desk three times with the knuckles of his left hand.

'Those are difficult questions, tough for me to have to answer, DC McCusker,' he said. 'You know, when I spoke to Irwin he said that whoever did this removed her tongue. I tried to find out whether they thought she was alive when it happened, but he would not be drawn on that detail,' he said.

Aoife did not react. It was possible that Moore got information from Irwin, but then again, it could have come from anywhere, the lion's share of the details were already on the front page of the papers. He was toying with her.

'I was at Mother's place until about 3.30 p.m. She cooked me up a fry for my Friday lunch, like she always does. I was here, in the Bad Bet from then on. Nelson can corroborate, as can my pals from Glasgow,' he said.

'The only people I know who would want to do this terrible thing is a so-called Dissident who wants to pull this great country back into its violent past. I would say this was the work of some degenerate Fenian,' he said. He held her gaze, his smile gone, let the sectarian jibe hit home. She didn't react, but didn't break his stare.

Moore opened his desk drawer, took out a black remote control and pointed it in her direction. She glanced over her shoulder and the flat-screen TV on the opposite wall came to life, the pre-match build-up, same channel as the big screen in the bar. The muffled commentary was keeping time with the images on the screen, the players lining up, ready to go on the pitch. A cheer erupted from the bar below as the camera panned along the Rangers team.

Irwin was right, he had it covered. The conversation was going nowhere. She moved to the door.

'Great thing, this Smart TV, you can get all sorts. Look, you can even play a video off your phone,' said Moore.

'Goodbye, Cecil. I am sure we will be in touch again. If you have any questions, or any information you think will be of use to the enquiry, please get in—' She stopped, frozen, looking at the flat screen. It had changed. The football was gone, instead she was seeing the inside of what looked like a hotel room. It was familiar, she had seen it before, a man was sitting on an armchair, hunched over a coffee table. She could see the top of his head, a bald spot, bright and clean. Another rustle of recognition, and of dread.

This was wrong, not possible.

That was Charlie Donaldson.

On the screen Charlie sat up straight, showing his face to the camera that was positioned above him. On the table were the makings of cocaine, chopped and prepared into two lines. Charlie bent down and moved his face from left to right across the surface of the coffee table and lifted his head with a jerk. One of the lines of coke was gone.

He repeated the process, mopping the residual powder off the surface of the table with his middle finger and applying it to his gums.

She knew what was coming next because she had been there. It was the hotel room in Derry where they had stayed for a night last year. One of only two trips away, before she'd realised that Charlie was substance dependent as well as a drinker. On cue, she walked out of the bathroom, a towel wrapped around her. The pair of them went down together in a tangle. Her towel was off, and she landed

141

unceremoniously on her back, laughing as Charlie slowly approached her on all fours like a dog. Charlie was on her, she pulled at his belt as he unbuttoned his shirt off and threw it across the room.

The picture paused, a frozen smile on her face.

CHAPTER TWENTY-TWO

Sheen looked up from his stool at the bar in Muldoon's.

'Do you mean the Sheens from Dockview Parade?' said white top.

It was his childhood street. A spark of excitement, fizzing and intense, ignited in Sheen's chest. He had been right to come to Muldoon's; already he was close. A few words in the right ear, he would have a name. The barman set down two pints of fizzing lager with a single knock, one at each of Sheen's elbows.

'Dockview Parade sounds right,' said Sheen. To his right, from further down the bar, a light rustle of movement, like a blackbird in a hedge. It was the other punter, with the newspaper, taking a look.

'The Sheens from Dockview have long gone, mate. They left after that car bomb. The one that killed the kids. Their son was killed. The peelers had to shovel the bits into black bin bags. Some woman found a hand in her sheets that was hanging out to dry, two streets away,' said white top.

'You're fulla shite,' his twin said, and then punched white top, hard and fast, connecting with the ball of meat that bulged on his left shoulder under the stretched hold of his polo top. The hit made a dull, cold sound, like slapping a leg of lamb. White top rocked and as he did so, his beer slurped over the edge of his glass and spattered onto the floor. He turned on his brother.

'Fellas!' It was the barman. Sheen could hear the gravel in his voice. So did the twins, who stepped away from each other. Sheen shifted round, found his pint, lifted it and sucked in a good draw. It was bitter, creamy and moreish – the best he'd ever had. Every Irish pub in Islington had served him a pale imitation. Fake, like him, maybe.

'Aye, our Uncle Mick used to know them,' resumed black top.

'This Uncle Mick of yours, is he around? I mean, could I have a word with him?' asked Sheen.

'Uncle Mick can't leave the house no more,' said white top.

'It's his breathing, it's no good,' said black.

'But we might be able to bring you round and visit him. Just for a wee while mind, he's not a well man,' said white top.

'Suits me, I don't have a lot of time. I am on a business conference, the other side of town, near Balmoral. I need to get back within the hour,' said Sheen, about to get off his stool.

'You houl your horses, Mr Businessman Sheen,' said black top, raised his palm. Sheen stayed on the stool.

'We need to talk about a donation, something to help our Uncle Mick. He doesn't have two sticks to rub together, and as I said, this might take a lot out of him, you know?'

Sheen sighed, reached into his jacket and took out his wallet. They had taken the long way round, but had got there all the same. Every grass he had ever hooked in, every lowlife and bottom feeder prepared to talk about the big fish: money. It always came down to money with these people.

'Not here. Later,' hissed black top.

Sheen looked up at black top, his eyes wide and surprised, innocence melting across his features. He slipped his wallet back into his jacket and the twins set two empty pint glasses on the bar. The newspaper on the end of the bar shuffled gently once more. Sheen could feel eyes on him, but when he stole a glance to the right, the paper was like a wall.

'We'll go, this way,' said white top. He started towards a door with an unlit exit sign over it, at the end of the bar. Sheen hesitated. How many fools had left Belfast pubs during the troubles in the 1970s and ended up on butcher's hooks, getting sliced to pieces? His chief inspector in London had a point, he needed to be careful digging round in Belfast's history. Not all of it, maybe not any of it was his. He reached for his mobile. Time to call Gerard.

'Uncle Mick's place is only a street away, mate,' said black top, gormless smile on his face.

Sheen returned his phone to his pocket, took half a dozen steps and surveyed his surroundings. He looked at the curving arm of the bar. The muffled sounds from the stalls rose and fell like waves. The barman was drying glasses, setting them in rows along the shelf above his head. All normal, he had nothing to worry about. White top banged the door open and strode through. Sheen could see

145

what looked like a brick alley way beyond. It made sense. Twenty minutes, chat with Uncle Mick, a few quid, back in the hotel before Aoife could get suspicious.

The door was slowly closed in white top's wake. Sheen quickened his pace and pushed it open. He heard the broadsheet newspaper rustle once again from his right as he passed the solitary punter at the end of the bar before he stepped through the door, black top close enough behind him for Sheen to smell his beer breath. Sheen saw the bricked-up exit over white top's shoulder a second too late. He heard the door close.

A hard knock exploded between his shoulders, full of force and like an enormous strike from a fat wooden mallet. Air forced from his lungs, he tumbled forward, feet tangled, the grey paving stones surged up to meet him, too fast. He raised an arm. A flash of heat exploded from his elbow, then numbness.

His face was mashed into the paving, mouth was full of new wetness, warmer and bitterer than the aftertaste of the stout. He gasped for air, coughed as he inhaled wet warmth into his windpipe, and sprayed the grey stone with blood. He had to react, now.

Sheen rolled to the right, pulling the deadness of his right arm under him. Pavement grey rotated to bright sky. He hit a brick wall, black top loomed above him, an Eiffel tower of a man, eyes wide and livid, the closed-over door of Muldoon's useless fire exit behind him. He scrambled to his knees, eyes on black top. He stepped forward, ate up the small distance between them. Sheen braced to rise and slam into him with all he had, but a dense supernova of pain, silent and furious, exploded from his right kidney.

He cried out, heard the music from the bar rise in volume momentarily as though in synchrony with his pain. The music dulled, but his pain did not. A dull throb from Hell pulsed up his back, and through his pelvis. Sheen collapsed, head between his knees. It was white top, visible behind him, upside down and backing away. He launched towards Sheen, whose rear end waited. White top was the kicker, Sheen the ball.

'Bust his hole!' shouted black top, from Sheen's right. Sheen watched him run in, blood from his split lip trickled up his sinuses, down the inside of his nose, building. It dropped and Sheen rolled his body to the right, jack-in-the-box fast, his back screamed. White shirt's toe connected with the brick wall hard enough to shower Sheen's head in dust. The wall responded as only a wall will, reversing the force of the kick back through white top's foot and back up his leg. The cry from white top was something between a professional tennis player serving an ace and a big game beast getting speared.

He staggered back, pogoing like a one-legged man dropped from the back of a train, and Sheen dragged himself up, hurled himself at him, gripped the upturned sole of white top's boot, pushed. White stopped the one-legged bogey and went flying. Sheen followed him up, used their shared momentum to make distance from black top, still behind him. White top crashed into a crate of empty beer bottles stacked two deep in plastic crates along the far wall.

Sheen rounded on black top, his elbow slicing like a sickle. If black top had a blade Sheen was a dead man, his heart and vital organs open for the taking under his raised left arm. He needed black top to step in, otherwise Sheen would saw uselessly in thin air, probably unbalance. That would be bad. The twin was younger and stronger. Sheen's back had felt like it was hit with a Range Rover. Thankfully, black top was also a mouth breather; he did not disappoint.

He charged, and Sheen's elbow connected precisely as planned with the ridge of black top's nose. It cracked like a green twig in a campfire. It sent him back, but not down. Sheen panted, more blood expelled from his mouth. Black top's right arm vaulted out, like it was on a piston. His palm stuck to the brick wall and he steadied himself.

Jesus Christ, that piece of meat could take a hit.

His flat brown eyes went out of focus, but then rested on Sheen, full of hate. His nose, crooked as a hill street in San Francisco, oozed a single globule of blood. Black top's tongue slowly appeared and licked it away, leaving a light red smear for a moustache. Probably concussed, but still moving for now. A good kick in the bollocks should finish him.

White light flashed, like a clean, brilliant bedsheet pulled over his world. A tin whistle, screamed without melody, pitched at the top of a thousand lungs. He was Saul on the road to Damascus, blinded and falling, the white sheet turned grey and the screaming whistles faded, replaced by something else, *slap, slap, slap*, getting closer, as Sheen's world turned from grey to black.

The slap of his feet echoed up Dockview Parade as he sprinted after the ball, the sharp pant of his breath, the orange glow of the concrete streetlamps, already on but it's not yet fully dark. A car turns the corner up ahead and he darts up on the pavement, skips a few more strides out, lets it pass, then he's back on the road, eye on the ball. Kevin will kill him if he loses the ball. Still, he slows, because the car screeches to a stop. A door slams and he hears the sound of feet, heavy, grown-up strides, running away. Then the world turns white and when he looks up, he is down, dozens of small fires are burning on the road, and black snow falls on his hand.

'Hey boy! You OK? Hey!' Sheen blinked awake, saw the grey landscape of Muldoon's backyard, his blood on the ground. Dockview Parade, the fires and the burning ball gone.

'Alive at least, you buck edgit.' Sheen responded with a groan. Yes, he is alive, the pain tells him so. He opened his eyes, sees the man's face, red-cheeked, a brown tweed cap on his head, eyes furious-looking and huge behind his thick lenses. The reek of beer from his breath wafts on Sheen. Sheen strained to place him. He has met this man before. But his mind is too slow.

'Buck fucking edgit, you,' he said, then his face lifts away.

'Yes, I'm OK,' said Sheen, but this was far from true. Pain pounded from the back of his head like a meteor had struck. Pain pulsed from his right kidney, low and long, like a fat double bass string being played. Sheen groped the ground for purchase, raised up a few inches and collapsed on one elbow and ejected his cooked breakfast, the stout, everything he contained in an unholy stew of hot bile and sour foulness that projected over a beer keg and up the wall. At last he stood, his world in mescaline hypercolour, but head clear.

The man stood, squat and stocky between him and the twins. It was the punter who was at the end of the bar, behind the paper. But also the same man Sheen met on the

149

plane this morning, the one who recited Yeats, and who threatened him so politely. The old boy had probably just saved his life. Sheen stepped forward. Time to even up the odds, explanations could wait.

The twins were stood shoulder to shoulder, filled the width of the bricked-up backyard in front of the old boy. Both bristled as he approached. White top held a thick brown glass bottle by its neck, like a nightmare ice cream. Its base was a jagged mouth of protruding glass. That was what the bastard had hit him with. His head hurt like hell, but it could have been worse, a lot worse. One slice from the end of that bottle could have had an artery in his neck. Black top sported a brass knuckleduster on his right hand. Brass balls, worn and evil-looking, protruded half an inch over the line of his knuckles. No wonder Sheen had hit the floor like a sack of coal when he'd thumped him from behind. If black top had punched him in the back of the neck, Sheen would have been communicating with the world through blinking. Lucky. He had been very lucky again.

The twins could stand the sight of their prey no longer. Both men moved at once, collided shoulders and came to an almost immediate standstill again. They looked at each other, black nodded to white, who moved half a step forward, eating more distance between himself and the old boy and Sheen, the bottle in hand, shards facing out.

'That'll do you, Nesbit,' said the old boy. 'Enough from the both of you. Drop that bottle—'

'Fuck you off, old man,' said white top. Then, to Sheen, as he inched forward, another half step, 'You're a dead man, Brit, a dead ma—'

It took place so fast that Sheen almost missed the move.

The old boy, stock-still until white top reached touching distance, seized his upheld hand, holding the broken bottle and twisted it away a fraction. He pushed up off the momentum, jabbed his head into white top's face. Sheen heard a slap crack sound and watched white top's head whip back, a spray of claret hit his twin in the same instant. White sagged, slack jawed, eyes dead like stones. His nose was now a snap for his brother's. His long body loosened and turned to jelly.

Black bellowed and swung the knuckleduster through a wide right at the old boy, round the slackening form of his brother. The old boy pulled out of the headbutt and pushed white top's arm up and back, the broken bottle held loosely, but still in play. The jagged mouth connected with black top's right fist, breaking with a low clunk and crunch. The old boy dropped white top's arm and stepped back. Black top let out a howl, hoarse and horrible, clutched his right arm in front of him and stared at it like it was a new species of monster. White top's knees now gave way entirely and he collapsed in a limp pile, the crates broke his fall once again, face down, no movement.

The brown bottle was embedded by the neck in the meat between black top's thumb and index finger. Blood coursed from the wound, a fountain of red pumping down black top's arm and dribbling to the concrete below. Sheen could hear it patter. Sheen reached in his pocket, searching for something to tie black top's arm. He needed a tourniquet; he could bleed out.

The old man stepped back and to the side, giving black top space. His anticipation, like his headbutt, was perfectly timed. Black top staggered past, his ruined hand held aloft, knuckleduster now dark with blood. He blundered through the fire exit and back into Muldoon's and was gone. The whole dance, from the old boy's first hit to black top's bloody exit, had taken no more than ten seconds. Sheen returned his attention to white top. He was out cold. The old boy grunted as he heaved him free from the crates, and turned white top on his side, arm beneath his body, mouth open, tongue out.

'That's the recovery position. Good idea, you don't want him swallowing his own tongue,' said Sheen.

The old boy straightened up. 'Very clever, Seamus Heaney,' he said. 'Now maybe you can think of what I can tell their Uncle Mick, who happens to be a friend of mine?' he said.

The old boy walked past him, back into Muldoon's. Sheen followed. His body cried out for mercy with each step and he could feel a tight egg at the back of his head. Sheen stopped, surveyed the damage, the vomit, and the blood on the floor. Maybe he did not speak the lingo here after all.

CHAPTER TWENTY-THREE

Aoife stared back at her own face, still projected on Cecil Moore's big television screen, and reached out, groped the hard corner of the door, tried to steady herself on legs that had become boneless. She over-balanced, stumbled, banged her head on the corner. The pain, searing and eye-watering, fed her rising fury. She glared at Moore, reached for her weapon, lips pulled back in a snarl.

'You bastard!' she screamed. She would kill him, shoot the fucker right here. Her finger moved from the guard to the trigger and she stepped forward.

'Put that gun down,' said Moore. His voice was calm, reasonable.

'Down, I said. One push on this remote and that home video will be on the big screen downstairs. The regulars will be pissed off for the first ten seconds, but after that they'll be queuing up for copies. They will get one too, whether that gun goes off or not, Nelson will see to it. You have three seconds,' he said, then started counting. 'One.'

How had this happened? Did Charlie stitch her up? Was he in on it? He wanted to tell her something yesterday at lunch, before she had walked off. She had been angry with him for being pissed and incoherent. No wonder the sod wanted to get blitzed, right now all she wanted was oblivion.

'Two,' he said.

It was the drugs. Moore was the king pin for coke in Belfast. He must have got to Charlie through the drugs. One way or the other Charlie had brought this on himself, and now her. Pull the trigger now and Moore dies, but she would lose. Life in prison is no place for a copper. She'd be better eating her own gun, if she could get out of the Bad Bet alive. But what about Ava? The thought snapped her back to her senses. She holstered her gun.

'Very sensible. You are a smart woman, and you will go far. Together, we will go far,' he said.

'You need your head examined,' she said. 'Just cos you made a dirty bloody video of me with a married man, you think I am going to be somehow beholden to you? Go ahead, show the pub, upload it for all I care,' she said.

Moore shrugged, nodded. 'Getting caught at it might even do your career a bit of good. Drugs, on the other hand, now that takes it to a whole new level. You, DC McCusker, were not having a love affair with a married man, you were involved in a seedy drug and sex fling with a bent copper, and you know as well as I do what the press and your superiors will make of that. And I'd be surprised if they let you keep custody of that wee mulatto child you look after,' said Moore. She ignored Moore's racist comment. For now.

Bent copper? So Charlie was in on it, from the start. Moore must have read her, no more poker face games now.

'Ah now don't you fret, your boyfriend didn't know about the camera, but he worked for me, still does. Sick man that Donaldson, drugs and gambling, bad mix. Lots of debts, on both counts. I am the poison, and I am the remedy you see. In exchange I get a little information here and there, the greatest form of wealth, apart from good art that is!

'Which is where you come in, DC McCusker. See I wanted Charlie in Serious Crimes, but the poor fella has reached his use by date, no good. He told me not to worry, he told me he knew just the person, a woman, and a taig, no less. A ticket for promotion if ever there was one in these fucked-up times we have found ourselves living in,' he said.

'I was promoted on my own merits,' she said, sounding weak and unconvincing to her own ears.

'Aye, keep on telling yourself that. Charlie was right about one thing, you're a good peeler, maybe the last of them, no vice. Very hard to control that sort of asset,' he said. 'So I knew I needed a wee insurance policy, something to keep the peace pipe burning, DC McCusker. And now I have you, a friend no less, in Serious Crimes,' he said.

Tears, hot and hateful, filled her eyes, shaming her. She was trapped, career suicide and losing Ava on the one hand, throwing away every principle and becoming Moore's bitch on the other. She was totally screwed. She looked at the awful still image frozen on the screen.

'How can I trust you? You have a thousand copies. All it takes is one to leak and it's over,' she said.

'There is one copy and one copy only. This is it,' he said, showing his mobile. 'No hard drive copies, no USB copy, no online copy. You have my word,' said Moore. 'You don't know if you can trust me, but you will. We need a professional understanding to work together, DC McCusker. If it leaks, the arrangement is null and void. You lose, I lose, the kid loses. So this stays with me at all times, and if I remain safe, so does our wee secret. If not . . .' he tailed off.

'Get that off the screen,' she said.

Moore did as she asked, football returned, sound muted.

'Don't worry, DC McCusker, this will work out fine, and don't concern yourself that I will be making this thing my bedtime viewing, really not my taste.'

Aoife looked at this man who was blackmailing and threatening her, and whom she was powerless to oppose, and said nothing because right now, for the first time in her life, she understood what it meant to be powerless.

Moore rummaged in his desk drawer, took out a cheap pay as you go Nokia mobile. He tossed, she caught. 'We keep in touch,' he said. 'Once again, my take on Mother's death. It was some looper Dissident from Ardoyne or the Bone across the way. Those Fenians are animals, you know? I want to hear that spoken in public, by you, Aoife, before this day is out. A test of our new relationship. I want to hear on the evening news. Keep it simple. IRA filth, up to their old tricks,' he said. She bit her bottom lip, eyes hot and wet, and stared at the painting on the wall, a woman with no head to think, no legs to run, prostrate and on public display. She nodded once, barely.

'Good girl. Now, off you trot, the match has started. Rangers will get a hiding, but you never know your luck, the other scum might have a bad day,' he said, breaking into a laugh now. She did as he bid, turned and walked out to the commentary of the match and Moore's deep laugh. She floated down the passage, and down the stairs, a ghost in her own body, dead and beaten.

Once in her car, she drove on autopilot and found herself back at SecuriTel. She rolled her window halfway down, sucked in the fresh sea air coming in off Belfast Lough, then soaked tissues with a bottle of water and applied the cool wad to the hot, nasty welt on her forehead. Aoife took stock. Charlie's betrayal, if true, was one thing, but the CCTV was something else, way beyond anything Charlie could have arranged, even if he had wanted to. It was high quality, industry standard, and the sort of technology she had heard of MI5 and Special Branch using in Northern Ireland. After today she would not be surprised if Moore was in cahoots with both. She squinted, as the sun was reflected from the side of the glass building. SecuriTel's logo loomed above her. The camera was still watching from its vantage point above.

That fat pig Danny Burgoyne, his accent was not Donegal, or Leitrim.

It was Derry.

Same place as the hotel where she and Charlie had been stitched up.

I rarely get to see people in the flesh.

Burgoyne had seen her before, on the CCTV recording he had probably helped set up. Not a coincidence that he was in the office on Saturday. Burgoyne was Moore's man, which meant Moore had a copy of the recording and he was hunting the killer. Information she now needed to shield from her team, until she found a way to deal with Moore's blackmail, adding lie upon lie, deeper and deeper by the minute. And next, she must obey her master's voice, blame republicans for the murder. Doing so would add fuel to a fire that could burn out of control. To refuse meant losing her job, her reputation, Ava. What a mess, what a godawful, dangerous mess.

CHAPTER TWENTY-FOUR

A tea towel filled with ice, the cubes pointed and unforgiving against the swelling on Sheen's head. It hurt like hell, but Sheen pressed it harder. The barman worked his way quickly across the length of the pub floor with a mop, bucket in tow, heading in the direction of the front door where black top's blood led. Sheen could see a path of bright wetness in his wake. He had given Sheen the ice pack without comment, before fetching the mop.

The old boy had resumed his place on the stool at the end of the bar and Sheen took one next to him.

'Give us your wallet, please,' said the old boy. Sheen dropped the fat leather sandwich on the bar between them. The old boy flipped it open and thumbed out two twenties. He closed the wallet with a flip and held the money up between two pork sausage fingers. The barman approached.

'For your trouble, Colm,' he said. Colm the barman nodded once and took the money.

'That's them barred now, sorry, Billy,' he said.

'Their own fault, as per usual,' replied Billy. 'Though having DCI Banks here dander in and wave a wallet full of money around didn't exactly help,' he said to Sheen. 'Mine's another pint by the way, and a large Bushmills to chase it,' he said.

'And a pint of water for me,' said Sheen.

Colm set to work.

'I want to thank you for helping me out there,' said Sheen.

'So say it,' said Billy.

'Thank you,' said Sheen.

'Welcome, Seamus,' said Billy.

Sheen gritted his teeth, heard them squeak and tasted the residue of his own bile. 'As I said when we met earlier, that's not my name. If I'm buying you a drink, maybe we can start again. My name is—'

'I know who you are, Owen Sheen. I recognised you on the flight today, and when you blundered in here. Name's Murphy, Billy Murphy.' Billy paused, appraised him. 'You have the look of your da, you always did,' he said.

'You mean, we have met, before?' said Sheen.

'I remember you, if that is what you mean.'

'And that's why you helped me just now, with the twins?' said Sheen.

The ice had started to melt and a cold finger of water trickled from his scalp down the back of his collar. He repositioned the pack with a wince, waited for a reply.

'Your da was a good man. He never deserved what happened,' said Billy.

Colm the barman set down their drinks and Sheen passed him a ten pound note. Colm thanked him, went to the till and deposited it. No change.

160

'Is your da still living?' said Billy. He drained a gulp from his fresh pint, and chased it with a sip of Bushmills; one drink opaque black, the other dark varnish fire in a glass.

'Dad's dead, this year,' said Sheen.

'Sorry to hear it,' said Billy, rocking his head forward and to the side once, half a nod, half a shake.

'So does everyone your age round here know how to handle themselves like you?' said Sheen, taking a sip of his ice-filled pint of water, the liquid running cold fire down his raw throat.

'My age, you say?' said Billy. 'In my day, I did some moonlighting for a local loan shark at the docks. Lots of bad debts on the waterfront.'

'You collected the money?' said Sheen.

'There was rarely money to collect, son, this was Sailortown. I said I did some moonlighting. I settled the debts whether money could be repaid or not,' he said, and cracked his knuckles, deep bony breaks.

'Then you'll understand why I am back, why I was willing to take a risk with the twins,' said Sheen.

Billy grunted and took another pull on his drink. 'I heard you spin a tissue of nonsense to them, same as you did on the plane to my wife this morning. I wonder if you have any truth in you at all, young Sheen.'

'I want to settle an old score, clear a debt, and you know what I am talking about,' said Sheen, grabbing hold of Billy's arm as he was about to raise the pint to his mouth again. Rough textured tweed, hard muscle beneath. Sheen let go.

Billy Murphy turned in his stool. 'You mean the car bomb, the one that killed your brother, that nearly killed you?' he said.

Sheen recalled his dream, or, perhaps, his newest memory: the sound of his feet running, the slam of a car door.

'Yes,' he said.

'A bit of honesty at last then,' said Billy. He paused, gulped his pint and put it down, half empty now. 'You're not the only one who lost that day. My nephew was playing football in the street with your brother,' he said.

Sheen took a second to make sense of what he was saying. He had been the only child that survived, meaning Billy's nephew was blown to pieces, just like Kevin. He'd had no clue. Yet again, his barren memory offered him only frustration and humiliation. 'I want the bastards who did it. I don't care if they are in prison or in government, I want them,' said Sheen. He had slammed the ice pack down with a muffled rattle on the bar. Half melted cubes dispersed across the dark wood.

'No doubt you do. It surprises me it took you this long to come looking, being a peeler and all. I might have balanced that book a long time since,' said Billy.

'But you didn't, did you?' said Sheen.

Billy eyed him. 'I had my own family to consider, and believe me I have settled my share of scores in this town over the years. Plus in Belfast, a man does well to understand his own limits. Discretion can be the better part of valour,' said Billy.

Billy knew something, his copper's sense told him so, and Sheen was close to hearing it.

'Give me a name, Billy,' he said.

Instead, Billy said, 'There was a lot of rumours at the time of that bomb, conspiracy bollocks. Some said it was loyalists with the help of the Brits who planted that device.

Others blamed some Marxist splinter group like the INLA. They had no scruples, and they had the form for it. No class, you might say,' said Billy with a dry chuckle.

'Some said it was a mistake, that the IRA had the car bomb primed and ready for a target in the city centre or for a British foot patrol and it was abandoned or went off early,' said Billy.

'I know all this already. I want the truth,' said Sheen.

'The truth is nobody knows, and the truth is just the truth, Owen Sheen. That bomb was never claimed, no one done time for it. Nah, what you want is a name,' he said.

Sheen listened. This was it, the moment he had waited for.

'Ask yourself who benefited from that bomb? It was one of the last plays in the Troubles. Before it there were tit for tat sectarian killings, the whole place was on the edge of civil war. That bomb was a wake-up call, and it sickened people, turned the bulk against violence. Gave loyalists pause for thought about killing any more innocent Catholics. Remember Protestants died too. One woman nine months pregnant with twins. You could say it set the stage for peace,' said Billy.

'I don't follow,' said Sheen.

'The truth doesn't always make sense, you know. The Brits got their message not long after when the boys blew up Canary Wharf, hit them where it really did hurt them, in their pocket. After that the Peace Process got properly moving, everyone willing to talk the same language, round the same table. But it was always the IRA who was one step ahead, leading the loyalists and the British government by the nose,' said Billy. He laughed again, the same dry, mirthless chuckle he had used earlier. 'From bomber jackets and DM boots to limousines and Armani suits, that about sums up some people on that side. Men like Jim Dempsey, for example,' he said.

Sheen knew who he meant. Dempsey. He was a middle-ranking republican, an administrator in the new Northern Ireland Assembly, but big behind the scenes, a political operator who got things done. A ruthless man, some had named him in connection with a fire bombing for a hotel in the 1970s. Dempsey denied ever being in the IRA, but he never sued the journalist who wrote the piece.

'Dempsey planted the bomb?' asked Sheen.

'Never said that,' said Billy, slowly shaking his head, and then raised his Bushmills and took a knock, a proper one this time, not just a sip. 'Dempsey benefited,' he continued, cheeks flushing a deep scarlet with the drink.

'But a man like him was too fly to be involved directly. By the early 1990s he was a poster boy for the political side of things, and earning more air miles than the Pope. He got someone to do the dirty work, same story the world over,' he said. Billy's voice dropped to a hoarse whisper, though their end of the bar was empty. 'Word about town was that it was one of his crew that was responsible.'

Sheen shook his head, not understanding Billy's meaning.

'One of the men that Dempsey commanded in St James, they operated in a team of three. These guys were loyal to Dempsey as much as to the IRA, and they were dangerous boys.'

Sheen nodded, this was better. 'Who are they? Where can I start looking?' he said.

'Start looking in Milltown, you'll find two of them

164

stacked on top of one another. Kennedy and Mooney were both dead and buried by the time your brother was murdered,' he said, still whispering, holding his whiskey glass in one fist. Most of it had been drained.

'That's two, you said there were three,' said Sheen. His pulse was racing now.

'The last of them is a guy called Fryer, John Fryer. He was alive when Sailortown happened, and active. He was put away shortly after, something unrelated. Got out on early release under the Good Friday Agreement, with the rest of them,' he said. His voice had dropped even lower, as though by uttering his name this Fryer might appear from the fire exit behind them.

Sheen's heart quickened further. He clenched his fists. 'Please, tell me he's still in the country, I have to find him,' he said.

'Keep your bloody voice down,' said Billy, his big eyes scanning the room. 'You'll have no problem finding Fryer. I know where he is,' he said.

'Tell me. If I look in his eyes, I will know if it was him,' said Sheen.

'Lot of good it might do you. Fryer went loop the loop, lots of these guys did. He is in Belfast Heights, the psychiatric hospital. The guy was cutting himself up after he was released. He ended up killing his pet dog, then decorating his apartment with it,' said Billy.

Sheen pushed his stool back and stood up. He opened his wallet, no notes left.

'Thanks, Billy. When I'm next in, I'll get you another pint,' he said.

Billy ignored the small talk. 'This Fryer, he is a bogeyman,

Sheen. And Dempsey is very powerful. After what happened today, you don't need me to tell you to be careful,' he said.

Sheen nodded, and then headed for the door, reached for his mobile, found it intact. Colm the barman looked up from his paper, said, 'See ya,' as Sheen passed, limping a little, his right side dragging with each painful step. Sheen returned the pleasantry, a local now after all, then pulled the door open and checked outside to see if Gerard was still waiting for him.

The car was gone, so he hit Gerard's number. Sheen listened to the ringtone, rested his hand on the cold metal surface of the table. No answer. Sheen killed the call, breathed in the waterfront air, salty, clean, but also faintly rotten. At last he had a name: John Fryer, and a place where he could find him: Belfast Heights. He pressed Gerard's number again, this time got a reply, told him to come. Sheen shuffled away from Muldoon's for a second time that day. A rough beast, its time come round at last, slouching through Belfast to be born.

CHAPTER TWENTY-FIVE

As Sheen and Aoife tucked into their Ulster Fry in TK One, Christopher had sat behind the wheel of the black taxi at a red light, no more than a mile away. He was waiting to take the left turn into the Kennedy Centre shopping mall at the top of the Falls road, John Fryer's shopping list in his pocket. The lunchtime traffic was murder.

Christopher could have gone somewhere more local near Bangor, but when he got behind the wheel of the black taxi and started the rattling old engine, this is where it had taken him: back home to the Falls road. Amongst the many other things that John told him at the Heights, he'd explained where to find this old dinosaur: in a locked-up garage in Poleglass, way out west. The garage door was no problem, and the key, as promised, was in a plastic bag under one of the front wheel rims. John Fryer had driven this taxi when he was first released from prison after the Good Friday Agreement. An old street soldier, suddenly wearing dead man's shoes, shipping punters from the west into the city, back again, cash in hand.

He had not lasted long before things took a turn for the worse. First the drinking, then the cutting and finally the incident with his dog, when he had bled it dry and painted himself into a safe corner in his council flat until he was eventually found by Jim Dempsey. After that he had been sent to the Heights, locked away and forgotten, until Christopher had discovered him.

It felt like poetic justice that the black hack should become the vehicle for his return to action. Against all the odds, its engine had started, coughing and spilling blue smoke, but back from the dead all the same. The traffic light ahead of him blinked amber and turned green, but after creeping a few feet forward he stopped again with a high-pitched screech, as a family walked across the road regardless, their dog off the lead. Typical westies.

Christopher's own canine history, just like John Fryer, was a less than happy one. Max, the next-door neighbour's evil Jack Russell had terrorised Christopher when he was a boy. The ugly bastard yapped day and night, but when Christopher's ball went over the hedge, he had to run the gauntlet, chased by the evil wee shite, its teeth bared, coming at him like a white cannonball. It never got him, but it had scared him, and Christopher had read enough psychology to know that a fear can generalise. First a fear of one dog, then a fear of all dogs. Max had never sunk his teeth in, but he had left his mark.

Christopher smiled. Max had turned up dead, when Christopher was eleven, bled out all over their back garden, the way a dog will if it eats rat poison in minced meat. Someone had fed it to him after saving up weeks of pocket money to buy. The neighbours had made a point of knocking his door, telling his parents what had happened, as though anyone gave a damn. Daddy had closed the front door slowly, he'd been wearing his uniform shirt, turned to Christopher who was watching from the living-room door and struck him once, the first and only time. Which was awful, but his silence was even worse.

A couple of years later another tragedy had hit the finger-pointing, door-knocking neighbours. The bitch had left their toddler unsupervised in the back garden with a shallow paddling pool during the hot summer of '03 (she'd gone indoors for less than ninety seconds, it was tight), but when she returned the replacement dog who had made almost as much noise as Max was face down underwater and not moving. Of course, this time the police came. Daddy had brought him out front, stood with his hand on Christopher's shoulders while he exchanged banalities in a hushed and reverential voice with his fellow officers. But when they departed, so too did Daddy's hand from Christopher's shoulders, never to return. He did not strike him. He did not even look at him. There was only silence that went on, and on. His mother had left the party by that point. She sat through the commotion and stillness alike in front of the telly, full blast, curtains closed.

Christopher blinked the thought of her away, looked to his left. Milltown Cemetery, gravestones and Celtic crosses peeping over a grey stone wall. It was empty and looked forgotten against the afternoon bustle of the road. But that was going to change. When their plan, starting with Jim

Dempsey, took shape, Milltown was going to get a whole lot busier and soon.

Someone leant on a horn behind him. Christopher shot a glance in his rear-view, a line of cars, more honks, clear and empty road ahead.

The lights had changed. He was holding up traffic.

Christopher raised a palm and took the taxi left, followed the road down, into the submerged car park under the shopping complex, oil, still air and the fumes from his taxi. He found a secluded bay by the wall, well away from the moving staircase that ascended towards the mall, and parked. He popped the glove compartment and took out Daddy's .38 Ruger, slipped it into the inside pocket of his coat, got out and walked towards the entrance.

The wide aisles of the mall were crowded. Christopher listened, heard the same snippets of conversations played over and over, talk of the blackout. Their fridges were off, meat was spoiling. Boilers were dead and no hot water. The NIE's worse than useless, not even answering the phone. Because this is west Belfast, if it were anywhere else, they would have it sorted. It's only us, second class citizens. Christopher savoured the worry and panic in the voices, but better still, he could hear it; the old anger was back. And there would be more, much more.

Some of the shops were shuttered and closed, and most open for business remained dark, with signs saying CASH ONLY in the windows, ghost workers illuminated in the pale light of halogen torches. The large supermarket, where he got Fryer's tobacco, and the pound of chuck steak he told Christopher they needed, were still lit. They must have a backup generator for the place. That could only last so long.

He found the Reebok trainers John Fryer demanded and the Celtic FC replica top he told him to buy in a sport's shop. Christopher checked the price. John said the trainers were cheap, but John was from a different era. Unfortunately for Christopher, John's trainers had become retro cool while he was locked away. They were not cheap any more. The Celtic top was more expensive than the trainers. Total rip-off. But John Fryer said only the trainers would do and they needed the Celtic top, so he would have to fork out. Outside a darkened electronics and lighting store (Light Fantastic), Christopher thumbed through the last of the cash in his wallet. Not a lot left. He could see the battery-powered strobe Fryer told him to look for, the sort of flashing light that could be fixed to the side of a home, or the post of a security fence. Like the meat, this was part of the plan to get inside Jim Dempsey's later, and a brilliant idea – but a pricey one. After this there would be almost nothing left of Christopher's cash, and no more in the bank.

Christopher nodded, but still did not enter the shop. Only right he should be broke. All great artists were. His reward would be the masterpiece of chaos that was in the making. He returned his wallet to his jacket pocket and made a move towards the entrance, but stopped. The gun, hard and heavy, was on his hand. No real need for it, but he'd packed it all the same. Daddy's voice, sudden and intimate, spoke.

He pointed a rifle at you, son.

Christopher flinched. Daddy had been quiet all day, yesterday too. With his return, Christopher now remembered a snippet from his dream this morning. Daddy's voice had been different then, choking and rasping, as only a hanged man could sound. And he had been angry, said nasty things. Christopher closed his eyes. Today Daddy sounded fresh as rain. And, as always, he was correct.

'Aye, he did,' said Christopher. John Fryer, on his feet at the dining-room table, his Armalite levied at Christopher, finger on the trigger.

And he had something to say about your granny. Questioned your God-given mission.

'Can I trust him?' asked Christopher.

Before Daddy could reply, another voice spoke, this one to his right side, not in his head. He felt as much as heard Daddy slip away, like fine sand escaping his fingers. Christopher clenched his jaw, opened his eyes, unable to keep the blade from his words.

'What?' he hissed. It was a child, maybe ten, her mongoloid eyes looking at him with amusement. She had her fair hair tied with a green ribbon, left hand a box with flyers, a bucket with a coin slot in the lid in the other.

'Wanna donate to the Irish language, mister?' the retard said. She shook the bucket of money, her tongue escaping from the side of her mouth with the exertion. Christopher snatched a flyer, rooted in his pocket and gave her a handful of copper shrapnel. She smiled but didn't thank him.

'You're welcome,' he said, turning back to Light Fantastic.

'Who was you speaking to there?' she said. Christopher glanced round. There was no one watching. He lowered his face to hers, hands on his thighs. She was still smiling, her eyes twinkling.

'I was speaking with God. And he said you need to learn some manners. Now fuck off,' said Christopher.

172

Ten minutes later, he threw his purchases on the back seat of the black taxi, reached for the keys and found a balled-up piece of glossy paper in his pocket, the flyer from the mongoloid. Christopher frowned, smoothed it out.

Lean Leat go Liofacht! Irish Summer School Saturday 10th July to Monday 12th July. Ages 5 to 10. Culturlann Centre, Falls Road, Ireland.

He knew the place, headquarters of Belfast's Gaeltacht or Irish-speaking quarter, not far from here, further down the Falls road. The retard kid was probably one of their pupils. The place would be full of them this weekend, ugly wee gibberish talkers like her. Christopher tapped the open page with the nail of his index finger, each touch counting the beat of his thoughts, an idea germinating, terrible, beautiful. He could taste the stale, oily air of the underground car park, hear the muffled hum and honk of traffic from the road outside, but his mind was elsewhere. He was in the armoury, back at the house in Bangor, doing an inventory. The plastic explosive he had scavenged from the arms dump was barely enough fireworks for what was planned for Jim Dempsey's cronies and Uncle Cecil in the next few days, and the almond-smelling 808 was barely enough to blow a dustbin lid off. He had detonators, but what good were they with nothing to detonate? Oh, for the want of a nail.

Christopher's finger tapped, his eyes far away, looking for what he knew, in his gut anyway, he was going to find, the answer that would let him create something spectacular, and awful, the thing that would tip the balance and create a landslide, carry Belfast, the whole worm-eaten country, into the pit. During the Troubles, there had been such events, seminal moments, points of no return. This would be even bigger, but only if he could find what he needed.

Christopher's finger stopped tapping. A smile creased his face, cold as a crack in packed ice. The cans of petrol, standing in the armoury, their purpose now clear. When he had purchased them, he had not understood. But Daddy had known. And it was Daddy who had told him to bring them home.

What was it the mong had asked him?

Wanna donate to the Irish language mister?

'I believe I do,' said Christopher, his smile widening. He put the key in the ignition, gunned the engine. Blue smoke belched, its big sound filling the low space. He reached to close the door and stopped, hand on the half-open window. Christopher got out and approached what he had seen resting in the darkened corner, the taxi's engine still rattling. Before Daddy spoke, Christopher had already seen its purpose. A sign, if any more were needed that his was meant to be.

You need that for the new mission. You can borrow it.

Resting against the wall on its plastic hand grips, was a two-wheeled trolley, the kind used by premises staff to move heavy items. Also the kind of thing used by delivery men. Hanging off one handle was a white cotton coat and hat, the kind Christopher had seen fishmongers wear.

'I see it, Daddy, I see it,' he said. It was heavy, solid steel, and Christopher grunted as he lifted it up and into the back of the taxi. It fitted, barely, wedged on the floor between the back doors. Christopher stood back and scanned the back of the cab. Unless someone went snooping it was hidden from view. He threw the cotton coat and hat over it. Christopher jumped in and slammed the door, noted that the trolley was also invisible when looking in the rear-view. He crunched the taxi into reverse and pulled out. When Daddy spoke, he hit the brakes, the squeal piercing in the concrete bunker.

This spectacular is on a need-to-know basis, and John Fryer does not need to know. Do you understand?

Christopher said yes, he did. Need-to-know only. Daddy asked him if he was ready, whether he had the stomach and heart for what must come?

'Thy will be done, Daddy, thy will be done,' said Christopher as he drove the taxi from the underground shadows into the daylight of a Falls road afternoon.

CHAPTER TWENTY-SIX

The first thing Sheen did after Gerard had dropped him back at his hotel was swallow three painkillers. Then he set to work on his idea board. He had just pinned the last photograph to the board when there was a knock on his door. He limped over and put his eye to the peephole, saw Aoife outside and did a double take. He saw Aoife's face in extreme close-up. There was a red crease encased by tender-looking bruised flesh on one side of her forehead. Sheen opened the door.

'What happened to your face?' she said.

Sheen stood aside to let her enter, which she did. 'You first,' he said, pointing to her forehead.

'I walked into a door, actually,' she replied. She looked him in the eye and Sheen could see no lie there.

'Seriously?' he said. She pulled off her coat and dropped it on the bed next to his leather jacket.

'Aye, I was in SecuriTel's main office. I got the recording, opened the door to leave, and turned to say something to the creep that gave me it. The door was on one of those weighted spring things, very quiet,' she said, then pointed to her forehead, looking honestly embarrassed.

'You're a bloody muppet, mate,' he laughed.

'Probably, but you didn't get that lip walking into a door. What's the story, Sheen? Did Nelson or one of Moore's boys come and see you?' Sheen gave her a questioning look, and then shook his head again, no longer smiling. She meant that skinhead meat packer who had been skulking about the Tiger's Bay community centre earlier.

'Nothing like that,' he sighed. What the hell, she was no mug, and the truth, as Billy Murphy had just instructed him, was just the truth.

'I got hit with a bottle on the back of the skull, blanked out for a second or two and woke up with my face on the concrete. Got this and a rose on my head for the trouble,' he said, pushing his tongue against the swell on his lip, making it protrude momentarily. Aoife looked at it, and then her eyes narrowed.

'Was it those football hooligans? The Celtic and Rangers lot that I saw throwing bricks and bottles near the Albert Bridge on my way back?' she said. Sheen raised his eyes to the ceiling in a way he hoped looked both resigned and bashful. It was a gift and he was happy to accept it under the circumstances.

'Honestly, I doubt they had me marked as a target, I just got in the way,' he said.

'Bollocks to that, you were assaulted, Sheen. If you can ID one of them we can have them for this, on top of anything else they have been lifted for,' she said.

'And what good will that do us, the case? I was in the wrong place at the wrong time and frankly, I should have known better,' he said. She moved a step closer.

'Let me see. You said you passed out, you're probably concussed,' she said, now taking his hand in hers and leading him to the bed. It was cool and lithe. Sheen obediently followed and sat down.

'No, I am not,' he said. She was standing in front of him, her chest at his eye level. He could see the trace of a white bra under the thin cotton of her shirt, her holster and weapon snug under her arm, shielded by the gentle swell of her left breast. Her fingers went to his head.

'Oi! Steady on!' he shouted, flinched.

'Sorry! Sorry, I just needed to check the skin was not broken,' she said.

'Well?' he said.

'No, you must be Irish with this thick head, but there's an evil bruise. It needs ice,' she said.

He pointed to the plastic glass he had filled from the ice machine near the lifts on the bedside table where he had set it. In fact, he had not applied anything to his head since leaving Billy Murphy at Muldoon's. She worked her fingers down the side of his head, both her palms loitering cool and smooth on the side of his face, rasping against the dusting of stubble now formed and then she removed them, the caress of her touch gone.

'Maybe this will shake a few memories loose, then,' she said and stepped out of his space. As she did, Sheen's thoughts filled with the name Billy Murphy had gifted him: John Fryer. Aoife's warmth was whisked away, like smoke up a chimney.

'Maybe so,' said Sheen. 'This is what I have done so far,' he said, pointing at the wall opposite the bed.

He had replaced a reproduction oil depicting Victorian Belfast with the large cork noticeboard. A line of A4 white paper ran from left to right and on it Sheen had started a timeline, starting with the death of Esther Moore on the far left on Friday afternoon and progressing forward. Colour pictures of the crime scenes were pinned to pages, notes and headings orbited the prints.

'Tells us where we are, and gives us, gives me, an overview of the scene details. These things are often important,' he said. 'What about the recording? Not Moore, I take it?' he asked.

'Not Moore, though we have a voice at least,' she said.

'Still, I say we take a trip down to interview Moore ourselves. What Irwin does not know won't hurt him,' said Sheen.

'No,' she snapped. Sheen paused, surprised at her abrupt response. She looked back at him sheepishly. 'There's no need, because I just visited him. Thought I should check on his alibi, so I went down there. His pub is close enough to SecuriTel, it made sense. He's golden, and the oily bastard was not giving up a grain. There is no point going near him,' she said.

Sheen stared at her for a second, looked at the gash on her forehead. 'Bit stupid, going there alone,' he said. A bit underhand more like. Underhand like slinking off to Muldoon's to pursue a hidden agenda?

'Because I am a woman, is that what you mean?' she said.

'Because Moore is a dangerous guy, you said so yourself, and because we are supposed to be working this case together,' he said.

'Snap decision, one of those things, I didn't have time to come and get you,' she said.

'I'm not competing against you,' he said.

'Get real, Sheen. Irwin plans to throw me to the dogs at the first opportunity, having you turn up was a bonus,' she said.

'Forget Irwin. You thought to check the alarm company, not me. This is your town, you have the edge, and so far you have come closest to giving us the break we need,' he said.

'I don't think my big idea will take us far, not unless we have a named suspect's voice to compare it with.' She took out her phone and played him the recording.

Sheen nodded to the board, happy to focus on the case. 'Then let me speak you through this,' he said. No reply, Sheen carried on. 'The headline for me is one word: contradiction,' he said.

'Why?' said Aoife.

Sheen pointed at the image of Mrs Moore. 'When I first saw Esther Moore this morning, and the way she was posed, it made me think of something, could not place it at the time. Now I see it. There was a spate of torture killings here in the 1970s, mostly Catholics. One guy was dumped in Tiger's Bay. He had his throat cut with a butcher's knife. The cut was so deep it almost severed his head from his body. They carved UDA into him, a sick taunt, or a way of claiming the victim,' he said. 'His body was laid out prostrate, with arms outstretched, like in prayer, a final insult after death to their Catholic victim,' said Sheen.

'So let's say she was laid out in a similar way. So what?' said Aoife.

'Not similar, she was arranged in exactly the same way,' he said.

'So what are we saying? Some extreme Dissident group is dishing up the worst of the past and serving it back to Cecil Moore?' she said.

'I don't believe this is the work of Dissidents. Mrs Moore was laid out as though in worship, but not because of her religion or politics. She was prostrate before the words on the wall, written in her own blood,' he said.

'The Nietzsche quote: From Chaos Comes Order,' she said.

'Nietzsche was a nihilist, in its purest form. They think we have no loyalties, we are without purpose, apart from maybe to destroy, and then die,' he said.

'The killer laid Mrs Moore in worship of nothing. That is the point, the contradiction. She is a loyalist who has been served up in worship of the absence of loyalty,' he said. 'This killer has taken something from the past that was fixed and darkly full of meaning,' he said.

'And he has turned it round. Killed a loyalist's mother like loyalists once killed random, despised Catholics,' she said.

'Exactly. Now take a look at this,' he said, and jabbed his finger on one of the printed images from the substation.

Aoife shook her head slowly, the crease formed between her eyebrows, right on cue. 'What exactly am I supposed to be seeing here?' she said.

'Look at the graffiti,' said Sheen.

'That's weird,' she said.

'Why?' said Sheen. She had clocked it, he knew she would.

'It's confused, jumbled up,' she said.

'It's a mess, chaotic,' he said. He ran his finger slowly

over the image, reading the acronyms there as he did so. 'PIRA, UVF, UDA, INLA,' he said.

'All paramilitary groups, active in the Troubles, but from both sides,' she said.

'It's a mixing pot, all the players in one place, all the old loyalties merged and melted. There's no doubt that it has been done by one person, and I think this was the work of the killer, the man who planted the bomb,' he said.

'Look, did you notice this?' he asked, his finger traced the shape of the letter A, then followed the path of the circle which enclosed it. She squinted, and then nodded as Sheen's finger completed its orbit.

'Yeah, I see something, not sure,' she said.

'I recognise it from the streets round Highbury, from when I was a kid,' said Sheen. 'A for Anarchy sign. The punks used to paint it on their leather jackets, remember?' She shook her head. Sheen had a few years on her. He needed to explain. 'Anarchy's the message, chaos over the IRA, the UVF above all the old allegiances. Chaos rules over all I suppose,' he said. She turned and walked over to the bed, sat down on the corner and started to shake her head again.

'It's creative, but this is not police work, not as I know it. You think this joker is serving up the past, mixing it, making it confused? That's not a motive,' she said.

'It could as easily be glue-sniffing teenagers spraying the contents of their frazzled brains on the side of the substation followed by a Dissident head case planting a bomb sometime later.'

Sheen shook his head. She was wrong. 'This is just beginning, Aoife. The writing on Esther Moore's wall said as much,' said Sheen.

Before she could reply, Aoife's phone rang and she answered it. It was Irwin.

She listened, nodded. 'Yes, sir, we will get on it right away. We'll see you back at Ladas after,' she said. She finished the call. 'Irwin said our footprint from Esther Moore's has turned up a match on the database,' she said. 'Local, a place called Belfast Heights. It is a psychiatric hospital. A car was petrol-bombed there last night, the place was evacuated, total mayhem. Boot print found beside the car,' she said.

Sheen's stomach dipped, but he kept his voice under control. 'Why would our killer want to cause havoc up there, even if we assume he's a Dissident,' he asked. But the awful, sinking sensation in his gut told Sheen that he might already know. Maybe it was nothing, but the gooseflesh on his arms and on the nape of his neck told him no, don't believe it.

'Irwin wants it checked out, and after he wants us back at Ladas Drive,' she said. Aoife grabbed her coat, headed for the door. Sheen swept up his jacket from the bed, walked to the open door where Aoife waited and turned out the light, leaving the curtained room in gloom.

CHAPTER TWENTY-SEVEN

Outside the entrance of Belfast Height's secure wing, the car had been removed, but Aoife could see the place where it had burnt. The compressed gravel of the drive was charred in a wide circle and the sandstone wall of the building was blackened. The press was there, one reporter she recognised from Ulster Television and a cameraman. They were seated on a bench that was wrapped round a tree, eating from paper bags.

'Come on, before they spot us,' said Sheen, walking quickly up to the main entrance.

Some looper Dissident, from the Ardoyne, or The Bone, wasn't that what Cecil Moore had said?

I want to hear that spoken.

In public, before the day is out.

She crunched over the gravel, held up her warrant card so the man seated behind a small counter on the other side of the glass doors could see it. He buzzed them in, looked from her, then to Sheen, a shadow of confusion passed over his features. Their faces, she had forgotten how they must look standing there side by side, the welt on her forehead and Sheen's fat lip.

'We need to speak to whoever is in charge,' she said. The man at the desk nodded, fast and businesslike, and picked up the phone on the desk. He was muscular, short grey hair, the desk space before him clutter-free and clean. He lodged it between his chin and shoulder as he pressed a button on the phone's keypad.

'Speaking as one former copper to another,' he said quietly, looking up at her with the phone still cocked in place. 'It's a shambles. Never lost an inmate, not in my years here. Cuts, that's the cause of it. Want the same job done with half the staff,' he said. 'Afternoon, Gladys, I have two police officers here at front desk. They need to speak to Mr Kinnard. Thank you, I will,' he said, replacing the receiver and standing up. 'I will buzz you in, then you walk straight on—'

'Sorry, just a second, what was that you said? About losing someone?' she asked. Sheen had stepped closer.

'One of the inmates, I mean patients. During the evacuation, took himself off,' he said.

They followed the directions and were met by the hospital manager in the corridor outside his office. Phillip Kinnard was a man in his late thirties with glasses and a weak moustache. Added to the weary face and the blue woollen jacket, and Aoife's overall impression was a secondary school geography teacher too long at the receiving end.

'Pleased to meet you. Phillip Kinnard, the manager,' he said, holding out his hand. Aoife shook and introduced

185

herself, was about to do the same for Sheen when he spoke up.

'The prisoner, inmate, or whatever you call them here, what was his name? The man who's missing,' said Sheen, his voice half raised. Phillip Kinnard did not reply immediately. He took stock of Sheen like a man who was used to working with the mentally ill.

'We currently have one patient not yet accounted for. Most unusual. It has never happened before,' he said.

'Have you notified the police?' said Aoife.

'This man represents a danger to no one. He has been under sedation level medication for the best part of ten years. He is probably sleeping in a ditch close to the hospital grounds. Our staff has been combing the area all morning. We will find him,' he said.

'Answer my question, please,' said Aoife.

Phillip Kinnard removed his glasses and pressed two fingers on the bridge of his nose. 'No, we have yet to file a missing person's report. It has not yet been twenty-four hours, and as I said we will—'

Sheen barged past her, almost knocked her over, and grabbed Phillip Kinnard by the lapels of his jacket. 'His name! Tell me his name!' Kinnard's face was a grimace of horror and surprise, his eyes mole-like without the magnification of his glasses.

'Sheen!' she shouted, pulling at his shoulders. 'Sheen, let him go, what the hell do you think you are doing?' she said.

'F-F-Fryer!' answered Kinnard. Sheen stopped shaking, but he still had a hold of him. 'J-J-John Fryer is his name. P-Please, let me go,' he said. Aoife pulled on Sheen's shoulders again and he dropped him. Kinnard slumped into one of the plastic chairs against the wall outside his office.

'He's been loose since last night and it's not even been reported?' said Sheen, standing over Kinnard.

'I am s-s-sorry, I was following protocol,' said Kinnard, shrinking into the chair. Aoife stepped forward and pushed Sheen back a step, stood between him and Kinnard. She looked at him, searching his face for an answer to explain this outburst, seeing only stone and rage.

'Mr Kinnard, the fire which caused the building to evacuate last night, we now believe it was started by someone we very much wish to speak to. It is important that we see any CCTV footage you might have and speak to anyone who was present yesterday evening,' she said. Kinnard nodded. This he could do. They followed him into his office, municipal furniture and a Narnia-like view of the rising granite head of Cave Hill from the big windows.

'Of course. It was my car that was destroyed,' he said, glancing from her to Sheen as though the fact would in some way exonerate him from Sheen's wrath.

'I want to see John Fryer's file. Get it now,' said Sheen.

Kinnard picked up the phone. He spoke to Gladys, told her to bring Mr Fryer's file, a pause then a repeat that yes, she should bring it at once, please.

'Is your CCTV outsourced, Mr Kinnard? Do you use SecuriTel?' she asked.

Kinnard shook his head once. 'No, too costly, it is managed in house,' he said, nodding towards his ancient PC. Aoife spotted the silver cord protruding from the back of the computer, recognised it as an input feed from the CCTV cameras. Another lead fed from the computer, this one connected to a DVD backup. 'The PC is pretty old, not a lot of memory, so we have a three-day holding storage there, then it gets copied onto disc,' he said, gesturing at the DVD burner. 'It has enough space to take three months of feed, and then we wipe it clean and start to copy over it. Unless, of course, there is a need to preserve footage,' he said.

'This is the footage you are interested in,' he said, motioning her to come over to his side of the desk to look at the screen. Sheen followed.

It was all but useless.

Black and white images, updating every two seconds from a camera angled to watch the door, not the staff parking area. At about 2 a.m. it recorded a flash of white light, and then a glow could be seen coming from the far left of the screen. If this was it, there would be no way of seeing who started the fire.

'No other cameras out front?' she asked.

'There are, but none that watch over the car park,' he said quietly.

'We are going to need copies of what you have, please, last forty-eight hours,' she said.

'What about where you evacuated the inmates? Do you have that covered?' asked Sheen.

'No, just the entrances and exits, not the assembly area,' he said.

'Then what bloody good are you?' said Sheen, who had lumbered over to the window. 'I want a list of every visitor Fryer had in the last year, I want copies of the CCTV which shows who he met and I want to speak to any member of staff who were present, and I want it today,' said Sheen.

'Easy, he has only had one visitor. We can check the

log,' he said. A tap on the door, then a lady with a silver bun walked in without waiting to be told. Gladys, Aoife assumed. She had a thick brown paper wallet in her hand. 'Ah, thank you, Gladys,' said Kinnard.

Sheen walked over and tugged it from her. She observed him coolly, before she turned to Kinnard.

'Anything else, Mr Kinnard?'

'Yes, please get me the visitor log for the past year and see whether you can rouse Adeola. He was on late shift last night, but this is important,' he said.

Sheen had sat down, a dog with a bone. He had opened the file and was flicking through it.

'Who is Adeola, Mr Kinnard?' asked Aoife.

'Adeola is one of our ward nurses. He has cared for Mr Fryer for some time and was working last night. When he wandered off,' he said.

Sheen scoffed, his nose in the file.

Five minutes of heavy silence ensued in Kinnard's office. Sheen spent it flashing through the pages of the folder, then slapped it on his empty chair and returned to his vantage point at the big window. Aoife had checked the cheap Nokia phone, expecting some kind of taunt or command from Cecil Moore, but found none, and also watched Sheen, who had been transported to his own personal realm. Whatever it was, it had something to do with the missing patient, John Fryer. She reached across and lifted the brown manila folder with Fryer's case history.

She flicked through the folder, noted his age, height and weight, then his address at time of committal, Divis Tower. She knew it. It was close enough to where her mum had lived, and died, where she had spent her early days as a child in the St James's Road area. It might be a worthwhile place to start looking, assuming John Fryer and his disappearance was important. She flicked further back, looking for more on Fryer. She stopped, several pages in, a detail catching her eye.

HMP Maze. The H-Blocks, in other words.

Fryer had served time. He was a prisoner, PIRA. She glanced up at Sheen, who was still off with the fairies, staring out the window. He must have seen this when he read the file, but his anger and exasperation, it had started as soon as he heard a patient was missing, intensified as soon as he heard John Fryer's name. Meaning Sheen knew that John Fryer was a patient, even before he realised one was missing from the Heights, and he knew he was a former prisoner. She read on, running a finger through the file as she scanned the information, found what she was seeking: the date, not of Fryer's release, but when he was imprisoned.

November 1994.

It was possible. He had not been in prison when the Sailortown bomb exploded, which made him a likely suspect. Looking up from Fryer's file, she could see the bruise on the side of Sheen's mouth, remembered the ice pack on his table when she had visited him in the hotel. Hit with a bottle, he had said. But who was it who had introduced the explanation about the Celtic and Rangers fans? Not Sheen, she was pretty sure about that. She had suggested it, and he had gone along with it.

Perhaps there was another explanation, why a man on his first afternoon in Belfast would get a fierce enough hiding to almost put him in hospital. Such as going to the wrong places and asking the wrong sort of questions. She touched the bump on her head absently, aware that she was doing it only when she winced at the pressure applied there by her fingertips. Both of them had gone looking, and both had got more than they had bargained for. Sheen's subterfuge was out. How long before her own was brought to light? And what exactly did Sheen plan to do if he found Fryer? The stone-cold look on his face suggested he was not planning to shake his hand. It did not exactly bode well for her, or her first murder investigation.

A crisp rap on the door. It was Gladys. Her eyes fell on Kinnard, hunched behind his desk, but this time she walked to Sheen and slapped the log, a thick, soft-backed A4 jotter, into his chest, turned and strode off.

'At least your logbook goes back further than three months,' said Sheen, looking over at Kinnard.

'Should be at least a year. We retain all back copies, of course,' said Kinnard from his chair.

'You said John Fryer had one visitor? Did this person visit him weekly, monthly?' asked Aoife.

'Adeola will be able to give more detail, but from memory, Mr Fryer was visited by one man on Friday mornings, though until relatively recently, he received no visitors whatsoever, poor man,' said Kinnard.

Sheen was flipping pages, moving from near the end of the journal, back towards the front. He started shaking his head. 'You people are a joke,' he said.

She stood next to Sheen and looked at the book. Sheen's finger found John Fryer's name, skipped the weeks in turn. Each entry was completed in similar handwriting, but each week, a different name, as though a different visitor signed in to see John Fryer. Most names she recognised, though none had visited Belfast Heights.

'By the looks of this, you have had some famous ghosts signing in over the past months. Theobald Wolfe Tone one week, Bobby Sands another, Gusty Spence, Gregory Rasputin, the list goes on,' said Sheen.

'Not recently,' said Aoife, taking the book from Sheen and leafing forward, finding the most recent dates which led to yesterday, Friday 9th July.

'Nothing for three months,' said Sheen. For as long as the CCTV cameras would take to complete a backup and rerecord over all the previous footage.

The door rapped again, and Gladys appeared with a very large black man standing at the door.

'Mr Kinnard,' she said, addressing only him. 'Adeola is here,' she said.

'Bring him in,' said Sheen.

She ignored him. Kinnard said, 'Yes, please bring him in,' and told her no there was nothing else she could help them with right now. Gladys called Adeola in by name and he slowly entered, shifting from one gum-shoed foot to the next, a block of a man dressed in a faded blue hooded tracksuit, at least six foot five inches and, Aoife guessed, twenty stone in weight. Kinnard got off his chair and greeted him. Adeola smiled weakly, let Kinnard clasp and shake one of his huge paws in both his hands, and then returned it to his side. He nodded first to Aoife and then Sheen as they were introduced by Kinnard. When Kinnard explained that John Fryer was still missing, Adeola's smooth face creased with concern.

'Adeola, did you notice anything unusual about Mr Fryer's behaviour recently, anything different that might help explain his disappearance?' she asked.

'Mr Fryer not himself. He not spoken for so many weeks. He not moved unless I move him. I feed him, wash him, wipe him, everything. No more drawings with his chalks, nothing. It not make any sense that he wander off. I brought him out when the alarm sounded, in his wheelchair. Then someone tell me they need me to help a patient. Mr Fryer gone, wheelchair gone too,' he said, shaking his head. 'No way Mr Fryer wander off, no way,' Adeola said.

'The man, the one who told you to go and help the patient, did you recognise him?' asked Aoife.

'Dressed like a nurse. There lots of nurses in the Heights. The Secure Wing, the Old Hospital,' Adeola said, waving one hand in a slow gesture of multiplication.

'Fryer had a visitor, a man who came to see him on Friday mornings. Was that the same man, the one who told you to help a patient?' asked Sheen.

Adeola shook his head again. 'I don't think so. That man, I remember him. He had long hair, wore a baseball cap. He was blonde, like Goldilocks,' he said, now breaking into a chortle, then a wheeze. His smile faded away. 'No, not seen him for a time. Friday mornings, brought Mr Fryer his tobacco. They talked. That man, he has a crazy laugh like a kookaburra, but he the only one. He the only visitor Mr Fryer had,' he said.

'If we send an artist do you think you could describe these men, the visitor and the nurse?' said Aoife, turning to Kinnard on the last word.

He glanced at her then focused his eyes on Adeola.

'The Goldilocks man, yes. I remember his eyes. The other person . . .' Adeola tailed off, slowly shaking his head, a look of confusion on his face.

'OK, we can have that arranged. The visitor will do fine. Thank you, Adeola, you have been very helpful,' she said.

He nodded, heavy and slow, she could see the sleep in his eyes. 'This just don't make no sense. Mr Fryer, he scared of the dark, lights on in his room all the time. Why would he go off in the night-time? He even leave his Buzz torch. Never let that torch go after sundown,' said Adeola.

'Let's see his room,' said Sheen, already walking to the door and not waiting for an answer. Kinnard, Aoife and Adeola followed his lead.

John Fryer's room was more like a cell, one of many identical inlets on a corridor with a hard, plastic hospital floor, smelling of disinfectant and stale greens. It was too small for all four of them to crowd in, so she stayed at the entrance. Chalk drawings covered the walls, lots of red and pinks, and tones of flesh. They were crude but clear. Bloody wounds, close up and visceral. She shuddered. No books, just a battered pair of white trainers beside the bed, squashed at the heels and still laced up. There was an unopened packet of rolling tobacco and a full packet of papers in the middle of the desk that was fixed to the wall. The message on the outside of the door had clearly instructed no sharps. Sheen picked up the plastic torch which was on the bed.

'Dat Buzz,' nodded Adeola.

Beside it was a bloodstained gauze on the snake of sheets that partly covered the sponge mattress. He glanced at Aoife, and she got his meaning. She pulled on a plastic glove from her jacket pocket, removed a sealable, plastic evidence bag and carefully placed the bloodied gauze inside before closing it. Sheen looked round the cell, briefly studied the walls, looked beneath the desk, then returned his attention to the bed.

'We have searched here,' said Kinnard.

Sheen pulled the thin mattress up, and then flipped it, revealing the bare plastic of the frame. He hunkered down, looked under it, started to rise, but stopped. He pulled the sheet off the edge of the mattress and his fingers disappeared into a small orifice in the corner. He pulled his fingers out. Dozens of pink pills bounced along the underside of the upturned mattress.

'Recognise these?' he said to Kinnard, who was slowly turning white before her eyes.

Adeola answered. 'Mr Fryer's pills. Antipsychotic tranquillisers. He take them from me, with his water, every day he take them,' he said, shaking his head. He had started to sweat, perspiration forming beads on his broad forehead.

Sheen's face was like thunder. 'Apparently not. Looks like he was more alert, and a lot smarter than he led you to believe,' he said.

'No, no, Mr Fryer not even touch his smokes for so long, and he never without his smokes. He not well, not even speak,' said Adeola, still shaking his head.

Sheen ignored him, glared at Kinnard. 'Report John Fryer as escaped, not missing, escaped, Mr Kinnard, and do it now. I want those DVDs from the CCTV, and the visitor log is coming with us, his file too,' he said. He pushed past Kinnard, and Adeola, and Aoife stepped out of the way before he could push past her. He walked up the tight corridor, shoes squeaking like a rusty bike chain.

Kinnard stared at Fryer's busted mattress, the pills scattered across its surface. 'Yes, yes, right away. Ade, please clear up this mess,' he said, gesturing to the medication and bedding, and then he scuttled out, squeaking up the corridor after Sheen.

Adeola was on his knees, collecting the pills in one hand and deposited them in his outstretched palm. She turned to leave, but then he spoke. 'Mr Fryer not safe when he don't take the pills. He needs his pills. He cuts himself, blood, blood, blood. Mr Fryer, he think he is a cursed man. He has hurt people, but he no mean to, his self too. And he will hurt more people,' said Adeola.

'The police artist will be with you later today for the E-Fit. Please don't leave the grounds, Adeola,' she said, turning to go.

'Wait!' he said, looking at her now. His eyes were wide in his face. 'I am nearly done. Don't leave me alone here,' he said, and then quickly turned to his task.

Kinnard handed her the recordings and documents as she left. Sheen was already waiting in the front reception. He hit the green button, exited. She followed, scrunching towards the car as the door sealed closed behind her. Aoife paused, looked at the scorched earth where the burnt-out car had been.

Fryer was the reason why the car was petrol-bombed. Someone had gone to great lengths to break him out of the Heights. If it was Dissidents, then like the Semtex used at the substation, they wanted to bring some old stock back into circulation, a damaged and dangerous ex-prisoner.

Some looper Dissident, from the Ardoyne, or The Bone.

Aoife looked over at the tree bench where the members of the press were still bunched together. They spotted her looking and the female reporter started over, the cameraman in tow.

I want to hear that spoken.

In public, before the day is out.

Aoife fixed her hair and walked towards them. A statement would get Cecil Moore off her case, temporarily at least, until she could work out a way of uncoupling her fortunes from his and getting her hands on that bloody video. The reporter was within speaking distance, a microphone in her hand, the halogen light from the camera ignited, blazing like a second sun. Aoife fixed a professional mask, tried to recall her media training from the Northern Ireland Police College, and got ready to speak.

CHAPTER TWENTY-EIGHT

'This is Oswald Smith. He works for the Northern Ireland Office,' said Irwin, who then introduced Sheen and Aoife.

This guy's a spook, thought Sheen.

Oswald was the quintessential grey man. With his mostly receded hair, he could have been thirty-five or forty-five, older or younger. He was small in stature, his thin frame lost in his dark suit, but the man had a force, a presence, zinc eyes unblinking and appraising them in the meeting room at Serious Crimes HQ at Ladas Drive Police Station. Definitely a spook, but question was what was Oswald the spooky NIO officer doing here?

'DCI Kirkcaldy said Special Branch was sending someone to this meeting,' said Aoife.

It was as much as she had spoken since they left Belfast Heights. Sheen had not broken the silence, used the journey to regain his composure and evaluate how much he had given away. No way could she know about Fryer's significance to him and his family. Sheen had only become privy to that information through his meeting with Billy Murphy earlier in the day. But she was clearly upset with him. So silence it was, all the way across Belfast, interrupted only by her (illegal) checking of a small Nokia phone three times during the journey. Sheen assumed it was to do with her daughter, Ava. Perhaps she used a different phone for her personal business? Not unheard of. Sheen wanted to know why she had spoken to the press and what she had said, but it would have to wait.

'Suffice to say, DC McCusker, that I represent the broader voice of the security services in my role with the NIO,' said Oswald. He was English, but unlike Sheen his soft accent was hard to place beyond the fact that he had probably been public school educated. 'My colleagues in Special Branch suggested that I join you today to add a little intelligence-led insight about the possible role of Dissident republican paramilitaries in the recent spate of criminal activities experienced over the last twenty-four hours,' he said, hands palm down, thumbs touching.

Aoife interrupted him. 'That is our strongest lead by far,' she said.

Oswald looked at her, mouth half open. Irwin was glaring right at her, his colour deepening by the second. If she noticed, she did not show it. Sheen suppressed a smile. It must have been a long time since Oswald was cut short. She had some guts.

'We have Semtex used at the substation, a link to a firebomb attack last night at Belfast Heights. A republican, John Fryer, is missing. We believe that he escaped and was assisted in doing so by those responsible for the explosion.

We also have a circumstantial link to connect the murder of Mrs Moore and the substation bombing. Dissidents have already started to claim responsibility for Mrs Moore and the substation online—'

Oswald raised both palms from the table, cutting her off. 'Which Dissident group has claimed responsibility, exactly? I assume you are privy to the recognised code words in use to verify such claims? There are now no fewer than four active Dissident republican paramilitary splinter groups at work in Ulster. I can assure you, there are informants and agents hard at work in all of them, sending a steady stream of intelligence our way.'

Aoife said nothing. Irwin skewered her with a look. 'So let me spell this out for you, DC McCusker, DI Sheen and you too, DCI Kirkcaldy: there is no Dissident republican angle in this. None whatsoever. If there were, I would know about it. To publicise it as such runs the risk of giving war junkies and their supporters much-needed propaganda and risks adding to what is already an incendiary situation this 12th July weekend,' said Oswald.

Sheen glanced at Irwin. Oswald just demolished his main line of investigation.

'Is that clear?' finished Oswald, looking at each person seated round the table in turn.

'Crystal, Oswald, thank you for your assistance in clarifying this,' said Irwin. 'In fairness, it was only one angle, and we can play it down when I speak to the press later,' he said.

Sheen looked at Aoife. 'I spoke to the press, at Belfast Heights,' she said, voice as timid as the schoolgirl she had apparently regressed to.

'What?' asked Oswald and Irwin simultaneously.

'Just to the UTV crew, the local lot. I might have mentioned the Dissident link. Seemed like a good time to show we were on top of the case, and it is our best lead, or was,' she said.

Oswald looked at Irwin. Irwin stared at Aoife blackly.

Sheen gritted his teeth. This was his fault. He had lost his rag at the Heights, stormed off in a rage. If he had kept a lid on it, he would have also kept an eye on her, behaved like a partner. She would never have blundered into such a poor decision.

'I suggested that she speak to the press,' said Sheen. Oswald moved his head to look at him, very slowly, like a lizard appraising potential prey. Irwin's face twitched. His eyes flicked between Aoife and Sheen.

'I thought we should put out a clear message. We seemed happy that we had our ducks in a row. Aoife, DC McCusker, was against it. I pushed her to do it. Effectively, I pulled rank, if I am to be honest. I didn't want to speak to the press directly, given my transitional status and the role I will be undertaking in the months to come,' he said.

The men at the table were absolutely quiet. Irwin's face was a study of unmitigated disappointment. It was impossible to tell if Oswald believed him. He deftly pushed his chair back from the table and walked softly to the door.

Aoife spoke. 'I did not mention anything alarmist, only that we were following several lines of enquiry, Dissidents being one,' she said softly.

'For your sake, DC McCusker, I hope you are right,' said Oswald from the door. He exited and was gone. Now you see him, now you don't. The door clicked closed.

'In future, DI Sheen, you will leave press briefings to me or to one of my superiors. Is that understood?' said Irwin.

'Totally,' said Sheen.

'DC McCusker, you have disappointed me. I was led to expect more tact from someone who cut their teeth working Community Relations. Just so we are clear, you take your orders in this case from me, and only from me,' he said.

'Sir,' she answered.

Irwin sighed, pushed his face into both his palms. The angry man had gone, in its place an overgrown country schoolboy. 'No matter, we move forward. The Dissident angle is out, Semtex or none. Let's rethink, see where the facts are leading us. On the plus side, MacBride extracted a hair from the plug hole in Mrs Moore's bathtub. It is different from those which appear to correspond with Mrs Moore, though both have been sent to England for DNA comparison, fast track, but it will take no less than a day, probably more. Could be something, could be nothing,' said Irwin.

'Every touch leaves a trace,' said Sheen. Sheen went on to explain the physical links between Esther Moore's murder scene and the explosion at the substation: the boot prints, the fact that a Doc Martens box was the likely trigger for the booby-trap bomb, the discovery of the bra. Irwin nodded, but still did not look overjoyed.

'Paddy bagged the bra,' said Aoife.

'I'll have it sent away separately, see if we can get a trace that confirms it to be Esther Moore's. Without the DNA it is just a discarded piece of underwear in the long grass on a hillside,' said Irwin. He was correct. Sheen had seen good evidence discredited in court by barristers who cast reasonable doubt where none really existed.

'Any update on the young man we were looking for at Tiger's Bay, sir?' asked Aoife.

'Jamie Anderson, you mean? No. His mother is back, not been able to get in touch with him. Worryingly for a teen, his phone is not responsive, and the lad has his Mac password protected so she can't access it. Meaning we can't locate the phone. Not yet anyway. We've asked the phone company to send his records and triangulate the last time it was in use. Technically he is not yet missing but the mother is pulling her hair out. His picture's been mailed to all units,' said Irwin.

'Cecil Moore's man Nelson?' said Aoife.

'You actually saw Nelson McKinty talking to this lad, or take him away?' asked Irwin. He was looking at both Sheen and Aoife. Aoife glanced at Sheen. This was his call. It was he who first noticed Nelson on the move at the community centre and went after him. But he had not even laid eyes on Jamie Anderson, either in the centre, or on the street.

Reluctantly, Sheen shook his head. 'Not exactly, no,' said Sheen. There had been enough bending of the facts for one day, and already, enough blow back.

'Then you know darn well it's not enough. Still, that man Nelson is a pervert, like his master. I will send a uniform round to the Bad Bet, see if we can get him to account for his movements. If not, I'll bring him in,' said Irwin.

'What about Cecil Moore?' asked Sheen. He thought he saw Aoife tense beside him, just a fractional raising of her shoulders, or perhaps he was imagining things.

Irwin scoffed. 'What about him? You heard Oswald.

The Dissident angle is dead in the water, we halt any more probes into Cecil's underworld business deals with splinter republicans,' said Irwin.

'Known enemies, bad blood within the loyalist community?' asked Sheen.

'An abundance of both. Moore had a fall-out with a guy called Scotty Woods from the Shankill not long ago, but there is no way that bottom feeder would dare confront him, and definitely not by murdering his mother. Cecil's UDA and the UVF have a detente and the word down the jungle drums is that Esther Moore's murder was not a loyalist home job. In fact, all fingers are pointing at Dissidents, which leaves us back where we started,' he said.

'What if we release the audio recording from SecuriTel? We might get a name,' suggested Aoife.

'Oh, we will. We'll get the phone book. It'll send the press into a feeding frenzy, probably drive those responsible deeper underground. It's an option, but not our best, more likely to muddy the waters than not,' said Irwin.

'We have to find John Fryer, no matter what Oswald says. Fryer was broken out of the Heights for a reason. There is a clear link,' said Sheen.

Aoife explained the mystery guest on Friday mornings who stopped visiting in time for CCTV evidence to be recorded over, her suggestion an E-Fit be put together using Adeola's memory of the man. She also told Irwin she had bagged the bloodstained gauze, something to give them a recent DNA comparison, should it be necessary.

'The nurse who worked with Fryer, he said that Fryer's visitor had long blonde hair, called him Goldilocks,' said Sheen. He had forgotten about the Goldilocks comment from Adeola, and now he could see how it chimed in with the hair found in Esther Moore's bath.

'Then let's get that artist's impression done quickly, the E-Fit will be shared with all units, and a recent photograph of Fryer,' said Irwin. He shook his head. 'The streets are awash with ex-prisoners, throw a stone in west Belfast and you're going to hit a Provo that served time. Yet this guy goes to the hassle of creating a distraction fire and breaks Fryer out of the Heights? Why?' He looked at Sheen and Aoife as though for an answer, but neither could give it. 'If they're not Dissidents, then what are they? What sort of cause is this? Find me a link, something that connects Cecil Moore and his mother with John Fryer and Belfast Heights.'

Their challenge set, Sheen and Aoife both stood, she moved quickly to the door.

'But keep the heck away from any republicans, Dissident or otherwise. Assume Fryer's former employment is incidental,' Irwin said.

'Sir,' said Sheen. He looked round, but Aoife was gone. Sheen called down the corridor for her to wait. She stopped and turned, her eyes full of reproach.

CHAPTER TWENTY-NINE

'Next time I need you to take the blame for my mess-ups I will let you know. How dare you?!'

'Hey! No need to get us both killed. I'm sorry if I have upset you. Just thought that what happened was partly my fault. If I had kept a closer eye on things, you might not have spoken to the press the way you did,' he said, still fumbling with the belt. She glanced at Sheen, then at the speedometer, which was well over forty mph along the built-up city street. A blare of horns from behind, someone she cut up. Typical man. He saw himself as central in every problem, and himself as the required solution. If they could look after themselves for five minutes she would not be in the jam she now was.

'Don't you ever take what's mine, do you hear me? You'd no right.'

If she saw a smirk on Sheen's face she was going to belt him. She'd crash this bloody car if it meant doing it. Sheen was nodding, no smirk. He looked part penitent and part sullen, staring out the windscreen. She breathed out, suddenly aware she had a lung full of air. She scrubbed some speed off. The beat of blood slowed in her ears, her words replayed in her mind until they started to sound like someone else, angrier, less reasonable.

They sat in silence, city bound.

A winking row of red taillights blinking to life up ahead. Traffic was queuing to turn up the Castlereagh road. She pumped the brake. The guy did her a good turn and she was jumping down his throat. Probably he deserved it, but at least in part this anger was coming from somewhere else, and it should be directed at someone else. Charlie Donaldson for a start, but even Charlie was a relative innocent in all of this.

A vibration in her trouser pocket. It was a message from Cecil. Sheen stared out the window as they edged forward to the lights at the junction, arms crossed. She sneaked a peek at her phone.

Thanks for that wee message on UTV Live. If there is something I should know about, be sure to let me know. Love Dad. X.

Aoife deleted the message, followed the sluggish traffic as they inched closer to town, slow progress explained as they were waved through a police checkpoint. They were monitoring traffic flow from the east of the city travelling west. The blackout was clearly expected. By the time she got over the Albert Bridge and back into the city centre, it was almost six.

'Where are we going by the way?' asked Sheen.

Fact was when she left Ladas Drive she had no plan

other than to dump Sheen at his hotel. Or in the Lagan. The DNA tests on the hairs found in Esther Moore's bath would be another day at least, and there was no sign of Jamie Anderson, the possible witness to Esther Moore's murder. Meaning welcome to the biggest part of police work they never taught you at training college: the art of waiting.

'I need to make a quick call, check that Ava is still OK to stay over at her friend's house in this blackout. Then, maybe you and I should go for a drink?' she said.

Sheen checked his watch, continued his study of passing streets before he replied. 'Can't say I'm not tempted, but as I understand it, this guy Fryer once ran with a very small crew, Jim Dempsey being one of them. Why not take a trip up west, knock on his door, and see what he knows?' he said.

She knew the name but had never met the man. 'Dempsey? Irwin would skin us alive if we went sniffing round the door of republican aristocracy like him,' she said. That was an understatement. He would have her off the case, after what had happened today. Maybe tomorrow they'd try their luck, but Irwin had been explicit this afternoon: steer away from republicans.

Sheen nodded, looked resigned. 'Drink it is,' he said.

She found a parking spot on Linen Hall Street, adjacent to Belfast City Hall, its blue copper dome and white baroque arches visible above the brown sandstone faces of the surrounding buildings. This pocket of streets always reminded her of New York, more Brooklyn than Belfast. She phoned Marie, who said they had plenty of candles and that the girls were happy campers, preparing to tell each other ghost stories. A local takeaway had its own generator so they were going to get Chinese.

'Ava all right?' he asked.

'Dinner by candlelight, ghost stories before bed,' she said.

'Blitz spirit by the sounds of it,' he said.

'Germans bombed Belfast too,' she said.

'Drink?' he asked.

'Oh, yes, drink,' she said.

'I'll take you to The Kitchen,' she said.

The Kitchen Bar was five minutes' walk from where she parked near City Hall, an old pub rebuilt into the periphery of the recently completed Victoria Square shopping complex. On the big screen she could see but not hear highlights of the Celtic v Rangers match from earlier. Looked like Celtic had won, and she allowed herself a grim smile of satisfaction. The sectarian politics of Scottish football meant nothing to her, but Cecil Moore supported Rangers and that was enough.

She walked Sheen through the galley of the public bar to a softly lit lounge. Music played, not too loud, something vaguely jazzy. For the first time since leaving the Bad Bet in Tiger's Bay earlier, she felt her shoulders drop and her adrenaline level drop too, in its place a heavy fatigue, but also a pang of hunger. She found a space at the high wooden bar, and leant against the buffed brass rail that ran under it. Sheen got the drinks, and they ordered Irish stew, the only thing still on the menu.

They sat down in a table nestled by the end of the bar. It gave them a full view of the room, and the bar's second entrance directly across from their seats. Drinks arrived first, then food, shortly after. Half of her gin was already down by the time she started the stew. They both ate hungrily and without conversation, until her spoon reached the bottom of the deep bowl and she was using the side order of buttered wheaten bread to mop up the last of the thick broth.

'Nice?' she asked. Sheen gave her a thumbs up from behind his raised pint, most of which was also gone. She felt the tingle of the gin in her temples, down her arms. She should drink some water – she was probably dehydrated – and definitely leave it at just the one.

'Another?' she asked. Sheen shook his head, swallowing. 'Doctor's orders,' she said. Their drinks arrived and they lingered on their second. She settled deeper into her chair, then felt the weight of her personal protection weapon, heavy against the wooden arm of the seat. She sat up again, leant forward a little.

Sheen pointed at her gun. 'You not worried you'll shoot yourself in the foot with that thing? Know I would be,' he said.

'Better get ready, Sheen, because you will be issued with one. But you'll also get trained. Glock 17 has what they call a Safe Action trigger, two-stage. Basically, if you accidentally flick the side of the trigger, nothing happens. The firing pin is captured at half-cock at the end of a firing cycle. You got to fully grip and pull to make it go off,' she said.

Sheen yawned melodramatically. 'Fascinating,' he said and they shared a laugh.

She stopped, looked at him more seriously. 'Can I ask you a personal question?' she said. Sheen's smile faded, but he nodded, his eyes still warm. 'What would you do if you found him? I mean, whoever was responsible for the bomb that killed your brother?' she asked. It was a bold question and a bit unfair. She was already pretty sure what

John Fryer was to Sheen. But what did Sheen intend to do? Finding him was one thing. But if Sheen wanted to do more than build a case against John Fryer, she needed to know. It was not simply the success of their investigation which now hung in the balance. Fryer was paired up with a murdering psychopath. If Sheen could not control himself, it was her safety, and therefore Ava's, which was at stake. She wanted his unguarded response.

Sheen's face clouded. 'I am going to ask him, and he is going to tell me. And then I am going to have justice,' he said.

'Justice? That is a fairly flexible term, depending on who is using it, you know? Are we talking Belfast justice, or Met Police justice here?' she asked.

'He'll have his day in court,' he said quietly. If there was such a thing as seeing murder in the eyes of man, then this was not that moment. If he wanted to kill John Fryer, then he had not admitted it, perhaps not even to himself. She asked him how he could ever know, after all the time that had passed.

'Ridiculous, but I've always thought that face-to-face the truth would be in his eyes,' he said.

Aoife nodded, not because she understood, but because it sounded like the truth, for Sheen at least. But was it enough for her to trust him? Her mother had trusted her useless excuse of a father, then God and the Blessed Virgin, and look where it got her. She had trusted Charlie Donaldson, and now she was harnessed to Cecil Moore. Sheen's answer told her she could probably trust him not to explode like a suspect device, but there would be no more men on horseback in her life, riding in to

211

save the day and trampling you underfoot in the process.

'What?' she asked.

'You're doing it, that thing with your eyebrows. When you are thinking, or getting ready to argue your point, you get a little crease, right here,' he said, pointing to the space between his own eyebrows.

She raised a finger to the same spot on her own face, as though she could feel what he meant, vigorously rubbed between her brows. 'Is it gone? Thanks for that, Sheen. Love it when a man points out something as charming as a crease in my face. Am I insanitary too? Is that your follow-up line?' Her finger moved from theatrically rubbing between her eyebrows to examining more carefully the hurt on her forehead, still tender but less so under a layer of gin. Her other hand crept on its own accord to Cecil's phone in her pocket, and she forced herself to stop.

Sheen was off his seat.

'Where you going?' she asked.

'We are having one more drink,' he said. Which made it at least two too many for her to drive home. And a taxi to Randalstown would cost a fortune.

'You trying to get me blocked, Sheen? Hope I can trust you to behave like a gentleman,' she said.

'Of course you can. I'm the only gentleman in Belfast,' he said.

'I am not sure I believe you, Sheen,' she said. At least part of her hoped that she was right.

CHAPTER THIRTY

Christopher and John Fryer had not waited in the queue for long. Saturday evening and traffic was light. The PSNI fool at the police checkpoint on the intersection between Broadway and the Falls road waved them through. He barely looked at the black taxi. Christopher sitting in the back, John Fryer driving. Christopher saw John raise a finger from the wheel in thanks as they accelerated past. Their taxi was a perfect disguise. Like the Celtic FC top Christopher was wearing. The only thing more common than a black taxi on the Falls road was someone wearing a Celtic top.

A closer inspection would have turned up that John did not have a valid driver's licence, let alone a cab permit. The fact that John was wearing the bottle-green uniform of the disbanded RUC under his loose-fitting tracksuit would have been trickier to explain away, and the weapons stowed under the spare tyre in the boot would have been a different conversation entirely. But they had been waved through and John grinded the taxi up a gear. The blacked-out side streets of the Falls flicked past his window.

Christopher's Doc Marten boots creaked like virgin snow under foot each time he clenched and unclenched his toes in the back of the cab. Granny's blood had stained the yellow stitching. That would be the clincher, the one that would be simply impossible to explain away. Christopher smiled, *It's just so hard to keep that yellow stitching box clean, officer, I'm sure you can understand.*

The DM boots were a bit naughty of him. He knew he'd left footprints but he couldn't destroy them. It would be wrong. Anyway, he had turned up at Granny's dressed for the part and not a soul had seen him. He probably could have stepped out into the street, red in tooth and claw, and still walked away. The thought, though stirring in him some excitement and pride, did not strike Christopher as particularly amusing, and yet there it was, the sudden bubble of laughter in his throat, formed in an instant and impossible to contain.

As it broke, and he struggled for breath, Christopher decided, it felt like from some distance away, that the laughing – no, these spasms – were getting much worse, almost impossible to predict and control. And that was not all. Not a whisper from Daddy since leaving the mall this afternoon. But in his dreams, that was another matter. Daddy, a Bad Daddy, had appeared once again as he dozed fitfully this afternoon, just as he had appeared the night before. Christopher could recall mere snippets, but what he could remember, he wanted to forget.

And when, exactly, had this turning, this decomposition of his Daddy's communication started? Not while he was planning his mission, no, Bad Daddy and his rope-strangled words was a more recent arrival. It coincided, almost to the hour, with the appearance of the man who was driving the taxi tonight, ill-fitting Daddy's uniform and heavy with bad juju. And here was a final thought, just as it seemed like the spasm might never stop and he, too, might asphyxiate, like father, like son. The stronger Bad Daddy became, the weaker his True, Good Daddy would be. Daddy would go quieter and quieter until he was gone for ever. The spasm dropped him, a man carried on a tsunami, deposited on high land.

John stabbed a glance at him from the rear-view mirror.

'What's got you tickled, kid?'

'Nothing,' he said, which was, in fairness, the truth.

John muttered something under his breath, reached over the windscreen and turned the white sign round. NOT IN SERVICE now faced out, and Poleglass Glen Road faced him. Christopher eased himself back into the seat, calmer now, ready. The shadows of the evening had thickened, west Belfast in blackout. A tingle of excitement coursed from his loins down his legs, bad thoughts about a Bad Daddy all gone. This was his doing. Tonight he was God of this city. John Fryer's voice punctured his reverie, thick with fear, his eyes glaring from the rear-view.

'It's dark,' he said.

'We talked about this, John,' said Christopher, but he could feel his panic, like a ball of negativity growing in the taxi.

215

'Remember what I told you. Fear is for others now, their blood will flow,' said Christopher. He stretched his legs out along the double seat, a picture of nonchalance, but Fryer losing his bottle, especially at the first round, had not been part of the grand design.

John grunted, put the headlights on, full beam, the yellow tubes of light opening up the dusky road ahead. Christopher felt his mobile phone vibrate, fished it out, another alert for @TenDead81. @LoyalistTrueBlue wanted to do all sorts of medieval things to Christopher's online persona. Christopher smiled. The photo of Granny Moore had over fifty thousand reloads. People were starting a good old-fashioned ding-dong, albeit online, raking up old hurts and wrongs, fighting for the moral high ground, screaming for blood. Christopher killed the feed, put this phone away and took out another.

He logged on again, to his separate account, using an alternative email, and password, and this time @God'sPeopleUnderSiege and he typed:

An eye for an eye.

He followed @TenDead81. @God'sPeopleUnderSiege had no followers yet, but that would change.

The engine rattled away under his seat as the taxi started up the hill of the Glen road. A light fog had descended to the foot of the Black Mountain, momentarily in and out of view as the taxi hurtled along. If a patrol car passed them, they would get pulled over, Fryer was speeding, running in a panic while seated behind the wheel. John's eyes appeared again in the rear-view, frantic this time.

'It's too dark. I want to go back to your place. Now!'

'Relax, John, you are doing OK. We are nearly there.' But

John was not doing OK. The guy was calmer on the pink pills. But then he would have been fit for nothing at all.

Christopher leant forward and rested his elbows on his knees, fixed his eyes on the illuminated corridor of road the taxi was swallowing up ahead. 'Be cool.'

'You be cool, you fucking wee gabshite,' replied John. At last, in the headlights, just ahead and to the right, a break in the hedgy border of the road.

'Slow her down, John, then take this right,' said Christopher. His voice was steady and instructive. John obeyed.

They turned into a one-lane street, which gently rose ahead of them, growing steeper as it followed the contours of the Black Mountain. The right of the road was lined with trees. To the left, new build townhouses, high-faced and spacious. Lincoln View, in every way it was situated well above the rest of west Belfast. John Fryer had scrubbed off most of their speed, and that was good, but it would be better if he kept a lid on the panic.

'Dempsey lives here?' said Fryer.

'Him and those like him,' said Christopher. The road turned a sharp right, ahead a cul-de-sac.

'We stop here,' said Christopher.

Fryer turned, slowly stopped the taxi, lights still blazing, engine rattling.

'Kill the engine now, John.' The rattle-tattle of the engine died abruptly, but not the lights. Christopher waited, every second a chance they would be seen. He spoke. 'Now the lights,' said Christopher. His tone was soothing, but his eyes darted left to right for a sign they had been seen. Christopher heard a creak from the steering wheel as John's fat fists tightened round it, his knuckles

217

white. The lights burnt on. John Fryer was breathing in short gasps, tailing off to a wheeze. He gripped the wheel like a caught snake. Then his left hand slowly unclenched and he lowered it to the sticks under the dash. He twisted one of them and in the same instant the lights went out, total blackness. Good John, brave John. He knew he would do it. He wanted Dempsey.

But mostly he had turned them off because John was his. Not his friend, any more than a lion tamer was friends with the big cat. But nor was he Christopher's toy. He was much more dangerous, more lethal. He was his animal.

'Thank you, John,' he said. 'Let your eyes adjust. Take it easy, fella.' Soon the darkness softened and Christopher saw John's hands, still ten and two on the wheel. He was trembling.

'Tell me you can smell that, kid,' he hissed. Christopher did not reply, and John Fryer repeated his question, voice thick with fear. John turned his head, looked into the back of the cab, still clinging onto the wheel like a trawler man in a storm. His bull's shoulders were shaking. Christopher's heart took an involuntary skip. The man was terrified, and whatever haunted him, was in the back of the taxi, with Christopher. Or so Fryer believed.

'John, I can't smell it. I can't smell the Moley because it is not here!' Then he heard something. A voice, rasping, and throaty, it spoke his name.

Chrissssssstopher . . .

It was Bad Daddy, and his voice was coming from beneath the taxi, the noose round his neck, choking him. The same monster he had found hanging from the bannister when he had returned from school, feet knocking against the wall, urine dripping from the bottom of his trouser leg. Christopher snatched the leather straps on the roof of the taxi and raised himself aloft, feet on the seat. He held his breath. John's shoulders kept shaking.

Chrisssssssssstopher . . .

Christopher did not look down, kept his eyes trained on Fryer.

'It's close,' said John. The big man took one hand off the wheel, fist to his mouth.

Christopher closed his eyes and slowly lowered himself into the back seat. His testicles had shrunk, his manhood retreated. He opened his eyes, took a breath and forced his still-raised feet to the floor, first one, then the other. The DM boots creaked. Christopher cleared his throat, blinked away the awful thought of Daddy on the rope and spoke. 'Tell me you are OK, John. Don't be going la la on me now.'

'I'm ready, kid,' said John, stronger now, hands flexing from the wheel.

'Good man,' he said, but he was not looking at Fryer. Christopher was staring at the dark floor of the taxi. 'If it is going to take too much out of you, we can abort the mission.'

John turned and squinted at him. 'I'm OK, kid. Are you? You smelt it, didn't you?' Blood on John's thumb. He popped it into his mouth, sucked.

'I can't smell anything. You're bleeding, John,' he said flatly.

'It's just a wee nick. Good thing too,' he replied and opened the driver's door, got out. Christopher watched him shed the tracksuit, Daddy's bottle-green RUC uniform beneath. He opened the boot, retrieved the Ruger and the plastic bag with the light, battery and bag of raw meat. John walked off up Lincoln View, swallowed by the darkness and mist. Christopher settled deeper into his seat, the cold sweat on his back making him shiver. His phone pinged, but Christopher did not move to check it. He did not move at all.

He watched the darkness and listened.

CHAPTER THIRTY-ONE

The homes along Lincoln View were dark and lifeless. Large fronted semi-detached and detached houses, bay windows and deep front gardens. The streetlamps, spaced every twenty metres or so, would have kept this row well illuminated, but tonight they were cold and blank, silver swan necks presiding over pools of darkness.

The assuring metallic aftertaste of his own blood had thinned. His heart started to canter. He wanted a smoke, but mostly he wanted away from this dark street and all its shadows and black places. Fryer stopped at the last house on the street: Jim Dempsey's. It was a good choice, a safe choice. Fryer would have had the same one. But Fryer would never forget that alertness was the hunted man's first, and last, defence.

He peeked over the wall. The downstairs bay windows were mirror glass, probably bulletproof. The front door looked vault strong. Above it at an angle pointing down was a snub CCTV camera. Identical cameras were fixed to the two front corners of the house. Neither had red LED lights blinking, looked dead. A big sensor light was fixed to the wall above the downstairs front window, the size of a large seashell. No guard, none that Fryer could see, unless Dempsey had a man inside.

Fryer glanced down. The front gate was unlocked. Dempsey had retained the instinct for security but he had got out of the habit. His arrogance had gone to seed, sprouted stupidity and sloppiness. Fryer entered Dempsey's garden. The shell-shaped light stayed off.

Fryer set the blue and white strobe on the ground, and attached the battery. The lamp burst into life, twirling in its sealed unit, splashed blue and white light on Fryer's face, coating the front of Dempsey's house and filled the enclosed patio of the front garden. Fryer pushed it behind a potted plant, less light was reflected. This was all about suggestion.

He stood up, adjusted the RUC hat on his head and walked across the paved garden to the front door, feeling steady in his Reeboks, feeling good. Fryer kept his eyes off the camera. Still, if Dempsey looked through the front window, he would see through the sham: no police vehicle parked outside, Fryer at the door but uniform all wrong, a ghost from the past.

But if someone had grown fat and lazy and was ten long years a smug cunt, then maybe his plan would work. Fryer raised the big brass knocker, a black spyhole in its centre, and rapped it three times, gunshot-loud cracks in the silence of the night. Inside, a dog started to bark like mad. This was expected. Fryer turned his back to the door and flipped the catch holding the Ruger in its holster. A man's voice, from within:

'Who's there? Identify yourself,' he said. It was Jim Dempsey. If he was doing the asking, then he was surely alone, or else Fryer would be dealing with a guard at this point. The dog was still roaring. It sounded like a big male, maybe a Mastiff or more likely a Rottweiler. Fryer shouted out the name of the local PSNI commander that was on the Internet, plus a warrant number he had made up, but sounded right.

'Mr Dempsey, there has been an assault at the bottom of the street, young person stabbed. We are just checking door to door.'

No reply from Dempsey, but seconds later the dog stopped barking, like it had been switched off. Also expected. It must have a calm word. Which meant it had an attack word, would kill on command. From within, sounds of the door being unlocked. Fryer walked briskly to the gate, disconnected the lamp from the battery, threw them into the plastic bag, and turned fast, strode back to the front door, building up momentum as he did so. He converted his last step into a swinging kick, and hit the door with all he had as it opened a crack.

A sharp snap, then a duller, deeper bump and crunch as the door connected with the human head Fryer saw briefly. Then it was gone, the door opened genteelly, all the force spent. From the doorway he could see a man was sprawled and groaning on the wooden floor of the hallway. Candles burnt in saucers, scant light. Fryer stepped inside and closed the door with the heel of his trainer.

The dog was a Rottweiler, big, black and male. It was

223

safely contained behind a steel security gate at the bottom of the stairs, key in the door, but it was going ballistic, knocking its face against the steel bars. He returned his attention to Jim Dempsey, still on his back. Less hair, what remained white now, no grey. Lost a few pounds, his neck skin loose wattles, but this was his man. He was wearing a short-sleeved plaid shirt with a horse logo on the breast. A bib of bright blood had already spread across the gaudy fabric. He raised himself up on both elbows, blinking slowly. His nose was swollen and dented at an unnatural angle, eyes beginning to puff and blacken. He mumbled something, through swollen lips. Fryer stepped closer. Dempsey's eyes rolled, he blinked.

'I'm OK, I'm OK,' Dempsey was repeating. His eyes fixed on Fryer, awoke with recognition. He scurried backwards, pushing with his feet. Fryer holstered the gun. 'Hold it, Jim. You put your hands where I can see them.'

Dempsey stopped, sat upright, and raised both hands. He stared at Fryer, breathing hard. The bastard started to smile. 'John Fryer? And dressed up to the nines in an RUC uniform?'

'Got you to open your door, though,' said Fryer.

Dempsey's smirk dropped away. 'Does the hospital know that you are out and about?' said Dempsey.

'I question, you answer,' said Fryer, gun raised.

'Anything you say, John. Whatever it is, I want to help.'

'The dog needs to quiet. What's his name?' said Fryer.

'Cara,' said Dempsey, eyes still on Fryer from behind his bloody mask, but thinking now. Cara, Gaelic for friend. Fryer nodded. 'Now, what's Cara's calm word?' said Fryer.

Dempsey glanced at the dog, then back to Fryer. 'John, I'm not sure I understand. I think you are confused here. The dog is upset. Best way to calm him down is for you to leave.'

'Answer me, or hurt. Your choice.'

'No,' said Dempsey. 'We are just talking, right, John, just talking here? No need for that. We don't need to go that way.'

'So talk.'

'I don't know what—'

Fryer stamped his heel on Dempsey's outstretched ankle, like a man crushing a tin can. Dempsey's hands went to it, his leg bent. Fryer raised the gun over his head and slammed the butt of the Ruger down on Dempsey's raised knee cap. It cracked like a porcelain cup. Dempsey's hands changed from ankle to knee, his face contorted, ready to scream. Fryer stabbed the barrel of the gun into Dempsey's mouth, leant closer. He could smell the blood, a whiff of aftershave, sour sweat.

'Assume that I want no more noise,' said Fryer. 'And put those hands back in the air.' Dempsey gagged, and Fryer withdrew the gun, but only halfway. He put his hands up again, clean lines now streaked his bloodied cheeks.

'The calm word,' said Fryer. He removed the gun from Dempsey's mouth, jammed it hard into his crotch.

'Fuar,' gasped Dempsey. Gaelic again: cold.

'Does the dog obey the word or the man?'

'Word,' said Dempsey, breathing in tight gasps. No hesitation this time, he was learning. Fryer stood up, kept the Ruger trained on Dempsey's centre of mass. He approached the security gate.

'Cara!' he shouted. No response. The beast continued its hoarse hysterics, bouncing from paw to paw like it was electrified. His barks ascended to staccato howls as Fryer reached the edge of the steel door.

225

'Cara,' Fryer repeated softly, moving his body even closer to the bars of the gate. 'Fuar,' he said.

Suddenly, Cara collapsed to his haunches on the bottom step, totally at peace, stomach rising and falling, chocolate brown eyes fixed on Fryer. Waiting, watching. The word was his master. And Fryer had said it. He reached down and tore open the plastic bag of chuck steak, took a handful. He tossed it through the bars, watched as Cara devoured it. He was a beautiful animal, too good for Dempsey. Right then, Fryer decided to take Cara away. For however long his mission lasted, Cara, a friend, would be at his side.

'He's going to need a drop of water soon,' said Fryer, taking the zip ties he'd found in the armoury room in Bangor from his pocket. He skirted round Dempsey, crouched down quickly, pulled Dempsey's arms together behind his back and slipped a plastic noose round his wrists. He pulled the short end very hard. It zipped closed. Dempsey hissed.

'On yer feet,' said Fryer, and hauled him up. Fryer marched him through to the kitchen, pulled a chair into the middle of the tiled floor and shoved Dempsey down and zip-tied his ankles to the legs. Tealight candles flickered on the surfaces and floor, scant light and faint reflection. By the back door was a steel cage, blankets and a bowl of water, inside. The kitchen smelt of dog but not much besides. Fryer pulled out another kitchen chair and sat down close to Dempsey, set about making a roll-up.

'Smoke?' asked Fryer, sparking up his tab.

'Quit,' said Dempsey.

Fryer scoffed, exhaled a cloud of blue smoke, better. A cup of tea would seal the deal. He glanced over at the sparse worktops, not even a kettle. Here was a boy playing at being normal, trying to fit in. Fryer would bet that he forgot to put out the bins, and still kept war hours. Fryer's eye lingered on a crayon drawing of two stick figures, stuck on the side of the fridge. Beside it a photograph of Dempsey and a child wearing an Irish dancing dress. Over the stick figures, large letters: I LOVE YOU, GRANDA. Fryer looked away quickly.

'That's from my granddaughter, she's only nine. Her name is—'

'I don't need to know,' said Fryer. Dempsey shut up. His head sank into his chest. Fryer dragged hard on his cigarette, smoke cut his throat, squeezed his lungs in a hot, satisfying cramp.

'You and me need to have a wee chat, Jim.'

'Now, of course, John. We can and we should. But not like this,' he said, lisping. It was definitely going to get on Fryer's nerves. One of Dempsey's front teeth was sticking out at an angle, causing the problem. Fryer leant in and pinched the tooth between his thumb and forefinger, plier strong. He twisted, and yanked it free. Dempsey yelped, a fresh trickle of blood running down his chin.

'Healthy root if it bleeds,' said Fryer. He flicked it away. It rattled across the floor.

'I need you to know, I'm going to be taking the dog, Jim,' said Fryer.

Dempsey nodded three times.

'So, I am going to need to know his kill word. Better to have and not need and so on. Plus, I wouldn't fancy saying the wrong word at the wrong time, you know?' Dempsey blinked at him, no longer nodding. Fryer took a final pull from the smoke and held the smouldering butt up to Dempsey's face.

'The word,' he said.

Dempsey nodded again, but no word.

Fryer pushed the lit cigarette into Dempsey's cheek, hand on the back of his head. The fire burnt into the soft meat of Dempsey's face, charred pork and burnt fat. Dempsey squirmed in the chair. It took all of Fryer's strength to keep him from toppling over, as he emitted a high-pitched sound, cross between a scream and a moan. Fryer unplugged the butt from its black socket which continued to smoke. He blew on the tip and it glowed red, vicious and ready.

'Please,' Dempsey whimpered.

'The word,' said Fryer.

'Please,' coughed Dempsey.

Fryer sighed, and jabbed it back in.

Dempsey screamed and jerked. Fryer nearly lost him entirely, dropped the smoke. Fryer leant his weight into the cracked shell of Dempsey's kneecap, felt something slide and then give way. Dempsey gagged, coughed a sour spray of vomit, hit Fryer on the chest. It was fucking stinking. Fryer stepped back.

'Breathe,' said Fryer. He hoped this was not going to end in mouth to mouth. Dempsey sputtered and spat. Fryer sat down, rolled another one. 'Now, I'd prefer to smoke this one. But I do intend to take the dog, Jim. So I need the word,' said Fryer.

'It's like handing you a loaded gun,' said Dempsey, weeping, but not lisping at least.

'Already have one, Jim,' he said.

Dempsey shook his head, no more weeping, a moment of quiet, then he spoke.

'Madmaná,' said Dempsey, very quietly. Gaelic word for Madman.

Fryer raised an eyebrow. 'Bit obvious, no?'

Dempsey looked away. 'So what is it you so desperately need to talk to me about, John Fryer?'

'Let's start with ten years, locked up in that place like the Count of Monte fucking Christo. Doped up to my eyes. Because of you,' said Fryer.

'I had to. Don't you remember what you did?' said Dempsey.

Fryer ignored his question, tried to do the same with the image of Shane's final whimpering minutes, but the seed had been planted. 'Where was the Movement when I needed it? Fucking nowhere, I was dead to them, and you. But now I'm back.'

'Then you're ready to collect your pension, John. Money owed.'

'That's your answer for everything, isn't it? You and your Brit money, you make me sick,' said Fryer.

'It's IRA money, I swear to you, veteran's money, your money, John. From the First Ulster raid.' First Ulster, vague recollections of a big bank robbery reported while he was in the Heights, early days. Millions taken, nobody convicted. So that had been an IRA job.

'We got so much we could hardly launder it,' continued Dempsey, 'but the old channels were still live so we kept on using them. First Ulster money went out, a cleaning cost and freshly laundered currency, diamonds, sent back,' he said.

'And you were kind enough to keep my share here, even though you left me to rot in the Heights?' he said.

Dempsey hesitated, and then he said, 'No, not here. I don't have access. If you want it, we have to speak to the accountant.' Fryer knew who he meant. The accountant was the money man, in charge of managing IRA funds, Belfast based. A man named Quigley. Fryer had run with his brother. Good family, clever boys.

'But you need me as a go-between. Quigley will never deal with you alone,' Dempsey added quickly.

'We'll see about that,' said Fryer. The candles on the kitchen floor had sputtered out, two on the work surface remained, burnt low. He could hear Cara panting from the other room. The darkness, all around, was closing in, and with it, the terrible visitation which it almost always brought. On the air, under the charred wax and smoke, he caught the first waft of rot, getting stronger by the second. But no matter, the time had come. Dempsey must have read his eyes. He started to squirm, shaking his head from side to side.

'Dog's thirsty,' said Fryer. He trudged into the hall. Cara watched him, pink tongue lolling as he opened the gate. 'Come.' Fryer held him by the leather collar, walked him into the kitchen. He could feel the ripple of loose skin and fur under his knuckles, the power beneath. He pointed the gun at Dempsey, one wrong word and he would shoot. He let the dog go. Cara moved gracefully to his bowl in the cage, started to lap water.

'Cut me loose, John. Let me take you there,' said Dempsey.

'Trust you? Who gave me every filthy job, never did the dirty work? Who betrayed me, left me in the Heights?'

230

said Fryer. His roll-up was dead. He dropped it. Another candle had puffed out, smoke rose in a thin line, but all Fryer could smell was the coming of the Moley, its stench thick as monkey house air.

'You needed help, John. You still do.'

The final candle flickered, the darkness encroached. The Moley was here, in this house. Fryer's heart pounded, his palms were slick, but he did not move. Tonight it would feed, and he would not run, or bleed. He called Cara and he heeled.

Dempsey struggled in the chair. 'No! John, don't! I have something else, you need to know,' screamed Dempsey, but to Fryer, his voice sounded far away. He seized Cara's collar and shoved him, a scream in his own throat, and his eyes on the shadows.

'Madmaná!' shouted Fryer and the dog roared, leapt on Dempsey, toppled him. His cries were brief, replaced by a wet gurgle. He twitched and shook as Cara ripped and tore. Only when the floor was pooled with black blood, and the Moley had disappeared, did Fryer shout, 'Fuar!'

Cold.

And calm.

CHAPTER THIRTY-TWO

Christopher could smell the heavy dullness of spilt blood as soon as John Fryer opened the front door of Dempsey's house. It was thick enough in the air to taste it. Dempsey was in the kitchen on his back, in a pool of it. He stepped closer, took out his phone and started to take a few snaps, to upload. John, who had ushered him in, continued to light candles.

He heard a guttural, low, animal growl.

Daddy?

He turned slowly. There was a big, black Rottweiler watching him from inside a metal cage. The door was open, a nightmare come true. Christopher's genitals shrunk to nothing for the second time in under an hour. He knew that John expected Dempsey to have an animal, thus the raw meat. But the stink of blood, the body. He'd assumed that the dog was dead, killed before its owner. That was logical, but totally wrong. The dog continued to growl as it eyed him from the shadows. No, not big, it was massive.

'Cara!' snapped John, and then said something that sounded like Irish. The dog stopped growling, its shoulders deflated. 'It's OK, kid. He'll do you no harm.'

Christopher nodded, managed a nonchalant grin. 'Cool trick. Maybe you can show me how to do that?' he said, mouth dry as cork. Christopher's fingers moved over the screen of his phone, uploading the pictures of Dempsey's body as @God'sPeopleUnderSiege, tagging two of the followers of his other online persona @TenDead81. His eyes returned to the black dog, still staring at him. He needed to get out of this place.

'This is a nice job, John. It's going to make a big impression,' he said, again inspecting the remains of Dempsey's degloved face. It was hard to keep his voice from quivering. The dog started to lick its chops. The fur on its face was matted and dark. He looked again at Dempsey's mutilated corpse, and made the connection, just as John Fryer spoke.

'It was Cara. He did the business for me. All I had to do was say the word,' said John. He was smiling, and Christopher smiled back, hoped the gloom of the kitchen was enough to hide his eyes.

'We should go, John. Photo's uploaded. Won't be long before the PSNI arrive here. Probably best that we don't stay to open the door for them,' he said. Fryer nodded. The man had clearly no clue what an upload was, but he knew who the police were.

'Let's go, boy,' said John.

Christopher exhaled. He was getting out of here. He started to move towards John Fryer. The mutt padded past him, went over to John and waited obediently by his new master's side. Fryer had been addressing the dog, not him. They stood together: stocky man, stocky dog. It was watching him, the dog that just ripped out a man's throat and peeled off his face.

'John, do a quick check out the front door.'

John nodded, told the dog to stay. He walked out. Seconds later he heard the front door unlatch. Christopher moved slowly to the table and lifted Daddy's Ruger. He watched the dog. The dog watched him. He felt a vibration from his phone, then another and yet another. More alerts. The word had spread. A whispered shout came from the direction of the front door: John's voice.

'Clear,' he said. The dog glanced in the direction of the voice, just the smallest break of its gaze from Christopher.

In the same second, Christopher raised the gun and pointed it at the mutt. His daddy had taught him how to draw and handle a weapon, said it was essential. He had also taught him how to fire one. A deafening bang, followed by two more, yellow sparks spat from the muzzle of the gun. The dog jerked, tried to run, fell. He could taste the cordite, a high-pitched alarm bell ringing in his ears.

The dog was prostrate on its side, blood leaked from the three holes. Its breath was coming in fast, rasping gasps and its legs were scrabbling and scratching. John burst through the dining-room entrance. He looked at the dog on the floor, then at Christopher. Then he went down hard on his knees, and put a hand on it. The mutt's legs had stopped making a run for it. Dog gone, he thought, and swallowed hard and grinded his teeth. This would be a bad time to start laughing.

John glared up at him. 'No,' he said. Not shouting, sounding close to tears. Fryer repeated himself over and over, both hands cradling the animal's big head.

'That dog,' he said, jabbing the gun in the direction of the carcass, 'it went for me. It was going to kill me.' John physically slumped, then got up slowly. Christopher lowered the gun. 'Would you rather it was me?' Fryer did not speak. Instead, he locked eyes with Christopher, and in that moment Christopher got his reply. Fryer briefly returned his attention to the carrion on the floor, turned away and walked out of the dining room in the direction of the front door. Christopher could hear the whine of sirens, getting closer. Alone with Dempsey and the dog, the house was immediately as thick with silence as it was with the coppery fumes of congealing blood. He put the Ruger into his belt, saw that the mutt's mess had seeped over to kiss one of his Doc Martens. Christopher made a sound of disgust and flicked the filth off his boot.

He hurried out of the kitchen, picked up the plastic bag with the light from the hallway and scurried from Dempsey's house. He looked left and right at the gate. No police, but no John Fryer either. He headed for the parked taxi, looking for the man dressed like his dead daddy, who had disappeared into the mist of the Belfast night.

PART THREE

BLOOD ON THE RISE

CHAPTER THIRTY-THREE

Belfast, Northern Ireland, present day
Sunday 11th July

Dawn had seeped a grey brown light over the vista of Belfast city as Aoife parked up on Lincoln View. It had just gone 5 a.m. She had been jolted awake in Sheen's hotel bed (headache, sandpaper mouth) by Irwin's call an hour before. Sheen had been asleep on the two-seater sofa – small mercies. By the time she used the bathroom and borrowed his deodorant, Sheen was awake too and she had given him the update.

'Jim Dempsey has been murdered, and Belfast is fucked.'

In the inky light she could make out half a dozen pallet-stacked bonfires in the city below. They were taller than the terraced streets which surrounded them, one almost as high as the twenty-storey flats which were adjacent. Tonight, the pallets would be set to flame and the loyalist fires would burn, seeing in the Glorious 12th and in Belfast, the past would come to life and take over. She shivered in the breeze that carried the smell of burning, a residue of the violence across the Peace Line between the Falls and the Shankill, which had been reported on the news.

Four police Land Rovers blocked off access to the end of the street. In front of the vehicles, blue police tape was tied across the road, a uniformed officer standing guard, submachine gun held in both hands. A moment of déjà vu, it was almost identical to the scene she had arrived at the day before in Tiger's Bay.

They showed their warrant cards and ducked under the blue tape. 'The west of the city, Dempsey's street included, is blacked out. Made it a lot easier to get in and kill a man, who lived and breathed security for most of his adult life,' she said. Sheen stopped, and she waited too, her hair lifted in the cold breeze, gooseflesh prickling her arms. 'The substation explosion. If you can't turn out just one light, turn out all the lights. Meaning killing Dempsey was always their plan,' she said.

'Or the start of one,' he said. More acrid smoke on the breeze.

'Out of Chaos,' she said.

They reached Dempsey's house. A white forensics tent annexed the front door and part of the garden. A generator hummed, cables running off it, one powering a sturdy halogen lamp that illuminated the inside of the tent and the hallway beyond. They changed into protective suits and signed in. Aoife walked through the door, careful to follow the white plastic stepping plates.

She noted the remains of burnt-out candles on the floor, and the blood deposits, drops and splashes on the floor, marked by the CSIs. She stopped and pulled the open front door towards her, Sheen by her side. The chain was snapped, hanging on by a single screw, and there was a smear of blood on the inside of the door above it. She pointed at first one, then the other, and Sheen nodded. He got it, forced entry, but the door must have been opened first, the hinges and main lock looked undamaged. She turned her attention to the bottom step of the stairs where she could see a chewed rubber bone behind an open security gate, its key still in the lock.

'If he had a dog, and it was let out, how come it didn't guard him?' said Sheen.

Aoife continued into the house, following predesignated white steps before them. She saw blood, first a little, then, as she entered the kitchen area, a lot. Then she saw Dempsey's dog. Aoife stared at the black, furry hulk that was on the floor beside the dining-room table. What she initially thought was a dark rug beneath the dog's body was a congealed pool of black blood. The smell in the room was overpowering: thick and raw, the smell of slaughter. It summoned an echo of sawdust-floored butcher shops from her childhood. In the super bright glare of the halogens the dog's body looked hyperreal, like a prop from a B movie.

'That was one huge dog,' she said. Sheen grunted agreement. She reached out to touch the oily smoothness of the dog's head. The animal's eyes were part closed, a film of blue formed over one, no life light. There was a penny tag on the leather collar round the dog's neck, a name pressed into its smooth surface.

Cara: friend.

'Look,' said Sheen. He was pointing down at the tiled

kitchen floor. There, partially obscured under the pool of thick blood that had spread from the dog's body was a footprint.

'Looks like this is our boy,' he said, taking a few photos on his mobile. It was partial, but clear enough, same groves running from left to right, a boat-shaped tongue up the middle. The same person, or at least the same pair of boots, had been at all crime scenes.

Dempsey's body had already been removed. The story was still an easy one to read. There was an overturned chair across the room, next to the sink and cupboard units. On the floor, plastic box ties, once closed, now cut. They must have been used to secure him to the chair, removed when it was time to take the body away. And there was blood, a small lake of it, pooled on the white tile floor around the top of the upturned chair, splashes of gore on the cupboard doors, and spattered across the floor in an arc, where Dempsey's head had probably laid. He had struggled hard before he died. She glanced back at the dead dog. Its muzzle was caked with blood; she made the connection. Her stomach twisted. She needed air.

Aoife sidestepped past Sheen, who was busy taking shots, then stopped. There, next to the leg of the dining-room table, concealed behind a chair leg, were two pinched roll-up butts, squashed flat. On one she saw a brown spot, possibly blood. She took a plastic bag from her pocket and picked up the two butts. She recalled Fryer's empty cell, in Belfast Heights. There was an unopened packet of rolling tobacco, and the rolling papers resting on top. It was what had convinced Adeola that he was really catatonic. Fryer was a chainsmoker.

'Fryer's been here too,' she said, holding up the butts

so Sheen could see. 'There's blood on one of these ends. We can confirm it with DNA. Wonder if Irwin will tell us to keep our distance now?' she said, standing up to find she could hear Irwin from the front entrance. She stopped, dead.

Aoife stepped off the white forensic steps and moved across the kitchen floor. She stepped on some of the blood, felt it slippery under her feet, but did not stop moving. She did not care. She was staring straight ahead at what she had seen, on the side of Dempsey's fridge. She heard Sheen's voice. He sounded urgent.

There was a photograph on the fridge, secured next to a child's drawing and scrawled message: I LOVE YOU, GRANDA. She reached out and pulled the photograph free. It showed a little girl, her dark hair crimped in tight ringlets and festooned with green and orange ribbons. She was dressed in a green and sequin Irish dancing dress. Dempsey was next to the child, his arm round her shoulder. But it was not her, or him, that had brought her across the room in stunned silence.

There, mid-dance, captured in the background, was Ava. She was wearing her competition dress, her wiry hair worked into cane rows on her head, falling round her neck and shoulders in stiff braids. This was taken at the Culturlann, last year. Aoife started to shake, tears coursed unchecked, hot and angry, down her cheeks.

John Fryer and whoever was with him last night would have seen this photo if they had looked at the fridge. They would have laid eyes on her little girl. Those murderers had been allowed to see her, and even more absurdly, even though she understood it was neither true nor possible, she felt that she had allowed Ava to somehow witness the horror that had taken place in this kitchen hours before.

'Fuck,' she hissed, clenched the photograph.

'Aoife,' hissed Sheen, full of warning.

She turned round to see Irwin in the doorway. He looked at her, then focused on the photograph in her hand. His mouth opened, his colour already deepened.

'DC McCusker, you'd best have a good reason for contaminating a perfectly good crime scene. Outside, now!' he said. Then, as though reaching the heart of the professional misconduct before his eyes, he added, 'And for goodness' sake please stop crying like a schoolgirl on the job,' he said.

CHAPTER THIRTY-FOUR

As she emerged from the tent she could see members of the press had gathered beyond the parked Land Rovers on the other side of the blue tape. Irwin was at the front gate, saw her looking in that direction. His colour had returned to ruddy from its previous magenta.

'Oh, don't you worry, DC McCusker. I have already briefed them. Your expertise will not be needed there,' he said. 'Now explain to me what the heck I just walked in on,' he said.

Her tears were gone, but she felt her tendons and muscles tighten. Christ almighty she wanted to smash this man in the face. Instead, she took in a shuddering breath. When she spoke, her voice still had a quiver, but she managed to keep it steady.

'Sir, I found this photograph on Dempsey's fridge,' she said.

Irwin took the photograph from her and scanned it, then looked up. 'And? What am I seeing here?' he asked, handing it back. She pushed it back at him and he kept it.

'Look again, sir. The child in the background, she is my daughter,' she said. Irwin scrutinised the photograph again. 'Dempsey must have taken his granddaughter to the same Irish dancing competition that I brought Ava to, last year,' she said.

Irwin was still squinting at the photograph, looking confused. 'That child is half-caste,' he said. It was a statement, but his face made it a question. One she was not prepared to answer.

'Yes, sir, Ava is mixed,' she said. 'I am her legal guardian,' she added.

Irwin grunted, but as he watched her, his complexion mellowed. He continued to observe her, as though she was a new species of some sort. Irwin had large dark bags under his eyes, the whites tinged with red, but he was definitely not nursing a hangover. He ran a hand over his usually shining smooth face, and it rasped loudly.

'I have two daughters, bit younger. I can see how that would cause a person a shock. But try to keep your emotions under control from now on. This needs to be bagged and sent for prints, not that there will be any point now,' he said, his tone more gentle than before. He handed the photograph back to Aoife. She waited for him to say something else, but that was it apparently. 'Back to this,' nodding in the direction of Dempsey's house as he said 'this'.

'Looks as though the dog was used, somehow, to kill Dempsey,' offered Sheen.

'I worked that out myself. But I doubt whether that Rottweiler tied him by the ankles to the kitchen chair or kicked his door in. Body had signs of torture, teeth removed, cigarette burns on the face, smashed knee cap. But the dog killed him. MacBride's colleague who is running the CSIs said the pathologist will make short work of the autopsy. Which means the body will be released for burial in a couple of days. Given the current climate a high-profile republican funeral is all we need,' said Irwin.

'CCTV?' asked Aoife. Irwin shook his head. Aoife told him about the footprint, and the discarded roll-up, the spot of blood.

'Fryer disappears from Belfast Heights yesterday and a day later, Jim Dempsey, his former CO turns up dead. We have to go after him,' said Sheen.

'The DNA will tell us for sure. If he is involved in this murder, we will have him. But do nothing that will bring Oswald and Special Branch down on us. I want to know who's wearing the boots, DI Sheen, and I want a link, something concrete that connects John Fryer to Esther Moore,' said Irwin. 'Dempsey's neighbour called 999 last night. Rap his door, get a statement,' he said, yawning. 'I need to get a cup of coffee. This town has been destroying itself all night. Madness,' he said.

'We heard about the trouble over the Peace Line. A man was killed,' she said.

Irwin nodded. 'Not released his name yet, but it's all over social media. Scotty Woods, UDA, lower Shankill,' he said. She recognised the name. Irwin had mentioned the guy in passing earlier, called him a bottom feeder, a minor adversary of Moore, though part of the same paramilitary group.

'By nationalists? This is going to cause more trouble,' she said.

'Most probably, but he wasn't killed by the other side. The news says we lifted someone?' he asked.

Aoife told him it did.

'The shooter is a guy called Jackie Coyle, UVF, and he is telling very interesting tales. Says that murdering Scotty Woods wasn't the plan, things got out of hand. Claims he was ordered to petrol-bomb Protestant homes, point the finger at Catholics. Make Scotty look impotent. But also says our friend Cecil Moore was giving the orders via his boss Turk Bates. I assume you know of him?' he said.

Aoife said she did. The guy did not even try to pretend that he was involved in community politics. He was a criminal, and he owned a share of most of the drugs shipped into Belfast. On paper, he was Cecil Moore's political ally, but also his business enemy. She shook her head, said that it didn't make any sense. 'Why is Cecil Moore working with Turk Bates?' she asked.

'Think about who benefits if Scotty Woods is removed from the frame,' said Irwin. The picture suddenly cleared. Irwin was right. It was obvious. Cecil would be able to move in and take over UDA operations in Scotty's patch, and the timing was perfect. The public and the media were still distracted by his mother's murder, and while that was so, Cecil was beyond reproach. His move caused riots in the streets, and Cecil would be there to save the day, with the 'strong man of the people' act. Better to have people afraid, looking to him for leadership, increasing his territory, and his profit.

'Moore is unbelievable,' she said.

Irwin grunted in agreement. 'Pride before fall, DC McCusker. Jackie Coyle is up in Antrim Area Police Station and he's going on the record against Turk, Moore, the other lowlifes who were involved last night. I am going to lift Moore for questioning, and the others. In my experience one rat jumps, the others surely follow. With any luck Cecil Moore will be left holding the rudder and we can send him down,' said Irwin.

Irwin's phone chirped and he answered it, listened and then ended the call with thanks. 'That kid Anderson has turned up. Royal Victoria Hospital, in very bad shape, but he is alive at least. We will go and have a word, when you are finished here,' said Irwin. As Aoife and Sheen turned to knock on Dempsey's neighbour, Irwin called her name, and she looked back. Irwin's eyes were fixed on her, a roadmap of red blood vessels, burning in his pale face. She braced herself for the quip, or the final chastisement, but instead his face creased into a weary smile. 'Your wee girl's a lovely looking child. If I were you, I'd check in on her. If you know she's safe and well you will be able to do your job with a clear head,' he said. Irwin marched off before she could reply.

'Thank you, sir, I will,' she said softly. Her hands remained at her sides and the phone stayed in her pocket. For a couple of seconds, Aoife was too stunned to move.

CHAPTER THIRTY-FIVE

Aoife and Sheen were squeezed into the small sofa in the front room of Dempsey's neighbour, a man named Phelan Brown. A large wooden board, the size of a child's first snooker table, hung on the wall. A St Brigit's cross was embossed on its surface, composed of thousands of meticulously clipped and lacquered matchsticks, each one carefully glued in place. She had seen similar craftwork in the homes of many former prisoners during her days in Community Relations. The only other decoration was a framed colour photograph, about half the size of the cross. It was of a young man, small brown moustache, blue jeans, zipped-up green bomber jacket, smiling and leaning against a blue Cortina car. The image was grainy – she guessed pre-digital – just like his tash and stone-washed jeans.

Phelan Brown looked somewhere between his early seventies and dead already. He sat opposite them on a high-backed chair that looked as though it could be raised and lowered automatically. He was wearing a brown polyester cardigan which, like the sallow skin of his sagging cheeks, seemed to be one size too big. A long cigarette was burning in the glass ashtray on the arm of the chair, filling the room with its stinking, bluish smoke. He caught her looking up at the cross on the wall. She noticed his brown eyes were tinged with yellow.

'My son made that. Took him years,' he said, gesturing to the cross, then to the photo on the wall.

'It's very beautiful,' she said.

'I'd rather have my boy,' he replied, lifting the cigarette and drawing in the smoke.

'We understand you called emergency services this morning,' said Sheen.

Phelan took another drag, set his cigarette on the grooved lip of the ashtray and nodded once. He told them that he had just settled into the chair by his bed to complete the crossword, sometime between eleven and twelve. Did not know exactly when. He had little use for the clock. 'I had two candles set up by the bed, but the light was no good at all, so I moved over to blow them out, but I couldn't do it first time,' he said. His voice was a hoarse half whisper. Phelan took another suck on his smoke, this time holding the half-finished cigarette between his first two fingers.

'Did you hear something?' she asked.

'I thought it was a firework going off, but quieter, like it had been set off inside,' he said.

Aoife thought about Cara the dog, lying prostrate in a pool of blood. 'How many bangs did you hear?' she asked.

'Not sure,' he said, then produced a big white cotton

hanky from his cardigan and coughed three times, a dry bark.

She saw the pain in his face, as he smacked his lips, withdrawing the hanky. 'Can I get you some water?' she asked. Phelan Brown shook his head, his eyes pinching closed as he smoked.

'I thought it was just kids, you know, they're forever setting off bangers. Used to be Halloween, but it's started to happen all the time. The police should do something,' he said.

Aoife nodded, willing him to get to the point.

'It took me a few seconds to get over to the front windy. Was dark, nothing to see. I had already turned away, and then I saw this guy, from the corner of my eye,' he said, squashing the last of his smoke into the ashtray.

'Description?' said Sheen.

Brown shrugged his coat hanger shoulders, shook his head, his hound dog jowls quivering. 'I'll tell you what I saw, but you won't believe me,' he said. 'Your man was dressed up pretending to be a peeler, RUC uniform, the hat, everything,' he said.

'A police officer? Was he armed?' Aoife glanced at Sheen. This was new, and important. A renegade copper was not on their radar. This could explain the fact that Fryer's accomplice was a ghost. The only forensics they had was a boot print, maybe a single hair.

'Probably, aren't you?' he said.

'Can you give us a better description? Build, hair colour, white, mixed race, age?' she asked.

'Smallish, smaller than thon fella,' said Brown, nodding at Sheen. 'But big set, big barrel chest, walked like a hard man,' he said. 'Not sure about age, younger than me, older

252

than you? Probably white, but it was dark, you know? The hat covered his face, no idea about hair,' said Brown.

'This is good, Mr Brown, this is really good. Is there anything else you can remember, any detail at all? It might be important,' she said.

Phelan Brown looked suddenly weary. He paused, produced a packet of Regal King Size and a lighter from his other cardigan pocket, got another smoke started and set it down. 'Your man walked out of my view. I waited, and then I saw another guy, coming from the same direction as the peeler. He was running, looked like a wee scumbag, you know the type,' he said.

Aoife shook her head. She wanted his words. Brown's idea of a troublemaker was probably a teddy boy in drainpipe trousers and a razor comb.

'Obviously he was white. Wearing a Celtic top. Had a baseball cap on. Couldn't see his mug, but he looked young, younger than the other one. He was leaner, no fat on him,' he said.

The baseball cap was a match for Fryer's mystery visitor at the Heights, but in Belfast, a young man wearing a baseball cap and a Celtic top was not much to go on.

'That's it. I let my curtain fall and went over to the bed. Called 999 on the mobile. You know when the police showed up? Nearly three hours later. Some young guy was in here earlier, he said that I should have reported gun shots, they would have come sooner,' he said, shaking his head.

'Mr Brown, did you go to sleep immediately?' she asked.

'Awake,' he replied.

'Please think, was there anything else, something you might have seen, or heard, anything that could give us a better clue on who these people are?' she asked.

Brown shook his head. He paused. 'This is probably nothing,' he said. 'A few minutes later I heard a car, but it was bigger, you know, like a heavy vehicle engine. It started up and idled for a few seconds, then it must have driven off. This is a cul-de-sac, so you get used to the sounds of the neighbour's cars. This was different,' he said.

'A motorbike, maybe?' said Sheen.

'Or a Land Rover, like one the police use?' said Aoife. She felt Sheen look at her as she asked this question. He understood what she had meant. If it was a copper involved, a police Land Rover would be perfect as a getaway vehicle.

'Definitely not,' said Brown quickly, answering both questions. Her excitement ebbed, but she was not going to give up. Brown was the best eyewitness in this case so far.

'I'd say it was a black hack,' he said nodding, looking pleased.

'A taxi cab?' asked Sheen.

'Aye, that's what I just said, mate, a black hack,' said Brown, looking at Sheen like he had lost his mind. He turned his attention to Aoife. She managed to suppress the smile that was playing at the sides of her mouth. 'You know what I'm meaning?' he asked. Aoife nodded. It made sense. A black taxi was perfect, even better than driving a police vehicle. Ubiquitous and all but invisible, hard to notice in a place where every third vehicle on the road looked virtually identical. Like wearing a Celtic top, or a baseball cap.

'Thank you, Mr Brown, you have been very helpful,' she said, standing up.

'Not sure I have. In my day I would have went out and

tackled them myself, but my day is well and truly gone,' he said, raising himself up.

'We can see ourselves out,' said Sheen.

'No doubt, but I'm seeing you out,' he replied.

Sheen opened the front door and thanked Brown for his time.

Aoife stood on the threshold. There was a holy water font hanging on the inside of the door frame, its contents full. She turned around. Brown was leaning on the yellow radiator in the hall. 'You know, Mr Brown, the RUC's gone. We are the PSNI, different times,' she said. She was picking him up on his comment about the man dressed as a peeler. Brown had said he was wearing an RUC uniform, not PSNI. It was a small thing, but it mattered. For things to change, new messages had to be repeated.

'You must think I'm not wise. I know who you are. I am a committed peace processor you know. I wasn't messing with you when I said he was wearing an RUC uniform. That's exactly what your man was wearing, the old bottle green. I remember it well. They put my door in enough times looking for my son,' he said.

Aoife nodded, thanked him, and turned to go but stopped. Phelan Brown may need a body transplant but his brain was working just fine. He was standing in the doorway, the front door half closed.

'Mr Brown, you said something else earlier. You said that this man was pretending. Why did you say that, because of the RUC uniform?' she asked.

'That was part of it, but mostly because of what he had on his feet. He was wearing a pair of white trainers. No peeler that ever came to my door wore white trainers, you included,' he said. 'I heard what happened to Jim Dempsey. You just remember that I called the police last night. There were other people I could have called first, but I called you,' he said, reaching inside the door. Phelan Brown flicked his fingers at her, cold water rained in fat drops on her blazer and the top of her head. The holy water. A blessing. 'Now go and catch these boys,' he said, and closed the door.

She quickly made the sign of the cross and walked after Sheen.

CHAPTER THIRTY-SIX

It was half eight on Sunday morning. Fryer sat in the black taxi, parked on the Falls road, outside the Culturlann Irish language and Cultural Centre. His hands were caked with dried blood that was not his own. An orange plastic bag stuffed with money rested on the passenger seat beside him. It was crammed with bundles of mostly Sterling, also some Euros and Dollars. To pass the time he had counted three bundles. Each was a thousand. There were a lot of bundles, enough to make him a rich man.

Despite what he had just done to get the money, Fryer cared little for the contents of the bag. The person he was waiting to set eyes on, however, she was a different matter. For her, he potentially cared a great deal. So here he was waiting and watching, when he should be lying low. He had not foreseen his Sunday morning beginning like this. Already, Fryer's world had been transformed utterly, and he'd not even had a cup of tea.

Fryer had waited out the death of Saturday night at the dining-room table. Same spot as the night before, same ashtray filling up. Pale dawn light had edged out the darkness beyond the curtained window, but as he set fire to another smoke, Fryer knew he would not sleep.

His mind was a washing machine, full of soiled laundry, and its cycle was not yet done, black thoughts turning again in his brain, as they had done all night. Jim Dempsey's gurgling screams, his revenge served at last, but when replayed Fryer felt nothing at all. And though it had fed just hours before, Fryer knew the Moley would return. Whether Dempsey was living or dead, the Moley would want more blood. He reached into his pocket, felt the razor blade he found in the bathroom cabinet. Fryer had covered the blunt edge with a strip of sticky bandage, a makeshift finger grip, wrapped a waterproof plaster over the blade for a sheath. He had been caught out in the taxi last night when the Moley had visited. Next time, Fryer would be ready.

Slosh and turn.

Cara the big dog, panting out his last breaths as Fryer cradled his huge head. No way had Cara attacked Christopher. Not without the kill word. What sort of sick bastard would shoot a beautiful creature like Cara, just for the craic? What other reason could he have had? The kid's voice, as though in answer, incoherent and full of sleep echoed down the stairs. Reminded Fryer of the dream chatter during his time in prison and then while residing at the Heights. In the dead of night the kid had let go one of those laughs of his, shrill and scream-like, breaking the still of the house, Fryer had flinched.

Slosh and turn.

But most of all, it was Dempsey's final words before Cara toppled him and finished him.

No! John, don't! I have something else, you need to know.

What was it Dempsey thought was so valuable, he might trade his life for? Had Fryer been sold out? Was that how he had ended up in the H-Blocks, as he'd always suspected? Dempsey wasn't going to tell Fryer any more tales, but Quigley the accountant was the man to ask. If anyone banked secrets, apart from Dempsey, it would be him. And he knew where to find him: the money man ran a 7-Eleven convenience store on the corner of the Falls and Donegall roads. And anyway, according to Dempsey, the accountant had his money, his pension. Maybe that was a lie, but only one way to find out.

Slosh and turn.

Fryer stood up and stretched. His tendons and joints popped and snapped like an old ship on the swell of the tide. He reached for his Armalite on the table beside him, withdrew his hand. In the Sunday-morning stillness, a gunshot would wake the dead. Plus, all he wanted was a quick chat. The accountant was a clever man. He'd see sense, allow Fryer to make a withdrawal, money owed and information buried.

Fryer picked up the taxi keys from the small table by the front door.

The kid was in full voice once again, calling his daddy's name, dreaming away. It did not sound like a good one to Fryer. Good, maybe Cara had not died after all; maybe he was bearing down on him, hot breath on Christopher's face. Fryer allowed himself a humourless laugh that dried up quickly. He knew better than most about bad dreams. The kid was lucky that his were confined to sleeping.

He opened the front door and sniffed the air. The damp odour of the dead leaves heaped beneath the hedge in the front garden, the paraffin whiff from an oil heater on the air, but nothing else in the half light. He clicked the front door closed, and then took a step out, cautiously checking the road in both directions from his raised vantage point. All was quiet and entirely empty.

In the driver's seat of the taxi his fingers did their accustomed work. He popped the roll-up between his lips and sparked it, then wiped the condensation from the driver's side of the windscreen with the cuff of his tracksuit top. Fryer released the handbrake and the heavy taxi quickly rolled down the hill, swallowed whole by morning mist which had settled in the dip. After a few metres, he twisted the key and the engine whinnied, coughed and gunned to life, now a good distance from the kid's home. Let him sleep, and let him dream.

He had a clear run from Bangor into west Belfast, found the 7-Eleven still shuttered, no car parked outside. Best to keep moving. There was more chance of being seen if he stopped. Fryer took the taxi into the adjacent warren of terraced and semi-detached houses, the St James's Road area.

His old haunt.

He drove past the house in which his son Kieran had once slept as a baby. Fryer stopped, reversed and looked at the front door, now double-glazed glass, painted light blue in his memory. This was where he used to steal in at night and take Kieran in his arms, rocking the baby boy in the darkness, feeling safe from the Brits patrolling the streets, looking for men like him. Feeling safe. The Moley could never touch him when he nursed the little beacon of light that was his baby boy. Was Kieran's mother still there? He thought not. The place looked totally different, and even if she was, she held nothing for him.

Kieran was gone, dead, his light snuffed out.

Fryer started moving and the taxi took him deeper, deeper into the ladder of streets, this time pulling up outside a house on a tree-lined avenue, the high-fronted homes here telling of more prosperous days long gone. It took Fryer a few seconds to register, then it came to him, like a weighted and bloated corpse bobbing to the surface of his mind.

This was the home of the retarded boy, McKenna. Fryer could not remember his first name. He had forgotten that, hard to believe it, but it was true, even now, sitting outside the home where he and Mooney had lain in wait that day before picking him up off the street.

On cue, the PVC front door of the house juddered, and then opened. A grey-haired woman, dressed in a blue towel dressing gown, a lit cigarette in one hand, staggered out, and then steadied. Fryer remained stock-still, watching. He doubted she could see him from this angle. He did not want to take the chance.

It was McKenna's mother. Drink-worn and haggard, but it was definitely her.

Her eyes were half closed and black streaks of mascara were smeared in lines on each side of her face, a washed-up Cleopatra. In her other hand was an empty bottle of Teacher's whiskey. She slowly descended the steps leading to the small front garden, and lifted the lid of the blue wheeled bin, tossed the bottle in. Fryer heard

261

it clink and clank as it landed on other glass. She turned. Her bony shoulders sawed at her thin dressing gown as she climbed the steps, and shut her front door. Inside that house she probably had a framed photo of her son, on a table or on the mantelpiece, maybe black and white. Maybe she talked to it as one drink turned to ten night after night, but never enough.

She'd been a teacher, smart. Made a lot of noise about her son's disappearance, went to the papers. But in the mid-'70s one missing youth was no big deal. A drop in the ocean of loss and violence in a city gone bad. There were other noises too: her son was an informer, he had run off to England and she knew it, he was a rat, he got what he deserved. There was writing on the walls that said so. Fryer had daubed some of it himself. In a place like St James, tout was a label that stuck, never forgotten or forgiven.

Fryer sat in the taxi and waited, listening to the tick of the engine cooling and the sound of small summer birds singing and answering one another, celebrating the dawn, all things made new. He ran his fingers over the raised Braille of his scarred forearms, reading the lines, too many to name, his past engraved, no longer hearing the birds. He gunned the engine and pulled away, this time telling the taxi where he wanted it to go.

Fryer watched the accountant's big Peugeot saloon car slow and turn left into the narrow entry that was creased between the 7-Eleven store and the kebab shop on the corner of the Falls road where he had parked and waited. It was barely wide enough but he took the turn with the well-oiled assurance of a man slipping into a favourite pair of shoes. The car disappeared from sight.

Fryer had seconds to observe the driver and make sure it was the man he wanted, but that was all it took. The accountant looked older, of course, had lost most of his hair, but it was him. That same look of inherent tidiness was unmistakable, remaining hair neatly clippered, his face clean-shaven. Fryer saw a shirt with a collar and tie, square wire-rimmed glasses perched on his nose. He looked like a pharmacist. All he needed was the white coat. He used to wear the brown smock of the grocer and maybe still did.

No matter, it was just a costume, and shopkeeper was just a role he played. But he played it diligently, Fryer gave him that. Which was why, riots or not, Sunday morning or Christmas morning he knew he would find the accountant opening his shop. But should you get closer, look into the grey eyes behind those glasses, you might get a glimpse of another man, a different story.

The accountant, Quigley, had been, and Fryer was very sure still was, the IRA's Chief Financial Officer, the little guy who sat on the big table. By virtue of his rank, Quigley had a place on the IRA's Army Council, had held the post of Chief of Staff, the power of life and death. He had sanctioned the execution of informers and Special Branch double agents, men who ended up wearing black bags over their heads and shot behind the ear in South Armagh. But unlike grunts like Fryer, who had pulled the trigger, the accountant never spent a day behind bars, never had anything pinned on him.

Fryer carefully slipped the razor blade with the plaster out of his back pocket, removed the sheath, stuck it to the dash. He pocketed the razor, got out, walked across the Donegal road and looked into the entry. The accountant's car, about fifteen feet in, was empty. The back door into the 7-Eleven was open a crack. No handle on the outside, just a key slot. Fryer squeezed himself between the wall and the side of the car, and used his fingertips to grip the inside lip of the door. He tugged. It emitted a sharp creak, opened.

Inside it was black. Fryer hesitated, one hand dropped to touch the razor in his back pocket. He squeezed his eyes tightly closed, counted to five, then stepped fractionally in, opened his eyes. Better adjusted, now he could see the dimness of a storage room. Not full dark after all, not so bad. He could deal with this. For a short time, he could deal with this.

Fryer stepped inside, breathed in the cold odour of the many cardboard boxes stacked in neat rows on the pressed metal shelving units, lined floor to the ceiling. He tasted soap powder, the clean astringency of tea bags, and the sharpness of soil on new potatoes. But nothing else.

He scanned the room quickly. Straight ahead a gangway running along the mouth of the shelving units. About three metres ahead was a door, slightly ajar, where weak light seeped in from the still-shuttered shop. From that direction the muffed music, volume turned down, barely competing with the somnolent buzz from a fridge freezer. And that was all, no movement, neither from the shelving stacks to his right, nor from the shop beyond the door.

The accountant must be in the front, maybe counting out a float for the till. Fryer padded up the narrow aisle of boxes, quiet as a cat. He watched the door to the shop, mentally scolding the accountant for his sloppiness. Just like Dempsey, grown fat in his brain in the last ten years, his vigilance and awareness had weathered down to nothing.

Fryer stopped, watched the weak light from the shop, now less than five feet in front of him, and frowned. There was something not right, no sign or sense of life from beyond that door. It felt as vacant, empty as the rows of shelves (and how dark they were, dark as gullies) which Fryer had just walked gingerly past. His hand slid carefully into his back pocket, found the razor's plaster grip.

He drew it silently, waited, all senses on fire.

The music was closer now but not originating from within the shop as he had surmised, it was—

A toilet flushed, the sound muted but unmistakable, and coming from Fryer's left.

His stomach sank like an anvil in a net and he had a second to now curse his own sloppiness and rusted senses, suddenly ten years too old, his mind pill-worn and cell-numbed. Yellow light flooded from beyond a stack of boxes containing packets of crisps. They were stacked high, had looked as though they were against a wall. The music grew instantly louder. Fryer heard the distinctive click and pong of a ceiling pull cord and the light disappeared. The accountant emerged from behind the stack, holding a small black transistor radio in one hand that was moulded to look like a miniature ghetto blaster.

He stopped, stared Fryer straight in the face. His eyes flicked quickly to Fryer's right hand, which held the blade. He flicked off the radio, silence filling the small space between the two men. His cool, grey eyes surveyed Fryer, leaking mild curiosity, nothing less and nothing more.

Fryer felt the urge to shuffle his feet, resisted it, not breaking the man's stare.

'You know you should not be here,' said the accountant. Fryer felt his stomach flush. The arrogant wanker. Surprised on the bog by a man holding a blade, but he was chastising like a Christian Brother in school. 'Learn to lock your door,' said Fryer.

The accountant offered him a small shrug and a faint smile, and then shook the radio and moved out of Fryer's vision. A second later and he heard a soft knock, presumably it being placed on a shelf or tabletop Fryer could not see.

'You keep your hands where I can see them, mate,' said Fryer.

The accountant ignored this, observed Fryer over his glasses. 'I heard Jim Dempsey's dead, though I expect you know that. They'll be looking for you, John Fryer,' he said.

The money man knew his name. All those years locked away, but not forgotten, at least not by this man. Fryer was right to have come here for information; the accountant clearly banked it like currency and assets. He read Fryer's change of expression.

'Oh, yes, I know all about you. Now leave,' he continued, the tone reasonable, but also self-assured. Someone who had been giving orders his whole life. Fryer felt his scalp prickle. The room was feeling too small and his clothes too tight. He needed a smoke. He reached for his makings, remembered the blade in his hand, and stopped. The accountant followed his movements, and then continued, though at this stage it should be Fryer doing the talking, making demands and watching him squirm. 'And, I heard you killed his bloody dog, too. Disgusting. Though, let's be honest, John Fryer, hardly surprising, given your form,' he said, and then he smiled that smile again.

Fryer growled, stepping into the space between them, observing from behind his rising film of rage that the man's right hand, the one which had held the small radio, was still obscured by the boxes. He was mocking him. This little prick was calling him a dog killer. 'I. Never. Killed. That—' But he did not get to finish his objection.

The accountant moved, fast and precise, like a seasoned squash player darting to Fryer's right, too fast for Fryer to follow.

In his right fist, Fryer caught sight of a black snake, swooping up in a dark blur. Fryer had the millisecond that was left to see its arched head rearing over the accountant's hand, the two forks of its tongue visible for just an instant. He twisted his face away, but too late. The snake struck Fryer hard on the side of the jaw, connecting with a massive crack and crunch inside his head, clamping his teeth closed on his tongue. Two agonising fireworks exploded simultaneously: the first from the side of his face, the second in his mouth, rapidly filling with the metallic syrup of his own blood.

Fryer staggered, dropped the blade, and raised his right arm in defence, eyes up.

The accountant had a mini crowbar held aloft, ready now to dish out another strike. If the iron had connected squarely instead of glancing him, Fryer would already be on the floor and his jaw would be a broken biscuit. But one strike to the head and he would be out cold, probably permanently.

Fryer lunged forward, grasping the accountant's right wrist as he did so. His legs, rubbery but not entirely turned to water, mostly obeyed him. The effort set his face off, the jaw taking centre stage above his lacerated and fattening tongue. He twisted the accountant's arm with everything he had.

The smaller man turned under the pressure, Fryer rammed his right elbow into the accountant's face, aiming for his eye socket, missing it but feeling and hearing the hard connection of bone on bone. Quigley coughed out a cry, and in the slow speed of the struggle, Fryer noted what a sad sound that was, an old man's gasp, surprised and injured.

Fryer did not stop. He pushed the accountant's arm up and back over his head, the crowbar now raised between them like a solid, dark flame of hate. Quigley's arm shook, started to give. Fryer stuck his leg between the accountant's feet, twisting the man's arm viciously once again as he did so. He used his heft to turn him with the same movement, pushed him hard from behind, bundled the smaller, wiry man to the floor, and landed on top of him. He let out a large woofing sound and the crowbar slid fast along the floor and into the shadows, where it made a soft knock against something Fryer could not see.

Cardboard boxes, probably.

Fryer was panting like an animal in labour, a runner of bloody saliva drooling from his open mouth. His jaw was a live wire, and he could feel the growing tightness of a blossoming welt, big as an egg. He wiggled it left and right, found it serviceable, but groaned as a fresh bolt of pain lit up in his face. The accountant was slapping at the linoleum floor with his outstretched palm, making hoarse rasping sounds as he did so. Fryer pushed off him, and the man started to struggle for breath, respiration watery and shallow. Fryer straddled him, and patted him down as he lay on the floor. His breathing had started to open up. Fryer took his car keys, wallet and mobile and set them on the small shelf which Fryer could now see was next to the toilet door, the one where the accountant had found the crowbar.

'I want no more of that hospitality from you,' he said. No response from the accountant. 'For what it's worth, I don't have a problem with you, you know,' Fryer said, standing over the man.

The accountant raised his face from the floor, turned slightly to look at Fryer. Glasses crunched, one of the arms broken off. He had skinned one side of his forehead when he had hit the lino, but otherwise he looked to be OK, for the time being. The accountant nodded. Fryer heaved him up, one hand on the seat of his trousers and the other on the scruff of his collar. Fryer turned him round and quickly marched him over to where a shoulder-high stack of boxes stood next to one of the metal shelves. He shouldered the top box out of the way and it fell to the floor with a heavy slap. Fryer pinned Quigley over the boxes, one fist filled with his shirt, and pressed heavily on his throat.

'Dempsey told me that you have my pension,' said Fryer.

The accountant looked up at Fryer, caution in his eyes for sure, but the money man was also back, surfacing above the indignity of his predicament. Fryer could see him recalculating the odds, estimating how much Dempsey might have known and how much Fryer had managed to get out of him. At the end, it was a profit and loss calculation, distilled into one all-important question: how much will it cost? He obviously overrated Dempsey's staying power.

'Bollocks, listen to yourself,' he replied, a trace of that smile again on his face.

Fryer heard something, something moving. 'Dempsey said,' replied Fryer. But the words sounded weak, infantile. The same sound, a shifting sound from his right, where the shelves were hidden in shadows deep and dark. Fryer resisted the temptation to look. A trickle of cold sweat ran a finger down his back, into the crack of his arse. Instead, he glanced over the accountant's shoulder and spotted his razor on the floor in the doorway to the shop front. He quickly returned his eyes to Quigley. He had already proved more capable than Fryer had estimated, and as though in affirmation the smaller man raised himself off the box, weight on his elbows, as Fryer's hold on his shirt fractionally relaxed. Quigley was looking at him, question in his eyes. He must have said something.

'What?' said Fryer, and glanced at the blade again, a mile away in the thin crack of light. Another sound, like something wet shifting and sliding, again from his right, but closer now. Fryer held his breath, the better not to smell the air. The darkness, at first murky and dim, had now thickened like black smoke broiling off a burning tyre. It was closing in, slow and indefatigable. Fryer stole a look behind. It would be good to let go of this man completely, to make a run for it while he still had time, get across the floor, through that exit door, away from this blackness, from what lurked within.

'I said there's no pension for volunteers. Dempsey lied to you,' he said. Quigley shook off Fryer's hand, sat up. He straightened his crooked tie. He considered Fryer slyly. 'There's float money for the till in my wallet. Take it and leave. Here,' he said, and slid off the boxes to his feet, 'I'll get it for you.'

Fryer didn't shove him back. He took a step back, eyes searching the thickening darkness to his right. No longer able to hold his air, Fryer was now panting, heart banging, and he could smell IT, taste IT, thick and so very near, about to be born from that darkness.

'No! No, no, no, you fucking bastard you!' he screamed into the darkness. His eyes returned to the accountant, suddenly his solace. Fryer held him, saw the razor gleam from the floor, shoved Quigley aside and lunged for it. He plucked it off the lino, scrambled back to his feet, and dragged the accountant to him, all his strength back.

'Do you smell that?' he hissed. The Moley's stagnant, wild stink had overwhelmed the smells of dry cardboard and soap powder. Fryer emitted an involuntary sound, something between a moan and a cry, the hair on his arms and neck erect and electrified. His bladder was hot and massive and ached for release.

The accountant's composure dropped. He started to really struggle. Fryer's fear had jumped into him, a black spirit moving between men.

'Fuck off, let me go,' he said, choking the words out under the pressure of Fryer's iron fist, once again at his throat. Fryer pushed him into the boxes, drove a knee into his chest, feeling the hard steel of the blade between his fingers under the sponge of the textured plaster. The Moley was almost on him. He didn't want to, but it had to feed.

'I'm sorry,' said Fryer. He swiped the blade upwards, streaking it across the accountant's face. The blade raced cleanly through his left cheek, across the open cavity of his mouth, scratching the hardness of his gritted teeth, and sliced a deep score up the right side of the man's face.

No blood at first, just the accountant's eyes, boiling in his face in recognition and terror. Sudden silence.

Then his face fell apart, opening in a perverse gash along the trajectory of Fryer's razor cut. His left cheek was severed to the bone, the skull-like grimace of his teeth revealed. His right cheek sagged open, fatty yellow tissue revealed, intact, though only just. The blood came, sudden and furious, streaming down Quigley's face like a scarlet cloth.

He started to screech.

Fryer looked up, but there was no Moley, just the darkness, and the rich coppery sweetness of the accountant's blood in the air. Fryer mopped his brow, trying to blot out the screaming. He needed a smoke, badly. By the time he had sparked up his first, he'd stopped screaming, and started talking through a wad of kitchen paper Fryer had found in one of the cardboard boxes. Pain, it was the ultimate information laxative.

Turned out Dempsey was telling the truth after all. The loot from the big bank robbery had been washed and returned, mostly as diamonds, and other high carat gems. Whatever had not been cashed and distributed to retired IRA volunteers was stored in safety deposit boxes, mainly in England. Ready money was buried in disused arms dumps.

'Where is my share?' asked Fryer.

'Mosht of the Belfasst money has been given out, but there is a schtore. It'sh up the top of the old loney, near the dry well on the Black Mountain. You know where I mean?' asked the accountant.

Fryer nodded. He knew the loney. It was an old country lane that once ran from the lower Falls area all the way to the Whiterock road, ended up near a dry wishing well on the slopes of the Black Mountain, overlooking west Belfast. It was a courting place for young people in his grandfather's time. If there was an arm's dump up there, Fryer had never heard of it. The accountant was right about the well though, it had always been dry, even when Fryer's grandfather had been a boy. There were stories that it had been dug into the hillside by the ancient Celts, in search for gold. People used to say it was a gateway for the Si, the little people. They would gallop out of the hole on their horses under the moonlight to cause mischief.

'I wonder,' said Fryer, pointing his smoke at the accountant, 'I wonder if you are telling me a wee fairy story here?' he asked.

The accountant shook his head, and with wide eyes in a Halloween mask, he watched as Fryer ripped open one box, then another, before removing a plastic container of table salt. The accountant's eyes opened even wider, two poached eggs with black yolks, and he started to scrabble from the boxes he was still slumped over. His arms gave way and he ended up on the floor on his side. He got to his knees and started to whimper and plead, lisping and slipping over his words through his tissue wad.

Fryer stood over him. 'I am not interested in going hunting for the crock of gold, mate. I want my fucking money, and unless I can put a hand to it right now, this,' he said, flicking the lip of the container open and pouring a handful of white salt into his hand, 'is going into your face,' he said.

273

Fryer leant over the man, bringing his salt-filled fist within inches of the bloody carnage of his face. The accountant screeched horribly and raised his free hand up to cover his wounds.

'There's a shafe. I have the code,' he said.

It was built into one of the structural walls, and (once again) concealed behind a stack of cardboard boxes. Inside, Fryer found bundles and bundles of cash, wrapped in paper jackets and fastened together in the same currency, same denomination piles: sterling, euros and US dollars. Fryer was no genius at sums, but if there was less than 100K in that safe he was a blind donkey. He found a strong orange plastic bag with a supermarket logo on one of the shelves. He dumped the contents and filled the orange bag up with money. Fryer was nearly done, but not quite. He returned to the accountant who was still on the floor, his breathing slow and shallow.

'What else is there?' he asked. The accountant murmured something about not understanding, please, sorry. He was slurring, eyes closing. Fryer cursed under his breath. The Moley was gone, but the fresh blood only kept it at bay for so long. Dempsey knew something, something that was worth more than all the cash in that safe. And Quigley knew it too. He reached for the salt and let the accountant see it. He flinched and tried to sit up, big eyes again fixed on John Fryer. 'Last night I didn't know I had a pension owed, and you just made me a rich man. You best think hard, money man, or get ready to hurt hard. I'll leave you here to squeal and die slowly,' said Fryer.

'Dempshey. Dempshey sold you out, John. Not Jusht when he put you in the Heighsts, before, before. He shet you up with the British. He wanted you gone, said it wash time for peace, time for peace . . .' said the accountant, his voice beginning to drift off. He was losing consciousness. Fryer prodded him in the mouth, felt the sodden tissue paper give under the pressure of his fingertip. The accountant jolted back to life again, started crying, pleading.

So he'd been right about Dempsey. The bastard had hung him out to dry, but not before Fryer had done enough carnage to make the whole place so war sick all sides were ready for peace. The irony of it, it made his blood boil. But this was not it, the thing Dempsey tried to sell. If he'd told Fryer this, he would have been a dead man anyway.

'There's more. Tell me my business, and I'll leave. My word,' he said, salt grains sprinkling like fine snow on the floor from his fist. The accountant's eyes darted left and right, that clever fucking brain of his working overtime now for John Fryer. Then his eyes lit up, his eyebrows raised. He had something.

'You have kin, John. There is blood that is yours, family that you don't know about,' he said.

'Who?' asked Fryer.

'You have a granddaughter,' said the accountant.

And just like that, all at once, it was true. He did. Fryer had a grandchild. He felt it, as fully as though he had been in the waiting room in the hospital and received the news from a nurse.

The accountant quickly mapped it out. Kieran's child, he'd got a dark woman pregnant. She had been deported, and then Kieran had died.

'What's her name?' said Fryer. His heart was racing, but for the first time in so many years it was not from fear, or hate.

'Ava. The child's name is Ava,' he replied.

'Where does she live?'

'No idea,' said the accountant. Fryer raised the salt. 'But I know where she ish today,' he said. He told Fryer he could find her at the Culturlann, the Irish language centre on the Falls road, not half a mile from where Fryer now stood. The accountant said the child had been spotted in the area. She stood out after all. Her stepmother was a peeler. People talked.

Fryer nodded, that much was true. He let the salt cascade to the floor. Ava, it was a beautiful name. He set the accountant's mobile beside him. With a little luck he would be able to make the 999 call before he passed out. Fryer took the plastic bag with the money and headed for the exit. He cast one furtive glance into the darkest reaches of the storage room and flicked the last grains of salt on his hand over his left shoulder before he left.

CHAPTER THIRTY-SEVEN

Fryer scanned the pavement outside the Culturlann, a converted sandstone Presbyterian Church, one hand on the plastic bag filled with cash on the passenger seat next to him. This was Ava's money, and she was going to have it. He would meet her as she arrived. Today he was going to call himself a friend, an old friend who had lost touch with the family. He would hand her the bag, tell her it was for her, her and nobody else. He wanted to see her expression change when she saw the money. Then he would smile back at her and walk away, but he could be in touch. This was only the beginning. Ava was Kieran's baby, and Kieran had kept Fryer safe in the dead of night, a light in the darkness. The Moley could never touch him. It would be the same with Ava. This was Fryer's second chance, to be a grandfather, and to break the Moley's curse at last. He would defeat it with Ava, his blood, but this time there was no need to spill it.

Movement, as the doors leading into the Culturlann opened from within. A young woman carried out a metal sign advertising coffee and stood it at the entrance. Fryer checked his rear-view mirror, saw a convoy of traffic, including one black taxi, turn the corner at the Royal Victoria Hospital and drive towards him. A few pedestrians were walking from the same direction, older, not children. He turned his attention to the road ahead, saw what he was waiting for. A group of three little girls approached, a woman with them, on a mobile phone. One child was a ginger, proper carrot-head, pale and a face full of freckles. Fryer disregarded her, focused his attention on the girl beside her. Fryer laughed, his eyes wide, taking in every detail of her face as she came closer. It was her. This was Ava. She was so swarthy, skin the colour of caramel, accentuated by the frizzy hair that was held in two curly bunches on either side of her head. They were full of chatter, all three speaking at the same time.

Fryer shook his head in disbelief, reached for the bag full of cash beside him. This was just a down payment. He would find more for this child. He would provide for her, give her what he was never able to give Kieran. And be there in a way he had never been for that boy. He glanced back at the road ahead. They were closer. He gazed at Ava, the buttery smoothness of her beautiful skin. The child actually glowed.

'Like an angel,' said Fryer to the inside of the taxi, and opened the door. As he did so, his eyes rested for the first time on the third kid in the group.

He stopped.

Fryer's heart kicked and his stomach dropped. He knew

that face, seen her before, recently. She had black hair that bounced in ringlets at her shoulders.

'No, no, no,' said Fryer, feeling hope drain away like blood in a sink. The girl was Dempsey's granddaughter. She must be Ava's friend. He recognised her face from the photograph on the fridge the night before. Dempsey's words in his mind:

That's my granddaughter, she is nine. Her name is—

And his reply: *I don't need to know her name.*

Same child. There was no doubt about that. Fryer looked down at his hand on the bag. There was blood caked under his nails. The lines on his knuckles stood out like etchings. Fryer could hear the children's chatter, very near. He let go of the bag and closed the door. He couldn't meet her with this blood on his hands. And he could never explain to this child why Dempsey deserved to die the way he had.

Jim Dempsey, the bastard, had fucked him over yet again.

Fryer watched the girls skip into the Culturlann and pass out of sight, and then in his mind's eye he watched the true story of how things would pan out if he got out of the taxi and approached a nine-year-old girl offering money. Someone would call the peelers, and they would come fast. He racked his mind for another way, but each scenario ended the same. Even if he managed to speak to her alone, Dempsey meant he had to build on lies. The truth was he could never be a part of her life. He was good for nothing, just an old dog that had been trained to kill, but now long past its prime.

Fryer twisted the key in the ignition and gunned the engine, felt the vibration hum in his hands and scarred forearms as he pulled away without indicating or checking his mirrors. He clenched his jaw, did not look back. Fryer drove up the Falls, took the taxi down the Donegall road, Bangor bound. There was an ambulance outside the 7-Eleven. He slowed to a stop as a tattered old man tottered out in front of the taxi. Fryer looked at Ava's money, thinking, then revved the engine to life and turned the taxi into one of the side streets.

He stopped minutes later, engine still running, outside McKenna's house, suddenly unsure. He grabbed the money bag and padded over to the front garden. He opened the blue recycle bin and dropped the bag inside, left the lid yawning. Fryer mounted the steps to the front door and gave it three hard bangs with the flat of his fist, turned and jogged back to the taxi and drove off. He stopped a hundred yards down the street, made sure he could see her house in his mirror. It took her a while, but eventually the front door opened. She looked like death, even from that distance. She stared around, turned to go back inside, then noticed the open recycle bin and went to it. She passed out of Fryer's line of sight. He waited, counted the seconds, the idling engine buzzing in his hands.

He saw her. She climbed the steps. She had the bag; she had the money. Good. Fryer found first gear and moved off, still watching. He wanted to see her face, maybe a smile. Then he would know; he had done something good. She stared up the street, looked directly at the back of Fryer's taxi, where the blue exhaust smoke chuffed out and rose into the air. Something was wrong. She wasn't happy. She was weeping. In that moment, she looked like her son, after Fryer had smashed him in the face. Fryer jammed his foot on the accelerator. The tyres screeched, he sped off, but not fast enough.

'Come on, you stupid old cunt ye, COME ON!' screamed Fryer, but it was no use. The taxi moved in slow centuries and he could feel her eyes burn judgement into him, as he cursed himself for being so old and so stupid.

CHAPTER THIRTY-EIGHT

'Daddy?!'

Christopher awoke in a mess of bed clothes, his cheeks wet. He stared wide-eyed at the bedroom door. His daddy was hanging there, dressed in full uniform. His heels drummed the back of the door as he convulsed. *Drum drum drum.* Christopher closed his eyes. The memory of his awful dream replaced the terrible vision before him, his nightmare still raw and lurid.

Bad Daddy had been drumming there too, but this time it was the kitchen table, the one where they used to eat their breakfast together, after Daddy returned from night shift, when he was a little boy. He was drumming the beat of an Irish jig with his hands on the table, the way he did when he wanted Christopher to do his impression of River Dance. Daddy used to laugh, but in the dream he wasn't laughing.

Rap and pat, rap and pat, rap and rap and rap and pat, went his hands on the table.

His face was blue and swollen, black puffed eyes, one already popped from its socket and resting on his cheek. The same way Daddy had looked the day Christopher had come home from school and found him swinging from the bannister. In his dream, he was smiling horrifically, the jelly of his popped eyeball jiggling as he rapped and slapped the tabletop. A trickle of blood was running from his raw socket and had started to drip off his chin, dark and black, into his bowl of cornflakes. Round his neck, Christopher could see the rope from his dressing gown. It had cut deeply into his flesh.

In the dream, Daddy was having a bit of trouble with his voice. He was mouthing words he could no longer say through vocal chords which had been crunched like wafers in a paper bag. But Christopher understood. The same thing he had said, all those years before:

Let's dance.

Let's dance.

Let's dance.

From under the sheet Christopher heard Daddy's feet drum again and he moaned. Another *drum, drum, drum*, but this time from the window, not the door. Christopher peeked out. The blind swayed in the light wind, the balsa wood stick that kept its base rigid tipped to one side and then clanked against the sill: *drum, drum, drum*. Not Daddy's heels after all. It did not even sound remotely like it. Christopher let the sheet fall off him, looked again at the bedroom door. Just a layered mound of towels, his dressing gown over them, arms hung loosely on each side.

Christopher kicked off the bed clothes, made his way to the bathroom and relieved himself in the rust-stained bowl. At the sink his red-ringed eyes returned his gaze from the circular shaving mirror. The blonde stubble that had covered the point of his chin and lined his top lip was longer now than the hair on his recently shaved head. He picked up the disposable razor from beside his frayed-headed toothbrush but dropped it. It could wait. His beard would not grow much thicker than this, no matter how long he left it.

Movement in the room behind him caught in the mirror. Christopher spun round. The room was empty, nothing there. In the corner was an empty chair against the door leading to the copper boiler. Beside it a busted plastic mesh laundry basket, empty, but rocking on its side, like it had just been knocked over. Christopher watched as it very slowly rolled first to the left, then back to the right.

He laughed, not a spasm, just a scoff, but his heart now skipped along like he had just finished a fair paced run. He turned back to the sink, slowly adjusted the shaving mirror, and pointed it at the corner and the chair. Still empty, but before it had been occupied. Somebody had been sitting there. He'd caught just a glimpse, the pressed crease of a pair of bottle-green police uniform trousers, and the buffed tips of a pair of best parade shoes, catching the morning light. His eyes left the empty chair, returned to meet his tired reflection.

Bad dreams and Bad Daddy, and things were getting worse. John Fryer the common denominator. Fryer had tried to bring a killer dog into Christopher's home. Why would he want to do such a thing? Christopher had no answer, but what he did know was John Fryer would rather see him dead than that fat dog. He'd read it in his eyes.

Perhaps he would rather see Christopher dead, full stop? And what would happen when their mission was over, after Fryer had planted a bomb at Jim Dempsey's funeral, and when Christopher had done the same to Uncle Cecil and the Orange Order on the 12th July? There would be chaos, of course. But what would he do with John Fryer?

From downstairs, the sound of the front door closing, keys dropped on the table. Moments later the acrid whiff of a freshly lit cigarette. John had gone out, but now he was back. Christopher returned to his bedroom, dressed and headed downstairs. As he walked past the open bathroom door, he stopped, but didn't turn round to look into the very empty room. Even though he knew what he heard. The unmistakable creak of a chair leg moving, followed by the thin rasp of the plastic laundry basket's rim rolling in a half circle on the linoleum floor. He knew who had moved it. A figure dressed in a creased uniform, with urine-darkened crotch. Bad Daddy, no longer confined to his dreams, a terrible apparition drawn by the man sitting downstairs. Christopher walked slowly, heart racing, a decision made.

Their mission was on, but John Fryer must not return.

John Fryer was seated in the same spot he'd occupied the night before. Christopher bid him good morning. Fryer grunted in response, refused his offer of a cup of tea. The ashtray was full of squashed roll-up butts next to the Armalite on the dining-room table, same as before. But there was something else, something different. Fryer's fingers were stained dark with dried blood. And next to his Armalite was a tight roll of what looked like 100 euro notes. Christopher forgot about his morning brew, pulled out a chair and sat down.

'Trouble, John?' he asked.

Fryer raised his eyes, looked tired. No, beyond that, utterly defeated. 'Don't worry about it, kid,' he said.

Christopher reached for the roll of cash, felt its dry weight in the palm of his hand, before John Fryer's fat paw pinned it to the table, the money beneath. Christopher reluctantly let go of the cash, pulled his hand free. Fryer let him go, but he enclosed his fist round the wad.

'That's my pension money,' he said.

Christopher nodded as though he understood, eyed the roll, tried to calculate how much it was. 'This must have fallen outta the bag,' said Fryer, his voice bleak and emotionless.

The bag? Christopher licked his lips, his thoughts a firework display of many explosions, but together, this could be the perfect finale. Whatever had happened this morning, it had beaten John Fryer into a new man. A man, almost, without any fight left. That was a John Fryer he could do business with, the same man he'd met in the Heights and got talking, who'd agreed to follow him. This was a man who just might see the need for a change of plan, a kamikaze mission. Do not pass GO, and do not collect £200. Or euros. Christopher pulled his eyes off the money. The wad was thick enough to fill Fryer's hand.

'Do you need my help?' he asked, voice full of concern.

Fryer sighed, shook his head, and then, beautifully, he started to talk. He told Christopher about his morning adventure: the accountant, the money, the gems in the well. By the end, Christopher's mouth was dry.

'That bastard Dempsey betrayed you throughout your whole life. He deserved everything he got, John,' he said. Christopher reached over the table, squeezed John Fryer's billowing shoulder. This was it. The perfect time to reel the big fish in. He had him on the hook. 'There's a way we can get closer. Be sure to wipe them all out, John. But it means we don't come home,' said Christopher quietly. John Fryer did not reply. Christopher kept going, explained the plan. He waited, expecting Fryer to tell him to go to Hell. But instead the man shrugged, pushed his chair from the table, shuffled towards the stairs.

With his back to Christopher, he replied. 'I'll do it. Don't care any more.'

Christopher smiled, glanced at the table. The wad of cash was gone. John Fryer had it in one hand, the gun in the other, a dead man walking up the stairs one step at a time, wearing his expensive trainers.

'What happened to the bag?' asked Christopher, keeping his voice conversational.

Fryer paused, did not turn. 'I gave it away. I owed it to somebody,' he said, then kept going. Christopher sat at the table, listened to the toilet flush, and John's bedroom door close. He may not be able to get his hands on that bag, but he knew, roughly, where the so-called well was Fryer told him about. You could get old maps on the Internet. He would find it, watch as Belfast burnt below him. And then, who could say? With that sort of money a man could start again. When he was finished with Belfast and John Fryer, he could find another palace of hypocrisy that needed torn down. With the funds, he could make anarchy his life's mission. Daddy's voice, clear and true, gave him a jolt.

He's asleep, son. Let's pay a visit to the Culturlann, and make that donation to the Irish language.

Christopher quietly carried the materials he needed from

287

the armoury downstairs, starting with the heavy canisters of petrol. The garage was cool and smelt of old oil and creosote. He could also smell the bittersweet marzipan odour of the Nobel 808 that he set down carefully on the surface of the scarred wooden workbench. Not many tools, just an old screwdriver, and a pair of tarnished wire cutters.

That will do us, son. We have enough to work with. I can speak you through it.

'OK, Daddy,' he said.

He looked at the explosives, the canisters of petrol, the timer and detonator in front of him. He needed to work quickly. Christopher tapped the handle of the screwdriver against the wooden worktop: *bump, bump, bump.* He stopped. It sounded like Daddy's drumming heels.

Let's dance, son. What do you say?

CHAPTER THIRTY-NINE

After leaving Dempsey's neighbour Phelan Brown, Aoife told Sheen she wanted to wash up and change, which meant returning to Randalstown. He said he would meet her at the Royal where Jamie Anderson was waiting. She also wanted to call Marie again, to check in on Ava. She had tried her before leaving Lincoln View, but got no reply.

Aoife tossed her own and Cecil's mobile on her bed, and when she emerged from the bathroom fifteen minutes later, Cecil's phone illuminated in the darkened room, then blinked off. The message was more abrupt, less toying than those previous.

Find me Jackie Coyle's location, NOW.

Coyle was the man who had killed Scotty Woods and was now cooperating with police. He had named Cecil Moore, and Cecil had got a sniff of it, somehow.

Another text message: *Aoife, I need you help me.*

He might be arrogant, but Aoife could read behind this message. Moore was scared, his back against the wall.

'Finally, you bastard, you have bitten off more than you can chew,' she said, cold water dripping from a loose strand of hair on her naked shoulder. Moore had been on the radio this morning lamenting the plight of the Protestant people of Ulster, under siege and under threat. What would happen to him when those people found out that it was Moore who had planned the attack on their homes, killed their leader in the street?

Answer me. Remember our video.

She locked the phone and threw it on the bed. No more messages, and no more blackmail. She had worked honest days and nights to get to Serious Crimes. What in Hell's name had she been thinking even letting him in? She reached for the hair dryer and plugged it in beside the mirror. Another message pinged on the phone. Delete it, don't even read it. Of course, she picked up the phone and looked.

ANSWER me, you BITCH!

She threw the phone down again in disgust and turned on her hair dryer full blast, blotting out the world. Moore was going to get his response, but from Irwin. Now it was he who was going to have to give some answers.

By the time Aoife was standing in her kitchen, pouring a fresh coffee, there were a further six messages on the phone. She did not open them; instead she lifted her own smartphone and pressed Marie's number. It was just past nine o'clock. The girls should be ready to begin their summer-school classes. Marie answered on the third ring, and Aoife could tell immediately she was outside. She could hear the sound of the girl's voices in the background, chattering away at the same time, talking ten to the dozen. Aoife smiled. Despite everything this bloody Sunday morning, that sound made her smile. It felt good.

'Hi, Marie, just me. Wanted to check in. Everything OK?' she asked.

Marie said everything was dead on. She told Aoife they were heading up the Falls road now, coming up the Culturlann, with the girls, as Aoife suspected. Marie, also able to talk the back leg off a donkey, told her all about the previous evening's events: makeshift campfire on the living-room floor, telling ghost stories, eating sweets, followed by bedtime, which degenerated into some kind of game of musical beds by the sound of it. Finally Marie took a breath and asked Aoife if all was well with her?

'You dealing with that trouble over the Peace Line near Clonard last night? People on the road are full of the talk of it. You can still smell the burning in the air,' said Marie.

'I'm all right, Marie. I heard about the trouble, but no, not working it,' she said. Talk of the trouble ticker-taped Jackie Coyle's name across her mind, followed by the last message she had read from Cecil Moore: *ANSWER me, you BITCH!* She blinked the thoughts away. She could do this. She would prevail.

'You still there, Aoife? So what are you doing?' she asked.

Aoife gave the stock reply that she always used when someone outside the force asked about police business. She did not even hesitate it was so well used.

'They are keeping me busy, but nothing too exciting going on,' she said.

'Well, just watch yourself. This place always goes buck mad over the 12th,' said Marie.

'I will, thanks, Marie. I'll see you tomorrow evening, might be a bit later than planned, but I'll be there. My girl doing OK?' she asked.

'She's absolutely fine. Sure listen to the noise of them,' said Marie.

'OK, speak to you later,' said Aoife, but Marie had already hung up. Aoife raised her coffee and took a sip, wincing at the bitterness. She visualised Ava trotting in through the gates of the Culturlann, Marie's daughter by her side. Marie was a good friend and a great mother. She would have eyes on them, all the way in, she trusted in that.

Aoife shivered, goosebumps prickling her arms all the way to her shoulders. Cecil's phone pinged from the kitchen. She pocketed it. She felt her jaw tighten and pulse treble as she moved quickly from one disgusting message to the next, deleting each with a jab of her thumb, her anger and her resolution to destroy Cecil Moore deepening with each deleted message. She was a bitch, a cunt, a whore bag, and a Fenian cocksucker. She reached the final message.

YOU have made a mistake blanking me, Aoife. You will learn about loyalty.

Delete, for the final time. Aoife turned off the coffee machine and she walked out the front door, all panic and frustration gone. Now she was just angry. Angry that Ava was involved, but mostly, she was angry at Moore's final text message. A snake telling her that she needed a lesson on loyalty? He had used the death of his own mother to make personal gains against his own community.

Aoife got into her car and slammed the door, pulled Cecil's cheap phone apart and removed the SIM card. She accelerated quickly until she joined the M2. She rolled

292

down her window, first discarded the SIM and then thirty seconds later, the shell of the phone. After all, it was a throwaway. In a matter of minutes, both would be broken and gone under the wheels of weekend traffic.

'Fuck you, Moore, and fuck you too, Charlie Donaldson,' she shouted, letting the cool air blast in round her face. The car rattled like a space shuttle on re-entry.

She needed to get her hands on that video. Even if Moore was not to be trusted, if there were other copies, his phone was a starting point. The video was definitely there. What other choice did she have? Let Cecil put a collar round her neck and lead her about on a leash for the rest of her life? She was back and, despite everything, she was glad to be alive.

CHAPTER FORTY

Christopher pulled the sheet off his bed and treaded carefully past John's bedroom and down the stairs. He lifted the taxi keys as he did so, headed for the garage where he unlocked the door that led to the street, threw the bedsheet on the bench and went outside.

The steel trolley was still on the floor of the back of the black taxi, well concealed, the white cotton coat and hat over it. Christopher heaved the trolley out and walked it quickly to the open garage door and inside where the device Daddy had helped him make was waiting. The petrol canisters made the incendiary bomb heavy, but he managed to coax it onto the foot of the trolley, covered it with the sheet and wheeled as fast as he could to the taxi. Daddy had told him to set the timer and prime it only when ready – safety first. Christopher manoeuvred the bomb into the back of the taxi, took all his strength. He wedged it snugly between the sofa seat and the folded singles, sweating lightly with the effort. He remembered to close the garage door over, before he drove away. He felt the trolley shift a bit, pushing against the folded seats at his back as he descended the hill outside the house, but otherwise, it felt secure. Christopher glanced in the rear-view, saw it looming in the back, propped up like a draped casket in his black carriage.

As he parked the taxi on the street next to the Culturlann, Christopher could hear the muted rise and fall of small voices within. He glanced down the street, lots of parked cars but no traffic and no people. Ahead a steady current of vehicles passed the mouth of the street leading to the Falls road, but for now few pedestrians, just an old couple who made slow work of the crossing. Christopher waited for them to pass, then got out and switched from the front seat to the back of the taxi where he put on the white cotton coat and hat, removed the sheet to prime the bomb. The air was tainted with faint fumes from the petrol canisters, and sickly sweet marzipan from the sweating 808 plastic. He ever so gently draped the sheet over the trolley and it's now softly ticking cargo. Christopher opened the door, nudged the bomb from its standing position, and lowered the load so it was all but flat to the floor. He pushed it, inch by inch, out the open back door of the taxi, lowered it through the turn of its wheels until it reached the ground below.

He was sweating, only partly through the effort, his hands slick on the handles. He got out and tipped the bomb backwards, edged it out of the way and closed the taxi door with his foot. From behind him he heard the distinctive metallic rattle of a front gate being closed. Footsteps approached the clack of heels. It got louder. He stayed still, like a spider disturbed.

'Nice morning,' said a voice.

Christopher nodded to his right, from where the woman spoke, in time to catch her swish past in a cloud of floral perfume and fresh cigarette smoke. Christopher did not reply. He watched as she marched on up the pavement and disappeared into the Falls road. From the near distance the tinny chime of a church bell, calling the faithful, like this woman, to their knees. Where she was headed, others would follow. He needed to get moving.

He breathed deeply, forced himself to push the trolley on another few steps, then stopped again. What if he was challenged? It was Sunday morning. Not a typical time for a food delivery as his outfit implied. Also, there had been trouble last night over the Peace Line, the news of Dempsey's death. People would be edgy, especially the sort of people who staffed an Irish cultural centre in west Belfast. The doubts circled his mind like besieging Indians. He wished Daddy would speak to him, give him a word of assurance. He should had never come out this morning. He wished—

Christopher turned his head in the direction of the Culturlann. Moments before there'd been laughing voices of children, but no longer. Something was happening. A different sort of commotion was afoot. Several adult voices in the mix, then the piercing wail of a single child's cry. This was it, the distraction he needed. He hurried along, turned the corner onto the Falls road and straight through the open gates of the Cutlurlann. As he approached the glass annex entrance the door was opened from within by an acne-cheeked teenage girl who stood aside to let him pass.

She said something, not in English. Christopher kept his head down, quietly thanked her and pushed the trolley inside.

It was dim, despite three or four LED camping lanterns positioned on round tables across the central space. Two more stood on the ends of the coffee bar that ran along the back wall, white porcelain coffee cups reflecting their glow. A banner, green and white, written in Gaelic, displayed over the bar. There was a door, no handle or lock, left of the bar. It was probably a swing door into the kitchen, too much traffic. He disregarded it, turned his attention to the wall to his left where long gothic windows were shrouded with floor-to-ceiling blackout curtains, the kind used in venues that hosted theatre productions. Better. Christopher headed towards the far wall where the curtains were bunched exactly as he needed. The old church building echoed with the shrill cries of a child who was surrounded by attending adults. Nobody looked at him.

He set the trolley on its foot, put his ear close to the swing door and listened for signs of life. He heard none. He nudged the door and it swung fluidly open. The kitchen was pitch-dark inside, empty. Christopher carefully tipped the trolley forward and slid the bomb off the flat foot. He pulled open the surplus of the blackout curtain and inched the bomb along the smooth wooden floor using his foot and lower leg to steady it, and his body weight to shift its bulk. It disappeared behind the curtain, shrouded in its funeral sheet and still softly ticking. Even if the curtains were drawn, there was more than enough surplus to keep it concealed.

Christopher steered the empty trolley back through the main room, casual. The glass door was still standing open and he emerged into the sharp light. When that bomb exploded tomorrow afternoon there would be no escape. The curtains would fuel the inferno. Christopher started to whistle as he loaded the trolley back into the rear of the taxi, then paused and smiled. The song, it was an old rock tune that had been on the radio when he and John Fryer sat with their tea the day before. 'Light My Fire', The Doors. He puckered his lips to resume, but the laughter broke free like a freshly broken oil head. The best he could manage was to clamber into the driver's seat of the taxi and let it out.

Time to return the trolley we borrowed, son. The coat and hat too. We can't have people say we are common thieves.

Daddy's words cut through his paroxysm and he turned the key in the ignition, face wet but sombre.

'No, Daddy,' he said quietly, eyes downcast. The taxi's engine rattled under him, and Christopher pulled away, bound for the Kennedy Centre mall which by now would be open for business. Little did he know it, but this brief exchange would be the end of his many conversations with Daddy. Good Daddy at least.

CHAPTER FORTY-ONE

Sheen texted Aoife a little past 9 a.m. to say that he and Irwin were waiting for her at the Royal's High Dependency Unit.

Jamie Anderson had been found unconscious with multiple injuries on waste ground between the lower Shankill and the Clonard area of the lower Falls. Not far, in fact, from where Jackie Coyle, the bloke who shot Scotty Woods in the street, had been picked up a few hours earlier. Jamie's mother held her polystyrene cup of coffee as though her life depended on it, told Sheen and Irwin that she had no idea how her son could have ended up in no man's land between Protestant and Catholic. Jamie had no friends outside the Tiger's Bay area that she knew of, and those he was in touch with were more likely to be communicating online rather than in person. Nor did he have any enemies. The kid had never been in any trouble before, and the genuine shock she displayed told Sheen she was telling the truth.

The nurse on duty gave them a grizzly inventory of Jamie Anderson's injuries: both legs had been broken, one arm too, the other badly bruised, ribs cracked, two vertebrae in his lower back cracked, fractured jaw, broken nose, some swelling on the brain.

'All of the above were probably caused by the same blunt instrument. A ball hammer would be my best guess,' she said. 'The young man is fortunate to be alive,' said the nurse, speaking to them outside the staff tearoom. She was smaller by at least a foot than both Sheen and Irwin, wearing a plain smock, her complexion free from make-up. She had her hair pulled into a tight bunch on the top of her head. Sheen had spent enough time in hospitals in and out of his time in uniform to know that these people worked hard, twelve-hour shifts, something her red-ringed eyes confirmed. She spoke with a terse efficiency which told of weariness, but there was no irritation. She had the professionalism, Sheen noted, not to go over the line, even though he and Irwin were eating into what must have been a precious break. Sheen looked up from the small black notebook in which he had been writing her summary, ready to question how she could be so sure about the weapon. She cut him off before he had time to speak.

'Oh, aye, I can tell. I've seen enough injuries in this place over the years to know the difference between a Hurley stick, a baseball bat and a hammer,' she said.

Sheen nodded, fair enough.

'Looks like this young man was most likely set upon while taking part in the riots over the Peace Line last night. It explains where we found him, left for dead,' said

Irwin. He sounded unconvinced by his own synopsis and Sheen did not blame him.

The nurse shared Sheen's silent scepticism. 'I said he was lucky to be alive, but in my experience when people try to murder each other in Belfast, they usually manage it. At the very least I'd expect more severe head injuries, symptomatic of being jumped or stamped upon. That's how this usually plays out. Get them on the ground, then they jump all over their head,' she said.

'Perhaps Jamie Anderson was fortunate. Perhaps the attackers were disturbed before they could finish him off. We just don't know. It was chaos there last night. Trust me I was trying to restore order,' said Irwin.

'No, no, no, I doubt that very much,' she replied. 'Not unless this young man was tied to a chair, beaten up, and then carried to the place where he was found behind the Peace Line,' she said.

'Explain,' said Irwin.

'He has clear ligature marks on his wrists and ankles, deep enough to have caused lasting bruising and to have broken the skin on his ankles,' she said, passing an index finger over both her inner wrists to illustrate. Sheen thought of that scumbag Nelson, and what he was going to do to him when he found him. The nurse locked eyes with Sheen. He saw her recognition, and her judgement. She broke her stare and produced a packet of Silk Cut from the front pocket of her smock. 'I'm gonna leave the rest of the detective work to you gentlemen,' she said.

'I need a smoke and in this place that means a walk. The consultant has agreed you can speak with Jamie, but five minutes, no more. He has only just regained consciousness.

I don't want him distressed,' she said. She was looking pointedly at Sheen.

'We need a bit longer than that,' said Irwin.

'I get back in five minutes,' she said. 'You'll not get sense from the poor creature. He's doped up to the eyes,' she said.

'Thank you,' said Sheen.

'Ah ha, if you want to thank me then find whoever did this,' she replied, and started to walk off, her rubber shoes squeaking on the hard, plastic floor.

'I plan to,' said Sheen.

'You do that,' she said, and then turned round to face him, her blue eyes like clear lights fixing on Sheen. 'And you arrest them,' she said, nodding at Sheen. She reached the L corner at the end of the corridor and took it, feet squeaking, her parting words hanging in the air.

CHAPTER FORTY-TWO

When Aoife arrived at the hospital, Sheen and Irwin had been in the HDU for a little over five minutes. They had made very little progress.

Sheen nodded to her as she walked in, and noted, despite the clinical surroundings, or perhaps because of them, that she had changed. The black blazer and trousers had been replaced by a dark blue matching pair that better suited her complexion and blonde hair. He could smell a welcome waft of fresh perfume, apples, as she entered and he found himself inhaling it hungrily.

'This is Jamie Anderson,' Sheen said, speaking quietly.

Aoife looked at the boy, and her eyes creased with concern. Sheen shared it. The young man propped up in the big hospital bed had his neck supported by a thick circular brace, three out of four limbs encased in plaster cast, monitor buds sprouted from his chest and a blood pressure cuff was attached to one wrist. A fluid bag and morphine drip fed an IV into the bruised top of one hand, and he had an oxygen mask over his mouth. Sheen noted a half-filled bag of dark urine slung to one side of the bed. Jamie's eyes were black and swollen almost closed, his top lip was split and inside his partly opened mouth Sheen could see chipped teeth and dark cavities where others had been knocked out.

'He is only fifteen,' said Irwin, breaking the momentary silence which had fallen. Sheen detailed the injuries which were on display before them until Aoife held up a hand and asked him to stop, which he did. Only in Belfast, thought Sheen, is this a lucky outcome.

'Has he been able to speak?' asked Aoife.

'He's in and out of consciousness,' said Sheen.

'E-Fit image from Belfast Heights was emailed through,' said Irwin, passing her his phone. Sheen watched her, as she looked at the image he had already studied. Aoife's initial look of scrutiny now relaxed into something closer to what he too had experienced when looking at that face: mild surprise, almost a disappointment. Sheen had been expecting some kind of Lombardo-type mug shot, thick in the eyebrows, deep-set eyes, heavy stubble – a face that shouted thug, criminal, sub-human.

What they had was a young man's face, smooth and youthful and clean, long in the jaw, but with cheeks still holding a few ounces of puppy fat. His nose was ever so slightly turned up and rounded at the end. The chin tapered to a shallow point, adding to the overall ordinariness of the face. But what had really held Sheen, and what was probably holding Aoife, was the eyes: blue-grey and cold. Sheen had wanted to look away, but found himself transfixed nonetheless.

Aoife looked over at Sheen and he instantly registered their shared certainty. This was their murderer. Question was, who was he? Aoife handed the phone back to Irwin, who said he had emailed it to both of them. She sat on the edge of the bed and very gently took Jamie's sausage swollen fingers of his left hand in her own. Jamie moaned at Aoife's touch. She quickly withdrew her hand, turned and looked up at Sheen, her eyes wide pools of concern. Sheen nodded to her. They were running out of time and at least she got some reaction from the lad. When Sheen had repeated his name, Jamie Anderson had not even stirred.

'I think you woke him up, that's all,' said Sheen. Then he nodded again and added, 'Keep going. Talk to him. If at all possible, get him to look at the E-Fit.' It might be the break they needed: a name, just a name. Irwin passed his large-screened phone over to Aoife, which she took, obviously getting his intention. Aoife leant in closer to Jamie, tucking a stray strand of hair behind her ear as she did so, once again started to cradle Jamie's hand. The boy made another sound as she did so, this one thick and nasal. His lips were moving, and Aoife put her ear right up against his mouth. Words, or what passed for words, were spoken. Aoife slowly nodded. She had somehow deciphered it.

'Your mum is here. You can speak to her in a minute, Jamie,' she said.

Aoife introduced herself. The first question she asked was the most obvious one, but Sheen quietly cursed under his breath. He was pretty sure he had the answer, and right now they needed a different name, one that would lead them to Esther Moore's murderer.

'Who did this to you, Jamie? Can you speak?' she asked. Sheen saw his eyes were open.

Nothing from Jamie Anderson. The room was full of the background hiss of the oxygen respirator, the intermittent bleep and buzz from the monitor behind the bed. The boy was scared. The fear was palpable, present in the small room like a malign spirit between the boy and them.

'Do you know where you were, before the police found you last night?' she persisted. No words from Jamie. Sheen saw tears running from the boy's swollen eyes. He heard the sound of approaching feet, getting closer. They needed him to look at the E-Fit, and their window was almost gone.

'Jamie, my name is DI Sheen. I work with DC McCusker. We will catch the person who did this to you, but now we need you to look at this. We think it is the man who killed your neighbour, Esther Moore. Do you recognise him?' he said. He was breaking all the rules, asked a leading question, but needs must.

Aoife raised the E-Fit image up so it was in Jamie's line of vision, but the lad closed his eyes, started to moan and cry, shaking his head from side to side as best he could manage in the restricted hold of the neck brace. As he did so, the cast on his other arm clanked against the metal barrier on the other side of the bed, and the heart monitor beeped, a red light flashed. Aoife let go. The squeak of the nurse's approaching steps stopped, and then sped up. She was running. She must have heard. Sheen snatched the phone from Aoife.

'Jamie!' he snapped. His puffed eyes opened in response, the crying ceased, but Sheen saw the awful trapped fear in his eyes. The nurse was back in the room. He ignored her question of what was going on and thrust the E-Fit image in front of Jamie's half-open eyes.

'Do you know him, Jamie? Did you see him? Can you tell us his name?' he said. Sheen felt a vice grip on his arm, but he refused to be budged. Jamie's lacerated mouth opened, and he emitted a broken, high-pitched horrible wail, but his eyes were open too, and he was finally looking at the E-Fit. Jamie Anderson was nodding his head. He was nodding. He recognised the face.

'Sheen!'

All they needed was the name. Sheen asked him again.

'SHEEEN!'

He relaxed his arm, was instantly pulled away from the boy by the force of the nurse's grip. She shoved him hard in the chest away from the bed, went to tend to her patient. It was Aoife who had spoken. She was staring at him, her eyes full of accusation.

'He's the best chance we have,' said Sheen, hating the words as they left his lips. The nurse turned from the bed where Jamie had settled a little but was still crying. She pressed the morphine drip twice.

'Get out of here. You're sick,' she snarled at Sheen. He felt a small but firm squeeze on his upper arm. Irwin, eyes on the floor.

'That's enough, let's go,' he said, leading the way. Aoife had already gone. The nurse turned back to Jamie and Sheen watched as the boy's body almost instantaneously relaxed, like watching him die. Sheen was half out the door but he turned fast, walked back to Jamie Anderson's bed and spoke in his ear, quieter than he had before.

'Jamie, please, mate, if you can hear me, just say his

name. If you know it, please just say his name,' he said.

'Jesus Christ!' said the nurse, moving from the other side of the bed and coming for Sheen. She stopped at the foot of the bed, and Sheen was frozen too. Jamie Anderson spoke, his voice slurred and full of dope.

'The Devil, he's the Devil, he's the Devil,' he was saying, his words slurring into incoherence as he finally drifted away.

CHAPTER FORTY-THREE

Aoife picked up two tubes of white sugar and emptied them into the cup of bitter-smelling coffee that Irwin had just purchased from the hospital canteen. She stirred the dark brew with the flimsy white plastic spatula. It warped in the heat. Aoife removed the stick, bent it between two fingers, and then twisted the stupid bloody thing until it snapped in two. She threw it across the table, blew on the coffee and sipped it. It was filth, too hot and now too sweet.

Irwin sat down heavily on the booth seat next to her. It creaked. She could smell his stress sweat, mingled unpleasantly with the overcooked food odours that hung in the unventilated air. Sheen joined them, setting down a tray with three sorry-looking croissants on plastic plates, covered in cling film, and a cup of tea. Aoife poked a hole in one of the cling-film tents and pulled off a piece of pastry. It was hard and stale, greasy in her mouth.

'Well, that went well,' she said.

'It went as well as could be expected,' said Irwin.

'I think we can conclude that Jamie at least recognised the E-Fit,' said Sheen. He sounded less sure. Rightly so. What he did in there bordered on harassment of a vulnerable witness.

'Oh, he did all right, Sheen. You traumatised him with your questions, and what did we get?' she said.

'Well, after you walked out he told me a name. Said it was the Devil,' said Sheen. 'Which, in a manner of speaking, is a positive ID,' he said. Aoife raised her eyes, went back to work on the substandard breakfast before her.

'Sheen's correct, about the boy's reaction anyway,' said Irwin.

Aoife silently cursed. Irwin was deluded if he believed they had just got anything of value from Jamie Anderson. The only thing they had managed to confirm was that the lad was damaged mentally and physically and so doped up that he could hardly speak. Irwin was on his phone, seemed buoyed, despite the let-down they had just experienced.

'The good news is that our DNA test on the hair found in Mrs Moore's bath has come back, and we have a match,' he said.

She sat up, Sheen too. 'We have a name? Someone with a record?' she asked.

'No, afraid not,' said Irwin.

'You said you got a match. If the database gave us that, it should also give us a name,' said Sheen.

'The name was Esther Moore,' said Irwin. Aoife glanced at Sheen, but he also looked confused.

'The DNA found in the hair sample was a family match, to Mrs Moore, right?' asked Sheen.

'Yes,' said Irwin. 'It was a partial match to be exact. Meaning it could have come from a relation, a brother or sister, more likely someone more removed. Someone who had stayed there, not necessarily even this week,' he said. She started to understand. Meaning the hair was most likely already in the tub before Esther Moore was killed. The match was useless.

'Dead end,' she said.

Irwin said nothing.

Sheen spoke through a mouthful of croissant. 'Even so, the DNA is not our only lead. We have John Fryer. It's time to start digging around in his world, whatever Oswald says,' he said.

'We can, carefully, but I don't hold out much hope,' said Irwin. Sheen looked at him questioningly. 'I read Fryer's Special Branch file. He worked in a small cell and the two other guys in his old crew are dead, and now Dempsey is too. No spouse, no recorded children. The guy spent his life on the streets, on the run or in a cell. For the last ten years, all we know is that he has been doing solitary in the Heights, then along comes the mystery man and poof, Fryer disappears,' said Irwin.

'What about Esther Moore? Is it worth going deeper into her family? This is Cecil Moore we are talking about, after all,' said Aoife.

'Cecil has an alibi for his mother's death. I spoke to him myself yesterday and, in fact, I tend to believe him. Certainly, that man has no children,' said Irwin, the disgust evident in his tone. 'I am going to bring him in to answer for what Jackie Coyle has told us. I can dig around a bit more then, but my understanding is that Cecil has no living relatives, no siblings. He had a brother, but that's a non-starter,' said Irwin, sounding equivocal, and still chomping on the last of his croissant. 'Anyway, it would not be a path that I'd be prepared to go down, even if I could,' he added.

Aoife's heart skipped. When Moore was lifted it would be easy for him to show the video with Charlie Donaldson. Still, her gut told her to keep cool. It was not Moore's way to cash in his chips at the first hand. The game he played was a longer one. She had some time. But he was dangerous. She needed to get her hands on his phone.

'Why's that then?' asked Sheen, eyes peering from behind the white foam cup.

Irwin did not reply immediately. He looked sullen. He washed away a mouthful of food with a slurp of tea before reaching for another pastry. 'Cecil Moore is a scumbag, but he is also the black sheep. I can't speak for his dead mother, but Cecil's younger brother was police, RUC. A good man and a great copper – decorated, dedicated, life was the job,' said Irwin. He was pointing his half-eaten pastry in Sheen's direction, his face growing red. A flare went off in Aoife's mind, fizzing and fierce and white, then disappeared. She set down her coffee, closed her eyes. She had to think, to see. It was something about Esther Moore's parlour, something that MacBride the CSI had said when she and Sheen had visited the crime scene. She almost saw it, but the fading flare dimmed and died away. She opened her eyes, still frowning. Sheen had spoken again.

'Worth looking into?' asked Sheen.

Irwin shifted in his seat, made a humph sound, in that preparatory way he did when he thought he had an ace point up his sleeve and he was building up to use it. 'We can take a run up to Roselawn Crematorium later on, Sheen, see how much sense you can get from the poor guy,' he said, not smiling.

'Oh,' said Sheen, nodding. 'Was he murdered, in the line of duty?' asked Sheen.

'In a manner of speaking. The poor chap took his own life. Pressures of the job, I heard, plus he cared for his wife. She had, you know, some issues,' said Irwin, leaning in towards Sheen and tapping one side of his temple with his thick index finger. He meant mental health problems. Irwin's code was as universal as scribbling on an imaginary notebook when asking for the bill in a restaurant.

'You knew him well?' asked Sheen quietly.

Aoife could feel something growing, like the anticipation of a hatching egg, only this one held information. Sheen could sense it too. He glanced at her and she nodded once, quickly. He should keep going.

'Knew of him. Based out of Donegal Pass station. He once carried a primed bomb off a bus in Great Victoria Street, walked it away from a crowded area,' said Irwin. Then he added, after a second's pause, 'It was different back then, before,' he said, leaning on the last word. Sheen looked confused, he did not catch Irwin's pointed comment about the RUC, but Aoife did. 'When this police force was still the RUC, before Patten and the reforms,' he said. Aoife could hear the venom in his voice, especially at the mention of Chris Patten's name.

The English minister who had recommended the root and branch reform of the RUC. The report that heralded a change in name, badge, iconography, uniform, complete renewal. The accolades of the past and the celebration of hard-won achievements were consigned to the dust of a closed trophy cabinet.

Suddenly the flare glared once more into life, and this time she saw what it illuminated. It was an RUC uniform. Then MacBride's voice replayed to her, that tone of toying, mock lechery which he had used in Esther Moore's home, describing the kind of weapon which could have caused the injuries to the old woman's hand.

Something long and hard, DC McCusker, like a police-issue baton.

MacBride's comment had seemed only borderline relevant then, but it shone brightly now. The PSNI were not issued with that style of old, hardwood baton. No, not the PSNI, but the RUC? Yes, the RUC most certainly were. Irwin was still talking, but Aoife had not heard his last couple of sentences. Her heart was skipping in her breast. Irwin laughed, sounded dry and emotionless. She tuned in again, strained to listen and order her thoughts simultaneously.

'You know what the ironic thing about it is, Sheen? That man, Cecil Moore's brother, he was never got by the gun of a terrorist, never turned by some corner boy paramilitary waving a wad of dirty money under his nose. What killed him was progress. It was the police that he loved and gave so much loyalty to. We ended his career, and his life,' said Irwin. A final flash in her mind, and the entire landscape was illuminated, stark and unmasked. Aoife stood up, nearly knocked her now-lukewarm coffee.

'Steady!' shouted Irwin, lifting the remains of his own drink off the table, glaring at her.

'There is no Dissident connection,' she said.

'Yes, thank you, DC McCusker. Try to keep up, will you?' said Irwin, but she did not let him continue. There was no time, now she had it.

'You wanted to know why John Fryer, of all the former prisoners in Belfast, was the one our killer selected?' she said. Her heart was pounding now, all considerations of Cecil Moore and his vile blackmail forgotten, replaced by this pulse of raw excitement, a unique form of joy. She felt its power, and for that instance it was hers alone. 'Then with all due respect, sir, please shut up and shift your arse out of my way,' she said quietly. 'Come on, Sheen,' she said, moving out of her chair as Irwin, silent and staring, slid out of his place and stood up as she had instructed.

'Come on, where?' said Sheen. 'What just happened, Aoife?' he asked. But she was already heading for the door, hoping he would follow and not really caring if he did or not. She was rolling. At last Irwin's stunned silence broke. She heard his bellowing voice as she strode away.

'DC McCusker!?' he shouted.

Aoife did not answer. She turned and saw Sheen hurrying after her. Irwin stood with his arms by his side, face crimson. She addressed him. 'I have the connection,' she said, her voice steady and calm. 'It's not Fryer. It is Belfast Heights. That's your link, sir. That's where our killer met him. The Heights is our key, and I am willing to bet that it will open our killer's front door today,' she said.

315

CHAPTER FORTY-FOUR

Sheen let Aoife focus on the road as she sped from the hospital to the Heights. As she indicated left off the Antrim road and swung into the main entrance she explained the connection.

'So you are saying that whoever busted Fryer out of here must have met him here? As in he was one of the inmates?' he asked.

'Sort of,' she said.

'Right,' said Sheen.

'The RUC uniform, the police-issue truncheon, and the near match on the DNA – taken together they point us in the direction of Cecil Moore's brother,' she said, her voice raised to a half-shout to overcome the background whine of the straining car engine.

'Who we know is dead and buried,' said Sheen.

'Yes, but Irwin also said that his wife, Moore's sister-in-law that would be, suffered from mental health issues, and that it was a strain, a contributing factor in her husband's suicide,' she replied.

'Are you saying that Moore's sister-in-law is somehow behind this? The person who visited Fryer was definitely a man. Our E-Fit gives us that much for certain. Adeola was clear about that, if nothing else,' said Sheen.

'I think the bastard has been hiding in plain view since John Fryer walked out of here. We have his DNA from Esther Moore's bath and I think we are going to get his name. If we look in the right place,' she said, and then pumped the brakes without warning. Sheen felt the car skid on the stone-covered surface, the sound thunderous for a couple of seconds. He was thrown forward, the seat belt biting hard into his chest and shoulders.

'Jesus Christ,' he said.

Aoife stared straight ahead, the ghost of a smile playing on her lips. 'And this is it,' she said.

They had reached a fork in the road where deciduous trees and big shrubs formed an island. The lane they were on divided, one path leading right, the other to the left. A rectangular municipal sign, corroded at the edges to rust, read Belfast Heights Psychiatric Hospital in faded white letters. Sheen could see directions. He strained his eyes to read. Right, Secure Unit, below it details of regulation visiting times, the name of the Chief Executive and his qualifications. This was where he and Aoife had gone the day before, until very recently the long-term abode of John Fryer. On the left, he read what he had overlooked the day before: NON-SECURE UNIT, the same blurb and administrative details printed below.

'We were looking for our man in the wrong part of

the hospital, in the wrong visitors' book,' said Sheen.

Aoife smiled, started to nod. 'This is where our murderer must have found out about John Fryer. It's why he chose him,' she said.

'One hospital,' said Sheen.

'Two units,' she said. Aoife slotted the car into first and they moved off, another spin of the wheels, this time taking the left-hand path.

The non-secure unit was more modern than the secure, and looked more conventionally hospital-like than the Victorian castle feel of the secure unit across the slope of Cave Hill. But it had the same sterile odour of disinfectant muddled in with the gassy, institutional smell of unaired rooms.

At the reception desk Sheen glanced up, saw a CCTV camera. No doubt this place was running off the same shoestring budget as the secure wing, and probably the same self-defeating system of recording over and ultimately erasing any evidence which the eye above the desk managed to capture. They would be lucky if they had their man on camera. That said, if Aoife's hunch was correct, they may not need his face on the screen to catch him.

The woman who had buzzed them in listened as Aoife explained what they needed: the signing-in book used by visitors, and a full register of patients. She made a quick call during which Sheen heard his name being mentioned.

'Thanks for waiting, that's fine. Here's the visitor log. This one goes back two years. There are others, but I think they are stored in the basement area. We would have to ask the caretaker about that, and he's not in today,' she said. She was about 5',6", short brown hair, looked and sounded like she was from Eastern Europe, though her accent had the tell-tale dip at the end of her sentence that suggested she had lived in Belfast for some time, or at least mastered English in the city.

Sheen took it from her, and opened it at the most recent page, scanned down the list of names, flicking between the scribbled visitors' signatures and the largely capitalised names of the patients. He had moved through ten double pages, gone as far back as a full year of records, and was almost about to ask Aoife to double check what he had just surveyed when he found what he wanted. The signature was a spidery scrawl, totally impossible to make out, but the patient name in column two was printed and clear.

P MOORE

'Look,' said Sheen. Aoife was at his side. He felt her clutch the arm of his jacket and an absurd schoolboy tingle of excitement shivered through Sheen's legs and groin. Aoife took the ledger from him and turned it round to show the woman, one finger on the name.

'We need the records for this person, full name, home address, anything else you have,' she said.

'Please follow me,' she said, moving from behind her desk, and walked down the corridor to Sheen's right. At regular intervals along the wall faded impressionist prints hung. Their frames were screwed securely to the wall. The covers looked like plastic, not glass. She stopped at a door, a rectangular box with a fire extinguisher attached to the wall outside.

'This is the day manager's office here,' she said, sifting quickly through a fair-sized bunch of keys, which she produced from the pocket of her fleece jacket, then unlocked the door. She opened it and reached inside. A second later the light blinked to life, yellow, fluorescent. The room was windowless. The ceiling was low, felt like a converted store cupboard.

Sheen assumed she was going to go for the computer, but instead she walked to the single grey filing cabinet adjacent to the desk, turned the small key waiting in the lock and pulled open the drawer that was second from the bottom.

'This drawer and the one underneath have a full listing of all patients. Those deceased are removed, transferred patients take their records when they go, but we keep files for those discharged. I have been here for more than two years and nobody has died during that time, so there you go,' she said.

'Thank you,' said Aoife. She had already started on the cabinet, was flicking through the files rapidly. He knew what she was looking for, the name they wanted: P MOORE.

'Not a bother at all,' she said, smiled at Sheen and left. Sheen joined Aoife. She slammed the first drawer closed with a clatter, then jerked the bottom one open. The first drawer probably went up as far as R. If they were going to find what they came for, it would be at the bottom, or not at all.

Aoife slowed, the crease of concentration folded between her eyes sharply. She was quietly mouthing the names. 'McCloud, Morris—' She stopped abruptly. 'Bloody Moore,' she said softly. She was looking up at him, her eyes full of light, victory. Aoife reached in and snatched the file from the drawer. She raised herself up, shoved the tidy arrangement on the day manager's desk out of her way and slapped down the brown manila file. Sheen stood next to her, close enough to taste a mouthful of the apple perfume. She opened the file, and they both scanned the front page simultaneously, Aoife's finger tracing the lines of information methodically. Sheen read the first section, then scanned on down the page, searching. His eyes focused on what he wanted, just as Aoife's finger stabbed the same place on the page.

NAME: Moore, Patricia Ann
DOB: 1.8.60
DATE OF ADMISSION: 12.1.2013
DIAGNOSIS: Schizophrenia, Paranoid/Mania

He stopped reading, scanned further down the page and found the home address, a street in Bangor, Co. Down, about twenty miles out of Belfast along the coast. Then the final piece of the puzzle, the name to the face on their E-Fit, he was sure of it.

NEXT OF KIN: Christopher Aaron Moore (son)

No mobile telephone number, just a landline for the home address.
'That's our boy, Aoife,' said Sheen. 'You got him. Well done,' he said. He wanted to shake her hand, hug her, kiss her, but instead he nodded like a donkey and smiled. 'Bloody well done,' he repeated.

Aoife smiled back, but then her face returned to a set mask of concentration. She reached for her phone. 'Not yet. We need to get to this address,' she said. Sheen waited for long enough to hear Aoife begin speaking to Irwin on the phone. He quietly left the office and retraced his steps back to the reception desk. He had an idea, and they should have time for him to check it out.

'Hiya, any luck?' asked the woman. She flashed the same smile.

Sheen waved a hand, maybe yes, maybe no. 'You might be able to do something else for me, though,' he said, smiling back her. 'The patient we mentioned, Patricia Ann Moore. If she is available, I would really like to speak with her,' he said. This was thin ground. Speaking to a witness in an informal way was one thing, but speaking to minors or those who had mental instabilities was a no man's land, at very best perched right on the periphery of the PACE codes of practice. Something she hopefully did not know. She shrugged and her smile faltered, then faded away to a look of genuine lament.

'Well, you know, you could try, but I doubt you will get any words in return,' she said.

'Why?' asked Sheen.

'Patricia has gone. Lights are on, but no one has been home for at least a year,' she said.

'Still, I'd like to see her, please,' said Sheen.

The woman nodded, walked once again from her station and set off, this time going the other direction down the corridor. Sheen followed, reached into his jacket pocket for his phone with the E-Fit.

'It said on her file that she has a next of kin, a son. Does he ever visit?' he asked.

She slowed a little. He could see from her face she was thinking, and then she nodded. 'Used to, but not for a good long time. He used to walk her round the gardens when it was not raining,' she said.

'And?' asked Sheen.

'And after Patricia started to become more and more withdrawn, he visited less and less. It happens. She probably did not even notice,' she said.

She stopped. They were standing outside mesh-reinforced glass double doors. Beyond looked like a common room for the patients. Sheen could see men and women in dressing gowns, some walking slowly, and aimless-looking. Others sat in high-backed armchairs, thousand-yard stares. Suddenly, Sheen did not want to go any further. He wanted to prolong his conversation, flirt with the woman, and remain in the land of the sane.

'Do you recognise this man. Is this her son?' asked Sheen, showing her the E-Fit.

'That's definitely him,' she said immediately, not even a second of hesitation. She visibly shivered. 'I would recognise those eyes anywhere. Creepy.' It was enough. Sheen knew he had his man, and there was really no need to take this any further. Still, he pushed the door open and walked in.

'Thank you for your help,' he said.

'Welcome. Patricia. In her usual chair, right over there,' she said, pointing through the door to a chair which was facing the big window running along the east wall of the building. The door swished closed behind Sheen. The first thing that struck him was the view, nothing less than breathtaking. The wooded area that bordered the grounds dropped steeply away before him. Beyond was the whole of Belfast, opening into the wide arms of the harbour. Sheen tugged his eyes from the scene before him, as he walked round the armchair. The vista, so stunning in that clean, clear Belfast light of morning, was wasted on Patricia Moore.

The woman looked eighty, not in her mid-fifties as her file stated. Grey silver hair, thin, unkempt and too long, flowed in two rivers either side of her face and over her shoulders. She looked like one of Macbeth's three witches as he had always imagined them. Her blue eyes were open, saucer-wide, almost luminescent in her gaunt face. Patricia's mouth was slack. It sagged open on one side like a split bag of grain. He hunkered down and brought his face close to the vacant one in front of him.

'Mrs Moore,' he said softly. He took one of her limp hands in his, skin soft, hard wires and skeleton just beneath. Mrs Moore, the same name as their victim. One woman dead, one living dead. 'Patricia, I am from the police,' he went on, feeling stupid. One or two other patients had now stopped what they had been doing and watched his antics in mute interest. Sheen kept talking. 'This is about your son, Patricia. This is about Christopher. It is important that we speak to him. He may be in some danger,' he said. Sheen thought he saw something, the faintest glimmer of recognition in her eyes at the mention of Christopher's name. He had a regular little audience now. Sheen gently patted the woman's hand, and let go, relieved to remove it from his own. He stood up and walked to the door. As he pushed it open, Sheen froze, dead. The hairs on the back of his neck were raised, a shiver of gooseflesh prickled up his arms, down his back, creeping horribly.

She was laughing. It was shrill, piercing, and terrible. Sheen turned around. The cackling laugh rang out again. A male patient in dark blue pyjamas and green dressing gown frowned and slapped both his hands over his ears, started to back away from her. Sheen didn't blame him.

'Jesus,' he said, and got out of there, her laugh chasing him.

Sheen walked down the corridor and stopped to look at one of the prints which hung on the wall. This one was part of a Jackson Pollock, called Black and White, for pretty obvious reasons. The chaotic drips and slashes of paint seemed frenetic, yet also had their own form of order. If you could see insanity under a microscope, that is how it would look.

Christopher Moore had crossed that line. Sheen hurried back to Aoife, because there was more to follow. Just like that snippet of slash and drips, what they had been served up so far was just part of the picture that Christopher wanted to paint.

CHAPTER FORTY-FIVE

Cecil set his mobile down, on the desk by his first-floor window in the Bad Bet in Tiger's Bay. The parked cars lined the hushed pavement and all was calm, Sunday morning coming down. Cecil appeared serene too, but that was only on the surface. His mind was in full production mode, the gears and pistons whirring and hissing at an industrial pace. He had just finished a phone call from his man inside Springfield Road PSNI station. It had been a brief conversation, mostly one way, a simple warning which his man had delivered.

They were on their way, coming to lift him. There was not much time.

Jackie Coyle had squealed Cecil's name, claimed he had ordered the petrol bombing of the lower Shankill. Apparently he had named the whole crew he was working with, including the Turk and his nephews. But that was not Cecil's problem. The Turk could deal with all the other little piggys involved. No, it was Jackie Coyle who was Cecil's problem. Now there was no trail of breadcrumbs leading to his door. This was the word of a grass, plain and simple, no evidence to hold him.

Or perhaps not so plain, not so simple. He had watched many of his contemporaries go down hard in the 1980s, and do long stretches on the word of a tout. Back then, Cecil found it necessary to get his hands very messy on more than one occasion. He had culled both the weak and good men who knew them, because loose lips most certainly were not going to sink Cecil Moore's ship. Against all of Cecil's meticulous planning, his ship was taking on water, fast.

Cecil sighed. If it had been the petrol bombs on their own, as he had told them, then this would not be half as bad. But the man had put a bullet in Scotty Wood's skull. The whole shebang had turned into a bigger deal. Cecil had been explicit: no guns. Even in a safe pair of hands, a loaded gun tended to have the trigger pulled, sooner or later. It was as much as guaranteed. A black cat sneaked out from behind the wheel of a parked car and skulked across the street and under another motor.

He checked his watch. Nearly five minutes had passed since his warning call. He could probably make a run for it. But that was never going to happen. Cecil had not raised himself up to stand on the corpses of his enemies and, God forbid, some of his still-loyal friends, by running like a dog every time he took a hit, every time the water started to leak in and the sinking feeling started.

'He pulled open his desk drawer, rummaged past the spare packets of batteries and pens with lids missing, until

327

his hand came upon one of his burner Nokia mobiles, still in its sealed plastic packet. He opened it quickly using a pair of scissors, inserted the SIM card which came with it, and turned it on. Cecil frowned, his face a picture of pain as he punched the number he needed into the phone, raised it to his ear, waited. He licked his lips, but his tongue was as dry as a Baptist's wake. For the first time in the ten or more years since he'd stopped smoking, Cecil wanted a fag, a nice B&H tar stick that would tear through his chest like a bush fire and steady his nerves. Cecil could hear the ringtone on the other end. This was a special number, one that Cecil had kept in the back pocket of his mind for a long time. Politics, it was not for the faint hearted, that much was for sure.

BLEEEP BLEEEP

If that bitch McCusker had done his bidding when he had texted her, this might not have been necessary. He would have been able to get to Coyle through one of his boys in the PSNI, maybe.

BLEEEP BLEEEP

The wee bitch needed a correction, a reminder, to teach her how their arrangement actually worked in practice. She was worth reminding, that the girl was potentially very valuable indeed, more so, Cecil mused, than the determined little madam even gave herself credit for. She had legs as the saying went, oh by Christ she did, and in the world they were living in these days, with Fenians overrunning the police and Provos making laws in Stormont, yes, she was going to go very far. And Cecil would be there too, riding along. Yes, she was a long-term investment, like a gilt-edged bond, worth waiting for payday. No need to cash her in just yet, or at least not entirely. Not that she did not deserve it after what she had done. Bitch deserved it.

BLEEEP BLEEEP

But he would show patience. He would be the teacher, she would learn who was master. She would heel. Cecil had already broken her. This was just her youth, and maybe a bit of a wild streak that made her believe that she was not his. Sure it was the same bottle that convinced Cecil she was well worth keeping. Life was a funny thing sometimes. The phone had just started its eighth ring and then it was answered. Cecil's face suddenly brightened.

'What about ye mate?' he said, his voice full of banter, rich and familiar. Your best mate, calling you when you were not expecting it. The voice which answered was less relaxed, made no pretence of warmth. Cecil's smile widened. Despite the fact that he was going to use up a major favour, with the peelers about to lift him, he was starting to enjoy this.

'You should not be calling me,' hissed the voice on the other end of the phone. Taken by surprise, fair dues. This guy could be anywhere, but Cecil certainly hoped it was somewhere that Oswald needed to make excuses, scurry to a quiet place. This was the call he probably assumed would never come, certainly not this time on a Sunday morning, that was for sure.

'Do you hear me?' Oswald hissed, speaking in an urgent whisper. He was talking down to Cecil, like a man in control. But men in charge rarely sounded as panicked as Oswald did now. Cecil looked at his watch. Nearly ten minutes since his warning call. The peelers were close, probably driving into Tiger's Bay right now.

'Ach, Oswald, is that any way to speak to an old mucker? You'll hurt my feelings, mate, so you will,' said Cecil, cold steel beneath the syrup of his words. He allowed himself a pause he could ill afford, keeping cool, so cool. 'You really don't want to go offending me, not after I have taken the time to pick up a phone and call you personally,' he said. Cecil was no longer smiling, his eyes fixed on the road below. When they came, it would be from the main road, at the far end of the street. He had a good view.

'Please, do not use my name,' said Oswald. 'What is it you want?' he said. Still speaking in a hissing whisper, but all the authority gone now, pleading. 'I am at work, believe it or not. I did not mean to appear . . . discourteous. What is this about?' he said. Not exactly an apology, but not a kick in the arse off one. Good enough for now. Oswald knew his place.

And rightly so. Cecil had enough on the fucker to make Jimmy Savile look like Daddy Christmas. Oswald thought he was sitting at the big table when it came to that kind of jazz, but he had no clue. What others were involved in, it made Oswald's sins look like public school fumbling after lights-out. But the measure of a man's sin, like his ability to survive, is in his own mind. All of which meant that Oswald's arse, to employ an apt phrase, was owned by Cecil.

'The world is more full of weeping than you can understand,' said Cecil.

'What?' asked Oswald.

'Meaning you need to get your chequebook out, son, and get ready to pay the piper,' he said.

There was a pause, this time from Oswald. 'Is this line secure?' he said.

'Burner. Are you in NI?' asked Cecil.

Oswald told him he was.

'Sure, isn't life just grand? Now shut your mouth and listen to me,' said Cecil.

Cecil spoke quickly. Not his style, but this morning, he was as fast as a Chinaman in a whorehouse. He explained what he needed from Oswald with an eloquent lack of fluff in less than twenty seconds. Jackie Coyle must slip in the shower, cut his throat shaving, fall off a step – he must be gone.

'I cannot just walk in,' started Oswald.

Cecil cut him off. 'I have men inside. Your hands will not get dirty, but I need access. Think of a way, and fast, Oswald. Intelligence is your job, remember?' said Cecil.

'Yes, yes, there is a way. I know how it can be done,' he replied.

'Good man. Now, one more thing,' said Cecil. He outlined his second order of the morning, in the same careful, meticulous fashion as the first.

Oswald listened. When he replied, his voice wavered. 'Now that, ah, that's going to take a bit of time. I'm not really sure I can guarantee—'

'Yes, you can, Oswald. And you will,' said Cecil. Silence. He had been told.

'I was sorry to hear about your mother. I hope those responsible will be brought to justice,' he said.

'Cheers, Oswald, appreciate that,' said Cecil. Cecil knew exactly who was responsible for his mother's death. He recognised the bastard as soon as he saw his Fenian face on the video from the kid Anderson's phone. The voice recording from Burgoyne confirmed it.

'When all this calms down, I am going to organise another wee meal in Donegal, Oswald. Very fresh produce, totally organic, and I mean very fresh indeed. I will make sure you are on the invitation list. I'll let you know the usual way,' he said, and killed the call, not waiting to hear if Oswald was interested or not. His fingers worked quickly, switching off the phone and removing the SIM, which he tossed into a marble ashtray on his desk and coated it in flame using a mini blowtorch from the desk drawer. The SIM warped and puffed, then fully ignited in a fierce, brief orange light, before shrinking into a small shapeless lump of burnt black plastic.

'Nelson!' roared Cecil, waving his hand over the tray to shoo away the smoke. Heavy footfalls knocking the wood floor on the hallway approached his office. The door opened. Nelson sliced in, closed it. He was wearing his thick gold neck chain, a muscle shirt, black jeans and brown shoes. His man was an intelligent dresser, a little natural taste. Nelson nodded, the small gold hoops in his ears dancing briefly as he did so.

'Peelers are coming, any second now,' said Cecil. Nelson's eyes widened, his mouth slowly opened. Cecil raised his eyes, sighed. 'Not for you, for me,' he said. Another nod from Nelson, then a forming question on his face. Cecil held up both hands in a stop-and-listen gesture. There was not the time. 'It's being dealt with. Now listen, it's time to get our friend from the kid Anderson's video. Should have gone yesterday, but sure . . .' Cecil tailed off. He needed to remain on point, get Nelson offside fast, before the whole operation hit a snag and that bastard half-breed nephew of his walked. He gave Nelson a street address in Bangor, the place where he would find his nephew. Asked him if he needed it repeated, and Nelson shook his head. The sound of screeching tyres from the street below sounded like they had just rounded the far corner, the one that led into the main road. Then the whining roar of big engine vehicles accelerating hard, getting closer. It was time.

'Nelson, you find him, take him to the lock-up and start to work on him. No limits this time. You don't have to go gently on him like the Anderson boy, this is no punishment beating,' said Cecil. Another screech of tyres, just below, then the slamming of multiple doors, clipped instructions, the crackle of static radio, footfalls moving fast, probably heading round the back. Let them, the wall was wrapped in barbed wire and upturned broken bottles. Cecil had a hidden doorway, his side exit into the neighbouring house. He owned it too.

'Go out the hole in the wall, and get rid of this,' said Cecil, throwing Nelson the shell of the burner phone, which he caught in one hand. Cecil watched him leave, slicing out as he had come in, the sound of his heels on the laminate. The front door of the boozer rattled on its hinges after being banged hard three times. He had best get down there; those wankers would knock it in if he didn't. Cecil liked those doors, original features, from a time when working class Prods from Tiger's Bay could actually get a good job, like joining the RUC. This made him think of his Fenian-loving dead brother and he quickly skirted the desk, opened the office door and called Nelson's name. Nelson was at the top of the stairs. He stopped, turned his face to Cecil and waited.

'Bring two reliables, Benny and Ivan. I don't want this ballsed up,' he said.

'That's all?' Nelson asked, still waiting.

The peelers banged the door again, much harder this time. Cecil fancied he heard the off-key scratch of a pane of glass crack. A shout came from below, the usual open-up bollocks. He blotted it out, needed to concentrate. There was a decision to make. His Judas brother had owned a service weapon, but the question was did his half-breed nephew have it? He could not see one on the video from the Anderson kid's phone. Still, better to have and not need than be shot in the face.

BANG, rattle and shouts from below.

'One more thing,' replied Cecil. 'Go strapped, just in case,' he said. Nelson blinked once, turned and disappeared down the stairs, taking them three at a time. *BANG*, rattle, shouts. Cecil growled and stomped back into his office. He flung up the sash window, bellowed down at the assembled cunts in uniform under him.

'You fucking bang that door once more and I'll stick my boot in your hole!' he shouted. He rammed the window closed and bombed down the stairs, his mental drawbridge pulling up, and portcullis falling in readiness for the rigmarole to follow. He fiddled needlessly with the bolt of the pub doors, longing it out for a few more seconds. Eventually, he released it, opened up, and invited the scum in with a smile. The sound of the bolt releasing stayed in his mind. It reminded him of a bullet loading into the firing chamber of a gun.

CHAPTER FORTY-SIX

At the Kennedy Centre Christopher purchased two sturdy padlocks, essential to ensure that, for John Fryer at least, their attacks on the 12th July would be a one-way journey. Before he drove out of the underground car park, he returned the steel trolley and the white coat and hat where he had found them the day before.

As Christopher passed the City Airport, Bangor bound, Daddy spoke. Or, more precisely, Christopher heard his voice. It sounded distant, synthetic. More like a poor recording, being played again and again on a loop, getting fainter until it had faded to the sound of the taxi's wheels on the road.

Something's gone rotten here, I can smell it. Something's gone rotten here, I can smell it.

Christopher couldn't smell anything. He scanned the road on either side – nothing amiss. There was a left turn ahead. Christopher slowed. Both the main road he was on and the left turn would take him to Bangor. The latter was the scenic route round Crawfordsburn Park. It would take longer. It also allowed him to approach his place of residence indirectly, coming at it from the other side of the hill. Christopher flicked his indicator, took the taxi left.

Daddy remained silent as wooded parkland swished past on either side. He maintained a law abiding 35 mph round one sweeping corner after another. A tractor, pulling a flatbed full of hay, approached on the other side of the road, too fast. Christopher slowed and edged the taxi onto the verge, allowing the farmer more than enough space to get past. The road was a travesty, hardly enough room for him, but still, taking this detour was the right thing, he knew it. Christopher called his daddy again and again as he took the taxi through slow meanders. He wanted to know what had gone rotten. He got only silence and the sounds of the road.

If Daddy knew, he was not letting on.

CHAPTER FORTY-SEVEN

Aoife pulled into Ladas Drive twenty-five minutes after she had got off the phone to Irwin. Irwin said he would give her half an hour before putting the team on the road. He was, at least, good to his word. In the large car park adjacent to the station, she could see four fortified Land Rovers parked in a line. Uniformed officers dressed in black Teflon stood in groups of three and four near the open rear doors. Semi-automatics strapped to their chests or in their arms, their utility belts hung heavily with pouches and canisters. They were all men. Not one woman in the vicinity apart from her.

A tremor of exhilaration in her legs. This was it: her collar, the Something Big against her name. She was going to catch a killer. Irwin emerged from the side door of the station and bowled down the stone steps. He was wearing a thick black fleece jacket, a beanie hat rolled up on his head. It reminded her of a rolled-up balaclava mask.

'Get a vest on, DC McCusker. You too, Sheen,' he hollered, by way of greeting. The small smile he gave them told her that he shared her sense of impending triumph, her curtness and unprofessional words from a few hours before forgotten, for the time being at least. 'And hurry up,' he said.

Aoife and Sheen headed for the station. It had been a long time since she had worn a vest – not since she was on the streets in uniform – and for the most part, even then, it had been a stab vest.

Irwin's voice raised from behind them, his words only partly audible. She turned. Sheen did too. The uniformed sergeant was face-to-face with Irwin, red beard flecked with white, eyes fixed and angry. A hard gaze from what looked like a hard man. She caught a few final words from Irwin. It sounded like he was arguing for all three of them to tag along, clearly against the sergeant's wishes. DCI Kirkcaldy was not, strictly speaking, needed on the operation. Same for her and Sheen. She knew Irwin enjoyed being at the business end, but he had also just stood up for her. Without her, there would be no raid. No reply from the sergeant. He started shaking his head, in what looked like disgust rather than disagreement. Irwin had won. He turned to her and Sheen.

'You two will ride with me. I will talk you through the plan en route,' he said, his cheeks a glowing plum. He looked like he was enjoying himself.

CHAPTER FORTY-EIGHT

There was no way of telling where they were from the back of the windowless Land Rover. Probably along the stretch beyond the City Airport, halfway to Bangor. Irwin had given them the run-down. The address was on a terraced street. Rear access would not be easy, so they would station a unit on the parallel road to scoop up anyone who managed to get out the back door and over garden fences. Irwin said it was not likely; they had the element of surprise, and they would go in fast and hard. It should be straightforward.

Aoife asked about their credible evidence. The E-Fit, the DNA from the hair in the bath, the boot prints – ultimately doubt could be cast on these things in court.

'We also have the explosives used at the substation bomb, and enough circumstantial evidence to suggest John Fryer and Christopher Moore are in cahoots. If we find them with guns and explosives there is a bigger case to answer for. That's how I got the search warrant issued,' said Irwin.

'Oswald told us to back off John Fryer, said the Dissident line is off limits,' said Sheen.

'So it is. But, you see, the information I have been able to get is that John Fryer is not, and never was, a Dissident republican. Technically he is still in the IRA, and officially they're out of action. And whatever else Christopher Moore might think he is, he's not a Dissident. Technically, we are not going against Oswald on this,' said Irwin.

Aoife watched as Sheen's face darkened at Irwin's mention of John Fryer.

'We have to catch them. There's more to this than what has happened over the last two days. It's bigger,' said Sheen.

Aoife picked up this line, as Sheen went quiet, though part of her was not sure whether they were really sharing the same point or not. 'We believe that what has happened so far is just part of the picture. There is more to come. You can see that, can't you, sir? With the 12th July, things feel like they are just ramping up, not levelling out,' said Aoife. She looked at Sheen, wanting his support. It was he who had recognised the ritualistic details in Mrs Moore's killing for what they were. He should explain this. But Sheen's face was dark, brooding. His thoughts were his own.

'With a bit of luck and God's grace we will catch these dangerous men this afternoon in possession of guns and explosives. We can take our time and question the pair of them about what the heck was going on in their sick minds,' said Irwin.

The Land Rover slowed down, and then stopped abruptly. 'Let's go,' said Irwin. The armour-plated back doors were pulled open, clean light flooded in, as the occupants poured out.

CHAPTER FORTY-NINE

The gyppo was making gurgling noises, thick and watery. The blood was spreading from the three bullets holes Nelson had put in his string-vested chest, a dark crescent on the hallway carpet. Nelson could taste it, warm and metallic in the air, mingled with the sharp smell of fresh cordite from the rounds he had just used. Nelson's ears were ringing; his heart was smashing in his chest. How the fuck had he ended up in a house full of gyppos?

The gyppo coughed once, a bright red jet of blood spurted up from his mouth, then he was still. The woman, who Benny was holding by the hair in the living-room doorway, started to scream and struggle. Nelson pistol-whipped her on the front of the forehead, and her legs turned to cold spaghetti. Benny kept a hold of her dark mop, then let go. She fell, eyes wide, all whites. Her body started to twitch. Fuck's sake, another one probably nutted. Benny looked over at him. He wanted an answer, but Nelson turned his eyes to the front door, a few metres down the hallway to his left. A sound, maybe the screeching of tyres. Hard to tell. His ears were still ringing. He inserted a little finger in one earhole and jostled it around. Benny was staring at him, not moving, but Nelson could tell he was shitting it.

'I know,' said Nelson. Benny nodded. He knew better than to push him. 'Let me think,' said Nelson, but that was getting harder to do. The reek of the gyppo's blood was filling up the small hallway at the foot of the stairs, clouding everything. It had been over ten years since Nelson had topped anybody. Even then it had been a spray and run, not up close and real like this.

He blinked away sweat from his eyes, checked the front door again. They had hit the right house. He had double-checked the address that Cecil had given him. Another thought, this one even more frightening than getting the address wrong: what if he was past his best? Ten years away from the front line was a long stretch. A man could get rusty, and fuck knows Nelson had no answer for what was going on right now. From the kitchen, a chorus of crying, kids screeching for Mammy, Daddy. Jesus Christ.

'Shut those filthy wee fuckers up!' barked Nelson. He heard Ivan screaming at them, telling them he would shoot them unless they kept quiet. He meant it.

'Do you want me to call Campbell, boss?' It was Benny who had spoken. Campbell? It took Nelson two or more seconds to register what the younger man was talking about, before it clicked. Campbell was parked a street away. Their plan had been simple, beautiful. Get to the address through the back gardens, find the Fenian Christopher, text

Campbell saying dinner was ready and walk out the front with him. They had agreed to call only if there was trouble. The three of them, Benny, Ivan and himself, should have been able to take him, and take him alive.

Now he had two dead rice crispies and the fucker they wanted was nowhere to be seen. If Benny called Campbell now it would mean defeat, proof that he had lost his edge, not just the target. Thirty seconds, maybe forty, since three bangs had put down the string-vested big bastard who had come at him from the stairs with an axe in his fist. Hard to tell, though. What was certain was that time was ticking away, and he was out of answers. Fuck it.

'Phone him,' he said to Benny. He exhaled, feeling better already. That was the right decision. They were in the shit. It was time to get out, regroup, rethink and go after their man again. Benny nodded, relief etched on his face. The children had started up again, louder now, followed by a dull slap and scream, then Ivan's voice, full of threats. Nelson tried to cancel it out. That front door had drawn his attention again. His ears were slightly clearer now. He turned his body and raised the gun up in the same motion. Movement from behind the clouded glass. Someone was on the front doorstep. Benny had the call to Campbell bleating on loudspeaker, no matter. He crouched down on one knee, his gun still pointed up at the shifting shadows beyond the front door, his heart a Lambeg drum pounding in his chest.

'Campbell,' said Benny. Nelson did not take his eyes off the door, heard the panic and fear in the younger man's voice as he explained there was a problem. A problem, why of course, this was Murphy's law after all. Lady Luck was squatting over them, a filthy fat shit hanging from her arse, ready to drop any second. Nelson blew a ball of sweat off the end of his nose and gave Benny the last order he would ever issue.

'Tell Campbell to run for it,' he said. More movement. Benny looked down the hall. The kids were fucking wailing.

'What's happening?' said Benny.

A second later the door came in.

CHAPTER FIFTY

Christopher parked up on a corner a few streets away from the house that he and John Fryer had shared for the last two days. Now he could see what was rotten: a white PSNI Land Rover was parked halfway down the road to his right. This street ran parallel to the one Christopher had grown up on and, by his estimate, the Land Rover was positioned exactly where the back garden of his very own childhood home would meet that of its parallel neighbour.

Rotten indeed, but things were perhaps not entirely spoilt. He snapped his head round. Three subdued claps, like firecrackers exploding under a blanket. Christopher pulled down the driver's window, froze and listened. The PSNI Land Rover gunned to life, its headlights flashed on and it surged forward, headed for him. Christopher nudged the idling taxi into first, rid the clutch, ready. He could see its occupants. The driver's eyes were fixed only on the road. The passenger was speaking into a radio attached to his chest. Neither the driver nor his wingman looked at him. He took his foot off the clutch and killed the engine.

The Land Rover screeched around the corner, screamed past, took a hard right, disappeared into Christopher's childhood street. The sound of the engine dimmed. He heard a screech of tyres. Christopher glanced down the now-empty street to his right and quickly estimated the time and distance travelled. He nodded. The Land Rover had stopped outside his childhood home.

His thoughts were interrupted by the multiple snaps of many guns fired at once, thirty seconds of frenzy, followed by total silence, not even a birdsong in the sunshine. A metallic blue Range Rover pulled very slowly out of his childhood street where the action had happened. He had seen this vehicle before, a flash of recognition, but no more. The Range Rover picked up speed, burnt past him. The taxi rocked on its springs. He caught a glimpse of the driver through tinted windows, and made him. He was one of Uncle Cecil's boys. Both he and the Range Rover were from Tiger's Bay. It was where he had seen it before, parked outside the Bad Bet. All the pieces fell into place. Cecil's men had come to visit him, and so had the PSNI, both at the same time. But he had not been home. He started to laugh, jagged and wild, and continued to do so, long after the moment of hilarity had passed.

CHAPTER FIFTY-ONE

Aoife blinked and squinted into the sunlight, and watched as the uniformed men swarmed fluidly from the back of their Land Rovers across the street and into Christopher Moore's front garden, taking position under the front bay window, and crouched in the sheltered alcove of the main entrance. Irwin was ensconced in their midst. He looked erratic, a grazing farm animal in a pack of wolves.

Another member of the raiding team pushed past her, almost sent her flying like a standing pin in the bowling alley. The man was big, like a rugby prop forward, but one who played less and coached more. His shoulders and neck were one piece of meat, his triceps enormous red thighs suspended under the tight clasp of fabric from his black T-shirt. He was carrying a red steel battering ram in his right fist. As he tabbed up the narrow drive, Aoife could see that the words SKELETON KEY had been painted in white letters on the red cylindrical side of the metal ram.

She watched the men on the steps silently part for ram man, who paused on the edge of the alcove, a clear run-up to the door now in front of him. He turned to Irwin, who nodded back, but his expression held a question rather than an answer. He was unsure if it was time to go, and for the first time Aoife wondered whether Irwin had done anything as heavy as this before. But there was no time to ponder, not for her, not for Irwin. Three shots barked out from inside the house.

Aoife flinched and raised her hands to her head in an instinctive gesture of protection. She saw the same spasm move through the body of men, as though jolted simultaneously by an electric shock. Ram man had crouched, but stood his ground, ready. The sergeant glared at Irwin from his vantage point across the steps. The muffled sound of a woman screaming, from inside the house, then it stopped, a plug pulled. Irwin had his head cocked towards the door. He was panting, face full of high colour. The ram man was moving from foot to foot, ready to go, glancing from the front door to Irwin. A child's cry from inside the house, piercing and frantic. It filled up the void, before stopping as abruptly as the woman's scream.

Irwin's eyes widened. He mouthed, 'Go, go!'

Ram man exploded forward, swinging the steel from his side as he moved. It whacked thunderously into the door, hitting squarely on the lower hinges. The second and third hits were equally powerful. The rattling booms of their impacts delivered with incredible speed, hitting the Yale lock, the upper hinges. She heard the crack of splintering wood. The door collapsed inwards, hanging on by the screw of one hinge, a loose tooth no longer part of the mouth. Multiple voices shouting, 'Armed police,' the men surged forward in one movement, taking Irwin with them. From first impact to men inside, three seconds.

Sharp cracks in quick succession, too many to count, handfuls of firecrackers lit and tossed simultaneously, then silence. Aoife moved, racing on legs that felt too heavy, her feet in dream treacle, not on the road. She reached the bottom step, could smell the sharpness of spent rounds, heard cries of 'Clear!' from inside and then, 'Officer down!' Aoife paused on the steps, her Lundy legs betraying her. Sheen shoved past her, went inside, crouched down. Please, God, don't be Irwin. She forced herself to step inside, could smell the sickly blanket of coppery blood in the air, and could feel the uneven texture of spent shells and broken glass under her feet.

Children crying, from just beyond the hallway, piercing and filled with fear, but to Aoife they were peripheral. Her attention was locked on the heap of bodies, sprawled together at the foot of the stairs beyond Sheen. A man and a woman. He was on his back, big, his island chest filled her line of vision. There was a hatchet next to his outstretched arm. Full black beard, probably in his forties. Not their E-Fit, not Christopher Moore. The woman was slumped against a doorframe. Her face was slick with fresh blood. Eyes half open, white, glazed, tongue peeking out of her slack mouth.

A uniform hunkered over the man, placed his fingers under his chin, and then an ear to his mouth, called out

'Dead', and then turned to the woman. Aoife shifted her eyes away from this, looked down at Sheen, who was crouched over the head of a body that lay side on to her, legs poking out of the front room. Brown shoes, leather soles scuffed and scratched. Had Irwin been wearing brown shoes?

'Irwin!' she shouted. Sheen had the man's black T-shirt balled in his fist, face-to-face, but it was not Irwin. This was Nelson, Cecil Moore's man. Sheen was shouting, shaking his limp body, his hands painted red where he had grabbed the T-shirt.

'How'd Cecil know?!' continued Sheen. Nelson's head wobbled loosely with each shake of Sheen's clenched fists, his fat gold hoops dancing their own jig. His face was yellow, eyes cold and blank. Another violent tug and shove from Sheen, a trickle of dark blood ran from the corner of Nelson's mouth. He was dead.

'Speak to me, you bastard. Was it Jamie Anderson? You hurt that kid, didn't you, you hurt him?' he said, still shaking. Nelson's mute head rocked in macabre agreement.

Aoife rested a hand on Sheen's shoulder. He shrugged her away, then turned, saw her and relaxed. She shook her head. 'He's dead, Sheen,' she said. Sheen shoved Nelson's chest to the floor, letting go of his shirt. Aoife stepped back, away from the horror of Nelson's dummy-like body, but mostly away from Sheen.

From beyond the room, the same cry as before: 'Officer down!'

They ran into the dining area, greeted by a chorus of wailing from three children in pyjamas held back by one man

351

in uniform. Two men were face down in the small kitchen, arms outstretched and secured, guns trained on them. They were alive. She turned and saw another body spread-eagled on the floor, overturned wooden chairs on either side. The sergeant was on his knees, both hands pumping the man's chest, Aoife saw the thick black fleece jacket. She moved in another step. A younger officer was pressing blood-soaked gauze to a wound under his chin, trying to stem the flow of blood that was pumping through his fingers.

'Irwin!' she screamed. Sheen pushed by her, went to his knees and joined the sergeant on the floor, who fell back, panting. Sheen took over the CPR, maintained the gruelling tempo, did not stop to give Irwin the kiss of life. The sirens grew louder, and the house quieter, the children carried away, and still Sheen pressed and pumped, until the blood from Irwin's neck wound just oozed like sap. The officer pressing the fabric to Irwin's neck could see the truth, even if Sheen was blind.

He let go of the gauze, slumped to a sitting position on the dining-room floor, stared at his blood-red hand, which he held in front of his face. She heard the screech of tyres from outside, the march of approaching feet, coming to help. Too late.

'Sheen,' she said, but he did not stop, maybe he did not even hear. He continued to work, and Irwin continued to dance with him as he pumped and pressed the dead man's chest.

'Sheen!' she shouted, and this time he did stop. 'That's enough. Leave him. He's dead, Sheen. Irwin's dead,' she said, voice clotted with tears. And it was her fault. Maybe Jamie Anderson had given them something, but Cecil had the SecuriTel recording, had it before them. He must have recognised the voice of his nephew. It was why Nelson got to Christopher's house ahead of them. Aoife had known about it but said nothing, and now, Irwin was dead.

CHAPTER FIFTY-TWO

Christopher reran the facts in his head, still listening and watching from where he was parked at the corner of the street. He could see it all, as though in one of those real-life police camera shows following the action from above. Shots had been fired, police radioed for help, and then one of Uncle Cecil's men had managed to slink away, unseen. But what of wily old Cecil? Had he been in the back of that Range Rover? No, the sly old fox would not leave his den and face the risk of being shot, or stopped in a car with armed men.

So his plan for Cecil tomorrow on the 12th July was not entirely scuppered, it just needed a bit of bailing out. Trying to get Cecil at the Cenotaph at Belfast City Hall, a place he could always be relied upon to make an appearance, was now out. Cecil would be on the lookout. Too risky to try to get in close, leave a bag and walk away. So what he needed was a little inside info. What was Uncle Cecil's plan for the day? If he knew where he would be at a certain point, Christopher could plant a bag bomb, and get away undetected before Cecil had a chance to spot him. He asked Daddy for some help, waited for over a minute in silence, but heard nothing.

Christopher started the engine, pulled the taxi out slowly and coasted across the entrance of his childhood street. One quick glance. Police vehicles, parked on the road and pavement halfway down. Cops in black riot gear everywhere, bristling with weapons, but the majority was definitely at his house. Then the taxi passed the corner and they were gone. Christopher cruised, thinking. He and John had not been compromised, but they could no longer stay in the house he had rented for them. It was just a few streets away from this action. Police rapped on doors, and probably sooner rather than later, they would rap on the right one.

He stopped outside the rented house he and John Fryer shared, got out and noticed there was a helicopter circling, low and close. He gave John Fryer a wee wave. He could not be sure, but by this time he would be awake, and if he heard the gunfire, John would be watching. Good. He needed him ready. Time for a shave and a haircut. They would take what they needed to make tomorrow a success and hide out. John's lock-up on the outskirts of west Belfast would be perfect tonight. When Christopher had gone there and broken off the lock on the door to collect John's taxi, it was obvious the place had been untouched for many years. All they needed was one more night. Later bonfires would burn across the city and if last night was anything to go on, the streets would be on fire too. But more was needed.

Tomorrow they would bring the refiner's fire, to Dempsey's men, to Uncle Cecil, to the whole maggot-eaten city. It would be enough to melt away the impurities of this place. And as Belfast collapsed, he would take to the hills, find the loot and move on. Maybe someplace hot, like Brazil. Somewhere he could make a new plan. This mission would be over, but he'd acquired a taste for the work, no, the art.

'*Suffer the little children who must come unto me,*' whispered Christopher, turning a cold smile to the warmth of the afternoon sun.

CHAPTER FIFTY-THREE

Sheen and Aoife had finally returned to Ladas Drive after the bloodbath in Bangor as daylight faded on the 11th of July. Paddy Laverty had now assumed temporary command of the investigation and was sitting in Irwin's padded leather chair in his office. Despite the upholstery, Sheen thought he looked decidedly uncomfortable. Sheen knew his type. The heavily moustached detective was a door rapper and a hound dog, not a manager. The pen went to his mouth, down again.

He tapped it on the desk and looked from Sheen to Aoife. His eyes were hard. Sheen had just finished telling him their theory, the short version. The carnage was not over yet. Christopher Moore and John Fryer were on a mission to bring chaos to the country, and their crimes had so far played on past events.

'You're telling me that Irwin bought all of this?' asked Paddy.

Sheen hesitated. He had to be careful. 'Not at first,' he replied.

'But he believed in it enough to sanction a raid on Christopher Moore's home address,' said Aoife.

'And what a great idea that was,' said Paddy.

Aoife did not respond.

Sheen kept going. 'If we had found them together, in possession of weapons, explosives, it would have been enough. It still can be,' said Sheen.

'And Cecil Moore's men obviously agreed. They went looking, too. It's not over, Paddy,' she said.

'Let me acquaint you with some new facts. About an hour ago, uniform were knocking the doors near the raid house where Irwin was killed, got no reply. They got in, place was empty but it's where they were. We found their bomb-making equipment, explosives and timers and the like, evidence that they had cut their hair from shavings on the bathroom floor. Fact one: our boys have flown the coop, and we were too late,' he said heavily.

'Yes, meaning we're a step behind them. Close enough to spook them into running. It makes them even more dangerous. They might bring their plans forward,' said Sheen.

Paddy waited, and then continued to speak, without acknowledging Sheen's point at all. 'Fact two: a man was attacked in his grocery shop off the Falls road earlier today. Had his face cut clean in two. Money was taken. I happen to believe there was a lot of money taken, though he said a few grand. He's a player, money manager for the 'RA, or used to be anyway. Seeing the connection?' said Paddy.

Sheen glanced at Aoife. This was news, and so far he could not see what Paddy was trying to paint for them. Aoife returned his look with a tight shake of her head. No idea.

Paddy kept talking. 'He told us that the man who attacked him and stole the money was none other than John Fryer. Said that Fryer had more or less confessed to Dempsey's killing, was off his mind, said he was owed money, his IRA pension. Dempsey told him so, but men who are about to die make up their own truths,' said Paddy.

Sheen could see where Paddy was taking this. Logical, but completely wrong. 'You think this is about money?' asked Sheen.

Paddy blinked, taking Sheen in with his tired-looking, watery eyes. 'Did they teach you nothing in the Met, Sheen? It's always about the money, or revenge, or fucking love,' he said.

Sheen felt his pulse treble. They were going to be warned off Fryer, or sent in the wrong direction. Paddy could not see the wood for the trees. 'With respect, this has nothing to do with money. Christopher left without touching Esther Moore's rings and jewellery. But he took the time to mutilate her body and write a message for us on her parlour wall. The money is not relevant,' he said.

Paddy was staring at him, his jaw clenched. Sheen sat back in his chair, steadied his breathing. He had been almost shouting. He was angry, but not just because Paddy was refusing to listen, because his reasoning sounded so solid.

'The money man on the Falls road stated that he was down just under five K. Meaning he was probably down ten times that, if not more. We are not talking about robbing some granny of her Giro. This is proper money, especially for those who have absolutely none,' he said. Another new card, something he did not understand.

Paddy read the question that must have been written on Sheen's face. He started to nod. 'Old-fashioned detective work, Sheen, the type that solves cases based on the facts, not based on theories, or feelings. Fryer just got out of the loony bin. The man has no bank account, no assets, nothing. Fryer is going to want to eat, no? And if I had just broken out, I would be planning to stay out, maybe even enjoy my time. Christopher Moore's bank statement tells its own tale,' said Paddy, sifting through a stack of printed pages on the desk and setting ten or more between Sheen and Aoife so they could read them.

'Our boy does not have a job, been living off the life insurance of his dead father. The money was transferred into his account after his mother was committed. Good sum, but as you can see, it's nearly gone,' he said.

Sheen flicked through the pages, Paddy was right. The numbers dwindled from a five-figure sum several years before to just over £150 by last week. All cash withdrawals, no credits.

'Those two facts tell me that money matters. Follow the money, find the motive. Next is revenge. Christopher Moore gives his grandmother a terrible death for reasons best clear in his own sick brain, but given that she was Cecil Moore's mother, and Christopher's late father married a Roman Catholic, I think we can safely say that she never sat him on her knee and fed him sweets. Former colleagues of Christopher's father confirmed his family disowned him long ago. Apparently he had to discharge his weapon once after taking his boy to the mother's house. That was the kind of welcome they got,' said Paddy.

'Christopher befriends John Fryer, makes a deal to bust him out, they go on the rampage, getting their revenge. Christopher kills Granny, Fryer wipes out Dempsey, who was the man that had him locked up there in the first place, and then they cash in their chips, and get their asses out of Dodge,' said Paddy. He glanced from Sheen to Aoife, nodding slowly, reading what was probably a look of shared revelation on their faces.

'Oh, you didn't know that? Aye, Dempsey was his CO on the street, and then had him locked away. Would piss me off,' he said. Sheen gritted his teeth, stared at Paddy, and Paddy held his gaze. It was tight reasoning, and under different circumstances, Sheen would have been the first to back him.

'That leaves us love, and so far, there has been precious little of that in Belfast of late,' said Paddy.

'There is more to this. It's not a revenge murder or robbery. They will hit again, probably bigger next time,' said Sheen.

'Hit who? There is nobody left to hit, Sheen. You need to wake up. It's over. Fryer's old comrades are all dead, so is Dempsey. We knocked on doors down St James and you know what? Most people there don't even remember him. The man's a nobody, forgotten. The Belfast Taxi Company hasn't even got a record of Fryer. The two of them have taken the money and disappeared, exactly as they had planned all along. And we will be damn lucky if we ever set eyes on the pair of them in Belfast again. The work you did connecting the two of them was good, but you were slow, they were fast, and so far, they have been smarter. So, before I draw a line under this, I'll ask you again, who are they going to hit? Where exactly can I find Fryer and Christopher Moore?'

Sheen's mind whirled. He could see something, skipping just beyond his vision, like flickering lights, and with them the answer that he needed. It was there for an instant, then gone. He did not reply.

'So what? Are you saying we just let them go?' asked Aoife.

'No, I am saying we do our best to catch them, but there is only so much we can put into this. We are stretched to capacity. Fryer has no passport. Christopher Moore would be foolish to try to use his. We have to assume they know we are looking for them. So we will set up a rota of checkpoints at well-used border crossings, as well as others known for smuggling. If they try to leave the country, they will go that way, or they will head for the docks and try to escape on a ferry to Scotland, maybe bribe their way on a container ship,' said Paddy.

'Sir, listen—' Aoife started, but he interrupted her abruptly.

'No! You listen, both of you. I want these bastards caught. Irwin Kirkcaldy was a decent man and a friend of mine. You will follow orders. Get yourselves down to the docks. Start looking for these clowns. Fortune might turn in your favour.'

Sheen was about to argue, but he swallowed it. It would make no difference. He stood up and left the room. Aoife too. He hoped Paddy was right about getting lucky, because Christopher and Fryer seemed to have the luck of the Devil himself.

CHAPTER FIFTY-FOUR

'Turn it off,' said Sheen.

Aoife pressed standby on the television remote. The screen went black, and the Operation Room in Ladas Drive PSNI station went deathly quiet. The news had started by reporting that Jim Dempsey's funeral was scheduled for tomorrow. He was to be buried in Milltown Cemetery's Republican Plot, next to his old comrade Bobby Sands. Huge crowds expected. It ended with Cecil Moore, released without charge by the PSNI. Sheen and Aoife knew why: Jackie Coyle had somehow managed to hang himself in police custody.

Moore had been speaking on an improvised stage next to a bonfire in lower Shankill, the community he had turned up to save from attack. An attack he had organised. He said he would stand shoulder to shoulder with his Protestant brethren, and that he would march on 12th July to join the new Orange protest camp near Twaddle Avenue in north Belfast. It was the place where those who had been denied the right to march their traditional route stood their ground, the apotheosis of loyalists under siege. And a good photo opportunity.

'Drink?' asked Aoife.

Sheen nodded and soon, Aoife handed him a polystyrene cup of black coffee. It would be too hot, too bitter, but that was too bad. Only he and Aoife remained, Paddy had gone to be with Irwin's widow. They had spent the afternoon and evening trying to spot Fryer and Christopher Moore at different entry points at Belfast docks. No joy, just a steady stream of mostly men, coming from Scotland.

'Thanks,' he said, looking at the crime scene photos pinned to his board, now attached to the Operation Room wall. 'We wasted our time this afternoon, you know,' he said.

'Paddy's the gaffer for now,' she said. Which was true, there was a chain of command.

Sheen blew on his drink, took a small sip, and winced. He needed a mental jolt, something to move his brain up a gear. In the briefing with Paddy earlier, he had come close to something, something that was going to help. No matter how much coffee he had downed at the docks today, it remained beyond his reach, a ship on the horizon, moving further away.

'Paddy's in charge, but Paddy is still wrong. This is not about money. It was never about money. Fryer could have been living in the lap of luxury up on Lincoln View with Dempsey if he had played the game,' said Sheen.

'We are talking about fifty thousand, maybe more. A man might think he isn't motivated by money until he finds a bag stuffed full of it. People change,' suggested Aoife.

Sheen shook his head. 'Paddy said himself, these two are a team, and I think he is right on that. Whatever they have planned,' said Sheen, moving over to the board and tapping the picture of the blood-painted words daubed on the wall of Esther Moore's parlour room, 'I think they plan to carry it out together. Something that will create total chaos,' said Sheen.

Aoife's phone started to ring. It was her smartphone, he noted, not the small Nokia. Aoife picked it up. A short conversation. She listened and then said, 'Yes, good news. Thanks for the fast turnaround. Bye.'

Sheen nodded to her. He wanted the news, anything good.

'That was the London lab. The blood on the cigarette end found at Dempsey's came back as a positive match for Fryer,' she said. Her eyes were twinkling, but Sheen only nodded and turned his attention to the board. It was good news, but no breakthrough. Now they knew for sure that Fryer had killed his former CO, but it brought them no closer to finding him, or Christopher Moore. He dragged a chair from the table and slumped into it, elbows resting on his knees. He stared at the evidence board. He was down, but not yet out. Aoife was looking at her phone.

'Trouble along the Peace Line in west Belfast, same as last night, plus in Ardoyne in north Belfast, and other places: Portadown, Lurgan, parts of Derry. It's spreading. Looks like Freeloader is partly to blame. Young people calling each other out, egging one another on,' said Aoife. She sounded tired too. 'Rioting, it's the age old Northern Irish pastime, a close second to the all-time favourite: killing each other and burying our dead. The past's played out year in and year out, but this year it is even worse,' she said.

Sheen could see the flickering lights again, but this time they were headstones, reflecting the morning sun as they drove past.

'What was that you just said?' asked Sheen.

'What, about rioting?' she started, but got no further as Sheen interrupted her.

'No, no, the other bit, burying the dead. You said the past is played out every year, and each year the past becomes the present?' said Sheen.

Aoife thought for a second, nodded, agreeing. 'Close enough,' she said.

'That's right, that is exactly right,' said Sheen. He stepped over and took a closer look at the photo of the substation, the partially visible graffiti, a chaos of contradictions, the A for Anarchy straddled over all. 'We've been looking out for these men, but our answer is behind us. In the past. Tomorrow Jim Dempsey will be buried in Milltown Cemetery, same place a loyalist once attacked and murdered mourners at another IRA funeral in 1988. He tried to take out the entire republican leadership in one go, all filmed by the world's media, remember?'

'Jesus,' said Aoife. He could hear the change in her voice, recognition replacing exasperation.

'Only this time, a funeral will not be attacked by some freelance loyalist,' said Sheen. He turned, looked her full in the face and he could feel the excitement pass between them, like high voltage jumping between live wire and raw steel.

'It will be John Fryer, Dempsey's friend and one of their own,' she said.

Sheen nodded. 'And tomorrow the past will march on

366

the streets of Belfast wearing Orange sashes, beating the tribal drums, commemorating Protestant sacrifices. Cecil Moore will be there. He just said so on telly,' said Sheen.

'And so will Christopher, ready to serve up the past with a new spin. Cecil's own blood is going to attack the Order and murder him. Oh my God, Sheen, we need to find them,' she said, starting to move.

Sheen raised a hand, she stopped, but her face told him she wanted an explanation. 'Half of Belfast is blacked out; a fair swathe of the city is fighting in the streets. Paddy told us that Fryer's old haunts in St James drew a blank, and no more leads came from the house in Bangor. They could be anywhere. So we wait. Let them break cover tomorrow. We know where they will go,' said Sheen.

'Paddy told us to watch the docks,' she said.

Sheen shook his head, hoping he looked assured, but what he was about to suggest was risky. A formal warning, suspension, possibly worse. Not only for his career, but Aoife's. He needed to be sure, and he hoped he was right. 'New orders. Tomorrow you will follow the Orange parade in Belfast. Cecil will be there. Find him and tail him. At some point he is going to draw his crackpot nephew like a wasp to meat. I will follow Dempsey's funeral. With any luck I will spot Fryer before they even enter the church,' said Sheen.

Aoife looked like she was standing on the edge of a high diving board being told to jump. 'Paddy will have our heads on spikes. We could work through the night, keep looking? We might get lucky,' she said, but her proposal lacked energy, and she looked tired.

'If we deliver Fryer and Christopher Moore tomorrow, we

can write our own tickets,' said Sheen. Which was probably true, but only one man mattered to him: John Fryer.

Aoife nodded. He had won her round. 'I'll call and make sure Ava is OK and then I am going home for some kip,' she said. 'Do you want a lift to your hotel?' she asked.

'Please,' he said, reaching for his jacket. Aoife raised her phone to her ear and walked into the corridor. Sheen looked over at Fryer's image on the board, his dark, blank eyes. Ade, the nurse from the Heights, had said Fryer had thought he was cursed, being chased by a monster or bogeyman from the dark.

'Hope you have a torch tonight. I don't want any bogeyman getting you before I do,' said Sheen quietly, to the empty room. He turned off the light, followed Aoife. *No, John Fryer*, thought Sheen, *you keep safe this night, mate, because tomorrow, as God is my witness, you answer to me.*

PART FOUR

BLOOD WILL BE BORN

CHAPTER FIFTY-FIVE

Belfast, Northern Ireland, present day
Monday 12th July

Fryer's throat burnt, the lock-up garage on the edge of Poleglass was heavy with the stale smell of many roll-ups. The blue smoke of his last still gently twisted in the air, illuminated by the internal light of the taxi where he sat. The rest of the room was thick with darkness. Fryer's fingers went to work again, and very soon another one was between his lips, dry and papery and set to flame. Fryer sucked in the cutting heat. He needed to be cool. He stretched his cramped leg out the open driver's door, but after only a few seconds he returned it to the illuminated cab. He did not want it in the dark.

Not for the first time he thought about his cell, its cold comforts and safety. He sipped water from a bottle. Felt good, but it would be even better to see his three pink bedtime pills lined up, and he would take them. He glanced at the kid in the rear-view, lying on the back seat. Fryer could see the blue glow of his mobile. The kid's fingers worked away.

'Belfast is burning, John. They are at each other's throats across the city, plus Derry, Larne, Newry, Carrickfergus. Everywhere! Government is talking about sending in the troops. It's happening, just like Daddy said. And this time people won't bring soldiers cups of tea on the street corners.' He started one of his laughing fits. Fryer winced, watched as the kid's legs twitched.

Fryer pinched his cigarette, flicked it out the door, and gripped the wheel. The kid was getting worse, by the hour. Fucking sick, sick enough to murder a dog. Fryer felt his pulse quicken at the thought of Cara, prostrate and bleeding. That dog would have made a great companion in the dark of this night. A good dog can warm the heart of a cold man. Fryer blotted out the broken sound of the kid's cackling and closed his eyes. He was walking Cara in the Falls Park, the breeze off the Black Mountain lifted his hair pleasantly as he cracked a sweat in the sunshine. The leather leash, tight in one of his hands, held the weight of Cara, huge and straining, but obedient. Ava, his granddaughter, held his other hand. She was swinging his arm a bit as she hurried to keep pace, chatting away. Fryer told her that there was buried treasure hidden in a well up the Black Mountain. Gems for his gem, and they were going to find them together.

'Shut up!' screamed Fryer. He slammed his open palm onto the dash. The light over the windscreen flickered. Brief and total darkness, then came back on. The kid stopped. Fryer glared at him in the mirror.

'Sorry,' he said. His face was wet with tears, eyes still

glassy. But he had stopped laughing. 'No need to scream at me like that. Lose you temper and lose the argument, that's what my daddy—' he said.

'I'm not arguing, kid. And I don't fucking care what your daddy said either,' said Fryer. The kid said nothing. The blue glow from his phone winked out. The back of the cab was in darkness. Time passed. Fryer thought the kid had fallen asleep and when he spoke, his words were a slow slur.

'Tomorrow seal deal, John. Dirty job, has be done, suffer lil children, God's work, suffer lil . . .' The kid went quiet. He was gone. Fryer reached for his smokes, rolled one and then one more, stocked up.

Two hours later, the kid was still asleep. His breathing low and steady. No talk from him tonight. Fryer shifted his weight and removed the handcuffs and razor from his back pocket. He had lifted the cuffs from the armoury before he picked up the two backpacks and makings for the bombs they would use tomorrow. The blade was stained with the accountant's blood. He set both on the seat beside him, sniffed the air. No sign of the Moley, but if it came blood would flow, though not from his veins, not any more. Yes, Fryer would complete the mission. When the kid told him how the plan had changed, that there would be no coming home, it had been a relief. He had nothing to live for, and nothing to lose. But the kid was not his friend. He had killed the dog and, if need be, his blood would be shed.

'He will feed you if you come for me,' whispered Fryer. His eyes were full and shining. His thoughts returned to Cara, and Ava, and he did not fight it. The wind was gusting, fresh as sea foam off the Black Mountain. He let Cara off the leash, watched her sprint into a pool of black crows, who took to noisy flight, and Ava laughed and asked him to show her the buried treasure.

CHAPTER FIFTY-SIX

Cecil popped two ibuprofens into his palm from the foil-backed sheet. He was shaking ever so lightly. He waited a second, and then mouthed them, washing the tablets down with a full pint of cold water that was on his bedside dresser. The savage pounding coming from the sides and back of his head was momentarily superseded by a new spike of pain as the cool water froze his brain. He growled, blinking it away, leaving him with the deafening beat of his hangover headache throbbing like a red alert in a nuclear power plant.

He exhaled slowly, tasting the booze from his sinuses. It had turned into a good night of it after he torched the bonfire on the Shankill. Drinks a plenty round the fire, back to a house party, rum and coke well into the wee hours, then just straight rum shots. Finally, just coke. He chuckled dryly at that joke, and then abruptly stopped, a moan escaped him. Jesus fucking Christ his head was pounding. His heart was bunny-kicking intermittently, and his stomach felt the size of a snooker ball, and as hard. No point attempting breakfast, not yet. It would never stay down, and he was just about to put on his Boss suit.

He hesitated, popped free two paracetamol from another foil sheet in his open drawer. Swallowed them dry. His gut protested, but it stayed firm. Soon enough this would take the edge off things. By the time he got up to the protest camp at Twaddle he would have had a feed and be ready for a drink. And there would be one waiting for him up there. Oh yes, they had already texted him their thanks for what he had said in front of the cameras last night.

Cecil reached once more into his drawer and took out eye drops, put his head back and let the cold droplets fall into first one open eye and then the other. He blinked away the crocodile tears before standing up to face his reflection in the dresser mirror. Not great, but soon he'd look well. He reached for the hanger next to where his Boss was waiting and carefully inspected the Orange sash hanging there. The bright orange was bordered with purple silk, gold tassels draped along the edge of its outer V. On one lapel was the number of his Loyal Orange Lodge (LOL) in Tiger's Bay and on the other a purple patch with 'Sons of the Reformation' embroidered in orange letters. Literally, this was the sash his father wore and his before him. Cecil had believed he would never have the privilege of passing it on in the same way, but the way things were moving these days, sure you never knew. Some traditions would always be sacred; the rest, like so much in this world, were open to negotiation. Or, more precisely, subject to manipulation, in Cecil's experience.

He swished open his bedroom curtains and dull light filled the room. The drum in his head produced a massive wallop at this intrusion. He gritted his teeth, took the pain. He could hear the sounds of gradual awakening from the other rooms – his boys from Glasgow. A flushing toilet, chests being cleared loudly, mumbled mornings. Cecil was always the first man to rise, and you could put your money on it that he would be the last man standing. No tout had ever lived long enough to put Cecil Moore away, no Fenian had ever bested him, no peeler or spook had ever owned him.

Movement on the street below. Cecil squinted, trying to see. The black cat he had seen slip under the parked car yesterday was tapping at a carton of double cream the milkman had left. It rocked on its base, and then steadied. Cecil smiled. He thought about the Turk's man, Jackie Coyle, found hanged in his cell, and he turned his mind to what was in store for the very headstrong DC Aoife McCusker. The cat clawed the top of the cream, sending the plastic lid flying and the carton rolled on its side across the pavement, its contents spewing, thick and white as paint. Cecil started to laugh, watching him get the cream, despite his mother, the news about Nelson, and that Fenian nephew of his, who was still out there. Sometimes, you just had to have a laugh.

CHAPTER FIFTY-SEVEN

Sheen rose early on Monday 12th July and spent half an hour in his hotel room, watching the news. It was all bad: fierce rioting across Northern Ireland throughout the night, some of it still carrying on; a Catholic pensioner attacked in her home in Londonderry, her throat cut. A copycat of Esther Moore in Belfast, but this time they robbed the woman. Police stretched to capacity, talk of bringing in the Army as a support, outcry from politicians, but, as usual, no answers.

By the time he went down to the hotel lobby the breakfast buffet was set up in the darkened bar, its beer pumps turned inward. Sheen ordered a full cooked breakfast but the now-predictable fayre of the Ulster Fry turned his stomach, and he settled for a black coffee. Outside a slow stream of men and women, some wearing Orange sashes, passed by. Families too. Sheen shuddered at the sight of the children. Paddy's reluctance to listen to reason was putting innocent people at risk. Even with a coordinated police effort, finding Christopher and Fryer would be difficult. As it stood, it was down to him and Aoife, two on two.

His phone buzzed. Aoife, a message:

Outside, you ready?

Sheen exited the breakfast room and pulled open the thick glass door. The chilly air instantly wrapped him in an unwelcome embrace. The sky was a uniform, gunship grey, a cold rain half-heartedly spitting. Headlights flashed him, to his right. Sheen walked over and climbed into the passenger seat, slamming the door against the buffering wind.

'Morning,' she said. Her hair was pinned back off her face, revealing the arc of her nose, her high, proud cheekbones. She was dressed in a black waterproof jacket, dark blue jeans.

'You still OK with what we discussed last night?' he asked.

'Our jobs, which will be the least of our concerns if the shooting starts. But yeah, I'm ready,' she said and started to drive, heading west where she would drop Sheen off as close to Dempsey's funeral as she could. Aoife would return to the city centre and find Cecil Moore.

The Orange Order from the nine districts of Belfast was scheduled to assemble at 10 a.m. at the Grand Orange Hall, near Carlisle Circus, to the north-west of the city. The Order would march to Belfast City Hall, pay their respects at the Cenotaph and carry on to an open space in the south of the city for a day of festivities. Aoife would join the main parade at City Hall and look for Cecil Moore and his men. Find Cecil, and she would find Christopher. There would be thousands of people on the streets, and she would need to be lucky, but it was a starting point.

If the main parade drew a blank, they at least knew that Cecil had promised on television to join the Orange protesters in north Belfast near Twaddle Avenue, banned from walking their traditional route. That was where she would go next. Her timing needed to be good, and she needed to be careful. There was no easy way to hide in plain view like in the city centre. She'd have to hold back until she had eyes on Christopher Moore. Her window to act would be small, and it would be dangerous. Pulling a gun on Christopher with Cecil Moore close by could mean a firefight on two fronts. One shot, clean and true, as soon as she saw Christopher and deemed him to be a threat to life.

'You remember what we agreed, Sheen? If you spot Fryer you make the call, wait for backup. You are probably the only unarmed copper in Belfast, and you will definitely be one of the few people at that funeral who are not packing. Most of the stewards will have legally held firearms and, believe me, they have experience using them. And Fryer won't turn up to a gunfight with a knife,' she said.

'I'll make the call,' said Sheen. He resisted the urge to wind down the window or look away, sure she would see the rage in his eyes, the same way the nurse had read him so easily in Jamie Anderson's hospital room.

'And?' she asked.

'Then I'll duck and cover until the action is over,' he said.

'Good man. The Serious Historical Offences Team will need you fit and well next week,' she said. She had pulled up on the Glen road in west Belfast. Sheen judged it to be less than half a mile from the Holy Spirit Church where

Dempsey's funeral Mass would take place, based on the online map he had studied the night before. The pavements were clogged with people, all headed up the hill, same as him. 'Best that I drop you here. I don't want to get stuck in traffic going back into town,' she said.

'Listen, Aoife, the same goes for you. Be careful, I mean. If you see him, and you think there is danger, don't hesitate. Take the shot,' he said, opening his door.

'I can't just shoot Cecil Moore,' she said, then stopped abruptly, started to chew her bottom lip.

Sheen shook his head, unsure how they had arrived at this place. Aoife's neck and face, he noticed, had flushed a deep scarlet. 'You mean Christopher Moore?' he said.

She nodded, with a smile fixed on her face. She reached inside her jacket pocket and took out her phone, then quickly replaced it without checking it. It was an involuntary movement, the same thing that she had been doing on and off most of the previous day, with one exception. The phone she was constantly checking yesterday was the Nokia. It was the sort of model that he had seen used in London as a throwaway or burner. Impossible to trace and good for secrecy. And the last name on her lips had been Cecil Moore.

'Aoife, has Cecil got something—' but before he could ask her what he had on her, she interrupted him, smile gone.

'You just make sure you make the call and keep your head down,' she countered. 'If you play it right, Fryer can be taken alive, questioned properly. He will answer for everything he has done. That's what you want, right?' she said.

Sheen held her gaze, and then broke it. He felt his stomach heat like a griddle. So she knew. It should not have been a surprise really. But did she know that he had willed for his dad to die in the end, so his bond would be broken and he could come here, all for the bloody lust for revenge?

'I want to catch these maniacs, bring them to justice, before they have a chance to murder again,' said Sheen quietly. He was staring at his hands, balled into fists on his lap.

She opened the glove compartment and withdrew something fixed on a thin silver chain. 'Take this, Sheen. I am not much of a believer these days, but any port of call today. Plus, I can't give you a gun,' she said. It was a matchbox-sized rectangle of worn leather, a cross printed on one side, and an incantation on the other: 'Be gone infernal powers of darkness . . .' She dropped it into his now-open palm. 'It's the Brief of St Anthony, patron of lost things,' she said.

'You calling me a lost cause?' said Sheen.

'Aye, now off you go,' she replied, her mouth close enough to kiss. She touched his other hand and his fist relaxed. Sheen shifted the small talisman from his left to his right so he could open the door, taking care not to drop the icon as he stepped out into the wind.

CHAPTER FIFTY-EIGHT

Christopher awoke with a start from a dream in which he was drowning in the cold sea off Bangor pier. Bad Daddy, or John Fryer, or perhaps both had been there. They laughed and did not help him. Daddy had a noose round his neck, called his name:

CHRISSSSSSSSSTOPHER

'Christopher. Hey boy! You hear me?' It was John Fryer's voice. Christopher looked around. He was in the back of the black taxi, limbs stiff with cold. John had an unlit roll-up between his lips. It fluttered like the tail of a mouse in a snake's mouth. Weak light had seeped in, from beyond the lock-up's still closed door. The day, their day, had arrived. A momentary pang of regret followed on the heels of his excitement. This was soon to be all over. And after their bombs exploded today, who would know the truth, especially about the Culturlann? Only Daddy and he knew that secret, and Daddy had gone very quiet indeed. People may manage to work out the rest, but that last, glorious event might never be truly appreciated. Some might even wrongly assume that it was all John Fryer's doing. Christopher eased himself out of the seat. Pins and needles buzzed in his right foot.

'About time. It's well past nine,' said Fryer. He jerked his head and walked to the front of the taxi. Christopher followed.

'The backpacks are primed, kid, set to blow for 2 p.m., but those timers, they were never the best and now they are a lot older,' said Fryer.

Christopher nodded, but his mind was elsewhere. His mind was on the keys for the padlocks he had bought. He had planned to get up a bit earlier, get to them, pocket one. 'Need to relieve myself, John,' he said, and walked to the bucket in the corner.

He scanned the open boot of the taxi, spotted the two fat padlocks. They both had a set of three silver keys, two of which were on a thin wire hoop and the third inserted into the lock itself. Christopher plucked the keys from one of the padlocks and, as he made his morning water, he slid one of the keys round the circumference of its wire hoop, popped it free. This would be the way out. He pushed it deep into the small pocket at the front of his jeans. He finished at the bucket and returned the remaining keys on the hoop to its padlock. John Fryer looked round the back of the taxi just as he did so, took the now-smouldering butt from his lips and made a thick rattling cough, and spat on the concrete floor.

'Come on, you,' he said. A pause, as John's eyes searched his face.

384

'Just getting these,' he said, holding up the padlocks. His voice was calm, but his heart was not.

'Aye, hurry up,' growled Fryer.

Christopher scooped up the locks and made his way round to the front of the taxi. John slipped on one of the backpacks. They were heavy with nails and bolts. John had the bag on his chest, so the straps were slung over his back and shoulders. The best way for them to carry the bombs. John Fryer was going to drive, and Christopher would be seated in the wheelchair after John dropped him off. The information on Uncle Cecil's plan for the 12th had come straight from the man himself, courtesy of a news bulletin the night before. Cecil's plan for a show of solidarity at the protest camp at Twaddle was the answer. They knew where he would be and when he was due to arrive. The wheelchair and the Union flag would be a perfect cover as he waited. With the padlock key in his pocket, he would be able to free himself and leave the bomb. Now it was time to make sure that John Fryer could not.

Christopher pocketed the padlock that would be opened by the spare key, kept hold of the second and went behind John and pulled the straps together over the hillock of John's shoulders. He fed it through a thick plastic hoop secured with nylon stitching, and then did the same for the second. He snapped the U latch closed, pulled the keys from the lock. The straps were fully extended, and stretched tightly into the holding point of the lock the centre of Fryer's back. No wriggle room; no way he would be able to squeeze his head out, should he want to.

Christopher removed the second padlock from his pocket, and put both sets of keys on the roof of the taxi.

One set had three silver keys, one set had just two. He placed the padlock beside them and gingerly lifted his pack, slowly manoeuvred it over his chest, bag facing front. He nodded to John Fryer and turned. This was it, the moment when he would discover if his plan would work. Christopher took a giant breath of air and held it, the better to create a little more slack between the secured bag and his body. It should be enough to allow him to reach round and get to the padlock when the time came. He felt the straps pull and tighten over the front of his shoulders and John Fryer's breath on the back of his neck. He heard him lift the padlock off the roof of the taxi, then felt him feed it through. There was one last pull on the straps and the click of the hasp being locked. Christopher let his lungs deflate very slowly. From the corner of his eye he could still see the keys bunched on the roof of the taxi. Fryer was silent. Christopher waited. Fryer's hand would slowly pick up the keys and he would ask him, quietly, full of knowing slyness, where's the third key?

'That's you, kid,' he said, and Christopher felt a sharp tug as he pulled the lock. Christopher winced as the primed bomb rocked on his chest. He turned round and took both sets of keys off the roof of the taxi in one quick movement. John Fryer did not suspect a thing. He walked back to the slops bucket, turned and made sure John was looking and chucked the keys into it with a splash.

'Won't need these, John,' he said. He felt the padlock against his back, lower than where he had placed Fryer's. It would be easy to use the spare key.

John Fryer pulled on his tracksuit top. It covered the padlock at his back, but of course he could not zip it up.

The bag looked a bit out of place hanging on his chest, but not really suspicious. There were enough tourists on the streets of Belfast these days looking a heck of a lot worse. Christopher could see it now: John Fryer getting himself up close to where Dempsey's coffin approached the grave, maybe as it was being lowered into the red clay of Milltown Cemetery. Then John Fryer would start shooting. Oh yes, they would chase him, but if he got his timing right, they would chase him to Hell. Let a hundred people set upon him; when that pack exploded they would all be blown away. Welcome to ground zero Belfast, part one.

Fryer walked over and pulled open the steel door. Christopher shielded his eyes as pale white light filled the garage. John Fryer got into the taxi, started the engine. Blue, oily smoke churned from its rattling exhaust.

'I'll drop you on the Crumlin road, kid. There's an industrial estate about two hundred metres down from the corner at Twaddle Avenue. With a bit of luck someone will take pity on you and wheel you right inside. I'd take your time. Arrive too early, questions will be asked. Arrive too late,' Fryer shrugged, and for the first time since Christopher had met him John Fryer laughed, a dry chuckle, but not without some warmth. Christopher smiled, laughed with him, not one of his fits. Reminded Christopher of the first real joke he had shared with his daddy, the one about the man with a dog. Someone asks him if they are Jack Russell's? No, says the man, the dogs are mine. How his daddy had laughed – a real laugh, not faking it. It had felt exactly like this. Christopher looked at Fryer, so soon to expire. Surely, there could be no harm in telling him about the Culturlann, not at this stage with a bomb on his chest? He was prepared to make the ultimate sacrifice, no qualms. Plus, if Christopher didn't talk to Fryer, there would be no one else he could ever tell. He mentally called for his daddy, asked him if he should. There was no response. Christopher stood his ground, waited until John Fryer leant on the horn. He walked over and got in the passenger seat.

'Let's go, Daddy O,' said Christopher.

Fryer looked at him sourly and stuck it into first gear. The sky was monochrome grey and threatening rain, but Christopher's heart was sunshine. When the laughing spasm started, he did not even try to stop, despite John Fryer's insistence that he shut the fuck up.

CHAPTER FIFTY-NINE

Sheen joined the crowd of mourners, eyes open, on the hunt for John Fryer. Question was, would he be able to pick Fryer out, aged, and probably in disguise? Above him, seeming close enough to touch, low cloud moved stealthily over the top of the Black Mountain, not quite reaching the words printed out in plastic sheets. He had seen a message printed there on his first morning in Belfast, but now it had changed, keeping up with the times. VIVA GAZA had been replaced. Instead, it now read: RIP COMRADE DEMPSEY.

Sheen turned into the grounds of Holy Spirit, found a raised standing position, the doors of the church and entrance of the car park in clear view. The numbers continued to increase. It was like a crowded tube platform. He felt his personal space close up, gentle nudges from both sides as others shuffled to make space for new bodies. From behind him, the sound of a car door latching open, and then thudding closed.

The memory was suddenly in his mind, visceral and clear. The sound was the key that opened the lock. A car door opening and slamming closed, but this one in Sailortown years before, followed by the sound of feet running off. In the church grounds, the crunch of feet on the gravel, as the person who had just closed the car door (or, perhaps, it was a black taxi, one that had been parked and he had not noticed?) now approached. Sheen held his breath, waiting. Any second now, the owner of those feet would come up beside him and it was going to be John Fryer, but not as he looked today. He would be young, his hair still glossy and dark, the same man who had left the car bomb ticking while children played in the street. Sheen would turn and look him in the eye and he would know, with absolute certainty.

'All right, mate,' said a voice. It was an old man, not a young one, soft red features and wet eyes. He was wearing a tan-coloured raincoat, buttoned and belted, the smell of recently extinguished tobacco mixed with a stronger waft of mothballs hung around him. Sheen nodded, unsure of how best to respond. A London accent could attract attention, questions. The car park was almost full, and Sheen could hear the approaching sound of pipes playing, followed by a hushing down from the mourners. Hats came off heads. Dempsey's body was about to arrive. It was time to honour Ireland's dead.

'We were daft to have thought we'd put this sort of thing behind us. The past haunts us here, mate. Too many skeletons in the cupboard,' he said in a whisper, the high, hospital smell of mothballs wafting at Sheen with the words.

'Aye,' whispered Sheen in return with a nod. The man was right.

The funeral cortège had now turned into the narrow entrance gates. Dempsey's coffin, draped in an Irish tricolour flag, was balanced on the shoulders of six men, three on each side. He recognised the two who were walking at the front of the coffin. Most people would: leading republican figures, household names in Ireland, Britain and beyond. Photographers, laden with cameras and bags padded quietly to preferred vantage points, snapping hungrily. They wanted the picture which would paint a story of where the Peace Process had come to over the 12th July. Sheen scanned the faces of the mourners as all eyes locked on the coffin. No John Fryer.

Overhead, he became aware of the rattle and growl of a helicopter and, glancing up, he saw it move in a wide circle above them watching, probably snapping photographs of its own.

The coffin had stopped at the steps of the church where a priest had emerged from inside the open double doors, flanked by two kids, a girl and boy, both dressed in white robes. From within, Sheen heard the muted sound of an organ playing. He ran his eyes back and forth over the faces now forming a line behind the coffin. No alarm bells went off. He stepped aside to let the man in the tan trench coat get through. The photographers headed for the gate. They knew where the real action was going to take place, where Dempsey's body would be lowered into the ground, perhaps to the stiff applause of a volley of rifle fire.

The grainy film footage Sheen had once seen of the loyalist killer, shooting at mourners in Milltown Cemetery, played briefly in his mind. Stone had been trying to get away, headed for the M1 motorway where a van at first waited, then drove off, leaving him to his fate. All filmed by the world's media, who would also be present today.

If Fryer was going to appear, Sheen would find him at Milltown. He still had time, but he needed to get there quickly. Walking was not an option. He took out his phone, scrolled through the contacts until he found the name he was looking for, pressed it, and walked away from the church entrance, willing Gerard, the taxi man, to pick up. At last, he did.

'Gerard, I was wondering if you wanted to earn an extra few bob this afternoon?' Gerard paused for a beat before replying that he was interested. Sheen quickly summarised where he was and where he wanted Gerard to take him. He quoted a price, what he hoped would be generous money in any man's terms.

'And I am going to need you to wait for me, on the hard shoulder of the M1. That's where you'll drop me so I can access Milltown from the rear,' said Sheen. He held his breath, waiting for Gerard to back-pedal, tell him it was too risky, thanks but no thanks.

'I will be with you in twenty, agreed?' said Gerard.

Agreed.

CHAPTER SIXTY

Fryer had barked at the kid to shut up, but he had kept laughing, all the way from Poleglass. They had driven down the M1, avoided west Belfast. As he drove past the back of Milltown Cemetery, he slowed and scanned the area. This was going to be his access point. A helicopter rattled overhead, probably tracking Dempsey's funeral on its way down the road. Fryer's eyes locked on something and his jaw clenched.

There was a car parked on the verge of the motorway just ahead. Hazard lights on, taxi sign on the roof. It was the exact spot he planned to use. And now there was a car waiting where none had any business to be. He passed the taxi, shot a glance inside, but it was empty, and then he saw its bonnet was open, a man half concealed with his head in the engine, legs visible. Fryer's eyes followed the broken path into the cemetery until he focused on what he knew he would find. One odd man stood out, closer to the motorway, his back to the granite cemetery wall, wearing a tan jacket. The man watched the cemetery, scanned the motorway, and for a millisecond, Fryer and he locked eyes over the distance.

'Shit,' he hissed. The taxi was obviously a decoy. The man in the cemetery was Special Branch, maybe undercover army. Either way, his plan was fucked, and he would need to think of another way in. He could feel his heart hammering in his chest, the bomb bag suddenly too tight and too heavy. He reached for one of his pre-rolled smokes and sparked it up, sucked deeply. His heart mellowed a bit. Fryer glanced at the kid. The laughing had stopped, but his eyes were gleaming. The fake taxi, the two undercover guys – this was unexpected, but not insurmountable. Question was, how did they find out?

'You all right, John?' said the kid.

Fryer switched his attention back to him. 'Dead on, kid,' he said.

The kid started to fidget, and talk to himself, quickly and quietly, like a man in a trance. Fryer sighed, drove on, listened to the whispering patter of the kid's voice beside him as he passed Grosvenor Road, Divis Street and the bottom of the Falls, then Peter's Hill and the Shankill before coming off at Clifton Street and turning left up the Crumlin road. The kid had stopped talking. They sat in silence.

Fryer saw the entrance to the industrial estate on his right and pulled in. It offered them a secluded inlet. He stopped the taxi, got out and kept his head down as he got the wheelchair out and unfolded it. The kid went to the boot, took his Daddy's Ruger pistol and unfurled the Union Jack flag. He sat down slowly in the wheelchair, concealed the gun beneath the flag draped over his lap. Looked OK, nothing too suspicious. His shaved head made Fryer think of a cancer patient.

'We walk from here. I'll get you as close to the camp as I can,' said Fryer, pushing the wheelchair up the entrance ramp of the industrial estate and out onto the Crumlin road. The day had started to brighten, sunshine breaking through the low cloud. The kid glanced up at him, serious. Fryer caught a glimmer of something in his eyes, initially saw fear, but quickly placed it as something else: indecision. The kid wanted to tell him something. He thought of the decoy taxi, and the man who watched and waited at Milltown.

'You haven't been talking to anyone, like to one of your da's old mates, have you?' said Fryer, still pushing, but slower now. As he walked, the pieces fell into line, events he'd failed to question. His heart had been ruling his head after losing his chance with Ava. The peelers had done some fast work in finding the kid's family home. And the kid had been out and about on Sunday morning, Saturday afternoon too now he thought about it.

'The only person I talk to is Daddy,' he said.

'Don't fuck me around, kid. If there is something I need to know, I need to know it now. Partners, right?' he said. The kid stayed silent, the wheels of chair squeaked in time. Now he could hear the faint sound of music, the protest camp. Fryer stopped, rested his weight on the handles.

'I've asked Daddy if it is OK to tell you, John, but he has not got back to me,' he said quietly.

Fryer's fists tightened on the handles. This was it. The kid knew something. Maybe the peelers had been on to them

395

all along. Maybe the whole thing was a set-up. Maybe he'd been a stooge doing MI5's dirty work by killing Dempsey.

'This is goodbye. Talk to me,' he said. 'Who else will know the whole story, after we are gone? The glorious things we will set in motion?' he said. *Come on kid*, he thought, *spit it out.*

'John, there's another bomb. A final spectacular that will really set the night on fire,' he said.

Fryer's mind swerved to keep up. Not what he saw coming. The kid started to laugh. He kept repeating 'set the night on fire', again and again between fits of hysterics. Fryer could feel the wheelchair rock against his grip. 'Kid! Be cool. Fuck's sake, tell me what you know,' he said.

The kid sobered up but made no sense. 'Suffer the little children, John. It is God's will. Daddy told me so,' he said, then broke off into a high peel of giggling. It was like a wild dog, not a man. That phrase, the one about suffering children, the kid had said it last night. A firebomb, on children. Fryer let go of the handles of the chair and walked round so he could see the kid. He had a thick stream of snot running from one of his nostrils, his eyes deranged and full of confusion. Fryer pulled hard on the bomb bag, almost dragging the kid from his seat. But he already knew the answer to his question even as he growled it, his face pressed into Christopher's.

'Where did you put the bomb?' he said. The kid's eyes widened, and then, of course, the laughing started, but not before he spoke one more word, the worst word Fryer had ever heard.

'Culturlann,' he said.

Fryer let him go, stepped back and swung his right

arm in a tight, vicious arc. His elbow connected with Christopher's jaw. Fryer felt it splinter, and the kid's head jackknifed with elastic energy, left to right, and returned to rest on the bomb bag. His jaw hung open at a crazy angle, his eyes were rolled back in his head. Fryer grabbed the handles of the wheelchair, turned it and pushed it back inside the entrance of the industrial estate, vaguely aware that his arm had opened, hot blood from elbow to wrist. He dug into his back pocket, felt the cuffs, pulled them free, and latched one round the kid's wrist and clicked it tight. He locked its pair to the metal arm of the wheelchair.

He checked his watch. It had gone 11.30 a.m. Dempsey's funeral would be at the cemetery gates, but Fryer was not interested. It would take him twenty minutes to get to the Culturlann, and Ava. He got into the taxi, breathing like a beast, and took off. Fryer cursed and cried, and repeated the same thing again and again, as he drove like a man possessed, 'I will save you, I will save you, I will save you.'

CHAPTER SIXTY-ONE

At the same moment Christopher Moore dropped the spare keys for the padlocks into the slops bucket, Aoife spotted Cecil and his men during the wreath laying at the City Hall Cenotaph. Cecil had positioned himself close to the ceremony where the television cameras could pick him out. When the main body of the parade started moving south, Cecil and his men did not follow them. They slowly started north, and then veered west. She had kept her distance, and at the bottom of the Shankill road she lost them, spent twenty minutes wandering up and down between Peter's Hill and North Street, almost walked straight into them as they left a greasy spoon cafe, lively conversation in full flow.

Aoife ducked into a doorway, pretended to be on her phone. She heard them pass, and sneaked a look as they walked off. Cecil Moore was with two of his Glasgow pals she had seen at the Bad Bet and one younger man, bigger set, probably the bodyguard. Cecil was holding their attention as they marched off. The bodyguard watched the road, the others watched Cecil. They stopped. As Cecil delivered his punchline, rough laughter erupted from his companions. If Cecil was mourning his dead mother, or saddened by the loss of his henchman, Nelson, he was hiding it well.

Her phone lit up. A message from Sheen. He had left Dempsey's funeral, had gone ahead to Milltown. She was in the process of replying, looked up at the sound of a vehicle stopping. A black taxi, red taillights aflame, had halted a little further up. Cecil and his group got in. The taxi's engine laboured to life and it drove off without indicating, away from her and up the Shankill road.

Aoife pocketed her phone and quickly legged it across the road, searching the oncoming traffic for another taxi, or a bus, seeing neither. She turned and squinted after Cecil's taxi but it was gone. She'd lost him. Aoife started walking, then stopped, better to think. He could be going anywhere, but chances were Cecil was going to follow the Shankill up to Woodvale, then all the way down to the junction of the Crumlin road and Twaddle, where the Orange protesters waited. He had promised as much on the news last night. All she needed to do was head him off.

A taxi approached, one free space. She stuck out her thumb, and the driver slowed abruptly, and stopped to let her in – her lucky day. Progress up the Shankill road was slow, the drone of the taxi's engine competing with a crying infant beside her. Almost half an hour had passed by the time she paid the driver and got out, then walked the short distance along the Ballygomartin road to get to the junction with Twaddle Avenue. The Orange protesters were about five hundred metres away and, sure enough, there were Cecil and his cronies, about a further fifty metres ahead of her, walking and talking. Aoife slowed down, pulled out her phone. Sheen needed the update.

Five missed calls: two from Paddy Laverty, three from Marie, plus a text. She had not heard her phone beneath the din of the taxi journey.

CALL ME NOW!

Aoife stopped, staring at the three words, her heart a ball of lead on a rubber band, falling away into her gut, her mouth sandpaper dry. Something bad had happened. She stabbed at Marie's name on her call list, missed it, nearly dropped the phone, pulled it into her chest and managed to make the call, holding the phone to her ear, listening to it ring as Cecil and his group marched further ahead. Marie's voice, wild and urgent; behind it, outdoor sounds of shouting, disorder.

'Aoife! Aoife!' she said, panicked. Aoife's heart rebounded on its rubber band, walloping back up in her chest.

'Where's Ava!' she screamed.

'He shot that man. He shot that policeman. I think he's dead. There was a big explosion. The place is on fire. Everything is burning,' said Marie. She was speaking without pause, a flow of babbling panic, clothed in tears, her breath hitching and sobbing loudly into Aoife's ear. Aoife gritted her teeth, felt her fingers dig into her palm as she clenched her fist, struggling to retain control.

'Breathe. Answer my questions. Where is Ava?' she asked. Sobbing from the phone, gasping. Jesus was Ava dead? Then, at last, Marie spoke.

'A man took her. He has her,' said Marie.

Aoife uttered a high-pitched yelp, and then jammed her knuckles into her mouth, biting down hard, focusing on the clasping pain. 'The Culturlann's burning. Ava's gone,' she said. Aoife's head was racing. She closed her eyes, piecing together the fragments Marie had managed to relay. A bomb, a policeman shot, Ava kidnapped? It did not make sense. And that place was full of kids. Marie said it was in flames.

'Marie, where did this man go? Where did he take Ava?' she asked. Her baby girl, it was all that mattered. God forgive her, even if every other child was killed, Ava was all that mattered to her. Marie did not reply directly. Her voice had slowed now. Aoife could hear the flatness of severe shock taking control.

'They said that he just walked in. He was looking for Ava, was calling her name. He knew who she was,' said Marie.

'What do you mean, he knew her? Who was he, Marie? Where did he go? Speak to me,' she said, marvelling at the steadiness of her own voice.

'He shoved her into a black taxi and then drove it off, up the Falls road. He said he was her granda, kept shouting he was her granda,' said Marie.

'A black taxi? Was he on his own, this man, or was he with someone?' asked Aoife, but Marie said nothing. It was all she was going to get from her. Aoife killed the call, turned and started to run back in the direction she had just come. She'd done twenty steps then stopped.

Where was she running to? The Falls? It was three, maybe four, miles away and she had no car. Sheen. She pressed his number. He answered on the first ring. No time for long explanations.

'Sheen, I think John Fryer has just kidnapped Ava from the Culturlann. It's on the Falls road. There was an explosion. I can give you directions. Please go, I'm too far away,' she said. There was a three second pause, Marie's final words buzzing like a fat blue bottle in her brain. He said he was her granda, said he was her granda, said he was her granda.

'I heard it, and I can see smoke. I'll find it. I have wheels,' he said, thankfully without bombarding her with more questions. She shouted to him go. Another pause, sounds of Sheen running, his voice strained. 'Sure it was Fryer?' he asked. She thought about what Marie had said: the black taxi the man was driving, the fact there had been an explosion, a police officer gunned down, but most of all she saw Ava's photo on Jim Dempsey's fridge, and remembered her foreboding and inexplicable rage.

'Yes, it was him. I don't know why,' she said.

He said he was her granda.

'Get that bastard and save my little girl,' she said. The sharp crack of a gunshot broke her sentence off. She could see a commotion, close to the Orange protest camp. Aoife started to run, phone held in her fist as her arms pumped at her sides. She should be running to save Ava, but she was not, she was running into certain trouble, yet again too late, too slow. She could see Cecil and his men running too, ahead of her. She pulled her gun out, increased her speed. She was scared, more frightened than she had ever been, but it was not the gunfire that terrified her. She wanted to reach it, to find the danger, claim it. *Dear God, please take me. If someone has to die, please take me, not her, please not Ava.*

CHAPTER SIXTY-TWO

A shear saw blade of pain sliced its way into Christopher's mind, extracted him to an awful wakefulness. He swallowed. The saw sliced again. He did not want to open his eyes. He could taste blood. He heard a sound, a wave breaking on the Bangor shore. Followed it as it faded, let himself go under cold water. Then the hiss of the wave changed. He jolted.

SSSSSSSSSSSSSSSSSSTOPHER.

Bad Daddy's voice. This time Christopher opened his eyes and cried out in agony. Oh God, his face. A billion pins of white-hot acid traced every contour from left eye to the point of his chin.

SSSSSSSSSSSSSSSSSTOPHER.

Another hiss of approaching sound, but not a wave. It was the sound of a car, moving fast over a dry road. He was in the wheelchair, facing the fence at the entrance of the industrial estate.

'Daddy?' said Christopher, his voice a throaty croak.

YOU ALLOWED FRYER TO BESSSSSST YOU, BOY.

Christopher's eyelids fluttered. He frowned, tried to recall, but the pain in his face was cutting and cutting, wanting his entire mind. He closed his eyes to concentrate. John had been behind, pushing and talking to him but he had been talking, too. He strained to remember their final words.

He had asked John who else would know, about the final spectacular. John Fryer had asked him where he had planted the bomb, and he had told him, just before the laughing took him, and just before the world went black. His face continued to broadcast unheard-of agony. John had hit him, and left him. He should have listened to Daddy. He told him it was on a need-to-know basis.

FOOL . . . YOU FOOOOL.

'Oh no,' slurred Christopher. He fumbled past the bulk of the bomb bag on his chest, reached under the flag. The gun was still wedged between the chair and his leg. His mission was still on, but first, he needed to get the bag off his chest. He moved his other hand to reach into his front pocket for the padlock key but his wrist was yanked painfully against the arm of the wheelchair. He looked down: handcuffs, one loop closed round the frame of the chair, the other tightly latched to his wrist, biting into his flesh, swollen and purple round its steel seam.

The pain in his face was God almighty. His swollen wrist had not even registered. He recognised the cuffs. They had been Daddy's, and they had been on the floor of the armoury. His eyes widened. Daddy had come here and cuffed him, as a punishment. In response, Daddy's voice, hoarse and reproachful, spoke.

IT WASSSS FRYER. FRYER GOT THE BESSSSSST OF YOU. YOU FUCKING FOOOL ...

Christopher tugged on the cuff again, strained with all he had. The metal bit into him, but did not slip or give. It was tight as a rivet. Christopher kept tugging, twenty times, sharp, merciless movements, but it did not budge. He stopped, panting. His wrist was slick with blood. A ring of fire marked the manacle's hold, but it had not moved, and it would not. He tried to slow his breathing, tears streamed from his eyes, and he was now aware of how disjointed and slack his jaw was, unhinged from his face. This was bad, but he was not laughing, at least, not yet. He breathed, marshalled his dancing thoughts. The bag was core. It needed to come off, then he could leave it near the protest camp, just as he had planned, and if they tried to stop him, he would shoot until he was empty.

He raised himself up and off the seat as far as the handcuffs would stretch, and reached into his front pocket. Christopher stretched two fingers down into the cavity. He could feel the serrated edge of the key but managed only to push it deeper, out of reach. His legs gave way under the added weight of the bomb bag, and he sat down heavily, his mouth snapped shut. He heard a rasp of bone on bone, followed by a fresh supernova of pain from his jaw. Christopher screamed. His vision greyed, but as his chin touched the bag he jolted his head upright again. He raised himself on rubber legs and drove his fingers back inside his pocket. Bloody saliva dripped from the corner of his lolling mouth unchecked. He pinched the key between two fingers and fished it out, his breath coming in dry gasps, like a sick dog. Now he needed to reach the padlock and open it.

He carefully placed the key between his lips on the right side, emitted a high moan as he closed his mouth. He worked his right arm out of the jacket sleeve, until his elbow jammed against the upper arm. No place left to go. Christopher closed his eyes and rolled his right shoulder in a violent shrug, screaming through his pursed lips as the movement rocked his head and shook his crushed jawbone. His elbow stayed stuck. He rolled again, shifted in the seat and his right shoulder popped free. He gave a yelp of triumph, pulled his right arm completely out, threw the jacket off the left side of the wheelchair, giving him access to his back.

Christopher took the key from between his lips, and stretched his arm back, like a man searching for an itch. He had planned to do this standing up, but the extra slack he'd built in gave him enough to play with. The tip of the key scratched the base of the padlock – still too high. He shuffled down in his seat as far as the cuff would permit and then leant back until he felt the thick padlock press between his upper shoulders, pinned against the back of the seat. He pushed up slowly, pressing the lock in place and then it slid down, an inch at most, but all he needed.

He reached round, felt the nose of the key circle the base of the lock and ignored the pain, did not breathe. The key snagged and he pushed his right hand up, felt it slot home, righteous and true. Christopher turned it and the straps loosened as the bag fell from his chest. He sang out in triumph, pulled the sleeve of his jacket off his left arm and then took the strap off his right shoulder. The weight fell away. He moved the strap down his left arm, and then he stopped, staring at his wrist. The jacket, and the strap of the bag, were bunched and waiting to move off his arm, but there was still the cuff, locked securely to the steel arm of the chair. He took the nylon strap in his free hand and ran his fingers along its length. It was triple stitched to the body of the bag. No amount of tugging would stretch or tear it easily. He lowered his mouth, ready to chew through it, but froze as a bolt of pain squealed from his jaw. He should have brought a blade, but he had not, so now he needed to find one, or a shard of broken glass. It was Belfast on 12th July. There would soon be broken bottles on the street.

Now the laughter came, furious and unbridled. Christopher sobbed in agony through the giggles as his jaw grated and rasped in his head.

CHRISSSSTOPHER . . . CHRISSSTOPHER, I KNEW THIS WASSSSH TOO MUCH FOR YOU. YOU WASTER, HE GOT THE BESSST OF YOU. YOU LOSE, WE LOOOOSEE.

Bad Daddy's voice plugged his laughter.

'No, no, don't say that. We have time, we have time,' he replied. Christopher checked his watch. It was almost twelve. The firebomb at the Culturlann was set to go off any minute. John Fryer was probably too late – the timers, they were so old. Christopher's nascent smile dropped. He stared down at the bag on his lap. Same bomb, same timers. He needed to move quickly.

He stood up, let the Union flag fall, lifted the gun from the seat, and started to walk up the entrance ramp backwards, still attached to the chair. Despite the blooming pain the giggles returned, but so did Bad Daddy's voice. He cursed him, damned the day he was born, told him Hell was waiting. Christopher emerged on the Crumlin road, heard the beat of drums and the tweet of flutes from the protest camp. Thoughts of cutting off the bag had gone, likewise his giggles. His plan to steal the stash of treasure from the Black Mountain was now just a dream within a dream. There was only Bad Daddy's voice, repeating a new mantra.

KILL THEM ALL, KILL THEM ALL, KILL THEM ALL . . .

Christopher sat down and started to wheel himself along. The bomb bag rested on his left knee, partly shrouded by his jacket, and he turned the wheels with his one free hand.

Soon he saw the flag-draped entrance of the protest camp on the other side of a roundabout. The music came from speakers. A small crowd stood there: Orange sashes, Rangers football tops. Two women, one wearing a red white and blue plastic bowler hat, left the group and walked across the road towards an ice cream van, parked on the kerb. Christopher headed for the van. A horn blasted, and a second later a car screeched to a stop, its hot grill inches from his broken face. The driver shouted something, but Christopher did not hear it. All he heard was Bad Daddy in his head, repeating his final order, and his final furious insult.

KILL THEM ALL, CHRISSSSTOPHER. YOU USELESSS BASSSSTARD, KILL THEM ALL. YOU USELESSS BASSSSTARD, KILL THEM ALL . . .

Christopher kept on trucking, reached the business end of the ice cream van, where the two women now stood with their backs to him. Men moved in his direction, coming from the protest camp, their eyes on him. Christopher reached under his leg, got the gun. He was now within spitting distance of the two women. The one wearing the plastic bowler hat turned and looked at him. Her mouth dropped open, eyes on the gun. She started to shake her head, back away. She glanced at Christopher's face and her expression moved from shock to horror.

'No, no,' she said, colliding with the other woman holding their treats. Both went sprawling, ice cream in the air, and at that second, the group of men rounded the corner of the van, and stopped as one, looked first at the women on the ground, then at Christopher.

KILL THEM ALL, CHRISSSSTOPHER. YOU USELESSS BASSSSTARD, KILL THEM ALL.

'Shut up, Daddy!' he shouted, raised the gun at the woman with the hat, now sat upright on the pavement, her face smeared with ice cream. Christopher pulled the trigger and, before he had time to register the recoil, he saw the back of her head explode and hit the side of the ice cream van, a grey and red splash. She unfolded from the waist and hit the ground. There was a moment of silence, all eyes on the woman. This time Bad Daddy did not break it. Christopher raised the gun once more, took aim, and started to laugh.

CHAPTER SIXTY-THREE

'Aoife, Aoife!' Sheen shouted her name against the buffering wind coming at him across the open expanse of Milltown Cemetery. Sounds of commotion, the scratch and rustle of a phone being roughly handled, then the line went dead. He had heard something else before she had broken off: a gunshot. He marched in long strides through the marshy ground to where Gerard was still parked, his head half submerged in the bonnet of his taxi as though having engine trouble. Sheen whistled sharply. Gerard slammed closed the car's bonnet and got in. By the time Sheen opened the passenger door, his shoes and socks damp with water, the engine was running. No time for explanations. Sheen pointed once to the billowing tower of dark smoke, which was churning up from the near horizon.

'Culturlann, Falls Road, drive,' he said. It was all that was needed. Gerard hit the accelerator, and Sheen was pushed back into his seat as the powerful car tore away, raising long bleats from other drivers. In less than five seconds they were doing over ninety. The cemetery disappeared on Sheen's left as Gerard weaved the car in precise embroidery through traffic. He slowed only to take the roundabout at the bottom of the Donegal road, and then only a little. He took it at over seventy. He guided the car through a slip road at the same speed, took an impossibly sharp left, the tyres yelping in protest. The car held its course, as though on tracks. They were on Broadway, a road feeding into the Falls, and Sheen, who had temporarily lost sight of the tower of smoke, now saw it again, looming to his left.

The facts came into his mind in staccato instruction form, like telegraph messages in a war room. The smoke was coming from the Culturlann, the place where Aoife said John Fryer had been. He had taken her little girl, Ava, and Sheen had to find her, find them both. Gerard slowed as they approached the junction with the Falls road, broke a red light and turned the corner.

Sheen was out and running, made it fifteen metres, then halted. A building that looked like a sandstone church was engulfed in flames, the fire howling out of its gothic-shaped side windows. The open front entrance was the gateway to Hell itself. He could feel the heat from this distance, hot enough to bake the skin on his face. The way the flames were burning was super intense, as though being fed by a flamethrower within the walls of the building. He moved his eyes to the far side of the Falls road where a crowd of bystanders was watching the fire burn, more children than adults. Some of the youngsters were crying and being comforted, most were staring blankly at the raging inferno, shock etched on their faces.

Sheen switched his attention to a small huddle of people crouching at the kerbside on the far side of the burning building, a uniformed police officer with them. Sheen moved forward, feeling the heat start to singe his eyelashes, scorch the fabric of his clothes. He raised his arm to shield his face and sprinted the twenty or so metres up the white line, feeling his exposed hand roast as though he had plunged it into an oven. From within the furnace he heard a dull explosion, followed by a scream from the children to his right. He reached the other side, felt the welcome cool of the wind rushing the heat away from his head and shoulders. He nudged his way through the huddle of people and saw a second uniformed PSNI officer was slouched against the kerb, blood his only pillow.

The man was dead. His blank eyes stared into infinity from a soft ghost face. A red bib covered his upper body from a wound in the middle of his throat. In the distance, Sheen could hear sirens approach. The man's colleague stood up and brushed past Sheen without looking at him. A second later, Sheen heard him shout into his radio, reiterating the need for assistance. Sheen's ears sharpened.

'Suspect escaped in a black taxi. I exchanged fire. He was hit,' he said. Fryer had been shot. Sheen needed to find him, before it was too late. A young man, ginger hair, shaved close to his head, knelt down and put his face close to the police officer's half-open mouth.

'This guy's dead. He fucking killed him,' he said, his freckled face pale and drawn.

'Where did he go?' asked Sheen.

'He just drove off up the road,' he said.

A woman spoke, to Sheen's right. 'Someone said he took a wee girl with him,' she said.

The sirens were closer now. No time to stand and stare. Sheen crouched down, unclipped the dead officer's service revolver from the extendable coil which secured it to the holster. The gun was heavy and snug, but alien in his grip. As he did so, the people shrunk away from him as one, minnows in a fish tank. The other officer had his back to the group. Sheen turned, waved to Gerard and the car pounced forward, seconds later stopped beside him. Now the uniformed officer turned, alarm on his face. He spotted the gun. No time. Sheen got in.

'Drive. We're following a black taxi,' said Sheen, and Gerard nodded, already propelling them away. Sheen's hands were slick with sweat, his mouth paper dry. He moved the gun from one hand to the other gingerly, wiping them on his trouser legs, eyes frantically scanning the road ahead. From the back of his mind, a voice told him that this was lunacy, that he had just fled a murder scene, stolen a gun. He was putting the child at risk, because this was not really about saving Ava, this was about catching John Fryer. He slammed door after door in his brain, until the voice was gone. He held the gun, concentrated on the dimpled grip in his paw, still searching, looking for anything that would show him the way, and then he saw it.

'There!' he said, pointing with his free hand. There was blue, oily smoke filling the road, from something further up. Their progress had slowed to just over the legal 30 mph limit. Traffic was stacked up ahead. Gerard moved to pass a people carrier with black-tinted windows that was next in line, but quickly swerved back into his own lane, almost colliding with a bus in the opposite lane.

'Sorry,' he said softly. He tried again, managed it this time. Passed the people carrier, a white van and small red Hyundai car in a single smooth acceleration. He tucked the big saloon back into the line of traffic, a cacophony of horns in their wake. Sheen opened his window, tasted the filthy smoke. He leant out, straining to see, but it was no good, there was a fully stacked skip lorry, two spaces ahead. A sudden burning of red taillights and the skip lorry ground to a stop, its load rocking, chains clanking heavily. Then he saw it, the source of the smoke. A black taxi, old style, swerved into the lane of oncoming traffic, which screeched to a stop, or swerved off the road to avoid being hit.

'Go!' shouted Sheen. Gerard followed the taxi, first on the wrong side of the road, then across the small hillock of a mini-roundabout before turning a hard right, up the steep hill which it was now climbing.

'Where are we?' said Sheen.

'Whiterock Road,' said Gerard. The taxi, for all its smoking signs of ill health, was tearing up the hill ahead of them, making good progress, getting away. Gerard rammed the saloon into a lower gear and the engine growled and kicked into life, pushing Sheen back in his seat.

'Where does this take us?' said Sheen.

Gerard did not answer immediately. The road between them and the taxi shortened, then the black taxi pulled away again, swerving into the other lane, overtaking two cars. No safe way for them to follow.

'It takes you the long way round to north Belfast, or west, through Turf Lodge,' shrugged Gerard. Despite everything he had been asked to do, he remained impassive, so cool.

Sheen glanced at him. In a place where everyone had a past, for the first time he thought about what Gerard's might be: almost certainly not an airport taxi driver.

'Or up there,' he said, nodding up at the green slope of the Black Mountain. The taxi hurtled across an intersection, through a set of red lights. A car in the cross-section lane skidded to an emergency stop, giving Fryer clear passage, but the one coming from behind it was too slow. It smashed into the back of the stopped car and knocked it into the oncoming lane. More screeching tyres, and the bumped driver was now smashed from the front by an oncoming removal van. Horns blared, rubber burnt – it was mayhem.

Beyond the intersection, Sheen watched as Fryer's taxi pulled off the main road, without slowing down, heading up an even steeper incline, to the foot of the mountain. He turned to Gerard, who nodded, eyes fixed on the road. They accelerated into the madness, but braked hard, barely avoided what happened next. A battered flatbed truck full of rusted scrap metal entered stage left and collided with the car that had first rear-ended its neighbour into oncoming traffic. The momentum of the impact part crushed the rear of the car, but the flatbed kept coming, mounted it like a ramp, and was tipped up on two wheels for a second of sweet balance, before it crashed to earth. Its cargo of rusted metal smashed massively, spreading across both lanes. No way through it. Sheen strained to see beyond the rising dust, but the taxi had disappeared entirely from his sight.

CHAPTER SIXTY-FOUR

Aoife sprinted hard, her mobile still held in one hand, her service weapon in the other. A small crowd of men was streaming out from the entrance of the protest camp on her left to where an ice cream van was parked on the kerb at the other side of the roundabout. A woman emerged from behind the van, screaming hysterically. Cecil was still at least twenty metres in front of her. She lost sight of him as he rounded the corner and disappeared behind the ice cream van. Seconds later she arrived, skidding to a stop, eyes wide.

Left: a woman was flat on her back, a black blood halo spread on the pavement behind her head, eyes blank and open, dead. More people from the camp now arrived by her side, stood gawking. Splattered gore, red, mingled with milky grey, was slowly dripping to earth down the side of the van. The remains of any brains she might have had. Right: Cecil and his men, all panting hard, looking at the mess on the van and the dead woman. His bodyguard had a gun in his hand, but his face said he had not yet arrived. Dead ahead, a skinhead man in a wheelchair with a gun in his right hand, and a bag on his lap. He was laughing, high and jagged, the only sound. His eyes were dancing, his jaw horribly askew. It was him. This was Christopher Moore. She stepped forward, gun raised, and pointed at their killer.

'PSNI! Drop your weapon, now!' she shouted.

Christopher's eyes, unblinking and glittering, fixed on her. He was still laughing, and the gun was still in his hand. She took another step, her gun aimed at his centre of mass. Sheen's words played in her mind.

Don't hesitate. Take the shot.

'Throw it down, Christopher. I will shoot you!' she said. Her finger was on the trigger, part compressing it, her palm slick with sweat, his laughter spearing her ears. She took a breath and closed one eye, aimed for his heart.

'Arrrrrhhhhhh! Bastard!!' It was Cecil Moore, coming from her right. He charged at Christopher, head low like a bull, fists at his side. Christopher's eyes flashed to him, the laughter still spilling forth. His expression transformed to one of pure salvation. He pointed his gun at Cecil.

Aoife lunged into the gap between Cecil and Christopher and squeezed the trigger. Her gun barked once, but the bullet entered the bag on Christopher's lap with a hard thud. She squeezed again, a clean shot. Christopher rocked back in the wheelchair, his face contorted, then a flash of orange from the eye of his gun. Aoife had time to think that this was the first time she had shot anyone, and then she was kicked in the chest by an invisible racehorse, stopping her dead. The air was driven from her lungs, but she squeezed her trigger once more, felt her gun recoil. Christopher's left shoulder exploded, leaving the fabric of his T-shirt frayed and smoking. He pointed his gun and it spat fire in slow motion. Aoife felt the horse kick her once more, left shoulder, and this time it turned her like a blow from a heavyweight fighter, the sound of the gunshot arriving just shy of the first blast of pain which exploded in her gut.

Cecil barged into her, his body briefly in extreme close-up, before his rough shove sent her down. Aoife landed on her side, skidded in the deposited slime that was running off the side of the ice cream van, then rolled and found herself beneath the iron undercarriage, looking up at its oily intestines. She turned, ignoring the white core of pain burning a hole through her centre. The world was a forest of feet, stampeding from right to left, and under the high-pitched din in her ears, she heard their panicked cries and screams. They cleared as one and then it was Cecil she could see, diving at Christopher Moore. Two shots snapped out, but Cecil did not stop, hands outstretched, going for Christopher's neck. The chair with Christopher in it overturned, and Cecil followed.

A super bright flash of white, blinding and sudden, filled her vision, followed by a blast of heat searing her face, scalding her eyes. Aoife turned and rolled, pure reflex. An explosion roared out. The ice cream van rocked on its springs over her head and a hot wall of air shoved her, powerful as the piston of a car crusher. She was wedged deeper under the van, into the cleft between the kerb and the underside of the vehicle. She cried out, but could not hear her own voice over the blast. The force pushing her stopped and she felt crashing overhead. Broken glass fell and danced in front of her eyes. Then there was only the distant whistle in her ears, her perforated ear drums mute to the world.

With it, the pain returned, crippling and awful in her stomach, a dull echo repeating in her ruptured shoulder. She touched her middle. Her hand came back red. Her heart was rolling in her chest like a snare drum about to announce a magician's prestige, but her head was light and weightless. She felt it rise up and start to float.

Aoife gasped, and opened her eyes (she did not remember closing them, but she must have). Cecil. She had to get to Cecil Moore, find his phone. She rolled her body round and started to crawl, crying out in pain as the rough surface of the pavement beneath her scraped her stomach. She gritted her teeth, blinked away tears, kept crawling, used her right arm, the left a dead weight at her side.

She emerged from under the van, chunks of windscreen glass embedded into her palm and lower arm. Three bodies to her right: Cecil's men who were still wearing their Orange sashes, splayed on the pavement and not moving, blood coming from their ears. Ahead of her was a mini wasteland: a buckled wheel, half its rubber tyre burning, a smoking shoe, and a human leg, impossibly complete and naked lay across her path like an obscene hairy log. She did not stop, clambered over it, pulled her torso after her, feeling it roll both firm and soft beneath her. Aoife had her eyes fixed on the smoking remains of Christopher's upturned chair, his hand protruding over the rim of the seat, held fast by the ring of a handcuff. Cecil must be near.

She reached the chair, her head now as weightless as a helium balloon and held only by the single hair of an angel. It strained to fly away from all of this horror. Christopher Moore was gone. Only his arm remained, a thick branch of super white bone marking its end point. She looked to her left and saw him, his shaved head slick with blood – limbs missing, but alive – his lips moving as he talked to the sky above. She turned from Christopher, found her quarry. She came to his legs first, but the rest of Cecil Moore was ten feet away. Aoife raised herself up on her right elbow beside Cecil's legs, whimpering and panting, trying not to look at the spew of his entrails that formed a slick path to the rest of his body. She gritted her teeth, sat up, howling at the massive twist of pain in her tummy, and quickly drove her hand into first one trouser pocket, then the other. She pulled out a roll of fifty pound notes from one, spare change from the other. No phone.

She tossed the money away and turned to face the grotesque path ahead. She set off, dragging her body after her, eyes on his jacket, not thinking about the way his chest was so unnaturally caved in, definitely not looking at the warm, squelching rope and liquids through which her right hand now dug and scooped. It was just inches below her mouth, its steam rising to greet her; offal and faeces filling the air. Aoife gagged. Nothing came up, just dry heaving, but she refused to stop. She heaved herself forward one last time and her hand touched the dry refuge of Cecil Moore's jacket. She struggled to a sitting position, wiped a hand down Cecil's sash, and started to check his pockets, her eyes half closed.

The front pockets of his suit jacket were still sewn closed, never used. She reached inside the right breast pocket, pulled out a foil-backed packet of painkillers. She dug inside the left and felt the weight of a phone. She slid it out and tried to focus on it, blinking to concentrate. It was the same phone he had used in the Bad Bet to cast the blackmail video for her. She pocketed it, and let herself fall back, feeling the crunch as her head hit the street, but there was no more pain, not even from her stomach. She turned her head and looked into Cecil Moore's dead eyes as the angel's hair snapped silently and the balloon streamed away. Was he telling her the truth? Did this phone contain the only copy of the video? Cecil did not reply. His face grew smaller as Aoife was lifted up, through the blue and into the black, her mind holding on to one word until the very last.

Ava.

CHAPTER SIXTY-FIVE

'It's OK, Ava. You're safe, baby. Everything's OK,' said Fryer. She was squeezed into a tight ball in the passenger seat. Fryer knocked the taxi down into second and pushed it up the steep incline of what used to be the old mountain loney. He had lost the private taxi, the same car that had been parked and waiting at Milltown. Fryer coughed, tasted blood, wiped it away. Not a bit of wonder the girl was frightened, he was a state. Some way to meet your granda this.

He gave the engine one final rev. They lurched forward before it conked out. Fryer pulled up the handbrake before they could roll back and groaned at the pain. The peeler had shot him in the side. More blood in his mouth. Fryer swallowed it, wheezed. The bag on his chest made it even harder, but that was not coming off. When he searched in his back pocket for his blade before going into the Culturlann it was gone. He must have lost it when he pulled the cuffs out.

Fryer got out, took his Armalite from the side well of

the door. He walked round to let Ava out, and then paused, saw billowing black smoke a few miles below. That was the Culturlann, the place where Ava had nearly died so horribly. He had saved her. Whatever else he had done in his miserable life, he had saved her, and now he was going to give her the gems, if they really existed at all. He opened her door and she shrunk away from him. Fryer asked her gently to get out now. But it was no good, she would not come. He glanced down the hill. They would catch up with him. Men like that always did.

'I said get out! I have a gun! Come,' he shouted. She flinched, stared at the gun, did as she was told. She was petrified, he knew it, but it was necessary. He slammed the door, grabbed her hand and walked laboriously up the mountainside, from grassy tuft to tuft. He stopped every ten paces to catch his breath, blood on his lips. Up ahead was a cairn of fist-sized rocks, waist height. This was the well, but not as he remembered it. Fryer held her shoulders, felt her tremble, her eyes on the dirt.

'Ava, I know I look like a bad monster, but I would never hurt you. Sorry I scared you. I need your help. We need to dig for buried treasure,' he said. She raised her pale green eyes to his, a flicker of interest now replacing the shock and fear. Fryer hesitated. Then he spoke, the clean mountain air on his hot brow. 'I'm your granda. I never knew, but it's true. I'm sorry I scared you, but I had to come and get you,' he said. He let go of her. If she wanted to run, he could not chase her. Fryer turned to the cairn, started to move the rocks. Ava did not run away.

'Help me. Please,' he said and she did. Fryer stepped away, watched her dismantle the marker. Her fear was forgotten, pure joy on her face as she completed a simple task. There was a metal plate, four feet in diameter

424

beneath. It was rested on the stumps of old bricks of the well. He bent down, pushed the lid, grunted. It did not budge. He checked his watch. It had gone 12.30 p.m. Time was running out, fast. He pushed it again and this time she joined him, her face set and determined. Fryer felt the plate shift, then it slid open with a hollow, metallic scratch.

'Thanks,' he said.

Ava stared at the black cavity, hands on hips, her frizzy curls danced in the mountain breeze. 'Are you going to put me down there?' she said.

Fryer laughed, and then started to cough, warmth and coppery wetness filling his mouth. He shook his head.

He walked round the mouth of the well and knelt down, reached into the blackness and felt beneath the overhang that extended round the circumference inside: soft earth, the crumbling base of the original brick well. It was pitch-black beneath, but Fryer reached inside, up to his elbow. He was not afraid; Ava was with him. He groped in the dark, followed the perimeter of the hole, found nothing but wet earth. He'd almost come back to the starting point and then he felt it. His fingers touched the cold edges of a metal box. Fryer lifted it out. It was heavy. He set it on the grass beside his gun. It was a black steel safety deposit box that had been doctored, edges welded together and a hinged lid fixed on the top, secured with a padlock, spotted with rust.

'Rock, please,' said Fryer. She returned with a pointed lump of granite, good. Fryer raised the rock and brought it down, three targeted hits, as hard as his sapping strength could manage. The final blow did the trick, the padlock sheared off and Fryer tossed it into the well. He opened the lid, and took a sharp intake of breath, coughed.

Inside was a single bar of gold, yellow and mesmerising, identification marks filed off. Next to it was a transparent freezer bag full of gems. Fryer lifted it out, watched as the sunlight caught the jewels and sparkled beautifully. The accountant had told him the truth.

Ava gasped. 'Are they real?' she asked. Fryer looked up, was about to tell her that yes, they were all real and they were all for her, but his world turned grey and she blurred in his vision. He slumped to the ground, saw the yellowed green grass in close-up. He tried to tell her to run now, take the gems and run, before it was too late, but instead he uttered a wet gasp. Fryer looked across the mouth of the well. There, coming from the loney was the man in the tan jacket, and he had a gun. He coughed, blood spattered across the grass. Fryer grabbed his Armalite, forced himself to stand. The world was a spinning disc. He was the single point of stillness. Fryer blinked. The scenery stopped rotating. He reached over to the hazy shape which he hoped was Ava's hair, held out the bag of gems, and felt her take it. Fryer smiled. He swayed, like a sapling in high wind. The man was close. He shouted, but what he said made no sense. He had a gun. It was pointed at them, at Ava.

'John Fryer! Look at me! You killed my brother. Look at me!'

Fryer stood in front of Ava, shielded her from this mad bastard. He raised his Armalite, pointed it at the man. 'Drop your gun, or I drop you,' said Fryer.

426

CHAPTER SIXTY-SIX

Sheen took another two steps forward, still pointing the gun at Fryer, who was now doing the same at him, the little girl, Ava, standing behind him. He was at the open mouth of a black hole in the hillside, small rocks scattered as though disturbed. Sheen's hand was trembling. He strained to focus on Fryer's face. It was definitely him. He recognised him from his photograph, despite the years and the shaved head. So this was his man: the one who had murdered his brother. Fryer called for him to stop, drop his gun, threatened to shoot. His voice was rasping and words slurred. Sheen saw blood on his lips, his face livid and corpse white. Sheen stood his ground, weapon raised.

'Let her go, Fryer!' he called. He looked from Fryer's face to the heavy-looking pack on his chest. Sheen thought about the explosion at the Culturlann and the substation – links in a chain. If Fryer had intended to kill his former comrades at Dempsey's funeral, he would have maximised the damage using a bomb, not simply the small rifle which he still pointed at Sheen. As though in response, Fryer spoke, his voice barely carrying over the rolling wind.

'This is a bomb. I can't take it off. Going to blow any minute now. Lower the gun, take her and run,' he said. Sheen hesitated. He believed him about the bomb, but if he dropped the gun, Fryer could kill him. And if he ran now, it would all be for nothing. Stalemate. Seconds ticked by, Ava's life in the balance.

'Answer me, Fryer. Did you plant the Sailortown bomb? It killed my brother, the other kids who were playing in the street that day. It nearly killed me!' shouted Sheen.

Fryer slowly shook his head, his face a mask of confusion. 'Sailortown? What the fuck has that got to do with anything? Who are you? Special Branch? SAS? I saw you at Milltown,' said Fryer. He was slurring now, and swayed like a man who had slid off his bar stool after too much whiskey. Sheen took another three steps, close enough now to look John Fryer in the eye.

Sheen said he was Historical Offences, told him to answer his question. Fryer's eyes momentarily lit when Sheen mentioned the SHOT. He started to sway, lids fluttering.

'I'll answer your question, boy, but first you listen and promise me something. If you need a sweetener, look inside that box, it's yours,' said Fryer, nodding to something gold, gleaming at his feet. Sheen did not take his eyes off him.

'There's a place called Coleman's bog in Monaghan. There is a cottage there, used to be . . .' his voice drifted off, his eyes closed and he stumbled, heading for the hole, but saved himself at the last second, and stood upright, but his arms were now limp by his side, the gun loose in his hand.

'Used to be, but maybe not now. Find it. There was a path. It went from there into the bog, deep into the bog. Follow it until the land turns to water. There is a flat rock, where God never wanted it to be, and under it is the boy McKenna. I killed him. It was my turn . . . Bring him home to his mother. Shhhhh Shhhe's waiting,' said Fryer, swaying, his face white as a clown.

Sheen took another step. He was almost at the edge, gun still raised. Fryer nodded to him, and then he cast his rifle into the blackness below with a single, lazy flick of his wrist.

'Ava! Ava, I am a police officer. Come to me now. You are safe,' shouted Sheen. Ava looked up at Fryer just once, then walked hastily round the hole, stood by Sheen's side. She had a plastic bag full of what looked like diamonds in her hand.

'Run, Ava,' said Sheen. 'Run as fast as you can, back the way you came and do not stop until you reach the bottom of the mountain. Go!' he said and she did, darting off. Sheen counted the seconds, waiting for her to get over the crest of the hill.

'Did you leave that bomb? Did you kill my brother?' asked Sheen, crying now.

Fryer nodded, then shook his head. 'Maybe I did. I did so much but don't remember now. All I know is McKenna. I'm sorry,' he said.

Sheen blinked away the tears and stared into John Fryer's eyes, and in his mind he heard a car door close and his feet hitting the street as he chased the football. He squeezed his eyes shut, put his finger on the trigger, and pressed.

Nothing. No blast, no kick. He opened his eyes, looked

at the gun. His index finger was only partly covering the split lip of the trigger, the central plastic safety catch still locked in place. Aoife's words, replayed but too late.

Safe Action trigger, two-stage. Basically, if you accidentally flick the side of the trigger, nothing happens.

Fryer stared at him, slowly shook his head. 'Time's up, mate,' he said. Sheen stepped back as Fryer stepped forward into thin air, and then he was gone, instantly swallowed whole by the darkness. Sheen dropped the gun, turned and ran. He got three paces. The hillside was rocked by an explosion, strong enough to kick him off his feet. He landed face first. Coarse grass scratched his cheeks and forehead as small stones rained on him. A brick landed with a thud inches from his right ear. He raised both hands and held them helplessly over his head. He looked back. Smoke drifted from the hole. Sheen got up and cautiously walked back to the edge. He cupped his hands, tasted the acrid smoke, chemicals and burnt meat.

'Fryer!' he yelled into the pit. 'John Fryer!' he shouted again. A mocking echo was his only reply. It shrieked Fryer's name, the voice of a condemned soul crying out from the abyss.

PART FIVE

BLOOD IS THE ROSE

CHAPTER SIXTY-SEVEN

Belfast, Northern Ireland, present day, three weeks later
Monday 1st August

'Ava?' Aoife's voice was slurred and full of dope but this was the first time she had opened her eyes for him, and he had visited her every day in the Royal Victoria Hospital. First in the Intensive Care Unit and, when her condition moved from critical to stable, in this small room off the main High Dependency Unit. An armed officer had stood guard twenty-four-seven since she was admitted. Paddy had insisted, bugger the budget.

He took her hand and gave it a very gentle squeeze. And leant in, resting his elbows on the crenelated blanket that covered Aoife's lower body.

'Aoife, this is Sheen. Can you hear me?' he whispered. She turned her eyes to the sound of his voice, rheumy and half comprehending, blinked once, and then she repeated the name of her daughter, her voice croaky and dry. It was not the first time. The nurses on duty had reported that Aoife asked the same thing each time she awoke, and each time she had been told that her daughter was safe. He needed her awake. They needed to talk. There was more than Ava's well-being to worry about. Sheen carefully squeezed her hand again as her eyelids started to sink. Once again they opened, like the ever-sleepy cartoon dog from the shows he had watched as a kid.

'Ava's safe. She has been staying with Marie. She told me to let you know that you owe her big time, said Ava eats like a horse,' said Sheen, smiling. Aoife smiled back, slowly, eyes blinking. She licked her lips.

'Here, try to drink some water,' he said, held a half-filled plastic beaker for her, fat straw standing propped within. Each time he visited he had brought her fresh mineral water, cold, plus applied a lip salve. She gave him a small nod, and managed a sip, and a swallow, then another. He pulled the straw from her lips, told her to take it easy. It would be some time before Aoife was back on solid food. She winced as she swallowed, then looked at the thick cast that covered her left arm and shoulder, before doing a slow take of the little room. Her eyes rested on the far wall where Sheen's jacket was hanging from one of the hooks.

'My coat?' she asked. After Ava, this was her priority. He knew why.

'They found Cecil Moore's phone in your pocket, Aoife. It was bagged, with your clothes, as evidence. I don't have it,' he said. Aoife closed her eyes, and her heart monitor picked up a little pace, beeping more rapidly as it did so.

'Aoife, I know he had something on you,' said Sheen. Her eyes remained closed. He did not want her to shut him out, and any more excitement might bring a nurse to them, so he told her. 'I got to the phone, Aoife, after I heard it had been found on you,' and she opened her eyes, watched him, alert now, a mix of fear and hope. 'I paid one of the technical support team who were at the scene. It was a risk, but I deleted everything on it, and I took the SIM,' he said. Risky was an understatement. So far the man he had paid had kept his mouth shut, but there had been a lot of questions.

Her eyes were wide open. She squeezed his hand once.

'I need you to tell me what I should do. Paddy Laverty is a meticulous guy. He is asking questions, especially from me. Should I make it disappear?' he asked.

Aoife closed her eyes, squeezed his hand, harder this time, and nodded. Her heart rate spiked. A nurse walked past the door, paused briefly, looked at the monitor. Sheen smiled and nodded. She walked on. Sheen looked back at Aoife. Her eyes were open again.

'Then it's gone,' he said. The small chip was stowed away in the little pocket of his jeans where it had been since the 12th July.

'Christopher?' she asked, her voice less husky now, but still slow and thick.

'He's alive, but only just. There are guys who stepped on landmines in Afghanistan with a better chance of playing Sunday league footy. He will likely end up in the Heights, secure unit. Can you can believe it?' said Sheen.

Aoife nodded. 'So chaos did not come to Northern Ireland after all,' she said. Then she added, 'By the way, what day is it?'

'It's been nearly three weeks, Aoife. It's the start of August. You've been awake a few times, but we nearly lost you,' he said. She stared at him, mouth a little open. He read the surprise, but also the fear, and the loss: time she had not known and could not regain. He understood.

'The trouble subsided, but Christopher and Fryer did manage to suspend the Northern Irish Assembly,' he said. She asked him to explain, and he quickly did. Unionists claimed that Fryer, who was never a Dissident, had therefore never really left the PIRA, and was still representing them when he killed first Jim Dempsey, and then shot dead a PSNI officer outside the Culturlann. They refused to do any further business with republicans in Stormont until someone proved that the IRA had really been disbanded and has gone away.

'So Christopher and Fryer brought down the government after all, just not the way they had intended,' she said, smiling ruefully. Aoife closed her eyes, and kept them closed, her breathing turned slower, deeper. Sheen placed her hand on the blanket. There was more to tell, but that was enough for one day.

Aoife's eyes fluttered open as Sheen stood up. 'Is Paddy pissed off? Did he discipline us, Sheen, for going against his order?' she asked.

Sheen gave her his very best relax and don't-worry smile, but did not answer her directly. 'He has insisted on an armed guard down the corridor twenty-four-seven. Those boys are killing it for overtime, so he can't be that upset,' said Sheen. She smiled weakly, her eyes closed again, and Sheen listened as her heart monitor dropped to the dreamy beat of a settling slumber. He stretched, checked his watch and decided that he had time for one more visit before he met with his new Serious Historical Offences Team.

Sheen reached down and gently smoothed the crease between her eyebrows. She did not need to know the rest, not now. After a tip-off, Paddy had searched her locker in Ladas Drive. Found a quarter kilo of uncut cocaine, just as the caller said they would. She was currently suspended, full pay, pending investigation. Having Cecil Moore's phone in her pocket helped complete a picture that already did not look good. Moore had managed to trap her yet again, even from beyond the grave. He hesitated, tasted her soft smell in the air. She'd warned him to never again take something from her she was not prepared to give. He was about to pull away, then instead kissed her tenderly on the mouth.

CHAPTER SIXTY-EIGHT

Sheen let the door of Muldoon's rattle close behind him, loud enough to cheat the music, and that, as before, was playing at a fair volume. A large yellow sign had been fixed to the pub's outer wall: PROPERTY ACQUIRED FOR REDEVELOPMENT. Similar posters were attached to the disused warehouses and half-derelict homes outside.

The pub was all but empty: the stalls to his left were dark and silent, the pool table stood in shade on its small stage, cues fixed to the wall. No happy hour in Muldoon's this Monday afternoon, and soon to be last orders if the sign out front was to be believed. Sheen traced his steps between the hazy squares of coloured light on the floor. The two regulars were on their stools, in shared study of the *Racing Times*, pencils in hand. As he got closer, Sheen could hear the muttered patter of their deliberations, punctuated by sips from the pints.

The barman, Colm, emerged from under the bar. He gave Sheen a nod. 'Stout?' he asked, and Sheen agreed. He squinted into the deeper shadows at the end of the bar and saw the man he had come here for. Billy Murphy's tweed hat was peeking over the lip of his *Irish News*, a headline about the stalled Stormont Assembly on the front page. Sheen smiled. He set a twenty on the bar where Colm was drawing his beer, glass at an angle.

'And two large Bushmills, please,' he said. Sheen took a stool beside Billy.

'Well, they say that a bad penny always turns up,' said Billy, the paper still held up covering his face. He slowly folded it closed and set it next to his part-finished pint. He looked at Sheen, his magnified eyes blinking slowly. An ancient turtle appraising a fool in his presence.

'Hello, Billy,' said Sheen.

Billy replied with a twitch of his head and then flicked the closed paper at his elbow with the tips of his fingers. 'Suppose we have you to thank for this mess?' he said. Colm set the pint of stout and Bushmills down in front of Sheen, plus change – an alarming amount of it, given the drinks he had just ordered. Sheen thanked him, then slid the big measure of amber over to Billy, who grunted, and nodded appreciatively.

'I think we have John Fryer to thank for that, or more accurately, politicians who are out to make hay from the death of a police officer and Jim Dempsey,' said Sheen. He took a draw from his pint, cold and dark and good. Billy did not reply. Elvis crooned out 'In The Ghetto'. Sheen reached into the small pocket of his jeans where an artefact from the hunt for Fryer and Christopher weeks before was secreted away. He had left another in an envelope for Ava, gave it to Marie with strict instructions that only Aoife open it.

'So, John Fryer just jumped down that well on the mountain, did he?' asked Billy.

Sheen drained half his beer in a wide swallow. He could sit here all afternoon with this frosty, friendly man. 'He really did. He could have killed me – he was wearing a suicide bag – but he chose not to,' said Sheen. In his mind he replayed the moment he tried to pull the trigger. The sound of the dry click as the gun refused. Then that awful, sinking feeling: he'd tried to kill a man. And yet, Fryer had been selfless, shielded Sheen from a death which was too late for him to avoid.

'What a hero,' said Billy, and then he finished his pint, setting it down hard on the bar. Colm looked over, and then went about his business. 'Did he admit it? I assume you asked him,' said Billy.

Sheen went to his whiskey, raised it a little so the light from the windows was trapped in the glass like molten rock. 'Said he didn't remember. Other things, yes, but not Sailortown,' said Sheen.

'You believed that? Jesus, you probably do believe in the Leprechaun after all, like you told my wife,' said Billy, shaking his head.

'I think it was the truth for him,' said Sheen.

'It was him all right,' said Billy. His face was set. 'I'm glad he's dead,' he said.

'Billy, I am sorry about your nephew. Nothing I could have done would have brought him home. I understand that now,' said Sheen.

Billy did not reply. He pushed his stool back and jumped down, walked away along the length of the bar. 'Going for a pish. I'll see you about, Seamus,' he said, his voice was thick and cracking, head down.

Sheen watched him stride off, turn the corner at the end of the bar. So much for goodbyes. '*Slainte*, Billy,' said Sheen and drained the Bushmills in one gulp, the liquid igniting in his stomach and spreading through him instantly. He stood up, took the stone from his pocket. If he saw Billy again, it was not going to be in this pub. Billy probably lived in a council house, soon to be relocated to somewhere like Poleglass, a million miles away from all he had ever known and loved in Sailortown. Sheen called over to Colm, asked him for a pen. He took Billy's *Irish News*, set the Bushmills on the front page and wrote a message in the blank margin:

My name's not Seamus. Thank you, Billy.

Sheen checked to make sure the two punters and Colm were not looking, saw it was all clear and quickly dropped the diamond into the whiskey. It fell to the bottom of the glass with a faint plink. Sheen made his way outside, breathed the stagnant freshness of the dockside air. He reached inside the small pocket again, pulled out the SIM card he had stolen from Cecil Moore's phone and walked over to the edge of the quay. He bent it between his thumb and index finger, and then folded it until it split in two and threw the bits into the muddy water. It was Aoife's secret, and he would protect it while she could not.

Sheen stared into the filthy water where the SIM had already disappeared and then glanced back at the decrepit shell of Muldoon's. Soon enough, all this would be gone, and with it the last remnants of a Belfast childhood he could not know. Sheen turned from the water, walked away. He didn't look back. It was the past, a land he no longer needed to know.

AUTHOR'S NOTE

Blood Will Be Born is a work of fiction. Any resemblance to real persons living or dead is purely coincidental, and any reference to real events is done so through the lens of fictional storytelling. That said, Belfast is a real place and many of the events in the book do take place in real locations. You can visit the Culturlann when you are next in Belfast. However, I have taken the liberty of changing things when and where it best suited my story. Hopefully readers who live in the real places mentioned will allow me this creative licence.

Other places such as Belfast Heights and Lincoln View are as fictional as the plot itself.

ACRONYMS AND ABBREVIATIONS

INLA: Irish National Liberation Army. Illegal Irish republican paramilitary splinter group with communist ideology. Aimed to take Northern Ireland out of the United Kingdom and create a United Irish communist republic.

IRA: Irish Republican Army. Sometimes also referred to as PIRA or Provisional Irish Republican Army in reference to a split that occurred in an earlier incarnation of the group. Illegal and the largest Irish republican paramilitary organisation which was active throughout the modern Troubles. Aimed to take Northern Ireland out of the United Kingdom and create a United Irish republic.

The Met: The Metropolitan Police Service. The police service responsible for the Metropolitan Police District of London which consists of all police boroughs apart from the 'square mile' of the City of London.

MI5: Military Intelligence Section 5. Also known as The Security Service, MI5 is the United Kingdom's domestic intelligence and security agency. Since 2007 MI5 has led security intelligence work related to Northern Ireland (previously PSNI).

PSNI: Police Service of Northern Ireland. The police force of Northern Ireland from 2001 to date.

RUC: Royal Ulster Constabulary. The police force of Northern Ireland from 1922 until it was replaced by the PSNI in 2001.

Special Branch: RUC Special Branch. Undercover police unit tasked with combating the IRA and other paramilitary groups by recruiting informers and working closely with MI5. Later replaced by C3 Intelligence Branch of PSNI, though still referred to as Special Branch.

UDA: Ulster Defence Association. Illegal loyalist paramilitary organisation dedicated to keeping Northern Ireland a part of the United Kingdom.

UVF: Ulster Volunteer Force. Illegal loyalist paramilitary organisation dedicated to keeping Northern Ireland a part of the United Kingdom. Smaller in terms of membership than the UDA.

ACKNOWLEDGEMENTS

Thank you to my family for their ceaseless support and words of encouragement. When I found it hard to believe, my wife Sacha, daughter Leila and son Jack kept the faith and knew it would happen. My three sisters Jennifer, Leann and Rosemary, my sister-in-law Nina and my parents were always there and never doubted. Thanks guys.

My mother-in-law Geri Dogmetchi gave valuable practical assistance as well as moral support. Thank you for the forensic science books and masterclass, for firmly guiding me to Crimefest 2016 in Bristol and insisting I throw caution to the wind and Pitch an Agent with *Blood Will Be Born*. Thanks for introducing me to Scott Bradfield's Online Novel Writing Course at the City Lit. Without Scott's capitalised, brilliantly caustic feedback and his command to Write Every Day, this would be something I still talk about doing, some day.

Thank you to my first readers. Your insightful feedback and positive encouragement was invaluable: Devinder

Guram, Han Bee, David Bailey, Charlie Hawes, and Geri. Thanks to Donal McCann for his skills as a photographer, and friend, in giving me a new public face, so much better than the real thing. Thanks to my friend Kenan Aksu for showing me the way back, no hurries, no worries.

And finally, thank you to my agent Lisa Moylett, who made this happen, and to the team at Allison & Busby for giving DI Sheen a home.

GARY DONNELLY is a writer and teacher who was born and raised in west Belfast. After attending a state comprehensive school, he read History at Corpus Christi College, Cambridge and has lived and worked in London since the late 1990s. *Blood Will Be Born* is his debut novel and the first book in the DI Owen Sheen series.

donnellywriter.com   @DonnellyWriter